Visiting time was almost over. Once the bell had been rung, everyone had to go, no matter how far they had come. Jo sat and gazed at him, longing to do something more than just squeeze his hand, knowing that she could not kiss those torn, misshapen lips. She kissed his hand instead, each finger and the palm, and held it against her mouth. Next time she saw him, she would be a fully fledged lumberjill, working – she hoped – in one of the forests of the south-east, and able to see him every week.

'I'll write to you, Nick,' she whispered. 'I'll write every day. And I'll come and see you just as soon as I can.'

Nick turned his head towards her. The dark brown eyes, once so alive, now as dead as pebbles, looked into hers. The bell rang loudly, an intrusion, and she hated the noise of it. She whispered his name again and, unable to say the word '*goodbye*', turned and hurried blindly out of the ward.

Not for anything in the world would she have confessed to anyone else the dismay she had felt on seeing his ravaged face. Not for anything in the world; not even to herself.

Lilian Harry's grandfather hailed from Devon and Lilian always longed to return to her roots, so moving from Hampshire to a small Dartmoor town in her early twenties was a dream come true. She quickly absorbed herself in local life, learning the fascinating folklore and history of the moors, joining the church bellringers and a country dance club, and meeting people who are still her friends today. Although she later moved north, living first in Herefordshire and then in the Lake District, she returned in the 1990s and now lives on the edge of the moor with her two ginger cats. She is still an active bellringer and member of the local drama group, and loves to walk on the moors. She has one son and one daughter. Her latest novel in hardback, *A Stranger in Burracombe*, is also available from Orion. Visit her website at www.lilianharry.co.uk.

PS I Love You

LILIAN HARRY

An Orion paperback

First published in Great Britain in 2002
by Orion
This paperback edition published in 2002
by Orion Books Ltd,
Orion House, 5 Upper St Martin's Lane,
London WC2H 9EA

Reissued 2007

A CIP catalogue record for this book is available
from the British Library.

Printed and bound by
Clays Ltd, St Ives plc

The Orion Publishing Group's policy is to use papers that
are natural, renewable and recyclable products and
made from wood grown in sustainable forests. The logging
and manufacturing processes are expected to conform to
the environmental regulations of the country of origin.

www.orionbooks.co.uk

For Ted, Mike, Brenda and Alison,
for their love and support

KTF

Part One

Chapter One

July 1941

As the late twilight fell, the London streets grew quiet. A few cars and taxis drove down Oxford Street, past the boarded windows of the shops. From open windows floated the sound of music – dance music, jazz, the crooning voice of Frank Sinatra, the warm tones of Vera Lynn, the lively sound of the jitterbug. In the deepening blue, moonlight glowed on the swollen bellies of the barrage balloons floating above the city. Later, there might be the criss-crossing tracery of the white swords of searchlights. Or the night might remain dark and quiet.

It was coming to the end of the second year of the war.

On the corner of Marble Arch, the high, ornate façade of the Lyons Corner House gleamed white against the purple dusk. From outside, it seemed silent and boarded against the raids that had torn London apart. But when the great doors were thrust open and the heavy blackout curtain pushed aside, an explosion of colour and light embraced the hesitant customer, drawing him in with a welcome echoed in the brightness of the seater's smile as she invited him to a table.

The chandeliers had gone, the exotic paintings been replaced by wartime posters exhorting caution and economy. But whatever changes war had wrought, the Nippy who came to serve him was the same as ever the Nippies had been – smart, clean, crisp and pleasant. And if the menu she held was shorter, and if you weren't allowed more than one kind of protein, it didn't seem to matter. Somehow, walking into a Corner House was more like coming home than visiting a restaurant.

'It's nice of you to say that, sir,' Phyl Bennett said to the young soldier who made this remark. 'It's what we try to do – make our customers feel at home.' She looked at his tired face. 'You been in action? No – don't answer that,' she added hastily. 'I know you're not supposed to say anything. Walls have ears, eh?'

He grinned a little wearily. 'Well, let's say I'm on leave. Going home to see me mum tomorrow. No harm in telling you that, I s'pose.'

'No harm at all.' Phyl took his order and hurried off to the kitchen. It tore at her heart to see these young men, no more than boys most of them, sent off to fight with almost no training. I bet he never meant to be a soldier, she thought. I bet he just wanted to be a motorbike mechanic or a train driver or something like that.

'A lot of chaps do want to be soldiers, though,' her cousin Jo Mason said when Phyl told her what she was thinking. 'Or sailors, or airmen. Like my Nick,' she added sadly. 'He was thrilled to bits when he got the chance to learn to fly, and now look at him.'

Phyl nodded. She hadn't seen Nick, but Jo had told her about the bandages that had swathed his head and body after he had been shot down in his Spitfire on the very day before they had been due to marry. 'Well, at least he's still alive. And you'll be able to get married the minute they let him out of hospital.'

She collected her order and went back into the restaurant. She still felt guilty that she and Mike had gone ahead with their own wedding. They'd planned a double wedding and when Jo had rushed off to Kent to see Nick, Phyl had wanted to postpone everything. But Jo, white and tight-lipped, had told her not to be so daft, and she'd been persuaded to go ahead. And, aware that Mike, too, would be sent away and

4

there was no knowing when she might see him again, Phyl had agreed.

I'm glad we did get married, she thought, waiting at the door of the restaurant for another Nippy to finish what she was doing at the till and move out of the way, but it does seem so hard on poor Jo.

The Corner House was as busy as ever. War had changed the customers, too, or at least the way they dressed. Instead of smart clothes, worn for shopping or for office work, many people now wore service uniform and there were sprinklings of khaki, dark navy and air force blue amongst the suits and colourful summer dresses. But the faces were bright and animated – men and girls having an evening out and enjoying a meal together. There are some things, Phyl thought, that even Hitler can't change.

The other girl had finished at the till and Phyl walked briskly across to the young soldier and set his meal before him. He looked up at her.

'That looks smashing. Here – what time d'you finish your shift? I suppose you wouldn't come out with me for an hour or so? Just for a walk or something,' he added hastily. 'There wouldn't be nothing funny.'

Phyl gazed at him pityingly. 'I'm sorry. I can't – I'm married, you see, and I don't go out with other fellers. Haven't you got a girlfriend, then?'

He shook his head. 'I did have, but she met someone else. Well, I don't blame her, we weren't serious.' He shrugged. 'It's OK. I just wanted a bit of company, that's all. You know how it is.'

I do know, Phyl thought, giving him another apologetic smile before hurrying away to serve another table. They're all lonely, and they all want a bit of company when they're on leave. It's easy enough to feel sorry for them and say yes, just for a walk, just for a chat. But I know what it can lead to. And she glanced across the restaurant at Maggie Wheeler, and thought what it had led to in her case . . .

They'd been talking about it only that evening as they'd got

5

ready for their shift. Maggie had been standing in front of the mirror, gazing in despair at her distending figure. She heaved a huge sigh.

'Gawd, look at that. Like a blooming elephant. I've let this frock out so many times now the stitches have got stitches in 'em. I'm sure old Turgoose has twigged, you know. I caught her looking at me yesterday. Might be a dried-up old spinster but she still knows a belly full of arms and legs when she sees one. I've got another week here and then I'm for the high jump.' She grinned wryly. 'That'll bring things on a bit!'

The other girls looked at her with sympathy. Shirley Woods tidied her cloud of dark hair under her cap and moved over to give Maggie room at the mirror. 'Has Mr Carter said anything, then?'

'Oh, yes, had me in his office yesterday afternoon. I never got a chance to tell you then. Nice as pie, he was, but there's nothing he can do about it. He told me at the outset, soon as it starts to interfere with me work, out I go, and anyone can see I've got a job to get past the tables now. Can't expect nothing else, can I?' Her mouth twisted ruefully. 'Get yourself in the club, get yourself out of it, that's the way it is. And they can't have me letting down the good name of Lyons Corner Houses, can they?'

'Well, I think it's a shame,' Etty Brown said loyally. She and Maggie shared a room at the hostel where Etty had lived after leaving the orphanage where she'd grown up. Small, sallow-skinned, with the dark eyes and slightly large nose that had made life hard for her with some of the girls at the hostel, and even with one or two Nippies – notably Irene Bond, who had joined Lyons at the same time as the other five – Etty was fiercely protective of big, yellow-haired Maggie. Her first experience of real family life had begun when Maggie took her to the house at the back of St Paul's, sprawling with brothers and sisters, and now that Etty and Maggie's brother Jim were officially engaged, the two were virtually sisters.

'It's awful the way people like Maggie are treated,' she went on. 'And the baby, too. It's not his fault – or hers – is it? And it's not Maggie's either.'

Everyone knew what she meant, but nobody – not even Maggie herself – could fairly say she was right. Maggie had asked for it, one or two of the other Nippies who didn't like her had said spitefully, and nobody could deny that she hadn't done much to avoid it.

Except for that once. And even Maggie didn't know the truth about that.

'So what did Mr Carter say?' Phyl asked. 'He didn't just give you the sack, surely?'

'Well, not in so many words.' Maggie did up the last straining button. 'It's going to be a race whether it's me or this frock that goes first ... No, you know what he's like, he always tries to wrap things up nice. He just said he was sorry but no one would believe it was just ordinary weight gain any more – specially with rationing the way it is! – and he'd have to give me me notice. So I said that was all right, I'd bin going to hand it in meself and that's what I'd do. Tell you the truth, it's bin getting too much for me anyway. I'm getting veins and when I gets home I'm almost too tired to lay on the bed.'

'I think he's been worried about you for a few weeks now,' Jo said. 'I've seen him looking at you, and he said to me one day didn't I think you ought to sit down and put your feet up at mealtimes? He never really wanted to get rid of you.'

'Course he didn't,' Etty said loyally. 'Why, you're one of the best Nippies we got. I wish I could be as jolly and cheery with the customers. You've always got a joke to share, and that's what they like.'

'Mmm. Pity I didn't leave it at just sharing jokes,' Maggie said with a wry grin. 'Wouldn't be in this mess now if I'd managed to keep meself to meself, would I? Me and my war work!'

It was hard not to laugh, even though everyone knew just how serious Maggie's situation was. She wasn't exactly an unmarried mother, because she was a widow, but anyone who knew her would know that her husband Tommy had been killed at Dunkirk – far too long ago for the baby she was carrying to be his. And anyone who knew her would also know that she'd gone with a lot of young servicemen after Tommy had died. Giving them some love and comfort before they went off to war, she'd said, but a lot of people would have just called her a tart.

'What are you going to do now?' Phyl asked her. 'Go down to your mum and gran in the country?'

'Yeah, I reckon so. Can't stop at the hostel with Et, can I? And Dad and the twins are in that men's lodging-house, I can't go there. Anyway, Mum and Gran have got our Evie's kiddies to look after, too, so I reckon I can help out there, and one more won't make that much difference.'

'Are you going to keep it, then? You won't get it adopted?' Phyl knew two or three girls who had had illegitimate babies, and they'd all had them adopted. 'Are you sure you'll be able to manage?'

'It's ever so hard, keeping a baby like that,' Jo joined in. 'You want to think about what sort of life it'll have, Mags.'

'I know. I haven't decided what to do, not really.' Maggie gave her hair a final brush and pulled on her cap. 'See, after I lost Tommy's baby, I didn't think I'd ever have another one. I mean, I never thought I'd find anyone like my Tom that I'd want to get married to. And now – well, it's like a second chance. And it'll be *my* baby. *I'm* its mum. I don't know if I'll be *able* to let it go, to be honest. The only thing is . . . ' She bit her lip and glanced down at the floor. 'Well, it's not knowing whose it is, see? I mean, it could be Davey's for all he was still wet behind the ears – he was a fast learner.' Her irrepressible grin broke out for a moment. 'Or Andy's – and Andy was kind of special, he was the only one I thought I might – well, I dunno what happened to him, dead by now I shouldn't wonder. So if it was either of theirs, well, I might want to keep it. But . . . ' Her voice trailed away and the other girls looked at her with sympathy.

'But it might be that other bloke's,' Phyl said. 'The one that – that—'

8

'Took me down the alley and raped me,' Maggie said bluntly. 'Yes, it might. And if it is – well, I dunno if I could ever feel quite the same about it. I mean, if it looked like *him*, every time I saw its little face, I'd be reminded, see. I don't know if I could ever feel properly motherly towards it. Even though it's not the poor little sod's fault. So . . .' She looked up and gave them a slightly twisted grin. 'I reckon I'll just have to wait and see, won't I? And then perhaps I'll be able to make up me mind.'

Phyl thought of the conversation as she looked across the restaurant at Maggie. In a week, the big yellow-haired girl would be gone, and that would leave only four of the six Nippies who had started together. And soon we'll be gone, too, she thought, for she and Jo had determined to join the services and, no doubt, Shirley and Etty would follow. And if all the other Nippies did the same, Lyons would be forced to do what rumour suggested they were planning, and go over to self-service, with the customers lining up with their own trays as if they were in a works canteen.

'You all right, Phyl?' Maggie asked as they met at the kitchen door. 'You look as if you're in another world.'

'Just thinking what it was like when we started here. We've had some good times, haven't we, Mag?' She grinned suddenly. 'Remember when Irene Bond spilt that soup down a customer's neck? She swore it was you jogged her elbow.'

'Well, so it was,' Maggie answered, her eyes crinkling. 'It was after she was so nasty to Etty that time. She needed taking down a peg or two, nasty, stuck-up so-and-so. Mind you, I wouldn't have done it if the customer hadn't already been rude to me, shouting after me when I went by when he wasn't even on one of my tables!'

Phyl laughed. 'We're going to miss you, Maggie.' She felt a lump come into her throat and saw that Maggie's eyes had filled with tears. 'Oh, *Mag* . . .'

'Blimey,' Maggie said in a creaking voice, brushing fiercely

9

at her eyes, 'being in the family way don't half turn you into a cry-baby. I turns on the tap at the slightest thing just lately.'

Phyl touched her arm. 'You go and have a good rest once you leave here,' she advised. 'You need it. And let us know the minute it's born, won't you? And if you do get a chance to come up to London, you make sure you come and see us.'

'Just try keeping me away,' Maggie said ruefully. 'I don't know how I'm going to manage down there in the country, Phyl, I don't honestly. Apart from a few summers hop-picking, I've never seen a field in the whole of me life!'

Phyl and Jo went home together after the shift had finished. It was over two months now since there had been a bombing raid on London, and a lot of the damaged buildings were under hasty repair. There were too many needing attention to do a proper job on any, Jo's father had said, but at least they were being made safer and bombed sites, which had become an adventure playground for the children remaining in the city, were being cleared of some of their dangers.

'They reckon there's unexploded bombs and all sorts under the rubble,' Phyl said as they picked their way through the streets. You never knew from one day to the next which way you might have to go, what with gas mains being mended and leaking waterpipes plugged up, or gaping craters left by explosions being filled in. The work seemed never-ending. 'They found a huge one down Pennington Street yesterday. Roped off the road for the whole night and people had to go down the shelter even though there wasn't a raid. Jean Somers, from the kitchen, told Maggie she and her mum weren't allowed home till eight o'clock this morning. That's why she was late and there weren't any sausages cooked for brunches.'

'It'll seem funny without Maggie at the Corner House,' Jo said, and Phyl nodded.

'Won't be all that long before we've left ourselves. There'll be only Shirley and Etty there then, out of our lot, and I don't suppose they'll stop all that long.'

10

'I dunno. I can't see Etty in the services, can you? She's so small. She looks as if a puff of wind'd blow her away.'

Phyl snorted. 'She's taller than me! Don't you remember how she grew and I didn't, when we were both in the kitchen? I thought she'd get to be a Nippy and I'd be left grilling cheese on toast. And it wasn't as if she even *wanted* to be a Nippy, till I persuaded her.'

'Well, she *looks* small,' Jo argued. 'I mean, you're not fat, our Phyl, but you've got a bit of flesh on you. Etty's like a wisp of straw.'

'She's strong enough, though, and brave, too. Look at the way she went down that hole and looked after them people who were buried. Got a medal for it. I reckon the services'll snap her up.'

The girls had planned to go home to Woolwich straight from work. Both had the next day off and wanted to take every opportunity to spend what time they had with their families. Phyl had had a telegram to say that her brother Ronnie was on embarkation leave, and Jo's brother Freddy had managed to wangle a forty-eight-hour pass. Norman was somewhere overseas, and young Alice out in the country, so the families wouldn't be complete, but it was the nearest they'd been for quite a while.

'Wonder where we'll end up,' Jo mused as she tried to decide which clothes to take with her. 'I know I'll be out in the country somewhere, in the Land Army, but it could be anywhere from Wales to Northumberland. It's exciting, isn't it – a proper adventure. And if you go in the Wrens you'll probably go somewhere like Portsmouth or Plymouth. I bet it'll be really interesting.'

'I know. It's even more exciting than when we first thought of coming to London and being Nippies. *That* seemed like an adventure, too, but we knew where we were going to work and live, and all that. Now – why, we could go anywhere, and anything could happen!' Phyl glanced across the beds at her cousin. 'You're not really thinking of taking that blouse, are you, Jo? I don't know what your dad would say if he saw you in that.'

Jo glanced down at the scrap of lace she held in her hands. 'Well, no, perhaps not. Though how he could pass any remarks when I'm over twenty-one and an engaged woman – a married woman, I ought to be by now – and we're only going to be with the family . . . But you're right. He'd have something to say. I'll take this old white one instead, even if it does make me look like a nun.'

'I just wish Mike and Nick could be there, too,' Phyl said wistfully. 'But there Mike is, somewhere out in Africa, and poor Nick's stuck in that hospital . . . Everything's turning out so different from what we expected, isn't it, Jo?'

Jo nodded, thinking of Nick in the hospital in Kent. She hadn't seen him for a fortnight now.

'I feel guilty I'm not going down there. I feel as if I ought to be there with him, every spare minute. And then when I am there, I just wonder if I'm wasting my time anyway.'

Phyl stared at her. 'Wasting your time? Whatever d'you mean?'

'Oh – nothing,' Jo said, and closed her mouth in a tight, grim line. She seemed to shrink into herself whenever the subject was mentioned, as if it hurt to talk about it.

Phyl touched her arm. 'Can't you tell me about it, Jo? We've always been able to tell each other everything.'

'There's nothing to tell,' Jo said tersely. 'Nick got burnt, that's all, and it's going to to take a long time to put him right. If they *can* put him right. We've just got to wait and see.'

'What do you mean – if they *can* put him right?' Phyl pleaded. 'How bad is it, really? What have they got to do to him? Hasn't he told you *anything* – what happened, or what the doctors say?'

'Oh, for heaven's sake!' Jo snapped. 'Why does everyone keep badgering me about it? He was *burnt*. Can't you imagine what they'll have to do?' She drew in a deep breath and sat down suddenly on the edge of her bed. 'All right. They're going to do something called plastic surgery. They take skin from other parts of the body and sew it on to the bits that are burnt. It's not like scalding your hand with the kettle, when it just hurts for a few days and then heals itself up. Nick's burns won't heal themselves up. They're too deep. And that means the places where they've taken the skin from have got to heal up and grow new skin, too. And it's going to take a long time. And he can't tell me about it because he can't *talk* properly. Because his – his face was – was too badly burnt.' She put both hands over her own face and began to cry, her body shuddering with each huge, harsh sob.

Phyl stared at her, appalled. She put out a hand and touched her cousin's shoulder, and when Jo didn't shrug her away she put both arms around her and held her close. Jo turned in her arms and clung to her and Phyl rocked her gently, resting her cheek against Jo's thick chestnut hair. They sat for a while without speaking and at last Jo's sobs began to diminish and she felt for a hanky and blew her nose hard.

'Oh, Jo, that's awful,' Phyl said softly. 'Why didn't you tell us about it before? Why didn't you tell *me*?'

'Because nobody could do anything to help,' Jo said wearily. 'Nobody could make it better. And I knew it'd just upset people, knowing – knowing what it was like.'

'Well, why *shouldn't* we be upset?' Phyl demanded. 'At least we'd know. We could share it with you. You ought to have said before, Jo.'

'I don't think I could have done. I couldn't talk about it. I only told you now because I – well, because I got too sick and tired of being badgered about it. You, Mum, Dad, everyone – always on about Nick. I couldn't stand it any longer.'

'Well, I'm glad I badgered you. You shouldn't keep things like that to yourself. Now you'll be able to tell me about it, whatever happens.' Phyl hugged her cousin again, and then asked, 'What about his mum and dad? How are they managing?'

'His mum's ever so upset. His dad's a bit better, he keeps saying that at least Nick's still alive, and that hospital he's in is the best one in the country for plastic surgery. And he's talked to the doctors and everyone about what they're going to do. They go in and sit with Nick every day.' She picked up the lacy blouse and dropped it again. 'I feel awful, not getting down there whenever I can. I mean, like tomorrow, I've got a whole day – I ought to be going to see him, but there's Mum and Dad and our Freddy ... And then I'll be going away soon, into the Land Army if they have me, and I don't even know where I'll be sent. It might be too far away to visit him.'

Phyl was silent. She'd been looking forward to her own new life, but this talk with Jo left her feeling anxious and disturbed. The separation was bad enough for her – the two girls had barely been apart since they were born – but she felt now that Jo needed someone close to her, to help her through. How was she going to manage if she was sent to the other end of the country and couldn't even visit Nick to sit and hold his hand?

'He knows you're going away, doesn't he? He knows you've applied for the Land Army.'

'Oh, yes, I've told him that, and I'll go and see him before I go, and I'll write to him, of course – someone'll have to read the letters to him at first, so I won't be able to say much but at least I can say that I – I – I love him,' she ended on another sob. 'At least he'll know that.'

'It's all any of us can do,' Phyl said quietly. Her own letters to Mike were full of her love, and so were his to her. 'It's not so bad as all that, Jo. So long as we can say we love each other. So long as we've got someone to love. And you know what else I think?' She sat up straight, looking at her cousin with bright, dark eyes.

'What's that, then?'

'I think, whatever happens, we've just got to make the best of it – and *enjoy* it, as much as we can. That's what's going to win this war, Jo – not taking everything too seriously and letting it get us down, but going out there with a smile and a joke, like Maggie does, and getting some *fun* out of it. You're going to *enjoy* being in the Land Army. And I'm going to enjoy being a Wren. And Nick *is* going to get better. They'll mend his face and everything, and he'll be as good as new. And you can write to him, and I can write to Mike, and we can still go on saying we love them because we *do*, and one day it's all going to come right again. *That's* what I think!'

Jo looked at her. She looked at the small, perky figure, the bright eyes, the short, dark curls, and she laughed.

'All right, Phyl, you win! I'll stop moaning and start enjoying this bloody war! And *I'll* tell *you* something. I can see you're going to enjoy being a Wren. You even *look* like one! A bird, I mean – *ouch!*'

She ducked too late as Phyl aimed a pillow at her head. The two girls fell across the bed, tickling each other and laughing hysterically. And down below in the kitchen, their landlady glanced up at the noise and rolled her eyes.

Nothing seemed to get these youngsters down for long, she thought.

Chapter Two

'Well, I reckon that's it,' Maggie said as she and Etty got on the bus outside the Corner House. 'End of an era, ain't that what they say?'

'Oh, Maggie.' Etty's eyes were full of tears. 'I don't know how I'm going to manage without you there.'

'You'll be all right, gal.' They clambered up the stairs to the top deck. 'Phew! I don't reckon I'm going to want to do this any more, specially not in this heat . . . You'll be leaving yourself before too long, anyway.'

'I don't think so. They won't want me in the services.'

'Don't be daft,' Maggie began robustly. 'You're as strong as any of us, for all you're only a tiddler. Or d'you mean . . . ?' She glanced swiftly at Etty's sallow features and then looked quickly out of the window. 'Sorry, mate, I never meant—'

'I know,' Etty said quietly. 'But it's true, isn't it? They won't want me. For all people say it's for people like me the war's being fought, they still don't want us where they can't help seeing us. Nothing but trouble, that's what we Jews are.'

'You're not to say that,' Maggie said forcefully. 'It's not true. Anyone who says that is just an ignorant pig – oh!' Her hand went to her mouth to stifle a giggle. 'Well, you know what I mean.'

Etty giggled, too, and then her face sobered. 'I really am going to miss you, Maggie, now you'll be going down to Devon, to your mum and gran.'

'I know,' Maggie said with a sigh. 'I'm going to miss you as well. But there's nothing much to keep me up in London now, is there? No job, no family – 'cept you – no proper home. All the same, I wish I didn't have to go. London might be in a bit of a mess just now, but it's where I'd rather be. I feel a bit of a coward, running away like this.'

'You're not running away,' Etty said loyally, and Maggie chuckled again.

'Can't run far anyway, can I, not in this state!' She glanced down at her swollen belly. 'Funny, innit, to think there's a baby in there. I bin carrying it about all these months and I don't even know what it is – boy or girl – or what it's going to look like.' She paused for a moment, then added quietly, '*Who* it's going to look like . . .'

They came to their stop and got off. The hostel was quiet. Many of the girls and women who lived there had been called up or had volunteered for the services. Mrs Denton, the manageress, popped out of her tiny office as they came through the front door.

'Your tickets have arrived.' She waved a couple of slips of thin cardboard at them. 'The tickets for the Underground shelter,' she added impatiently as the two girls stared at her.

'Coo, I'd forgotten all about those,' Maggie said, taking them. 'Thought for a minute you'd paid for us to go to the London Palladium. Well, a fat lot of use they're going to be – we haven't had a raid for weeks and I'll be leaving soon to go down to Devon.'

The manageress shrugged. 'That's your business, as long as you give me proper notice. I dare say there'll be someone else glad of them if you don't want them.'

'Oh, we'll keep 'em for now.' Maggie tucked them into her purse and turned away to go upstairs. After the last few raids, back in May, she and Etty had applied for the tickets to the tube station shelter and been given priority – Maggie because of her condition, and Etty to look after her. Not that she would have any idea what to do if Maggie went into labour, she said, but with any luck there'd be women there who'd had their own babies and would be able to help.

'I'm not having it down there anyway,' Maggie had said.

17

'First sign, and I'm off to hospital where there's proper doctors and nurses.'

But she was wrong. At ten o'clock that very night the sirens went to signal a raid, and with hundreds of others the two girls hurried down the escalator. Their bunks, with numbered labels pinned to them, were at one end of the platform and they stumbled over the people already camped on the platform to reach them.

'I don't reckon I give up work a minute too soon,' Maggie observed as they sorted themselves out. 'I never had no trouble carrying those trays till today, but now me back's killing me. I'll be glad to lay down, even on these monstrosities. You take the top one, Etty, I'll never manage to climb up there.'

'The bunk wouldn't hold you anyway,' Etty remarked, grinning, and swung herself nimbly up to the top bunk. Maggie snorted and inserted herself on to the lower one, grunting as she tried to make herself comfortable.

'We're not going to get much sleep here,' she grumbled. 'What with that flipping sing-song going on down the platform and that WVS woman coming round with tea every five minutes . . . And what's that they got down there, a blooming lending library?'

'That's right, ducks,' the WVS woman said cheerfully, pouring tea into Etty's mug. 'Only quiet corner in the station, that is. Would you like a nice romantic novel to read, while away the time?'

'I'd like to get some sleep to while away the time,' Maggie said. 'What with this flipping backache, and not knowing what's going on overhead . . . D'you reckon they're starting the Blitz all over again, Et?'

'I don't know—' Etty began, but she was interrupted by a sudden squeal from the lower bunk. She peered over the edge. 'What's up, Maggie?'

'I've got a pain,' Maggie gasped. 'Ow! Cripes, Etty, I think this is it.'

18

Frightened, Etty scrambled down to the concrete platform. She leant in over Maggie and caught her hand.

'You don't mean the baby's starting?'

'I bloody hope it is,' Maggie panted. 'I wouldn't like anything else to hurt this much ... My Gawd, Et, it's just about cutting me in half. I thought it was supposed to start gradual?'

Etty hadn't the faintest idea. She looked around desperately for help. A man was glowering from a nearby bunk.

'Cut the row, can't yer?' he demanded. 'Some folks is trying to get a bit of kip.'

'My friend's having a baby,' Etty said. 'She needs help—'

A woman reared up in the bunk beneath him. 'Started labour, has she? Cor blimey, some people don't 'alf pick their moments. Where's her hubby, then?'

'She hasn't – he's away,' Etty amended swiftly. 'And her mum's out in the country. She's only got me.'

'Why in't she out with her mum, then?' The woman came over, pulling an old grey coat around her and tying a belt from a brown mackintosh round her waist. 'Oh, never mind. Let's have a look. This yer first, darlin'?'

Maggie was sweating, her face ashen. She nodded wordlessly, then shook her head. The woman looked exasperated.

'Well, is it or ain't it? It's got to be one or the other, and you should know.'

'She lost one,' Etty explained in a low voice. 'Miscarriage when she was about four months gone.'

'Well, thassit, then, thass why this one's in a hurry, see? Second babies often come quicker. How long you bin like this?' she asked Maggie, but Maggie shook her head and then rolled it from side to side as a fresh contraction gripped her. 'Looks to me as if she's pretty far gone,' she observed to Etty.

'She was all right when we came down here. Said she had a bit of a backache, but that was all. I'm sure she never thought it was the baby.'

'Why not? She's a pretty big size. When's it due?'

Etty felt her colour rise. 'She – she's not really sure. She

19

thought at the beginning of September.' September would make it definitely the soldier's baby, and she knew that in her heart Maggie believed it was his. She'd hardly let herself hope it wasn't, and even if it was born now, at the end of July, that wouldn't prove it belonged to either of the other two. Babies could be early or late. Etty knew, too, that Maggie had almost made up her mind to put the baby up for adoption, and it would be easier to do that if she knew for certain it was the result of the rape.

'Well, it ain't going to hang about that long,' the woman said. She put her hand on Maggie's swollen stomach. 'Blimey, feels as if it's going to kick its way out. I reckon you're going to have this kid in record time, gal.'

'Do you know what to do?' Etty asked in panic. 'I've never – I mean, I haven't—'

'It's all right, gal. I've borne seven. There ain't nothing to it after the first eight.' The woman chuckled, a throaty, gravelly sound. 'Look, you go over and arst them at that tea-urn to save us some hot water. And any clean teacloths they got. And then go and see if you can find the warden, he oughter have a first-aid kit handy.' A deep boom resounded through the shelter and everyone looked up. 'Just as if we ain't got enough to do, they got to start dropping bombs on us,' the woman said dispassionately. 'Well, that's why we're here, ain't it? One thing about it, life ain't never dull these days.' She pulled a thin blanket from Etty's bunk and twisted it around the iron frame, giving the ends to Maggie. 'Come on, now, gal, you hang on to that. It'll help you bear down, see. And yell all you like, that helps, too, never mind anyone beefing about the noise. Yer entitled to make a noise when yer giving birth, see.'

When Etty returned with the first bowl of hot water and an anxious WVS lady, Maggie was hauling on the blanket and yelling at the top of her voice. The man in the bunk opposite had rolled over and pulled his blanket up around his ears, but most of the others near by were leaning on their elbows watching. One or two other women had come to help and

20

they were gathered around the writhing Maggie, urging her on with hoarse, encouraging voices.

'Give her a fag. It'll help the pain.'

'No, leave it till afterwards, she'll appreciate it then.'

'Tea,' Maggie gasped between contractions. 'Gawd, I'd kill for a cuppa Rosy Lee.'

The WVS lady thrust forward a steaming mug. 'Give her a sip of this.'

'Blimey, an angel,' Maggie panted. They helped her to lean up and drink from the mug. 'Cor, that's like manna from heaven – oh, my *Gawd*—'

Tea went everywhere as she twisted into another contraction. The woman who had seven children knelt and peered up Maggie's skirt, which was rucked up round her waist. They'd got her knickers off, Etty saw, and she felt humiliated for her friend, to be in this position with so many strangers looking on, but Maggie was past caring. Her legs flailed in the air and two of the women caught a foot each and let her push hard against them. Her scream split the air.

'Blimey, what's that?' someone called out from further along the platform. 'A bloody train coming in? What the bleeding hell's going on down there?'

Nobody took any notice. The mother of seven looked up, triumphant. 'I can see its head. It's coming any minute. Bear down now, gal. Give a real good push, now.'

'I can't!' Maggie roared. 'I can't, I tell you, I bleeding fucking *can't*!' She thrust so hard against the women that her body shot up the bunk and she banged her head on the frame. 'Aah! It's killing me! It's bloody *killing* me!'

'No, it's not. It's not killing you.' The woman at her head looked round and saw Etty, hovering desperately behind her. 'Here, you're her mate, ain't yer? You get in here and talk to her. Tell her she's all right.'

Etty didn't think Maggie was all right at all. She thought her friend was right and that the baby was killing her. But she knelt close beside Maggie's rolling head and put her hand on the sweating forehead and shouted into her ear.

'It's all right, Maggie. It's all right. It'll soon be over. The baby's coming, they can see its head, all you have to do is push.' She echoed the commands of the mother of seven, down at the other end of the bunk. 'Push now, push as hard as you can.'

'I'm *trying* to push!' Maggie screamed. 'I'm trying, I tell you! You think you can do any better, *you* have the bloody thing! Oh, my Gawd, my Gawd, my *Gawd*...' She arched her back and Etty watched in astonishment as the swollen belly shrank before her eyes. The huge lump seemed to travel along the bunk of its own accord, and then Maggie howled again, howled like an animal in its final extremity of pain.

There was a moment in which everything seemed to stop, a moment when the howl seemed to hang in the air, the pulsing lump of Maggie's belly pause as if for breath, and the women gathered around her knees and feet froze where they stood. And then the moment was broken. There was a concerted movement, a babble of excitement and finally, rising above the noise, the thin, uncertain cry of a newborn baby.

'It's born!' Etty cried, almost beside herself with excitement. 'Maggie, it's born, you've got a baby! *You've got a baby!*'

'Well, I didn't think I was going to have a bleeding piglet,' Maggie muttered, sinking back on to the thin pillow in sudden exhaustion. Almost immediately, however, she pulled herself up on to one elbow. 'Where is it? Let me see. What have I got?'

'It's a boy,' the woman who had borne seven of her own told her delightedly. 'A fine little chap. Not all that big – maybe a bit early, you said you thought it should be next month, didn't you? About five pound, I'd say. But he's a little smasher all the same.'

'Give him to me. I want to see.'

'Hang on, gal. Got to cut the cord first. Anyone got a bit of string and some scissors?' The ARP warden appeared by her side and rummaged in his first-aid kit. 'There. That's it. Now you got to wait for the afterbirth, see, but that'll come easy enough, you won't have no problem with that. Here, you can have your little boy now, give him a cuddle, eh?'

She passed the baby up into Maggie's arms. The two girls stared at him. He had a small red face, screwed up as if in fury, and his body was covered in grey slime, streaked with blood. An ugly lump of twisted matter protruded from his stomach. Etty looked at it doubtfully, then realised that it must be the cord which the woman had just cut. He had stopped crying and as they looked at him he opened his screwed-up eyes and looked into his mother's face. He had milky blue eyes and amazingly long lashes.

'Oh, my Gawd . . .' Maggie whispered, and held him gently against her breast. Tears fell on to the wet fair curls plastered against his skull. She lifted one hand and smoothed it over his head, and whispered again. 'Oh, my Gawd . . .'

Etty found that she was crying, too. She leant her head against Maggie's shoulder and shuddered. 'You won't give him away, will you, Mags? You won't never give him to anyone else?'

'Give him away?' Maggie whispered back. 'Not blooming likely. He's mine. *Mine*. My little Barry. My little boy.'

'Wouldn't you just know it?' Jo said wearily. 'Our one night home with the family, Ronnie on embarkation leave and our Freddy on forty-eight-hour pass, and we have to have a raid.'

The siren had gone at ten o'clock, just when the two families had been in the middle of a hilarious card game. Groaning, they'd gathered up the various bags and boxes – the insurance papers and ration books and wallets and purses – that always went to the shelter with them, and ran down the garden. There were two shelters to go to, one in each garden – but by common consent they all squeezed into the same one. Only Bill Mason and Stan Jennings had stayed outside, firewatching.

The first planes came snarling overhead almost before they had pulled the thick blackout curtain across the doorway. They huddled on the bunks, listening for the first explosions.

23

'Well, we're still together,' her mother reminded her bracingly. 'At least, as many of us that can be.'

'Yeah, what a party! All squashed together in a tiny Anderson shelter. There's not enough room to swing a cat, let alone have a knees-up.'

'My knees are practically up to my chin anyway,' Freddy remarked from his position on one of the low bunks. The two families were, as Jo said, squeezed in like sardines. 'But am I complaining?'

'Yes!' they all shouted, and Carrie Mason looked round anxiously.

'Talking of cats, has anyone seen Robbie? I brought him in with me. He's not under one of those bunks, is he?'

Those who could manage it peered beneath the canvas bunks and shook their heads. 'He must have slipped out again. You know he hates being down here.'

'He's more worry than all the rest of you put together,' Carrie said. 'I live in fear of anything happening to him. Alice would never forgive us.'

'Alice has got to learn what's important,' Jo said shortly, 'and a cat isn't.'

'Jo! How can you say that?'

'How can I *not* say it?' She glowered round at them. 'When I think of my Nick – and Phyl's Mike, God knows where – and our Norman – well, I'm sorry, but a cat's not the most important thing to me, even when it's our Robbie.'

Phyl put out her hand and laid it on Jo's arm. For Jo to say that, she thought, meant a lot – Jo was as fond of animals as her young sister. All the same, she knew that Jo would be as heartbroken as Alice herself if anything did happen to the big ginger cat. He was part of the family. She felt a tear drop on to her hand and saw the glisten of her cousin's eyelashes.

'Robbie'll be all right,' she said. 'He's got places to hide. He'll probably be back in a minute with a mouse in his mouth.'

Jo gave a small, choking giggle and then buried her face in her arms, her shoulders shaking. Phyl laid her arm across her back and Carrie, too, moved closer to comfort her daughter. Somewhere outside there was an ear-splitting crash and they all froze and listened, heads up. There was another, and another. It sounded as if a gigantic thunderstorm were going on over their heads.

'It's a few miles away,' Freddy said. 'They've gone past us, I reckon.'

'They'll be aiming for the docks, surely,' Ronnie pointed out. 'You think they've overshot?' He began to scramble off the bunk. 'I'm going outside to see.'

'No!' Carrie and May reached out simultaneously as their sons began to make for the door. 'Don't you go out there, too! It's bad enough your fathers—'

'Listen, Mum,' Ronnie said, 'we're going to be in a lot more danger where we're going next week – well, we *are*,' he added in a justifying tone as he caught sight of Jo's face. 'You know that. Look, none of us is safe in this war. Doesn't matter where or who we are.'

'You don't have to make it worse—' Jo began, but the boys were gone and their voices could be heard outside, talking excitedly but knowledgeably about searchlights and enemy aircraft. Boys! she thought ruefully. They're not boys any more, are they? A few years ago lads of their age would still be having to come in when their dad told them to at night. Now they were going off to fight wars, and how could you tell a fighting man what to do at home?

She glanced at her mother in the dull, flickering light of the hurricane lantern and saw the same thoughts expressed on the tired face, too worn for a woman of her age. It's no use fighting it all, she told herself. You just have to go with it, and do your best. It's all anyone can do, and heaven knows if it'll be enough.

The all-clear went at six in the morning and the families stumbled wearily up the garden path. Again by common consent, they went to their own homes where Carrie and May

25

put on kettles to make tea. They sat round in the two back rooms, drinking the scalding liquid.

'Reckon I'll just have a wash and then get off to work,' Bill Mason said, rubbing a hand across his face.

'Bill, you've not had a wink of sleep. Can't you go in later?' But Carrie knew he couldn't, or wouldn't. There had been many nights, long successions of such nights during the Blitz, when the men had kept firewatch all night and then gone off to work in the morning, sometimes without even seeing their beds. The thought that it could all be starting again was a disheartening one, but everyone knew that there was nothing else to be done. As Mr Churchill said, they would never surrender.

'The only place he didn't say we'd fight', Stan Jennings remarked in the next house, 'was in the bedrooms. And that's because he knew flipping well we'd never get the chance!'

At the insistence of their mothers, Jo and Phyl and the boys all went to bed for a few hours. The raid was over and there didn't seem to have been too much damage in the Woolwich area. It seemed a waste of time, when they had so little chance to be together, but they all had to set off back to their various destinations by evening, and it might be the last chance they would have to sleep in their own beds for a very long time.

'You can get a few hours' sleep and then spend the afternoon together,' Carrie told them. 'We'll have a good tea for when your fathers come home, and then we'll have to say goodbye.' She spoke bravely, but everyone heard the quiver in her voice. 'It means as much to me and May to have you safe under our roofs, whether you're asleep or awake,' she said. 'So just get up them stairs and let's all have a bit of peace and quiet!'

For once, they didn't argue. They did as they were told. Each of them was aware that they would soon be scattered over the country, perhaps even over the world – the boys to be posted to destinations unknown, even the two girls to face an uncertain future.

'We're going to the recruitment offices tomorrow to hear

where we'll be sent,' Jo told her mother. 'Me in the Land Army, and Phyl in the Wrens. Then we'll all be in uniform, bar our Alice!'

At that moment, as if he had heard the name of his absent owner, the big ginger cat Robertson strolled into the kitchen. He glanced at them all without interest, went over to his bowl where Carrie put the scraps of leftover meat or fish from their own meals, and then stuck one hind leg into the air and started to wash. Jo and her mother stared at him and then laughed.

'Well, you were right about one thing,' Carrie said. 'If anyone knows how to look after himself, it's that cat. And d'you know something else? I reckon as long as he's all right, so will be the rest of the family. He's our lucky mascot – that's what he is.'

'Well, it's up to you to look after him while we're away, then,' Jo told her. 'That way, you'll be looking after us all. As long as you take care of our Robbie, you'll keep us all safe.'

Chapter Three

'I'm going to be a *what*?' Jo stared at the woman in the Land Army office. 'A *lumberjill*? What the heck's that when it's at home?'

The woman smiled. 'Well, you've heard of lumber*jacks*, haven't you? You're going to be a lumber*jill*. The Women's Timber Corps, to give it its proper title.'

'What – felling trees and sawing up logs and all that sort of thing?' Jo shook her head a little. 'I thought I'd be on a farm – milking cows and ploughing. That's what I wanted to do.'

The woman sighed. 'Well, we can't always do what we want these days. And most of the girls who go into the Timber Corps do find they enjoy it. But that's not what it's all about, is it?' She fixed Jo with an eye that seemed to look right through her. 'Nobody's fighting this war for fun.'

'No.' Jo felt ashamed. She thought of Nick. 'But – my fiancé – he's in Kent. Will I be able to be near him?'

'I've no idea, I'm afraid. In any case, you won't be able to go home for the first six months, you've got to be trained. And he'll be away himself before long, I dare say.'

'He won't.' Jo debated whether to tell the woman about Nick, but decided not to. There were plenty of other girls in her position, with good reasons for not wanting to go too far away and, as the woman had said, everyone was having to do things they didn't want to do. And Nick's parents had taken a cottage in Kent now, to be near him, so he wouldn't be on his own while he went through all his operations.

But I ought to *want* to be near him, she thought guiltily,

unable to understand the feeling of relief that had washed through her at the woman's words. *I ought to want to move heaven and earth to be near him. I love him. We were going to be married. We still* are *going to be married as soon as he's well enough. So why can't I tell this lady how important it is that I get sent somewhere near him? Why can't I make her see?*

Because there's a war on, she reminded herself sternly, *because we can't all have what we want, and we've had it hammered into us so much we feel guilty for even thinking about it . . .*

She even felt guilty about the fact that she rather liked this idea of being a lumberjill. It wasn't what she'd expected – but it could be fun. Hard work, of course, but work that would be done out in the open air, in woods and forests. Something different, something she would never have had a chance of doing in the normal way of things.

The fluttering of excitement she felt outweighed the twinge of guilt. *I'll go and see Nick first chance I get,* she thought. *I'll tell him about being a lumberjill. He'll be interested. And I'll write to him every day. I won't let him even* think *I don't love him any more . . .*

Phyl, too, found some surprises awaiting her that day. First there was the news of Maggie's baby, told with great excitement by Etty, and almost before she'd had time to absorb that, she was stopped by the supervisor as she went on shift and told that Mr Carter wanted to see both her and Etty in his office.

'He hasn't told me what for. I hope you've been behaving yourselves.'

'Of course we have, Miss Turgoose,' Phyl replied, casting her mind back a little more guiltily than she would have liked the supervisor to know. She glanced at Etty, who was looking alarmed, and they put down their big silver trays and made their way to the office. Etty gave her a nervous glance.

'What d'you suppose it's about? He's not going to give us the sack, is he?'

'Of course he's not,' Phyl answered in surprise. 'Why should he?'

'Well, you know there's all this talk about self-service. They're going to do away with Nippies. And they're sure to get rid of the worst ones first.'

'Well, thanks,' Phyl said wryly. 'I hadn't realised I'd got such a bad reputation. And you're not the worst, Etty, not by a long chalk. In fact, I'd have said we were pretty well in Mr Carter's good books.'

'Well, yes, but . . .' Etty bit her lip. 'There was that customer last week who complained his Welsh rarebit was tough . . . I turned round and told him he was lucky to have Welsh rarebit at all. I know I shouldn't have done it, but—'

'Well, I'm glad you did,' Phyl said, laughing at the memory of meek little Etty answering a customer back. 'Even if we're not supposed to do it, he was a nasty, rough sort of man, not the sort that usually comes in here.' She giggled. 'Anyway, *you* can talk – what about that woman who put her hat on the table and let the feather trail in the milk-jug and then blamed me? Maybe she's put in a complaint.'

'You weren't rude, though, even though it was her own fault.'

'No, but you never know what someone like that might say. Anyway, we'll soon know.' She tapped on Mr Carter's door and gave Etty a friendly nudge in the ribs. 'Stop looking so terrified!'

Mr Carter was sitting at his desk, reading some papers, as they went in. He looked up at them both and smiled.

'Come in, both of you. Sit down.' He gestured towards two chairs placed in front of his desk. With nervous glances at each other, the girls did as they were told and he gave them both a considering look. 'Now, there's no need to look like that. I'm not going to tell you off. In fact, I hope you're going to be pleased with what I'm going to say.' He leant forwards. 'I've got a little proposition to put to you.'

30

Phyl stared at him. 'A – a proposition?'

'Yes.' He looked at her thoughtfully. 'I understand you've both registered for service, is that correct?'

They nodded. 'We all have. Jo's joining the Land Army and I've applied to join the Wrens. Etty and Shirley are still waiting but Shirley thinks, with her father being ill, she might get exemption.'

'And are you very keen to go into the Wrens?' Mr Carter asked Phyl.

Phyl flushed a little. 'Yes. But I'll go into whatever service they put me in, of course. I mean, I'd *like* to be a Wren but the main thing is to serve the country. If they decided I ought to be in the ATS, or the WAAFs, then, of course, I'd do it.'

'Of course.' He regarded her again and Phyl began to feel uncomfortable. What was all this about? Was he going to tell her that *none* of the services would want her – perhaps because she was too short? She felt the tears beginning to form at the back of her eyes. Mr Carter went on, rather hastily, 'Don't look like that, Phyllis. I'm sure that if you really want to go into the Wrens, they'll be only too pleased to have you. And I'm equally sure that any of the services would be pleased to have Esther in their ranks. But, first, I'd like you to consider what I'm about to ask.'

Phyl waited, her heart beating rather hard. She thought of Irene Bond, turning out to be a spy. Suppose Mr Carter was a secret agent of some sort. Suppose he wanted her – Phyl – no, it was impossible. She glanced at Etty and saw the same bewilderment on her face.

'How would you like', he went on more slowly, 'to continue working for Lyons, but in a rather different way? How would you like to go out of London?'

'Go out of London?' Phyl and Etty stared at the restaurant supervisor with a mixture of surprise and dismay. 'You mean be evacuated? But—'

'Not evacuated, no.' Mr Carter glanced past them to make sure that the office door was firmly closed. 'I'm asking you to treat this in confidence, Phyllis and Esther. Lyons have been entrusted with the responsibility of managing a very special war enterprise. We're to take charge of a large munitions complex somewhere in the country. I and some of the other managers are to be trained in handling high explosives and we'll be provided with staff to do the work. Some of them will be local, others will come from elsewhere, and some will be Lyons staff. I'd like you to be my key girls.'

'*Us?* But why?' Phyl's thoughts seemed to be running races in her brain. 'I mean, there's nothing special about us, we're just ordinary Nippies. Just waitresses. What use would I be with bombs and things?'

'You're not ordinary at all.' Mr Carter smiled at her. 'You've already proved yourselves heroines last year, during the Blitz. You've proved yourselves cool and capable in a crisis, and in your work you've proved yourselves to be quick and efficient. You have all the qualities we need. It would be essential war work,' he added.

Etty bit her lip. 'Would this munitions work count instead of going into the services? I mean, would they let us do it?'

'Yes, they would. There's nothing more important than making the weapons our forces need.' Mr Carter paused, looking thoughtfully at the slight figure before him. Etty Brown had always been so self-effacing that she had, as one of the other Lyons Corner House supervisors had once remarked, been in danger of disappearing altogether. Yet as he'd pointed out now, she had a lot of courage, and she also knew how to keep quiet. He'd never once heard her boast about her doings, even though the King himself had presented her with her medal. She would be ideal in the new task he had been set. And so would Phyl.

Bernard Carter had been as surprised as the two girls when he'd been told he was to have training in high-explosives work. It was a million miles away from supervising in a large London restaurant, inspecting the waitresses' fingernails and the length of their skirts and petticoats, making sure that everything ran smoothly in the Corner House at Marble Arch. But in the two years since war had begun to spread its deadly tentacles over the whole world, nobody's life had been predictable. Boys who were barely old enough to drive a car found themselves flying Spitfires and Hurricanes, girls who had never left home were being put into uniform and sent far away, children had been torn from their mothers and fathers to live with strangers.

Alongside all these, for a man whose life had been spent in London, working his way up in a chain of famous restaurants, to be transferred to managing a bomb factory seemed hardly a ripple in the stream.

'I'd like you there, Phyl and Etty,' he said. 'In fact, I'd have liked all of you girls who became Nippies together to be there – except for, well . . .' He stopped the name 'Irene' from passing his lips, although he knew that the two girls were well aware whom he meant. 'You were the best little group we ever had and I'd have liked to have been able to keep you together. But failing that, I'd like you to come to Elstow with me and some of the others who have been picked out for this work. Will you say yes?'

Phyl met his eyes gravely. She knew that in war you got very little choice, but if she refused Mr Carter would probably accept this and find someone else, leaving her free to go on with her plans to join the Wrens. However, he had chosen her, and in Phyl's view it was unpatriotic to refuse whatever service you were asked to do.

'Of course I'll come, Mr Carter. I'll do whatever I can to help win this war. We all will.'

'Yes, we will,' Etty chimed in. 'I'll come, too, Mr Carter.'

He smiled at her and held out his hand. 'I'm very glad. I'll let you have all the details you need as soon as possible. Now, you'd better go back to your work – but not a word to any of the others about this, you understand. It's all very secret. That's why we have to be extremely careful whom we choose.'

Phyl and Etty nodded and slipped out of the office, bewildered and excited. Outside, they paused and stared at each other, their eyes bright.

'Secret work!' Etty whispered. 'I can't believe he's chosen us. Well, me anyway. I can see why he'd choose *you*, but—'

'Don't be daft,' Phyl said, poking her in the ribs. 'You're the one with the medal! Well, it's not what I was expecting to do – I really wanted to go in the Wrens. But, like he said, it's war work and it's important, so it's what we'll do. And I tell you what, Etty – I'm glad we'll be going together. It'll make all the difference, having you there.'

Etty gazed at her. Even after all she'd been through in the Blitz, even after her heroism and after her trip to Buckingham Palace to be presented with her precious medal, she could still never be quite sure that other people actually liked her, and weren't just putting up with her. For Phyl to say what she'd just said meant more to Etty than all the medals in the world.

Her heart skipping, she went back to the big, bustling restaurant and nodded to Shirley Wood, who had been looking after her tables. Shirley came over and gave her a quick résumé of what orders had been made.

'So all you've got to collect is the fish and fried potatoes for Table 4 and curried veg and rice for Table 2. What did Mr Carter want? Not in any trouble, are you?'

Etty shook her head. 'No. Just a – just a chat.' She felt her colour rise and saw the mild interest in Shirley's eyes deepen to curiosity. Hastily, she grabbed a tray and joined the line of Nippies waiting for orders to be handed over the counter. She stared fixedly at the posters on the walls behind the serving staff and her colour rose still further when she realised what she was reading.

'Food is a Munition of War,' she read. The word 'munition' jumped out at her. Bombs were munitions, grenades and bullets and mines were munitions. She'd never thought of food as such a thing.

Well, would you believe it? she thought with a tiny, nervous giggle. I've been working in munitions all the time!

Jo was due to start her training in a fortnight's time. She finished working at the Corner House in a haze of tears, but as soon as she began to pack she felt the excitement rising within her at the thought of the new life she was about to begin.

'I've always wanted to live in the country and work with horses and things,' she told Phyl as they sorted out their belongings. 'How on earth did we manage to collect so much stuff? We'll have to give half of it away. I can't believe I'm really going to be doing it.'

'I know. I can't imagine it either – you, chopping down huge trees. And no pavements or shops or pictures. Won't you miss it all?'

'Don't suppose I'll get time,' Jo said cheerfully. 'Anyway, the pittance we're being paid won't leave much over for shopping, and I dare say there'll be village hops to go to and things like that. What about you, Phyl? Aren't you sorry you're not going in the Wrens after all? You were so set on it.'

'I know. But Mr Carter said he wanted me to go to this place, and it's war work just the same, so . . .' Phyl shrugged. It was difficult that she couldn't tell Jo what she'd be doing. Keeping her war work a secret had seemed exciting and easy to begin with, but she hadn't realised what it would mean to keep it secret from her friends and family. Even though they understood that some things couldn't be talked about, she knew that her mother and cousin were hurt that she wouldn't tell them. In the end, she just said vaguely that she thought Lyons were taking over the catering at some army camp or other, but she knew this sounded flimsy. Army camps did their own catering. 'I'm going to miss you ever so much,' she said to Jo now.

They sat side by side, without speaking, for a few minutes. Then Jo said quietly, 'It's Nick I'm most worried about. He doesn't seem to be getting any better and I feel I ought to be with him. He needs me. And with this Timber Corps, I'm not going to be able to see him for months unless they put me somewhere near him, but the woman in the office didn't seem to think that was very likely. I know I can write to him, but it's not the same, is it?'

'No.' Phyl thought of the letters she wrote to Mike, long letters written each day telling him about life at home and in the Corner House, telling him about the other girls, about the damage in the streets, the raids – anything she could think of – while at the same time remembering not to let out anything that might help the enemy should her letters be intercepted, and trying to keep cheerful. And telling him she loved him and missed him and wanted him home, till her tears flowed and dripped on to the page and left smudges in the ink.

Jo went down to see Nick a couple of days before she went away, and sat beside his bed in the hospital ward. All around her were other men who had been burnt, mostly in aircraft like Nick, and she could see almost every stage of their recovery, from the men – little more than boys, most of them – who had just come in and lay swathed in bandages, through those who had already started on their long journey of operations and skin grafts, to those who would soon be leaving. Some were still terribly scarred, and would remain so for the rest of their lives, and Jo turned her eyes away, praying that Nick would not end up so disfigured.

'I don't know exactly what I'll be doing,' she told him, stroking his one good hand. 'Felling trees, the lady said, and sawing up logs. It sounds funny, doesn't it? But there's one good thing, some of them use horses to pull the logs so I might be working with them, too. I'm looking forward to that.'

Nick said nothing. He still could only speak in grunts and growls, but he squeezed her hand and she smiled at him. What's he going to look like when they take those bandages off? she wondered. Poor Nick, it must hurt so much.

A lot of the time, he seemed half-asleep. They drugged him for the pain. She wondered sometimes if he knew she was there, or even who she was. But it was better than having to watch him suffer and hear him scream like some of the boys whose injuries were so terrible that no amount of drugging would take the pain away.

'I've got to go now,' she said softly, and leant over him.

'Oh, Nick, . . . I hate going away like this and leaving you. I ought to be here with you all the time. But . . . you know how it is. Like the lady in the office said, we just can't do what we want these days.' She gazed helplessly at his bandaged face. 'I want to kiss you,' she whispered. 'I want to kiss you goodbye properly. Oh, Nick, I'm going to miss you so bad.'

Tears dripped on to his bandages and she drew back hastily, afraid that the salt would seep through and sting his raw flesh. She bent her head to his hand, afraid even to lift it because of hurting the bandaged arm, and laid her cheek against the skin. With all the burns and the skin grafts, it would soon be the only bit of him that wouldn't hurt. It's not fair, she thought passionately, it's not *fair*. What did Nick ever do to deserve this?

She took his fingers between her lips, one by one, and bit them very gently. 'I love you, Nick,' she whispered. 'I'll think about you all the time. And I'll write to you.' Someone would have to read out her letters – a nurse, or even his mother – and she wasn't sure she'd be able to write all she wanted to say. 'I'll tell you what I'm doing, but really all I'll be saying is that I love you. Even if I just put it as a PS. And I'll come back the first minute I get leave, and see you again. Oh, *Nick*—'

The bell rang for the end of visiting time. Jo gave his hand one last kiss and stood up. She gazed down at the bandaged face and to her great joy saw his eyes focus on hers and felt sure he was smiling. Then he seemed to swim away through a blur of tears, and she turned swiftly and walked away down the ward, not daring to look back. If I look back, she thought, I'll never go away. I'll just stay here till they have to carry me out.

But at the door she stopped, unable to go without a final glance. Just in case he was watching, she turned and looked again towards his bed. She lifted her hand and blew him a kiss and gave him a last little wave.

It might have been just her imagination, but Jo could have sworn she saw the fingers of his one good hand flutter a little in farewell.

Chapter Four

The new factory was to be set up at a tiny village called Elstow, a mile or so away from Bedford. As Phyl and Etty travelled there by train a few months after Mr Carter's surprise announcement, they found themselves staring out at an expanse of grey, flat fields, still rimed with the snow of the bitter winter. There were hardly any hedges, and only a few snowdrops and early primroses brightened the banks of the ditches to say that spring was coming. The low ridged furrows, still iced with frozen snow, indicated that the fields had been planted with potatoes and the only things higher than the tips of the ridges were a few bare, straggly trees on the skyline and an occasional church tower.

'Blimey, this is a God-forsaken hole,' one of the other Nippies observed. Mr Carter had picked out several to start with Phyl, and the supervisors and managers from other Corner Houses had chosen some as well. They all gazed at the uninspiring landscape. 'It's like a flipping desert.'

'I heard this place we're going to is just a sea of mud,' a girl with short yellow curls remarked. 'There's only a few buildings there.'

'Well, it'll be up to us to get things going, won't it?' a third girl spoke up. Her name was Kaye and she worked at the Coventry Street Corner House. She had bright brown eyes and dark brown hair that tumbled in big curls and waves to her shoulders. 'I'm looking forward to it. I was getting fed up with serving mince and carrots to office workers.'

'I noticed you didn't mind serving the soldiers and the

airmen, all the same,' the yellow-haired girl remarked with a wink, and everyone laughed.

'Course I didn't,' Kaye said, tossing her curls and grinning. 'That's just being patriotic. It's our duty to make life as good for them as we can while they're at home, because they're heroes when they're away!'

Everyone laughed again, but Etty and Phyl glanced at each other and Etty felt tears come to her eyes. That's what Maggie used to say, she thought, only she went a bit too far. And she was lucky to come out of it alive.

The skyline was changing. Slowly, in the cold grey mist that hung over the icy fields, Phyl began to make out the shape of a large church with a tower that stood a little apart from the main building. A short distance away she could see a cluster of tall chimneys and a few other buildings, and then the huddle of houses that proclaimed they were approaching a village.

'I reckon this is it.' Kaye, who was sitting next to her, was also looking out of the window. 'Not that we'll know it, when there's no signs up anywhere these days!'

The train began to slow down and as the guard came along the corridor shouting 'Elstow! Elstow!' the girls began to gather up their things, chattering excitedly and staring out at the church and chimneys. There was little else to suggest that they were arriving at an important and secret munitions site.

'Well, there wouldn't be, would there?' Phyl muttered to Etty as they collected their few bags together. 'And Mr Carter told us it was still being built. But the minute they'd got a few buildings ready, they'd want to start making bombs and that's why we're here.'

They got off the train and stood on the platform, shivering and uncertain in the thin, scouring March wind. Phyl found herself next to Kaye again and the brown-haired girl gave her a friendly smile.

'You're from Marble Arch, aren't you? I've seen you out at the Club.'

Phyl smiled back. 'I haven't been there much just lately.

40

My husband's away and I don't like going dancing without him. I like going for the swimming in the summer, though, and I'm in the dramatic society. Well, I was.'

Kaye studied her. 'That's it. I've seen you in a play.' Her eyes sharpened suddenly. 'Here, did you know that girl Irene Bond, that there was some sort of scandal about? We heard talk that she turned out to be a spy, but nobody seemed to know the truth.'

Phyl coloured. 'I don't think she was a real spy – she just said a bit too much. We didn't know all that much about it really.'

'She went to prison, though, didn't she?' Kaye persisted. 'And wasn't there some other woman tied up in it, too? A shopwalker at one of those posh stores, wasn't she? I'm sure I heard she went to jail.'

'Muriel Chalk,' Phyl said uncomfortably. It had been in the papers, so there couldn't be too much harm in talking about it, but Mr Carter had kept them all behind one day and told them he didn't want to hear any gossip at the Corner House about the scandal. 'I don't know what happened to her. Anyway, I think Irene's out again now.'

'Well, it just goes to show what the posters say about keeping mum and all that,' Kaye went on cheerfully. 'Oh look, here comes a lorry. I suppose this is our transport to our palatial accommodation.' She heaved an old army kitbag on to her shoulder and gave Phyl a friendly smile. 'Come on. Let's see what delights the village of Elstow has to offer!'

The village of Elstow turned out to be prettier than they had expected, with a row of quaint old timber-framed cottages and an old pub called the Chimney Corner. The village was famous for making bricks, and the chimneys Etty and Phyl had seen were those of the brickfields. Next to them was the big abbey church with its separate tower and Mr Carter, who met the girls as they arrived, told them that it had another claim to fame.

'You'll have heard of a book called *The Pilgrim's Progress*,' he said, and some of the girls, who had been to Sunday

School in their childhood, nodded. 'Well, the man who wrote that book, John Bunyan, was born in this village and he used to ring the bells here. They say that he based the book on the surroundings of the village.' He glanced around at the flat, greyish-brown expanse of mud that surrounded them. 'I should think this was the Slough of Despond, wouldn't you? But we're not going to let it make us despondent, are we? We're going to be like Bunyan's Pilgrim, and work steadfastly for the victory of good over evil, never giving way to temptation or the Giant Despair but coming out at last into what Mr Winston Churchill has called the broad sunlit uplands of victory – in other words,' he added, looking rather pink and embarrassed by his speech, 'we're going to work as hard as we can and make sure we help our forces to win the war!'

The girls clapped and Kaye leant close to Phyl and whispered in her ear, 'Does your boss always talk like that?'

Phyl shook her head. 'I've never heard him do it before. He was lovely, wasn't he? He sounded just like Mr Churchill.'

'Well, so long as he doesn't smoke cigars around the place!' Kaye said. 'I've heard you're not allowed to take cigarettes or matches or even jewellery into the work areas in case of starting a fire.'

'How can jewellery start a fire?' the yellow-haired girl asked.

'It can strike sparks. We'll be working with high explosives, see. Anything can set off an explosion.'

The other girl shivered. 'It sounds dangerous! I think I'll hop on the next train back to London.'

'Where, of course, you're as safe as houses,' Kaye said mockingly. 'Come on, Jenny, you're not a coward. And you know how good you are at stuffing sausage rolls. Stuffing bombs'll be just the same, only bigger.'

The girls were to live in large wooden hostels, obviously erected for the purpose. The one that Phyl and Etty were to be in had three floors, mostly bedrooms taking from one to four beds, with a big common-room on the ground floor.

There would be other workers coming, too, Mr Carter told them, and many of them would be billeted in the village or in Bedford itself. Meanwhile there were just a small number of munition workers and a number of builders, all housed on the site so that work could proceed as quickly as possible.

'Are there air-raid shelters, too?' someone asked nervously.

'Of course, but the raids seem to have stopped for the time being and we hope that we'll be able to get all the construction work finished quickly. This is to be a large site and the aim is to produce up to ten thousand bombs a week.' Mr Carter paused while they all gasped. He frowned slightly. 'You must all understand that the work here is secret and mustn't be talked about to anyone. You mustn't even tell your family or friends where you are or what you're doing. You'll all be required to sign the Official Secrets Act, and this means you're bound by law never to discuss what you're doing. The consequences of doing so could be very serious.' He paused again and Phyl wondered if he was thinking of Irene, who had given away gossip she'd overheard while waiting at table in the Corner House and might well have been responsible for the deaths of many servicemen and even civilians.

'All the same, although we'll all have to work hard we shall still pursue the Lyons policy of taking care of our workers and giving you enjoyment as well. There'll be film shows, possibly even touring live shows, concerts and competitions. We know that people work best if they're happy and we'll try to make sure you are as happy here as possible. So if there's anything upsetting you, please don't hesitate to come forward. And please remember that the work you are doing will be helping us to win the war. Take a pride in your work, take pride in yourselves, and your country will be proud of you.'

He stood back and the girls clapped again. They moved off to their hostel and sorted out which rooms they were to have. Phyl and Etty found themselves sharing a four-bedded room with Kaye and the girl called Jenny, who had also worked in Coventry Street. They smiled at each other as they unpacked

43

their few possessions and put them away in the small lockers and the one wardrobe.

'Well, here we are,' Kaye said. 'Almost like being in the army after all, isn't it? That's what I was going to do – join up. Then this came along, and since I don't care what I do so long as it helps win the war I said yes.' She took a battered teddy-bear from her kitbag and sat him on her pillow, arranging his arms and legs carefully. 'This is Ambrose, by the way. I've had him since I was little. He goes everywhere with me.'

Phyl smiled and thought of Jo's sister, her young cousin Alice, who had refused to be evacuated without her cat Robertson. She'd had to go in the end, and by all accounts she'd found herself a cat in the country that she was almost as much attached to. Auntie Carrie had said more than once that it was going to be as much of a job to get her to come home without Solomon as it had been to get her to go away without Robbie.

Etty had never had a pet or even a teddy-bear of her own when she was a little girl. There had been a dolly her mother had made her before she died, out of some rags and a mophead, which she'd called Esmerelda and carried around for a while, but some boys found it one day and tormented her by throwing it to each other, always just out of her reach, and then stuffed it in the fire where it had died horribly, its limbs twisting and contorting in the heat. After that, she'd never had anything of her own to love.

Until Jim came along, she thought, her heart warming at the memory of Jim's tender kisses and his gentle hands. But Jim was far away in the army now and his letters came all too rarely. She kept them in a bundle, tied with a bit of pink ribbon, and read them again and again.

'I see you're engaged,' Kaye said suddenly, and Etty realised she'd been gazing at the ring Jim had given her, with its tiny diamond, and blushed. 'What's his name?'

Etty told her. 'He's Maggie Wheeler's brother.'

'Maggie Wheeler? Didn't she used to be Maggie Pratt? Her hubby never came home from Dunkirk.'

'Yes, that's her. She took me home to tea one day when we first worked at the Corner House, and he asked me to go for a ride on his motorbike. He took me out in the country. We used to go nearly every weekend after that.'

'So where is he now? Serving?'

Etty nodded. 'He's in the army. In Africa.' She covered her mouth with her hand, afraid she had said too much, but Kaye gave her a sympathetic look.

'It doesn't hurt to say that. We know our boys are out there. You must get worried about him.'

Etty nodded again and Jenny, who was sitting on her bed rubbing her legs, said, 'My brother's out there, too. What did you say your Jim's name was?'

'Pratt. Jim Pratt.'

Jenny examined her feet critically. She was a small, slight girl with short, yellow curls and blue eyes. 'My brother's called Tony. And our name's Harris. Perhaps they know each other.'

'Come on, Jen,' Kaye said, 'there must be hundreds of blokes out there, thousands. It's not like being at a party.'

'They might have met each other,' Jenny argued. 'After all, *we've* met, haven't we?'

There seemed to be no answer to that and Etty concentrated on arranging her things. They were pitifully few. A photo of Jim, a pretty blue and silver casket that had once held some of Lyons' chocolates and in which she kept her shell necklace and the brooch Jim had given her, which for some time they'd counted as an engagement ring, and two or three other oddments. She put her little bundle of letters into a drawer with her underclothes and then looked out of the window at the endless mud.

It was more empty than Etty had ever believed a landscape could be, completely different from the busy streets of London, grim though they had become with so many buildings destroyed during the Blitz. She wondered if she would ever be able to get used to such an endless, flat expanse, and such a huge upturned bowl of sky.

Phyl, too, was gazing out of the window. The talk of boyfriends had brought Mike very close in her thoughts and she suddenly missed him unbearably. What a dismal place this is, she thought. And to think I could have been in the Wrens, somewhere like Portsmouth perhaps, where things were happening and there'd be a feeling of being a part of the war.

She remembered her words to Jo about making the best of things and getting some fun out of it all. Well, Mr Carter had said the site would be like a real little town soon, with its own roads and railways, its factories and offices and canteens, and its own social club. There'd be dances and concerts, and perhaps even visits from famous singers and comedians for things like *Workers' Playtime* on the wireless. There was bound to be fun to be had, and if there wasn't, well, she'd *make* some!

'Come on,' Kaye said, pulling at her arm. 'There's tea being served in the messhut. Let's go over there. A cup of Rosy Lee is what we need.'

Phyl grinned at her. 'Rosy Lee! That's what Maggie Pratt's dad always called it. He's a proper Cockney, born within the sound of Bow Bells, and he talks practically all the time in rhyming slang.'

'Just like my old man,' Kaye declared, and winked at Jenny. 'Maybe they know each other!'

Jenny pulled a face at her and laughed, and the four girls linked arms and swung out of the hostel together, making for the Nissen hut where they would be served their meals until the proper canteens were built. Phyl felt the warmth of Etty and Kaye, one on either side of her, and her brief loneliness vanished. She might have been parted from the friends she had made at Marble Arch, but she'd already made new ones. Perhaps it wasn't going to be so bad at Elstow after all.

On the day that Phyl and Etty arrived in Elstow, Maggie was wandering restlessly beside the little river running below a little wood near a Devonshire village. The winter had been almost as bitter in Devon as in Bedfordshire, but here the spring had begun and the hedgerows and high Devon banks were studded thickly with primroses the size of half-crowns, with patches of violets growing between them so that the lanes seemed to be clothed in the royal colours of purple and gold. Along the banks of the river the pebbles and boulders, which had been fringed with glittering ice, were lapped now by swirling brown water that had come down fresh from the melting snow on the moors.

Maggie sat on a rock and stared into a deep pool. A small bird, brown with a white bib, darted across the water in front of her and dived beneath the surface. Further downstream, a heron stood motionless near the bank, its neck hunched into grey shoulders, long beak outstretched ready to pounce. It was very quiet.

I could be a million miles from London, she thought. A million miles away from the war. You wouldn't think, sitting here and looking at all this, all these flowers and birds and the little fish darting in the shallows, that there was a war on at all. You wouldn't think there were such things as air raids and tanks and people killing each other. You wouldn't think anyone would want to do it.

She touched the water with her fingertips, feeling the cold silkiness of the water pulling at them. Until she came here, she had never seen a stream that flowed as this one did, swelling sinuously over smooth round rocks, tumbling in a glitter of broken spray against a clutter of pebbles. In London, the Thames was wide and grey, flowing sulkily between banks of dark, heavy buildings or dropping out at low tide to leave stinking mud where small boys would search for flotsam and jetsam. That was funny, she thought, there were two men on the wireless called that. Flotsam and Jetsam. They played the piano and sang clever comic songs. She'd heard them only the other evening.

There was neither flotsam nor jetsam on this swiftly flowing stream, only bits of trees – branches or occasionally logs – that were swept up when it was in flood and got caught in little eddies. And the water was clean and clear, not like the murky Thames. You could drink this water.

Maggie sat on her rock and looked around at the peace and beauty of the scene, at the crystal water and the newly greening trees and bushes, at the primroses and the violets and the darting birds. She thought of London, dirty and noisy, and she felt a great wave of homesickness wash over her as the river washed over its stones, and she put her head into her hands and wept.

An hour or so later, her face washed by river water, her step as springing as ever and a smile on her face, she walked back up the garden path of the cottage she shared with her mother and grandmother and the children. Flowers were coming out here, too, the yellow trumpets of daffodils and fritillaries like purple bells with zigzag patterns on their drooping heads, but mostly the garden was given over to vegetables and the hens that foraged free amongst them. It was Ginnie's job to look after the hens, helped by young Billy and the even smaller toddler, Freddy, who had been drawn from his dead mother's arms in the rubble of the bombed house.

Thankfully, Freddy had no memory of that terrible night. He followed his brother like a faithful puppy and now that the hens were just starting to lay again they searched the garden every day for eggs, carrying them in with great pride and infinite care, to be put in a bowl in the stone-flagged larder.

'There you are, Mags,' her mother greeted her as Maggie came into the dim little kitchen. 'I was just saying to your gran, our Maggie ought to be back from the village any minute with that shopping. Did you get all we wanted, love?'

'They didn't have no lard, and the butcher only let me have half a pound of liver, mean old sod. He knows we got kiddies and all.' Maggie put her shopping basket on the table and sat down on a kitchen chair. 'I'm parched, Mum, there ain't a cup of tea going, is there?'

'Your gran and me had ours an hour ago. I'd've thought you'd be home earlier.' Ivy Pratt felt the teapot under the knitted cosy. 'It's nearly cold.'

'I don't care. It'll be wet and warm, that's all I need.' Maggie watched as her mother poured tea into an old cup and added a dash of milk and a saccharine tablet. 'How's he bin?'

'Good as gold.' They all glanced towards the cot in the corner, its rails once painted white but now battered and chewed half-bare. 'Been sitting there watching us like a little angel. Dropped off to sleep half an hour ago. I dunno, our Mags, how you come to have such a good baby when all mine was holy terrors. Never stopped screaming, you didn't, from the minute you was born till the day you turned twelve months old. Ain't that right, Ma?'

Ada Pratt nodded. Her teeth were out as usual, grinning from their accustomed place on the end of the mantelshelf above the fireplace. Ada had settled into the cottage just as if she'd always lived there, making that corner hers just as she'd kept the corner by the range in their London home all to herself. Aged nearly ninety, she looked just as Maggie always remembered her, a stout, wrinkled body with a collapsed face and a mouth like a crimped jam pie, clad always in a rusty black dress with a crocheted shawl about her shoulders and a black umbrella ever to hand, even though these days she seldom went outside the door.

She rarely smiled, which was probably just as well considering that she only put in her teeth at mealtimes, and she had a caustic remark to suit most occasions, but Maggie knew that her life had been bitterly hard and she admired the obstinate courage that had brought her grandmother through first the loss of her husband in the Boer War and the need to take in washing to bring up her young family, and then, when she ought to have been able to enjoy her old age in some comfort, to come out of a bombed basement cursing the German pilot who had smashed her home.

'Proper little tartar, you was, Mags,' she said, agreeing with

49

her daughter-in-law. 'Thought about putting a pillow over your face a few times, I did, only your dad wouldn't hear of it. All right for you, Sam, I told him, you're out at work early in the morning and not back till evening, we got to put up with her all day. Why don't you take her to work with you one day and see how you get on, I arst him, but he never did.'

'Gran!' Maggie said, shocked. 'You've never told me that before. If I'd known that, I'd never have gone off and left you in charge of my little Barry!'

'Well, I never done it, did I? And I ain't going to smother *him*. He knows how to behave himself. Like your mum just said, bin as good as gold all morning. Anyway, you drink up your tea, there's a letter for you.'

'A letter?' Maggie swallowed her lukewarm tea and stood up. The envelope was propped up on the mantelpiece, guarded by her grandmother's teeth. She might just as well have clamped them over it, she thought, ripping open the cheap brown envelope and taking out a sheet of scrawled handwriting. 'It's from our Etty.'

'Etty? Oh, that's nice. How's she getting on up in London, and how are the other girls? Has she heard from our Jim lately?' Ivy stood at the low sink, scrubbing potatoes. 'I bet she gets more letters from that young scallywag than we do.'

'She's not in London.' Maggie read on, her brows furrowed. 'She's in the country somewhere, doing secret work. She can't even say where she is.'

'*Etty?* Doing secret work?' Ivy dropped a potato back into the cold water. 'I can't believe it. What sort of secret work? You mean she's a spy?'

'No, of course not. How could she be a spy in this country? You have to go abroad for that. And she doesn't say what sort of secret work. It wouldn't be secret if she did, would it?' Maggie read the letter again, shaking her head. 'I dunno. It sounds queer to me. From what she says, it seems like Mr Carter's there as well and some of the other Nippies from other Corner Houses. I can't make it out.'

'And she don't give you no hint about where she is?'

'No. Just that it's in the country somewhere. They can't be setting up a Corner House out in the country, surely.'

'Well, how are you going to write back to her, then? And what about our Jim, what's he going to do? He'll want to know where she is. And she's our Barry's godmother, too.'

'She's given me a post office address. A box number. Oh, just a minute – Bedford, it says. PO Box Number Two, Bedford. But she can't say no more than that.'

'Bedford?' her mother repeated. 'What on earth can she be doing that's secret at Bedford? It don't make sense.'

'What does make sense these days?' Ada demanded scornfully. 'You know as well as I do, our Ivy, the whole world's gone right off its rocker. *Nothing* makes sense any more. Why, if you come in and told me they'd got chimpanzees doing secret work in London Zoo, I'd believe you. In fact, they prob'ly have. It's just the sort of daft idea they'd get.'

'Never mind all that.' Maggie folded the letter and put it back in its envelope. 'I'll write back to her this afternoon, see if we can't find out a bit more.' A faint murmur came from the cot and she got up and went over to bend over it. 'Hullo, my little treasure. You waking up for your mummy, then, are you?'

The baby opened his eyes and laughed at her. He stretched fat little arms upwards and Maggie caught his fists in her fingers before lifting him. She buried her face in his neck and he chuckled and squirmed.

Barry was six months old and as fair and as fat as his mother. He had been born with golden curls plastered to his hard, round little skull. His eyes had remained blue, just like Maggie's, and he had her rosy features and beaming grin. He looked exactly like her.

There was not the slightest resemblance to anyone else and Maggie still had no idea who his father might have been.

Chapter Five

Of the six girls who had started work together, there was only Shirley Woods left now at the Corner House. There were other Nippies and Sallies as well, of course, but although Shirley was friendly with them there wasn't the same comradeship that she had shared with Maggie, Etty and the two cousins. At this rate, she thought wryly, I'm even going to start missing Irene Bond!

After her first shift once Phyl and Etty had left, she made her way home feeling depressed. Everything's changed, she thought, and none of it for the better. Like Mum and Jack, all that way away in Wales – although to be fair, Jack did seem to love it there, with all the animals. But it didn't make life any easier for her, especially with Dad the way he was after his accident.

Alf Woods was now having epileptic fits two or three times a week. Sometimes Shirley would come home and find the furniture knocked aside, a sure sign that he'd had a seizure, and her father either slumped exhausted in a chair or trying to wash clothes that had become soiled with urine or worse. When this happened, he was almost too ashamed to look her in the eye, and would sit all evening staring into space, disgusted with the body that was letting him down so badly.

'You'd be better off putting me away,' he told her. 'Put me in the loony-bin with all the others. That's where I belong now.'

'Dad! You're not to talk like that!' Shirley spoke with real anger, born of a fear that this was exactly what might happen.

52

'You're *not* mad. You're just the same as you ever were, it's just that now and then—'

'Now and then I has a fit. Oh, yes, that's all. Just a fit, nothing to worry about. I might bite off me own tongue, I might shit and wet meself, I might roll about on the floor and not know what I'm doing – but I'm not *mad*, it's just a fit. *What the hell's the bloody difference?*' he roared at her. 'I can't control it, I don't know when it's going to happen – except I get that horrible smell a minute or two before – and I can't do nothing about what I do while it's on me. I can't even walk down the street any more in case I has a turn. And I'm frightened to stay at home by meself in case I falls in the fire – not that we can have much of a fire, with coal rationed the way it is now. I'm frightened all the time, Shirl. What sort of a way is that for a bloke to live? A bloke like me, what's always bin proud of being a working man doing a good day's work in charge of a big crane down the dockyard? How d'you think I feel now, dependent on my daughter to bring home a wage? I tell you, it's a pity that car didn't finish me off, 'stead of just banging me on the head and leaving me with this lot.'

'Dad, don't,' begged Shirley, in tears. 'Don't talk like that, please.' But she, too, was frightened. Every day when she came home, she turned the corner half expecting to see the house burnt down, or came through the front door with a sinking heart, afraid of what she might find. Even the days when her father hadn't had a seizure weren't much better, for she knew he had hardly dared put on the kettle in case he might be gripped while he was lighting the gas, and she knew that he would probably be sunk in his chair, overwhelmed by depression.

'Why don't you go to Wales?' she suggested. 'Owen's auntie would be pleased to have you there, and you'd be with Mum and Jack. It's so peaceful there, and you'd have nothing to worry about. It'd do you so much good.'

'How can I go to Wales? I couldn't go on a train, frightened I might start rolling around at any minute. And I couldn't look the Prossers in the eye, not once I'd had one there and they'd seen what I was like, messing meself like a baby. Anyway, I can't leave you here all on your own, Shirl. I know I'm no more than a bloody handicap now, but I'm still your father.'

'You're *not* a handicap!' Shirley gazed at him helplessly. Almost the only shred of pride he had left in himself now was the belief that as her father he was still some protection for her. She wanted to tell him that he needn't worry, that if he went to Wales she could join up in one of the women's services and go away herself, but she knew that if she told him this he would feel utterly worthless, of no use to anyone. And she dreaded to think what he would do if he felt that.

'I'd miss you like anything if you went, Dad,' she said, trying to choose her words carefully, 'but I really do think you'd feel better in yourself if you were away from London and with Mum again. You miss her so much. It's part of what's making you poorly.'

'I'd missed her before I had me accident,' he said, 'but I didn't have fits over it. It was that bang on the head what caused them, and you know it, Shirl. Now, look, if you're fed up with having me under your feet, you only got to say so. I know I'm no use. I'd get meself out of your road straight off. You've only got to say the word.'

'*No!*' Shirley's voice, normally so soft, rose almost to a shriek. 'Dad, you *know* you're not a bother. It's just that I worry about you. I'm scared you'll be ill while I'm at work, and really hurt yourself. I wish I could be here with you, but I can't. And if Mum knew—'

'You're not to tell her,' he broke in. 'If she had any idea – well, you know she'd be back here like a shot, and what about our Jack? He'd never settle back in London now, not till the war's over, anyway. No, we just got to carry on the best we can, Shirl, and if I bangs me head on the fender one day and finishes off what that car started, well, it'll be God's will and nothing else.'

Shirley got up and went out into the kitchen. She stood at the sink, filling the kettle through a blur of tears. It was breaking her heart to see her father like this. He had always been so strong, the sturdy rock at the centre of the family. She could remember when Jack had been a baby and they had begun to realise there was something different about him, that he wasn't learning to walk and talk as a toddler should, that his funny little baby nose and slanting eyes weren't ever going to change. Some people, she knew, would have sent the baby straight into a home and tried to forget him, but Alf and Annie Woods wouldn't even consider it.

'He's our baby,' Annie had said, cuddling little Jack against her. 'And he's got a sweet nature.'

'He's our son,' Alf agreed. 'We brought him into the world and we'll take care of him. You don't just turn babies away because they're not what you expected – you take what family you're sent.' And he'd had sharp words for anyone who drew aside as Jack stumbled along the road when he was bigger, and slurred out his words when other kiddies could chatter nineteen to the dozen.

Now Alf seemed to have crumbled, and he was the one that needed looking after. But most of the time he was still strong and as capable as he'd ever been. It was just that these turns came on him almost without warning, and he felt trapped and useless. And it was making him afraid to do anything. It was making him afraid to live.

When that thought entered her head, Shirley felt really frightened. She wanted to ask for help, but who was there to ask? She couldn't even ask her brother Donald for, like so many young men, he was away in the army. He'd been away for two years now and there didn't seem to be much chance of him coming back until it was all over. Sometimes, in her darkest moments, she thought he would never come back at all.

She sighed, and put two spoonfuls of tea into the pot, aware that their ration was almost used up. One for each person, and one for the pot, Mum had always said. Now Lord Woolton's slogan was one for each person and *none* for the pot.

'Come on, Dad,' she said, coming back into the living-room with the tray. 'Have a cup of tea and look on the bright side. You haven't had an attack for three days now. That's really good. And what's more—'

She stopped abruptly as her father gave her a strange look. His eyes rolled up into his head and he sniffed suspiciously. 'There's a funny smell—' he began, and then his body slumped sideways and he fell to the floor in a tangle of jerking, twisting limbs. His face distorted and his mouth frothed, and Shirley snatched the teaspoon from his saucer and thrust it between his teeth, then grabbed cushions from all the chairs and piled them around him to stop him striking the furniture or the fender around the grate.

'Oh, Dad,' she said, watching helplessly as he writhed at her feet. 'Oh, *Dad* . . .'

To Phyl and Etty, and to the other girls working at Elstow, there seemed to be no end to the constant arrival of materials or to the trucks that left daily, loaded with ammunition. And as the site grew to the size of a small town, it was obvious that the powers that be did indeed see the war going on for years.

'They wouldn't be doing all this if it was all going to be over by Christmas,' Kaye said on their first morning as they passed gangs of men labouring to build roads and new factories in the sticky grey mud. 'This lot means business.'

They came to the building where they were to work. Although not much more than a huge Nissen hut or aircraft hangar, once they were inside it was a different story. Just inside the door was a dressing area, where coats and shoes must be left, and everyone was issued with clean overalls and rubber plimsolls. They had to queue up to be inspected – 'Just like Lyons!' Kaye whispered with a giggle – and the supervisors came along the line, looking at each girl with an eagle eye.

'Take off that ring,' a girl just along the row from Phyl was ordered brusquely. 'You've all been warned about that. And *you* – you've got earrings on. You can put them in the box over there till after your shift.'

'But they're real gold,' the girl protested. 'I don't want 'em pinched.'

'You shouldn't have brought them here, then.' The supervisor came to Phyl and looked at her hands. There was a pale indentation on her third finger. 'Are you married?'

'Yes, I am,' Phyl faltered. 'But I took my ring off.' She touched her throat and the supervisor sighed with exasperation.

'And I suppose it's on a string round your neck! Look, you girls, when you're told no jewellery, that's exactly what it means – *no jewellery*. Even if it's under your clothes, it can still strike sparks. D'you all want to be blown sky-high? Because that's what'll happen. And that goes for cigarettes and lighters and matches as well, anything that could start a fire. Even nail varnish, so you can scrub off that nasty red stuff straight away, Kaye Maddox, and don't let me see you with it again.'

She clapped her hands for attention and the girls further along the line, who had been whispering and giggling together, hastily pulled themselves together.

'Now, look, you've all worked for Lyons one way or another and you know what discipline means. Or, at least, you *think* you do. But I'm telling you now that your lives up in London have been spoilt and pampered compared to what they'll be here at Elstow. When you worked in a Corner House, the worst that could happen to you was a blowing-up by your supervisors. Here, the worst is a blowing up by tons of gunpowder and dynamite. If you break the rules here, you won't just get the sack, you'll risk getting killed, and killing a lot of other people at the same time. Killing your *friends*. Do you understand that?' There were a few nods and subdued murmurs. 'So remember the rules and stick by them, and while we're on the subject of rules, don't ever, *ever*, talk about what you're doing here. In a minute you'll all be signing the Official Secrets Act. That means gossip isn't just gossip any more, it's *treason*. A few remarks passed where they shouldn't be turn you into a traitor. And you know what happens to traitors, don't you? Traitors get hung.'

Etty felt her face grow pale. She thought of Irene Bond and Muriel Chalk. Nobody really knew what had happened to them, although people said that Irene had only been put in prison for a few months' hard labour. But Muriel had just disappeared. Had she been hanged?

Phyl shuddered, too. She fished out the ring, strung on its bit of pink ribbon round her neck, and went over to put it in the box, as ordered. Someone wrote her name on a scrap of paper and gave it to her, and she folded it away into her pocket. She went back to Kaye, feeling subdued and a little sick without Mike's ring to give her courage, and found her friend scrubbing at her nails with polish remover. It smelt like peardrops.

'I don't know if I'm going to like being here,' she said.

'Oh, it'll be all right. Once they know we're sticking to the rules, things'll cheer up a bit. Didn't your Mr Carter say there'd be concerts and things? We'll have some fun, you'll see.' Kaye finished her scrubbing and put the top back on the bottle of remover. 'I don't reckon they'll have much trouble, anyway. Nobody wants to get blown up, after all.'

Phyl nodded. All the same, she didn't much look forward to working with gunpowder and bombs. I'd rather be back in the Corner House, she thought. I'd even rather be in the kitchens where I started, grilling cheese on toast with Etty.

But that was the way of life when there was a war on. Nobody had any choice any more.

'Like this?' Jo said.

She grasped the long-handled axe in both hands and swung it high above her head to bring it down hard against the stump of the tree. The other girls, all clad in their new breeches and pullovers, watched with interest. The axe missed the tree completely and the force of it pivoted Jo in a circle. She staggered, almost fell, then stumbled a few steps before regaining control. The instructor gave her a sardonic look, while the other girls dissolved into laughter.

'No, not like that,' he said. 'And the rest of you needn't go all historical, you won't be no better when your turn comes. Look.'

He took the axe from Jo and swung it neatly to make a sharp cut in the stump. A second chop, and he had cut a perfect V. 'Now, you start on the other side and the tree'll fall that way, see, and you won't kill all your mates.'

Jo tried again and this time she hit the tree and was pleased to feel the axe cut deep into the wood. 'It won't come out,' she said, tugging. 'The tree won't let go.'

Grinning, the instructor took the axe again and showed her how to make a shallower cut, so that it would be easier to release. 'Nobody expects you to fell it with one blow,' he said. 'You're allowed to make quite a few chops.'

Recovering from their mirth, the rest of the girls tried, too. For this first lesson, they hadn't been given real trees, only stumps a few feet high. Here in Culford the woods were used for training only, and when each batch of girls was considered fit to do real work they would be posted to forests all over England and Wales. They'd be expected to be in training for about a month.

'You know, this is fun,' the girl next to Jo observed. She was tall and well built, with a freckled face and a mass of red-gold hair which tumbled to her shoulders. 'I reckon I'm going to enjoy this job.'

'We'll need shoulders like prizefighters'.' Jo grinned back. 'I can feel my muscles growing already!' She flexed her arms. 'Ouch! That hurts.'

'It'll hurt even more in the morning,' another girl joined in. She was small but stockily built and had mousy hair cut in a short bob, which made her face look completely square. Her eyes were a pale, muddy grey but she had a cheery grin and a happy expression. She had a Birmingham accent. 'I remember when I first started work, I was sore all over for the first week or two. Then I got stronger and it was all right.'

'What did you do?' Jo asked.

'Worked in a book warehouse, shifting boxes of books. Not a lot different from this, when you come to think about it – paper coming from trees. S'pose that's why books are so heavy.' The girl stepped forward in her turn and swung her axe as if she'd been doing it all her life, making a smart cut in the stump. 'Mind you, it'll be different when we're working with real trees.'

'I think it'll be exciting.' Jo imagined herself deep in the forest, yelling 'Timber!' and watching a huge tree crash to the ground. 'Only a bit sad, seeing all those lovely trees chopped down. But as long as it helps the war work. What's your name? Mine's Jo Mason.'

'I'm Suzy Beech.' The girl giggled. 'Had to come in the Timber Corps, didn't I, with a name like that!' She looked at the red-haired girl. 'You're Poppy, aren't you? Is that short for something else?'

'No, my proper name's Margaret.' Poppy tossed back her curly mane. 'Apparently my grandad took one look at me when I was born and said I was as red as a poppy, and I've been called that ever since I was little. Poppy Marsh, that's me, all the way from Nottingham.'

'Nottingham! Isn't that where Sherwood Forest is? I suppose you'll be going back there.' Suzy winked. 'Maybe you'll meet Robin Hood.'

'Dunno. If I do, I'll ask him why he hasn't joined up. Don't have no time for these conscientious objectors – nothing but a lot of cowards. You get some working on the land, I've heard.' Poppy sniffed. 'I just hope we don't have any in our unit.'

The instructor shouted across at them. 'Come on, you girls, you're not here to gossip. I want all these stumps down before teatime, so put your backs into it. Tomorrow we'll be criss-cross sawing and if you've still got breath to natter while you're doing that, you'll be put into the heavy gang.'

By the end of the afternoon, the girls were exhausted. They climbed stiffly into the lorry which was taking them back to camp, and when they scrambled down again they could scarcely walk. They staggered into their huts and fell on their camp beds. Jo was next to Poppy, with Suzy just across the way. They lay moaning for a while, then Jo rolled off her bed and stood up cautiously.

'I'm for a cuppa. They said there'd be some in the messhut. Anyone else coming?'

'I haven't got the strength,' Suzy moaned. 'I thought I was strong but that flipping axe and all those tree stumps have knocked me sideways. You'll have to get them to fix up a tube so I can just lay here and suck.'

Poppy eased herself into a sitting position.

'I've got aches where I didn't even know I had muscles. How long did you say we'd feel like this, Suze? A couple of weeks? I'll never stand it!'

'At least it keeps us warm,' Jo said. The ground was still hard with frost, and the tree stumps slippery with ice. 'What did you do, before you came here?' she asked.

'Worked in a Lyons teashop. I used to—'

'A *Lyons*?' Jo asked, amazed. 'Which one?'

'In Nottingham, of course. I was a—'

'Well, if that don't beat the band. *I* worked for Lyons, too! I was a Nippy in Marble Arch Corner House. What did you do in the teashop?'

'I've been trying to tell you,' Poppy pointed out. 'I was a waitress, too, only they didn't call us Nippies. Matter of fact, I had the chance to transfer to a Corner House, but I didn't want to go to London and anyway I liked the teashop, it was small and friendly. I didn't want to go to a big Corner House with a thousand other people working there.'

'Corner Houses are friendly, too—' Jo began, but Suzy interrupted. She had levered herself up and was bending stiffly to pull on her shoes.

'Don't you two start arguing. You're in the Timber Corps now, and we're all equal. It doesn't matter what we did before.'

Poppy looked at Jo and pulled a face, and they both

61

grinned. 'She's only little,' Poppy said, 'but she knows how to be boss. Well, I suppose we'd better do as we're told, eh? And I don't mind someone else serving me my tea, I can tell you! It makes a nice change.'

Over the next few days they learnt more about each other. Poppy lived in a three-bedroomed semi-detached house in a nice area of Nottingham, with her parents and two brothers. 'Only, Pete and Graham are both away now, in the army,' she explained. She had a boyfriend called Neil, but it wasn't serious, and a dog called Scamp who seemed to matter rather more. Her dad had served in the First War and been gassed, and his lungs had never been the same since, and her mother was in the WVS.

Suzy came from Canterbury. She lived with her mother. There were only the two of them, her father having died years ago when Suzy was a baby, and it had been a hard decision to leave home, but in the end there'd been no choice. She was hoping to be posted somewhere near home.

'Have you got a chap, too?' Poppy asked, her mouth full of currant bun.

Suzy shook her head. 'Don't want one. Mum says it was the best thing that could have happened to us when Dad died. She knows what men can be like.'

The other two stared at her. 'What d'you mean, what they can be like? My dad's a smasher. Well, he can be a bit awkward at times,' Jo amended, thinking of the way she'd had to sneak out with Phyl to watch the Coronation, on the day when they'd decided to become Nippies, 'but everyone's dad's like that. He's good as gold, really.'

'Well, mine wasn't,' Suzy said, and closed her mouth tightly. The other two exchanged glances and Poppy changed the subject.

'There's an army camp not far away. I wonder if we'll get asked to the dances?'

'I shan't go,' Jo said. 'It wouldn't be fair on Nick. He's my fiancé,' she explained, and when the other two looked questioningly at her, she added tersely, 'He's in hospital in Kent. Got shot down in his Spitfire.'

'A pilot! Gosh – that's romantic,' Poppy exclaimed. 'How long's he going to be in hospital? Will he be going back to his squadron soon?'

Jo looked down at the table, feeling her eyes fill with tears. She hated telling people about Nick. It seemed to bring back all the anguish of that moment when she'd first seen him, lying heavily bandaged in his hospital bed, and of all her visits as she'd gradually realised just how badly he'd been burnt and how long it was going to take before he was better.

'No. He won't be going back,' she said in a quiet voice. 'And there's nothing romantic about it. He got shot down the day before we were supposed to be married.'

There was a brief, appalled silence. Then Suzy touched her hand. 'Is he in that hospital where they do all the plastic surgery and skin grafting? I've got a friend who nurses there. She says some of the men are ever so badly burnt, but they can do a lot for them.'

'Yes,' Jo said. 'Yes, that's where he is. And I'm not going to be able to see him for a whole month, all the time I'm here. He's got all those operations to go through, and I can't be with him.' Her voice trembled and broke.

'But that's awful!' Poppy exclaimed. 'Why, we're not all that far away here. You could get a train from Bury St Edmunds and be back in a day. You could go at the weekend.'

'I can't. You know we're supposed to stay here all through our training. They never let girls go home the first month in case they're homesick and don't come back.'

'Well, I wouldn't take any notice of that,' Poppy said robustly. 'Not if it was my chap. Look, we'll cover for you, won't we, Suze? We aren't working on Sunday. You could go then.'

'We're supposed to be going to church.'

'For cripes' sake! God won't mind you going to see your boyfriend instead. He'll be pleased. Look, if anyone says anything we'll say you've got a headache, or your period or something. You just get up early and go. *I* would.'

Jo gazed at her. I would, too, she thought. If it was Poppy or Suzy telling me this, I'd say just the same. So why haven't I thought about doing it myself?

Sunday morning dawned bright and sunny, with warmth already in the air. The girls were allowed to lie in, with a day off from the physical jerks they did at six-thirty every weekday morning. Jo woke with the blackbird's song and slipped out of bed, dressing swiftly in her breeches and shirt. She tiptoed to the door of the hut and then glanced over her shoulder. All the other girls seemed to be asleep, but Poppy's eyes were half-open and as Jo looked at her one of them closed again in a wink.

Jo grinned and slid through the door. There was nobody about in the camp and, since it wasn't a military establishment, no guard at the gate. She walked rapidly along the lane, her back tingling, half expecting at any moment to hear a shout. But nobody called out, and soon she was at the little railway station and the man in the ticket-office was looking blearily at her.

'You're up and about early, gal.'

'I've got a family visit to make.' She asked for her ticket and produced the money. Poppy and Suzy had clubbed together their own first week's wages to make sure she had enough. There would be a change to make, and a long wait at the station, but she could be at the hospital just before midday. Coming back, she'd need to catch the three-thirty to be in camp in time for supper.

Despite the early hour, the train was full. There were always soldiers and air force men going somewhere, she thought, wedging herself between a large sergeant and a private, sweating in their heavy serge. Probably they were taking advantage of their own opportunities to see wives and girlfriends. The compartment was stuffy and smelt of bodies and breath. Most of them were smoking and the air was blue with smoke.

Jo hadn't ever started to smoke, and neither had Phyl, but several of the other Nippies did and she was accustomed to smoke at the Corner House. But this morning, in this close, fetid atmosphere, it seemed too much to bear. She felt sick and dizzy, and was thankful when it was time to change trains. She almost fell on to the platform and took a deep breath of fresh air.

'You're looking a bit pale.'

Jo turned with a start. The man who had spoken to her was tall and suntanned from working out of doors. He had a calm face and bright hazel eyes that looked as if they could dance with merriment. He was wearing the brown breeches and green pullover of a landworker. There weren't many men who wore these clothes – it was a Land Army uniform, mostly for the girls – but Jo had seen one or two about the camp, and racked her brains to try to remember something that had been said about them. Something Poppy had said, she thought, but couldn't remember what.

'I'm all right. It was just so stuffy and smoky in there, and the train was swaying a lot.' She brushed some smuts off her pullover and looked with distaste at the black streaks they left behind. 'Ugh. And I started out so clean and tidy, too!'

The man laughed. 'I've seen you before. You're in the Timber Corps, aren't you?'

'Yes, that's right.' Jo looked at him more closely. 'Are you at Culford, too?'

He nodded. 'I'm in one of the other gangs. How are you getting on? Are you enjoying it?'

'Oh, yes. I'm worn out every night, but I love working outside and in the woods. We did criss-cross sawing the other day – I've never laughed so much in all my life.' She described how she and Poppy had each taken one end of the big saw and chanted 'See-Saw, Margery Daw' to help them get a rhythm. 'Once you've got the idea that all you have to do is pull and push and the saw does the work, it's easy, but we were trying to *make* it do it at first. The saw nearly bent itself double and so did everyone else, laughing at us.'

He grinned. 'I was just the same, with my partner. It looks so easy, you'd think anyone could do it, but there's a real knack. Same with everything, I suppose.' He paused for a moment. 'How long have you got to wait for your next train? Have you got time for a cup of tea?'

Jo hesitated, then nodded. 'I've got an hour at least – and that's if it's on time! Thanks.'

They strolled along the platform to the little buffet, where they were given thick mugs of strong tea. The man bought a couple of sandwiches and offered Jo one. She shook her head, then changed her mind.

'I didn't have any breakfast,' she confessed as she bit into the bread and fish paste. 'I slipped out early.' She blushed, realising that he must know she wasn't supposed to have left the camp. 'I'm going to see my fiancé, in hospital.'

'In hospital? Sorry to hear that.' He asked about Nick and Jo told him, briefly. He shook his head. She thought he was probably about twenty-six or twenty-eight, a bit older than Nick. She wondered why he was in the Timber Corps.

'My name's Josh Taylor,' he said. 'Short for Joshua.'

'That's from the Bible,' Jo said, and he nodded. 'My name's Jo Mason. Short for Josephine. I'm from London – I was a Nippy before I joined up.'

'What, in one of the Corner Houses?' She nodded. 'I used to go in them quite a lot. I worked in the City for a while, before – before the war.'

Jo gave him a curious look. He was strong and fit, as far as she could tell, and most men of his age were in the forces by now. Unless there was something wrong with him that meant he couldn't be accepted. Or unless there was some other reason.

'Which train are you waiting for?' she enquired. 'Are you going to see your family, or your girlfriend, or something?'

He smiled. 'I'm going to see my father in Brighton. It's my last chance before going away. I've just got my posting – a village in Shropshire. Won't be able to get home much from there.'

They found a bench and sat down, drinking their tea and sharing Josh's sandwiches. He was easy to talk to, Jo found, pleasant and companionable, with plenty to say but not forcing his opinions on her. She told him about her days as a Nippy and how much she'd enjoyed working for Lyons.

'They treat you like a family. There's a social club at Sudbury, where we used to go every weekend for sports and dancing, and whenever a girl gets married they give her a wedding cake. The supervisors are really nice – most of them, anyway – not a bit like foremen in factories. Not that I ever worked in a factory. I helped in the local greengrocer's shop with Mum before I joined Lyons, but my cousin was in a factory and she hated it.'

'I was an accountant,' he said. 'I had a job in Brighton and then got transferred to London. Then war broke out and . . .' He paused and looked at the remains of his sandwich. He seemed about to say something else but Jo, feeling embarrassed by his silence, rushed in.

'Were you there in the Blitz? Wasn't it awful? We never knew what we were going to see when we came out of the shelters in the morning. Houses bombed to bits, people killed, bodies lying about It was horrible. Our lodgings went one night, and our landlady was in them.' Her voice was sober. 'Phyl and me – Phyl's my cousin – were on night shift at work, firewatching, and when we turned the corner to go home there was just nothing there but a black, burnt-out shell. And poor Auntie Holt – we always called her Auntie – she was laid out in the church hall with all the others that had been killed that night.' Her voice broke and she brushed fiercely at her eyes. 'Sorry – I didn't mean to tell you all that. I don't usually tell people, it always makes me cry – dunno why I should suddenly come out with it now.'

'It's all right,' Josh said gently. 'I'm glad you've told me. And there's nothing wrong with crying. It'd be a poor thing if you couldn't cry over someone you loved.'

'Yes, I suppose we did love her,' Jo said thoughtfully, finding a handkerchief. 'I mean, she wasn't one of our family, just our landlady, and we weren't there all that long – but she looked after us as if she were a mother. And Phyl and me were both upset when she was killed. It seemed so unfair.'

'War's like that,' he said. 'It doesn't care who gets killed. Fairness doesn't come into it any more.' There was a short silence and then he said, 'So where's your cousin now? Phyl, did you say her name was?'

'That's right. She's in Bedford. Lyons are doing the catering for an army camp there.' She fell silent again, and then said quietly, 'We were supposed to be having a double wedding, her and Mike, and me and Nick. But Nick got shot down the day before and now he's in hospital having skin grafts and things.'

He turned and looked at her, his brown eyes shocked. 'Skin grafts! He was badly burnt, then.'

'Yes,' Jo said. 'Yes, he was.'

They were silent for a while, but it was an easy silence. Then they began to talk again, quietly, easily. By the time Jo's train arrived – no more than half an hour late – she felt as if they knew each other well, had known each other for years.

She got up and stood facing him as the train steamed slowly alongside the platform. 'Thanks for the tea and sandwich. It's been nice talking to you.' The phrases sounded stilted and not at all as she wanted them to sound, but what else was there to say? 'I hope you have a nice time with your family.'

His brown eyes looked down at her gravely. 'And I hope you find your Nick feeling better about things. He's got a hard job in front of him.'

Jo nodded. She looked at him, at his eyes, his firm lips, and then put out her hand. He took it in his and she felt the warm, dry strength of his fingers. He smiled at her.

'Thanks for your company, Jo. Maybe we'll see each other around the camp.'

She nodded again and turned to climb aboard the train. She didn't really expect to see him in the camp. He'd be leaving next week anyway, to go to Shropshire. Then they'd never see each other again.

He was still standing on the platform when she found a seat and looked out through the window. The engine gave its warning bellow and started to move forwards. Jo saw Josh lift his hand, and she raised hers in reply, not at all sure whether he had seen her or not. Then the train began to move and he was lost in a puff of steam and smoke.

Jo turned her face away and looked ahead, along the line, along the way that would take her to Nick.

There hadn't been time to let Nick's parents know that she was coming, but Jo was surprised to see them coming out of the hospital as she arrived. She'd expected to find them beside his bed, making the most of every possible moment. To her dismay, as she drew closer, she saw that Mrs Laurence was crying.

'What is it? What's happened?' Fear tore at the edges of her voice. 'He's not – he's not . . .'

'Jo!' The Laurences stopped and Mr Laurence stared at her in surprise. 'We didn't expect to see you here today. Did Nick ask you to come? Did he tell you . . . ?'

'Tell me what?' She looked from one to the other, her fear growing. 'He didn't tell me anything – he doesn't know I'm coming. What's happened? What's wrong?'

She looked at Nick's mother. Mrs Laurence had taken her son's injuries badly right from the start. But her tears this morning were for something new, Jo was certain of it. Something had happened and she wanted to shake the other woman's arm to get it out of her. 'Please, *tell* me.'

'Nothing's happened,' Mr Laurence said heavily. 'At least, nothing we didn't . . . Look, Jo, it might be better if you didn't go in to see Nick this morning. Go back to your camp. Leave it for a week or two.'

'But why? Why shouldn't I see him? And I can't leave it – I'll be going away soon. I might be hundreds of miles away, the north of England, *Scotland*, even . . . Look, what's going on? What's the matter with Nick?'

Nick's parents looked at each other. Then Mr Laurence sighed and said, 'They've taken the bandages off, Jo. That's what it is. It's – well, Nick's mother found it a bit hard to take, and I'm afraid you might as well.'

Jo stared at them. 'Taken the bandages off?' It ought to be a good thing. It *was* a good thing. It meant he was getting better. But . . . 'What – what does it look like?' she asked in a small, fearful voice, and knew that they didn't need to answer.

There was a long silence. Mrs Laurence sobbed into her hanky. Jo looked at her and wished she could think of something to say. At last she said quietly, 'I think I ought to go and see him, all the same. It's not going to make any difference after all. And I've come all this way . . . I wasn't supposed to come out this morning at all. And if I don't go in soon . . .'

'Visiting time will be over.' Mr Laurence nodded. He laid his hand on Jo's arm. 'You go on in, Jo. And afterwards, come round to the cottage and have a bit of dinner with us. You'll have time before your train goes back, won't you?'

Jo walked away from them and into the hospital. She found her way to Nick's ward, her legs shaking more with each step. Despite her brave words, she wasn't looking forward to seeing Nick's face with the bandages off. I mustn't let him see it matters, she told herself as she walked along the endless corridor. It *doesn't* matter. It doesn't . . .

The nurse who met her at the door was one Jo had seen before. She was small and pretty, with curly blond hair tucked under her cap. She looked about twenty but was as brisk and efficient as a much older woman. She nodded sharply when Jo told her who she was, and led her to a bed that was shrouded by curtains.

'Why are the curtains drawn?' Jo asked. 'Has he been moved? He was over there last time.'

'That was weeks ago,' the nurse said, as if Jo had been neglecting her fiancé by not visiting before. 'And the curtains are drawn because he prefers it. Just for the moment.' She poked her head through them and said in a softer voice, 'There's someone else to see you, Nick.'

Nick? Jo looked at her in surprise. Surely the nurses were supposed to address their patients more respectfully – with their ranks and surnames. But she was too concerned about Nick to bother about hospital etiquette. She pushed past the pretty young nurse and stepped through the curtains, a bright, loving smile pinned to her face.

'Nick! Surprise, surprise! I've nipped out of camp specially to come and see you. I hear they've taken your bandages . . .' her voice faded '. . . off . . . Oh, *Nick* . . .'

There was a moment, an eternity, of silence. The nurse had disappeared. Jo and Nick stared at each other – Jo with wide, frightened eyes in an appalled face, Nick with fury and resentment and hostility.

Jo made a huge effort and dragged her tattered composure around her. She looked for a chair and sank down on it, knowing that if she didn't her legs would give way completely. Unable to tear her eyes away from the ravaged face, she felt for the good hand that had been their only means of communication and held it tightly. The rage in his eyes was even more frightening than the dreadful face that had once been Nick.

'Oh, Nick,' she whispered, and tears spilt down her cheeks. '*Nick* . . .'

'Well?' he said jaggedly, his voice so distorted by the contortion of his mouth and jaw that she could barely make out the words. 'Say it. Go on. Tell me how ugly I am. Tell me you don't want to see me any more. I won't blame you. I don't want to see myself.'

'Nick, no! I'm not going to say that. Of course I want to see you. Whatever you look like—' She caught herself up. 'It's only till they've done the surgery,' she said gently. 'You'll be all right again then.'

'Not like I was before,' he said. 'I'm never going to look like that again, don't kid yourself. I'm always going to be ugly, Jo,

71

whatever they do to me.' He turned the ruined face away. 'I might as well have gone down in flames in the first place,' he said bitterly. 'There's not going to be much point in anything now, is there?'

'Nick! You mustn't say things like that. Of *course* there'll be a point. We – we're getting married. We've got all our lives to look forward to. I love you, Nick.' She pulled her chair closer. 'You've got to believe that. I *love* you.'

The face turned back to her. 'Do you? Do you really? Even – even like this?' The dark brown eyes, the only recognisable part of Nick that was left, stared at her. 'Suppose I always look like this. Will you really want to marry me? Will you really want to walk down the aisle with me? Will you even want to walk down the *street* with me?'

Dark brown eyes that had once been so merry, so full of laughter, and were now so hard and bitter. Jo felt the ache of tears again in her throat. She shook her head blindly and brought his hand to her lips, kissing it fiercely.

'You mustn't say such things. You mustn't.'

Nick stared at her. She forced herself to look again at the mutilated face, the thickened, puckered skin, the rawness of the burnt flesh; the torn, misshapen nose, the lips that no longer made a mouth.

'Shall I tell you something?' he said, and she flinched at the caustic note in his distorted voice. 'I can say whatever I like. I've been a flier. I've shot down enemy aircraft and I've been shot down. I've been nearly burnt to death. I can say *anything I bloody like*, and there's nobody, Jo, nobody, not even you, not even God Himself, who can tell me any different. It's about all that's bloody left to me.'

Visiting time was almost over. Once the bell had been rung, everyone had to go, no matter how far they had come. Jo sat and gazed at him, longing to do something more than just squeeze his hand, knowing that she could not kiss those torn, misshapen lips. She kissed his hand instead, each finger and the palm, and held it against her mouth. Next time she saw him, she would be a fully fledged lumberjill, working – she

72

hoped – in one of the forests of the south-east, and able to see him every week.

'I'll write to you, Nick,' she whispered. 'I'll write every day. And I'll come and see you just as soon as I can.'

Nick turned his head towards her. The dark brown eyes, once so alive, now as dead as pebbles, looked into hers. The bell rang loudly, an intrusion, and she hated the noise of it. She whispered his name again and, unable to say the word '*goodbye*', turned and hurried blindly out of the ward.

Not for anything in the world would she have confessed to anyone else the dismay she had felt on seeing his ravaged face. Not for anything in the world; not even to herself.

Chapter Six

At just ten months old, Barry Wheeler was on his feet and walking round the furniture. Maggie was so proud she thought she would burst.

'It must be the country air,' his grandmother said, watching him admiringly as he tottered unsteadily between the chairs. 'None of you ever walked till you was a good eleven months, and our Evie was nearly fourteen months. He'll be running about before he's that.'

'Three months, that's how long it is,' Ada said through her gums. 'Three months from crawling to getting up on their feet, and he bin crawling nearly that long now. Mind you, he's fat, he might take a bit longer.'

'He's not fat! He's just well built. And chubby. Babies are meant to be chubby.'

'Whatever he is, he'll soon get it down now he's almost walking,' Ivy said. 'Well, the peace is over. He'll be into everything now. You'll need eyes in the back of your head, Mags.'

Maggie nodded. She said, 'I been thinking about things, Ma. I didn't ought to be sitting here on me backside all day doing nothing. It ain't right.'

Ivy looked at her. 'I wouldn't say you was sitting about much. You do the hens with Ginnie, and you've started on the garden, growing veg and that. And you got Barry to look after, and you helps with the other little 'uns.'

'I know, but you and Gran do that as well. And I could dig the garden in me spare time. I ought to be doing more, like the others – Jo and Phyl, and Etty. They're all helping the war effort and I'm doing bugger all.'

'You're not thinking of joining up!' Ivy was shocked. 'You got a kiddy, Mags! You can't just go off and leave him.'

'I don't want to go off and leave him. But I ought to be doing something.'

Her mother pursed her lips and stared down at the baby, who was holding the arm of the chair with only one hand. Any time now, he would let go and take his first few steps. They watched with bated breath.

'You thinking about getting a job, then? I dare say there's some work going round about here. They'll be wanting pickers for soft fruit soon, or you might be able to pick up a shop job in Tavistock. You could bike in every day.'

Maggie shrugged. 'I want to do more than that, Mum. Something to help.' She looked down at Barry, who let go of the chair arm, overbalanced and toppled sideways to lie chuckling on the floor. Everyone, even Ada, smiled, and Maggie reached down and lifted him on to her lap where he began to play with her necklace. It was one Tommy had given her when they'd first started going out together. 'I want to do something for my Tom.'

'So you *are* thinking of joining up.' Ivy drew in a deep breath and Maggie knew she was gathering together her arguments. *Going off and leaving a kiddy. Me and your gran taking all the responsibility. Already got young Ginnie and poor little Billy and Freddy to look after* . . . Maggie rushed in quickly, before they could start flooding out.

'No, I'm not joining up. I'm not going away. I'm going to see about doing some nursing.'

'*Nursing?*'

'Yes. Up at the big house. It's been requisitioned for an army hospital. They're bringing blokes there what've been injured and got to convalesce. I saw the notice in the post office. I've applied for an interview.'

The two older women gazed at her. 'But you don't know nothing about nursing,' Ivy said at last.

'Well, I can learn, can't I? Nobody knows about nothing till they start learning. And it's mostly convalescents, people who are getting better. Anyway, they wants all sorts there, cleaners and all, so there ought to be some job I can do.' She grinned suddenly. 'I can carry in their tea, if nothing else!'

'Well, I dunno . . .' Ivy looked dubiously at Barry, who was now struggling to get down and practise crawling again. 'It means me and your gran got to take charge of him. You couldn't take him with you.'

'You wouldn't mind that, though, would you? Not really? It could be your war work. We all got to do our bit, Ma. I mean, things ain't getting no better, are they? Even down here in the country . . . Look at the way Exeter got bombed a few weeks ago, there's practically nothing left in the centre, just like Plymouth. We got to do *something*. You wouldn't really mind looking after Barry a few hours a day, would you?'

Ivy gave her a smile. 'No. I wouldn't mind a bit. He's a little love, and I been dying to get him to meself. You're right, Mags, we all got to do our bit and if you want to go and do some nursing, you go and do it and good luck to you. Me and your gran and young Ginnie will look after Barry.'

After Maggie had gone out, taking Barry for a walk to the village pond to feed the ducks, Ivy and her mother-in-law looked at each other.

'Could be a good thing,' Ada said, opening the tin in which she kept her sweet ration. 'P'r'aps she'll meet someone up there. Oh, botheration. There's only toffees left. You knows I can't eat toffees, Ive.'

'It was all they had. Put 'em on the window-sill, they'll go soft in the sun, turn into fudge.' Ivy frowned. 'Tell you what, Ma, that's what does bother me a bit about our Mag going to work up the big house. You know what she's like.' She glanced over towards Barry's cot. 'We don't want no more little bundles of joy, do we?'

At the end of their month's training, and before they went off to their postings, the lumberjills were given a forty-eight-hour pass. Jo went home to Woolwich and, to her delight, found Phyl there as well. The girls fell on each other and hugged tightly, something they would never have done before. They drew apart and laughed, a little embarrassed.

'You look smashing,' Phyl said enviously. 'You're brown already, and it's only April! Sure you haven't been on holiday on the Riviera?'

'Oh, yeah, with all the film stars as well. Only last week I found myself chopping down a tree with Clark Gable. Nice bloke, but not much good with a cross-saw.'

Phyl wrinkled her nose. 'Now you're talking a foreign language. Tell you what, Elstow's not as bad as we thought it'd be. Last week—' She stopped suddenly and clamped her mouth shut. There was a moment's slightly awkward silence while the family looked at each other and tried to think of something else to say. They all knew that nobody was supposed to talk about their jobs, even at home.

Phyl stared at the floor. She wasn't even supposed to say she was at Elstow – 'Bedford' was all they were allowed to tell people. Now she'd let the cat out of the bag before she'd been home five minutes.

'How's our Alice?' Jo enquired, trying to cover the awkwardness. 'I've been writing to her but all she talks about is that boy – what's his name, Ossie? – and the cat where she lives.'

'Solomon,' Jo's mother said. 'She seems as fond of him as she is of our Robbie. I'm frightened to read her letters out loud when he's in the room in case he gets jealous.'

Everyone laughed and looked at the big ginger cat, who was licking his paws and looking quite unconcerned. Jo picked him up and nuzzled her face into his fur. Her mother gave her an uneasy glance. Jo seemed altogether too bright and cheerful, she thought. It didn't ring true somehow.

'And how's Nick? You been to see him again?'

'A couple of times,' Jo said casually. 'Now he's got the bandages off they're going to start on the surgery soon. It means quite a few operations. I wouldn't be able to see him very much anyway, so it's just as well I'm going to Shropshire. He's in good hands.' She thought of the pretty nurse. Her name was Amy, and she seemed to be around every time Jo had visited. Her blue eyes were cool, but when she spoke to Nick her voice was gentle, and she was the one person he didn't seem to mind touching him.

'Phyl and me thought we'd go up to Marble Arch tomorrow,' she said, changing the subject. 'See Shirley – she's the only one left at the Corner House now. She's on morning shift, Phyl checked.'

'That's all right, you go. So long as you can get home in time for a good meal all together before you have to go away again.' Carrie sighed. 'It's all goodbyes these days, isn't it? You and Phyl, our Alice, the boys. It's hard to keep track of where you all are sometimes.'

'At least it's hellos as well,' Jo said bracingly. 'Every time we go away, we come back again.' She stopped, thinking of all those who didn't come back, thinking of Nick. 'Anyway, you know me and Phyl will,' she went on uncomfortably. 'Phyl's all right over in Bedford, serving teas to soldiers. And there's nothing much going to happen where I'm going.' She thought of the posting she had received, of her hopes to be near Nick, of the terribly long way away she was going to be instead. 'I don't suppose they've ever had any bombs at all up in Shropshire.'

Shirley was serving a table full of airmen when someone nudged her and she turned to see Jo and Phyl grinning at her from one of her tables. She gave a squeak of delight and almost dropped her tray.

'I didn't think you were going to make it! It's almost time for me to go off duty.'

'That's why we came now,' Jo said. 'So we can sit and have a good old chinwag. Give us a pot of tea and whatever you've got that passes for cake these days, and we'll hang on till you can join us.'

Shirley did as she was told and hurried through the rest of her work, serving the last few customers and clearing tables with a speed that impressed even Jo and Phyl, who could serve and clear a table as fast as anyone. In less than half an hour she had disappeared into the back regions and then materialised beside them, dressed in her ordinary clothes. She sat down and another Nippy, grinning, came and asked for her order.

'Funny to be on the other side of the counter, sort of thing,' she said, pouring herself a cup of tea. 'So how are you two, then? What's it like being a lumberjack, Jo?'

'Lumber*jill*,' Jo said. 'It's not bad, to tell you the truth. Nearly as good as being a Nippy – now I've got used to all the quiet, anyway. It's a bit different from London, I can tell you. I've never heard anything as quiet as it is there in the night—' The other two burst out laughing and she defended herself. 'All right, so it sounds funny, but you *can* hear quiet! It's almost solid – like the blackout. All you can hear is owls, and they sound really weird – spooky. They don't all go tu-whit, tu-whoo, you know, some of them scream, really *scream*, and one of the girls thought it was someone being murdered the first time she heard it! We've got used to them now, though. And then there's foxes barking, and—'

'I thought you said it was quiet!' Shirley broke in. 'It sounds worse than the Blitz.'

Jo grinned. 'Stop taking the mickey and have one of these cakes. I must say, Lyons are still doing okay, this is nearly as good as a pre-war tea.'

It wasn't really. The selection of cakes was smaller and the menu carried a longer list of what you couldn't have than what you could. Only one serving of protein and all the dishes starred, so that you could have one two-star dish and one one-star dish, or two one-star dishes . . . it was almost too complicated to bother.

'So how about you?' Phyl asked Shirley. 'How's your dad these days?'

Shirley made a face. 'Not too good. He has a couple of

these fits, or seizures or whatever they call them, a week, and he never knows when they're going to happen so he's frightened to go out or do anything on his own. The doctor keeps trying him with different tablets, but none of them seem to do much good and some of them make him feel sick or get headaches, so it's even worse. I've tried to get him to go to Wales to be with Mum, but he won't go, he says he can't leave me on my own.'

'But wouldn't you be better off? I mean, it sounds awful, but if you knew he was safe you could do what you want to do – join up, or something.'

'I know, but I can't tell him that, can I? He already thinks he's nothing but a nuisance. And all the time I'm here, I'm worrying about what's happening at home . . .' Shirley glanced up at the clock. 'I'm sorry, I'll have to go soon. He gets worried if I'm late.'

'Oh, Shirl. We've only been here five minutes.' Jo looked across the table at her and saw the anxiety in her face. She reached across to touch Shirley's hand. 'We'll keep in touch, won't we? Write, and that. And you'll let us know if – if anything happens.'

'Course. And you tell me all about what it's like up in Shropshire. D'you know, I'd never even heard of it before – had to look in Donald's old school atlas.'

The three girls gazed at each other, aware that they might not meet again for a long time. Even Phyl, who was near enough in Bedford to be able to get home quite quickly, might not have much chance to visit the Corner House. And in these days of war, nothing could be certain. You didn't know what might happen next – to anyone.

'It's been good,' Phyl said in a queer, strangled sort of voice. 'Being Nippies together, I mean. We – we've had some good times, haven't we?'

'Smashing times,' Jo agreed, her mouth twisting a little. She forced it into a grin. 'Remember when Phyl dropped blancmange down that customer's neck? I thought she'd die right there and then. The look on his face!'

The other two smiled, a little tremulously. 'It was lucky Mr Carter was on duty that day. If it had been Miss Turgoose, she might've got the sack.'

'It was the customer's fault, though,' Shirley said. 'He sort of turned round and jerked just as she was putting it on the table, and he knocked her arm. I saw it myself. Anyway, he took it in good part, said it was nice and cooling, and he was happy enough with a free meal to make up for it. And it wasn't *much* blancmange, only a spoonful or so.'

They fell silent again and then Shirley stood up briskly and said, in a slightly louder tone than usual, 'Well, I'd better be off. I promised Dad toad-in-the-hole for tea and he'll be looking forward to it.' She looked at them, then bit her lip and turned away hurriedly. 'Cheerio. And – and good luck.'

'Cheerio, Shirl,' the other two said. 'Good luck to you, too.' And then she was gone, weaving her way swiftly through the tables. She turned briefly at the door and brushed a hand fiercely across her eyes before diving out into the street.

Phyl and Jo were silent for a moment or two. Then Jo said miserably, 'That's that, then. We might as well go, too, Phyl. I promised Mum I'd be back in time for a last evening at home.'

'Me, too. We thought we might have a game of cards all together. Like old times.' It wouldn't be like old times, because the boys were away now and Alice was in the country, but you had to keep up some semblance of what life had been like before the war. What everyone hoped life would be like again – even though they knew in their hearts that it could never be quite the same.

They finished their tea and paid the Nippy who had served them. Then they went outside, feeling as if it might be for the last time. They stood for a few minutes watching the crowds and then turned to look at the great façade of the Corner House itself, remembering the day they had first come as eager, apprehensive 'rookies', the fun and the anxieties of being a Nippy, the friendships that had been forged, the lessons learnt. Maggie and Tommy. Shirley and Owen. Jo and Nick, Phyl and Mike, Etty and Jim. And Maggie's grief when Tommy had been killed, leading her to actions that had seemed quite reasonable and sane to her and completely crazy to the others. Leading to a night when she had been left for dead in the middle of an air raid. Leading to baby Barry . . .

Life had seemed so easy, such fun, when Jo and Phyl had come to London on that Coronation day, five years ago, and first got the idea of being Nippies. Now, although there was still fun to be had, they knew that it was a dangerous and precious thing as well and not, after all, to be taken lightly.

'Let's catch the bus,' Phyl said, and they stood at the bus stop and waited until the next big, red double-decker rolled along. They climbed aboard. The clippie was moving down the aisle, collecting money and snipping out tickets from her little machine.

She stopped and stared as Jo and Phyl climbed on to the platform. Then she turned a bright, angry red.

'What are you two doing here?'

'My godfathers!' exclaimed Phyl, who had picked up this expression from Jenny. 'It's *Irene* – Irene Bond.' She smiled. 'From Nippy to clippie, eh, Irene? We just came up to say cheerio to some of our old mates before we go to do our patriotic duty. Funny we should run into you as well.'

She slipped into a seat and Jo sat down beside her and offered up their fares. Still scarlet and tight-faced, Irene clipped out their tickets and then, without a word, went back to her little cubby-hole under the stairs. Jo and Phyl looked at each other and grinned.

'She didn't like that, did she? Us seeing her on the bus. When you think she always set herself up as something better than any of us – Lady Muck, we used to call her. I bet they won't have her in the services, not after what she did.'

'Well,' Phyl said, 'I suppose we ought to have a bit of charity. She's paid for it and I don't suppose she'll do it again. The least we can do is give her a smile when we get off.'

They did. But Irene wouldn't return their greetings. She

wouldn't even look at them. They got off the bus and walked away down the street, shrugging.

There were more important things to worry about these days than the one Nippy none of them had ever been able to make friends with.

The hospital was to be used for Canadian servicemen. They arrived in Jeeps and field ambulances, scattering bars of chocolate to the village children. Maggie, who had been taken on as an orderly, made up countless iron beds and felt as if she were in a film as she walked between them, listening to the Canadian accents.

'Is that a Devonshire accent you've got?' one of them asked as she brought him a cup of tea. He pronounced 'shire' as if it rhymed with 'wire'. Maggie laughed and shook her head.

'Gawd, no! I'm a Cockney – from London. Got bombed out in the Blitz.'

'Gee.' He gazed at her. 'Bombed out. Gee, that must be something. Guess you had a pretty bad time up there in London.'

'Yes, we did, I suppose. But we knew it was coming.' We didn't really know what it would be like, though, she thought, remembering the devastated streets, the ruined buildings, the crying that seemed to come out of the ground as people dug frantically for buried relatives and friends. 'It was so tiring,' she said thoughtfully. 'We never seemed to get any proper sleep.'

'Sleep!' He laughed. 'You don't sleep much in the army either. Not when you're fighting. You might not get the chance to wake up again.' He stretched luxuriously against his pillows. 'First chance I've had of a good night's sleep, in this place. Say, is this English tea you've given me?'

'That's right. Don't you like it?'

He sipped and made a thoughtful face. 'Sure ain't much like coffee.'

'Well, it wouldn't be, would it? But they've got coffee in the kitchens.' Maggie had seen the Canadians' provisions –

coffee, cigarettes, chocolate, all the things that were almost unobtainable now. The only good thing about them being allowed to bring such luxuries in was that they were generous with them and shared them about. She hardly ever went home now without a bar of chocolate for the children, or some fags for herself and her mother. And there'd been talk amongst the nurses about stockings. Proper silk ones, and that new stuff they called nylon.

She left the soldier trying to get used to his tea, and carried on serving the rest of the ward. The room was a large bedroom on the first floor, and there were half a dozen beds squeezed in there. The patients were mostly young officers getting over wounds and broken bones, looking forward to getting back into the war. They were incensed over Pearl Harbor and determined to help the Allies to win. Now that the whole world was at war, she thought it must be like conducting an orchestra and watching every country at once in case someone took advantage, like the Japanese had, and attacked some other country against which they bore a grudge.

But what a muddle it all is, she thought, pausing on the landing to look out over the huge, landscaped gardens, now being dug up to grow vegetables. What a flaming muddle.

Chapter Seven

By the time they'd been back filling shell cases with explosives at Elstow for a week, Etty and Phyl had almost forgotten what it was like to be a Nippy.

Learning the job had been the worst part. Until now, munitions had been a man's job and the girls had been brought in because of the call-up. The men who were to train them were surly, aggrieved at having to give up their jobs to slips of girls.

'It's not that we got any objection to doing our duty,' one of them said to Kaye as she stood beside him at the bench. 'But handling explosives and making bombs is men's work, no doubt about it. It oughter be a reserved occupation.'

'Go on,' said Phyl, who stood on his other side. 'It's no different from stuffing sausage rolls. Girls can do this work easy.'

He glanced at her with disfavour. Her brown curls were stuffed into a scarf, wound like a turban round her head, but her eyes were just as bold and her wide mouth as ready to grin. If he'd met her down at the village pub he'd have asked her out, and the fact that he fancied her irritated him all the more.

'I'm glad I never had to eat none of your cooking, then,' he said. 'This stuff can blow up in your face. It ain't a pound of sausagemeat.'

The girls were to work in a long Nissen hut, with machines that stretched nearly the length of the room. They were in motion the whole time, with shell cases and gunpowder and all the different parts coming through in a long, inexorable queue. You had to work swiftly, putting your bit together before it moved on to the next girl. Any holdup kept everyone waiting, and created a wave of muttering that spread all the way back down the line. If you weren't paying attention, you could get your hands caught in the moving parts. One girl almost lost a finger the first day and hadn't come back. She was still bandaged up.

'Look at that girl Vi the other day,' the man said, referring to her. 'That could've bin a lot worse, you know. Could've sparked off an explosion, killed a hutful of people. Bringing in a lot of girls. It's daft. Plain daft. This is precision engineering, this is. Men's work.'

'So how long have you been working in munitions, Nobby?' Kaye enquired. 'I heard that a lot of the blokes were pretty new to the job, too.'

Nobby Clark glared at her. 'Now, you look here, gal. There was a lot of us trained as engineers, did apprenticeships and all, back in the thirties. And then what happened? The bleeding slump. Factories closed down. Production stopped. Coal mines, shipyards, industries all over the bleeding country, shut down. Thousands of trained men with no jobs, and what was we supposed to do, eh? Take jobs where we could and *if* we could.'

He turned aside and Phyl thought that if he hadn't been in the machine shed where everything had to be kept so clean, he would have spat. 'I been a flaming milkman, I rode a bloody ice-cream bike round the streets with "Stop Me and Buy One" on it, I've worked a market stall and I've stood on street corners with me cap held out. And now – *now* – just when I thought I could do me proper job again, get back into engineering and machine work, along comes a crowd of bits of girls and tells me to 'op off 'cause they can do it just as well. It ain't no different to stuffing bloody sausage rolls!' This time, he did spit. 'And *I've* got to go and peel spuds and wash bloody socks in the bloody army.'

The girls stared at him. They looked at each other. At last,

Phyl said uncomfortably, 'It isn't our fault, you know. We've been told what to do as well. We didn't want to come and work here.'

'Nah,' he said, sounding a little less angry now that he'd had his say. 'Nah, I know that really, gal. It just gets up your bleeding nose, that's all. Well, I tell you what, if I ever gets near a bloody German I'll give him what for, and I hope I've got a bloody bayonet to do it with. Shooting's too good for 'em. I tell you, I'll screw it up his backside like I'm fitting shelves!'

He went back to showing them how to fit detonator caps, and how to cut shell-cases. They had to learn all the different jobs, so that they could be moved anywhere in the factory, and each job had its own dangers. Cordite didn't stay in neat little piles – it would fly up into your face and bring your skin up in angry weals and lumps. If it got in your eyes, it could drive you crazy with the pain. And some of the machinery was old and decrepit, liable to cause accidents of its own.

'You got to watch out when you get tired,' Nobby said. 'That's when accidents happen. Half the things that go wrong go wrong in the last hour or two of a shift, so just you remember that.'

Shifts were twelve hours long. Seven till seven, all day and all night, there were bombs, grenades and bullets being made. Mr Carter had said the aim was to produce four thousand bombs a week. Phyl shut her eyes and thought of all those bombs, together with the thousands of others being made at other factories all over the country, thousands and thousands of bombs being dropped on Germany. It's as awful for people over there as it is for us, she thought. I'm going to think about it every time I screw on a detonator cap. I can't help it.

She didn't, though. She watched and listened and when it came to her turn to try, she found her nimble fingers unexpectedly adept at the precise work. To her surprise, she found that she enjoyed it. It was satisfying to carry out work that demanded concentration, and when the results of the week's work were posted up on the notice-board in the canteen every week, she felt proud to think that she had helped the war effort.

'I feel almost like we're in the front line,' she told the other girls as they walked down to the pub one evening. 'We're doing something really important.'

The Chimney Corner was full of people, almost all employed at the factory. Nobby was in a corner with two other men and they looked up as the four girls came in and then looked quickly down into their pint mugs again. Kaye leant on the bar and ordered three shandies.

'Shall we embarrass him? Shall we go over and say hello and be all matey?'

Jenny giggled. 'He'll bite your head off.'

'Go on, he was nice as pie this afternoon. He's got used to us now, knows we can do the work okay.'

'He won't want his mates to know that, though,' Jenny said. 'You know what they're like. A few of 'em have come round, but there's still a lot got it in for us because we've taken their jobs.'

'Not our fault, though. We got to go where we're sent same as they have. And I'll tell you what, soon as the war's over it'll be us who're out on our ears. Look at all the girls that have got men's jobs now – us in factories, clippies on buses, girls making aeroplanes, working on farms. You name it, women are doing it. One of these fine days the men'll all come home and want their jobs back, and where will that leave us? Back at home in the kitchen, that's where, with some bloke telling us what to do just because he's a *man*.' She pulled a face. 'I'm going to make the most of it while I got the chance. Do my work and have some fun as well. We won't get the opportunity again.'

Etty looked around the pub. It was packed with girls and men from the rapidly growing factory. Even in the few weeks she had been there, she reckoned it had probably doubled in size. The tiny village was almost swamped by it, with just a few locals and almost everyone else from the hostels. The landlord, a man so stout he could scarcely reach the pumps, was beaming all over his big, round face and his wife, so thin that she could have made a shadow look overweight, was scurrying about with trays of drinks. I could give her a few tips there, Etty thought, and felt suddenly homesick for the Corner House.

'What's the matter?' Kaye asked softly in her ear. 'You're looking all forlorn.'

'I was just thinking about London,' Etty confessed. 'You know – the Corner House and the other Nippies. I was just wondering how they're getting on now. We've all got split up lately. They – they were like family to me.'

'Everybody's family's got split up,' Kaye observed. 'I don't know one that's still together. But that's the way it is, Et. There's a war on. And we got to do our best to help win it.' She picked up her glass and drained it. 'Come on. Let's have another one. It's another twelve-hour shift tomorrow, but for tonight we're *free*!'

Mr Carter tried to keep up the old Lyons custom in looking after the girls and the jobs they were doing. The standards of discipline in the Corner Houses had been strict, but the girls who worked there – the Nippies, the Trippies, the Sallies – were cared for far more than the average shopgirl or factory worker. The supervisors knew them all by name, they knew their family background, their problems and their joys. The social club at Sudbury gave them a life outside their work, where they could meet each other at dances or in sports. Phyl Jennings had been a leading light in the drama club, Jo Mason a star swimmer and diver, Etty quick and nimble on the tennis or badminton courts, Shirley a steady oarswoman in the rowing races. Maggie had just been generally popular, and even Irene Bond had shone on the dance floor or in the hurdling races.

These six had, for some reason, been better known to Mr Carter than many of the girls he had trained. Now only Phyl and Etty were still with him and he couldn't help taking a special interest in them.

Maybe it was because they *were* special, he thought. Phyl because she was such a little livewire. The first time she'd applied to be a Nippy, with her cousin Jo, she'd been rejected because she was an inch too short, and given a job in the kitchens instead. But she'd been determined – Mr Carter laughed to himself at the memory of her efforts to grow – and eventually won over the manager himself, who'd decided that she could have a uniform made specially for her. And not only had she made a first-class Nippy, as everyone had known she would, but she'd brought young Esther – Etty – with her.

What a little mouse Etty had been. Yet what a good little worker she'd turned out to be, quick and efficient, shy but friendly with the customers – and what a heroine during the Blitz! Lyons were lucky to have such girls working for them.

Bernard Carter knew a little of Etty's story – that she was an orphan whose mother had been Jewish, that she had grown up in an orphanage and then lived in a hostel. She seemed to have no family, but he knew that Maggie Pratt had taken her under her wing, and now Etty was engaged to Maggie's brother Jim.

'You're an excellent worker,' Bernard told her one morning, watching her deft fingers. 'But you mustn't overdo it. You're looking tired.'

Etty flushed, immediately feeling guilty, and Kaye jumped to her defence. 'We can't help getting tired, Mr Carter. We're on twelve-hour shifts.'

'I know.' He hesitated. 'I'm not criticising you. And I know that all work and no play . . . But perhaps it would be better if you didn't go down to the Chimney Corner quite so often.'

Etty's blush deepened. 'I only drink shandy—' she began, but he shook his head, smiling.

'It's all right, Etty. I'm not saying you're a drunkard! Just that one or two early nights a week would do you good.' He gave her a smile and laid his hand on her shoulder for a moment before moving on. Etty and Kaye looked at each other.

'Mean old sod,' Kaye said. 'Doesn't he realise a girl's got to have a bit of fun? We'd go mad if we stopped in and just did our knitting every night.'

'He didn't say every night. Just once or twice a week. He's right, Kaye – I do feel tired. And it's the job that matters most.'

Kaye looked at her more carefully. Etty's face was certainly pale – but she was naturally pale, that didn't mean a thing. And her eyes looked big and shadowed. 'Maybe you'd better stop home tonight,' she said. 'Get a good night's rest. You'll be right as rain in the morning.'

Etty nodded and went on with her work. She was used to long hours and hard work, but twelve hours a day, seven days a week just didn't give you a chance to catch up with yourself. It wasn't as if the twelve hours off was all spare time. You had your washing and mending to do, and everyone was knitting for someone – balaclavas or socks for soldiers and sailors, pullovers for boyfriends or brothers, gloves and mittens for Christmas presents.

'I tell you what does get up my nose,' Kaye said, 'and that's the fact that we don't get paid as much as the men. I mean, we're doing the same work so why shouldn't we get the same money? I don't reckon it's fair.'

'Yes, but that's the same in every job,' Jenny chimed in from Etty's other side. 'Men always do get paid more. I don't mind, meself. If we got paid the same they might start wanting us to pay when we go out with them. And they wouldn't feel like buying us presents and things.'

Nobby Clark came along the line then and scowled at them. 'Get on with your work and stop this nattering. You're paid to do a job to help win the war, not chew the fat over last night down the pub.'

'We weren't,' Kaye told him. 'We were talking about equal pay for equal work.'

He stared at her. 'Equal pay for equal work? What sort of

rubbish is that? You don't do equal work. You're not flipping trained for it.'

'We're being trained, though. We're getting better all the time. Everyone says so. And some of the girls are better than the men even without training. Some of these precision jobs need smaller fingers, like our Etty's. Look at her, she works as fast as any bloke. She ought to be paid properly.'

'Now, look,' Nobby said, pushing his face close to Kaye's, 'men have *always* been paid more than women. It's only right. Women only work till they're married, they live at home with their mums and dads, and they might put a bit into the housekeeping but all they got to pay for apart from that is their clothes and their lipsticks and stuff. They get paid for every time they go out with a bloke, and as soon as they've caught a husband they can knock off and stop at home and do bugger all while he works all the hours God sends to keep them and their kids. What do they need equal pay for? It ain't a question of what the job's worth, it's what a bloke's got to do with his pay that's important. Men *need* more pay. The country'd go to pot if we started paying girls equal.'

'The country'd go to pot if you didn't have women to do all these jobs now,' Kaye retorted. 'If we depended on men to do everything, we'd be slave labour under Hitler. Who'd make the bombs when the men are off at the Front, eh? Who'd make the guns and bullets for 'em to fight with? Who'd drive buses and build aeroplanes and—?'

'All right, all right,' he interrupted her. 'That's enough. The whole line's come to a stop through your arguing. You *don't* get equal pay and that's that and all about it. Now, get back to work, or it'll be the foreman's office for you, and I promise you, your feet won't touch the ground on the way!'

He stalked off along the line, his back rigid, and the girls watched him with round eyes and then turned to look at Kaye. She shrugged and pulled a face.

'Okay. We'll get back to work because that's what we're here for and I reckon I'm as patriotic as anyone else in this place. But I still think it's wrong. I still think if we're doing as good a job as the blokes we ought to get the same money. So there, Mr Clark – with knobs on!'

She stuck out her tongue in the direction of the departing overseer, and everyone laughed and turned back to their work. Etty's fingers, which had paused when the line came to a standstill, flew as fast as they had before. But Kaye's words had made her think.

Ever since she was a child in the orphanage, Etty had been treated as a lesser being – either because she had been an illegitimate baby, or because she was Jewish, or because she was just smaller and paler and quieter than other people. But since she'd become a Nippy and found friends who treated her as an equal, she had begun to think that perhaps she could be almost, if not quite, as good as anyone else. And that night during the Blitz, when she'd crawled down into the bombed cellar and helped the buried family to safety, she'd felt a strange surge of power, as if after all she was worth something to the world.

It's only because girls didn't do men's jobs before the war that they got paid less, she thought. But Kaye's right. If you do the same job, you ought to be paid the same. And if that means you pay for yourself when you go out, well, that's fair, too. I'd rather do that, she thought, than have some man pay for me and then think he's got the right to kiss me or maul me about.

Well, she probably wouldn't get much chance to put it right. Men still ruled the country and probably always would – they weren't likely to give women the chance to take over! But it didn't stop girls like her thinking about it.

Jo scarcely had time to think about her pay. She was just grateful to receive the little brown envelope at the end of each week and sort its contents into little piles.

'That's to send home to Mum. That's to save up for Christmas and birthdays. That's for things like hankies and darning wool and bunnies. That's me shilling a week hire for the pushbike to go to work on. And that', she said, surveying the little piles of coins on her bed and looking ruefully at the smallest of all, 'is me pocket money.'

'Doesn't leave much for high living, does it?' Poppy remarked from her bed. They had been put in the same billet, a small cottage in the village of Clun where they had been posted. Their landlady was a widow whose two sons were both in the army, and Jo and Poppy had their bedroom, with narrow iron beds and an old-fashioned washstand. There was an iron rail across an alcove where they could hang their clothes and a window that looked out across the valley to the forest-clad hills where they would be working.

'Well, we're not going to have much time for high living anyway.' Jo sighed a little, remembering the fun she and the other Nippies had had, going to the pictures together or out to the social club at Sudbury. You could still go to the club – Lyons had said that anyone who had been called up into any of the services was still entitled to belong to it – but she didn't think there would be much chance of that. More importantly, she couldn't think when she would be able to get all the way down to Kent again to see Nick. So much for asking for a posting near him, she thought bitterly.

The girls had arrived at Clun after a long day's travelling and on the first night they just dumped their kitbags in a corner, washed in the kitchen sink and fell into bed, exhausted. The next day, they were called early and got up to have a quick look round the village before starting work.

'It's not a bad place,' Suzy said, meeting them in the main street. She was billeted two doors away with an elderly couple. They wandered down to the old stone bridge and gazed down into the clear stream. 'There are a couple of pubs and a village hall where they have dances, and some shops. And there's an old ruined castle just up there, see?'

Poppy stared at her. 'Don't you think we've seen enough ruins lately? I bet Jo has, in London. If an old castle's all they've got to boast about, they don't know what war is!'

Jo grinned. 'There's something different about a castle, though. It's more romantic.' She looked about her, sniffing the clean air and feeling a stirring of excitement. If only Nick weren't so far away and so badly hurt, she could really enjoy it. 'Anyway, we'd better go back and get our breakfast. We'll be late for work otherwise and that'll never do, not on our first day. Tell you what, I'm quite looking forward to it. Wonder if we'll be allowed to fell any trees.'

'They'll want to see what we can do first. We've only had a month's training after all.' Poppy led the way past the stone cottages, back to their billets. 'See you in half an hour, Suze.'

Thirty minutes later the girls joined a crowd of other new recruits, standing with their hired bikes by the little stone bridge. There were one or two trucks parked there but nobody else seemed to be about. Although it was still only seven-thirty, the sun was already warm and Poppy had put on baggy khaki shorts. Jo looked at them enviously.

'Where did you get them? I didn't know they were part of the uniform.'

'They're not. They're me brother's.' Poppy giggled. 'From when he was a Boy Scout. I thought they'd be more comfy than breeches and long socks—'

'Well, you thought wrong, girl.' The voice behind them sounded curt and angry, and the girls spun round to see a broad, stocky man with a bald head burnt brown as a football standing beside one of the trucks. He was wearing heavy overalls and had a thin, roll-your-own cigarette hanging from his lower lip. His voice had an odd sort of lilt to it, almost Welsh but not quite . . . 'And you can just go back to your billet and change back into your proper clothes. *Now!*' he added fiercely, making them all jump. 'How d'you think you're going to get on up in the woods, working with brambles and nettles and adders and God knows what else round your knees? Gow, didn't they give you no training at all?' He turned and looked with furious exasperation at another man who had come out of the back of the other truck and was walking towards them. 'It gets worse every time. This crowd's out of the bloody pram.'

The other man was middle-aged, with straight black hair

and eyebrows that came so low over his eyes you could hardly see them. He looked as if he had a permanent scowl and Jo felt an instant dislike for him. So far, she thought glumly, the morning's not going too well, and we haven't even got on our bikes yet!

'Right,' the first man said, spitting the end of his cigarette into the river. 'My name's Huw Morgan and I'm in charge. You do as I say, see? And this is Spencer. You don't need to know his other name. Right. You can follow the trucks. We're going over there, see . . .' He waved a hand in the direction of the forest clothing the hills across the valley. 'And after today you'll be expected to be there on the dot of eight o'clock, so you better see how long it takes you to get there. Half the morning, I wouldn't wonder. Best part of the day'll be gone.' He spat again and turned away with an expression of disgust. 'Sending us bloody bits of girls! First hour'll be spent getting their breath back and the rest of the day filing their nails. Well, come on, won't do no good hanging about here. Is that girl back with her breeches on yet?'

'She's just coming,' Jo said, catching sight of Poppy dashing down the street. 'What will we be doing today? Will we be felling trees or sawing logs?'

Huw Morgan gave her a look of contempt. 'Felling trees? Sawing logs? You? Don't be dafter than you got to be. We got to get *into* the trees first, before we can start that sort of parlour game. We got to get some *roads* built.' He paused and took a small packet of tobacco and some flimsy papers from his pocket. They watched as he laid a neat line of tobacco along the paper and then rolled it and licked along the edge. He patted his pockets and found a box of matches and lit the cigarette, drawing on it deeply, keeping his eyes upon them the whole time. 'That's what you'll be doing,' he said at last. 'Building a few roads, see? And you needn't think you can knock off for a fag while you're in those old trees neither. It's strictly no smoking. Understand?'

The girls nodded, too stunned to speak. Huw Morgan and the other man swung the starting-handles of their lorries and hauled themselves up into the cabs. With a crash of gears and a billow of smoke from the exhaust pipes, the two vehicles rumbled off along the narrow lane.

The girls looked at each other.

'Whew!' Suzy said. '*He's* going to be a barrel of laughs – I don't think! And what about us building roads? They never said anything about that in training camp.'

Jo climbed on to her bike and giggled suddenly. 'Did you hear what his name was?'

'Morgan,' Poppy said. 'So what?'

'No. His other name.' Jo giggled again. 'Huw! Get it? *Huw!* I wonder if they call him Huw the Tree!'

Poppy and Suzy stared at her. Her face completely straight, Poppy turned to the other girl and shook her head.

'It's the thought of building a road,' she said gravely. 'It's turned her brain. Sad, really. I had hopes of that girl.'

Jo swung a hand at her head and she ducked. Laughing and feeling better, the girls mounted their bikes and spun away down the valley. It was warm and sunny, they were in a new part of the country, they were about to begin their war work. And it was going to be fun. Even road-building, under the curt direction of Huw Morgan and Spencer, could be fun. They'd make sure it was.

Chapter Eight

'This is worse than training camp,' Jo groaned as they staggered back into the village at the end of their first day. 'I thought I'd built up me muscles, but I feel like a jellyfish. I'm not going to be able to get out of bed tomorrow.'

'If you don't, you'll have Huw the Tree coming round to drag you out,' Poppy told her, and they pulled faces. 'Come on, Jo, it's only a few more yards.'

'It might as well be a hundred miles. I tell you, Poppy, I just want to lay down and die, right here on the pavement.'

'You'll be in everyone's way, then,' Poppy said unsympathetically. 'And who's going to have to sweep you up and decide what to do with the body? Come on.'

They reached the gate of Mrs Dell's house and pushed their bikes into the shed. On legs that felt as though they might buckle at any moment, they stumbled into the kitchen and collapsed on two wooden chairs.

'That's the first time we've sat down properly all day,' Jo told their landlady as she poured tea into two cups for them. 'All we got at dinnertime was a log or the ground. Honestly, I never thought it would be such hard work!'

'We had to go down to the sawmill first and load the trucks with big planks of wood. Then we had to unload them back at the woods and lay them on the ground to make a road. It got worse the further in we went – we had to carry them. They wouldn't take the trucks in. We laid about half a mile of road, I reckon—'

'A hundred miles, you mean,' Jo interrupted, rubbing her back.

'Half a mile,' Poppy repeated firmly. 'And tomorrow we've got to chuck sawdust all over it – tons and tons of the ruddy stuff – so that it'll bed down into a solid mass. Otherwise the foreman says we won't be able to get into the forest at all once it starts raining.'

'He's right,' Mrs Dell said. 'Proper quagmire it is, in those old woods. Well, you'll have earned your teas and if you want to have a wash in the sink, I'll get them on the table for you. There's a kettle of hot water on the range and a nice bar of Lifebuoy ready.'

Mrs Dell was a small, round, comforting woman, built like a doughnut. Her cottage was small, crammed with mementoes of her life – a row of photographs on the mantelpiece, a small model of Blackpool Tower, a Coronation mug with several pencils stuck in it. In the back room, where most of the living was done, there were a square dining-table with four chairs, and two armchairs by the range. Leading from it was a lean-to scullery with a small enamelled gas cooker with bent legs, a couple of cupboards and a deep white sink.

Jo washed first and came back into the room. She looked at the photographs.

'Is this one of your sons?' She picked up a portrait of a young man in soldier's uniform. There seemed to be two photographs of the same young man. 'I thought you had two. Don't you have any pictures of the other one?'

Mrs Dell laughed. 'Bless you, they're pictures of them both! They're twins, you see. Like as two peas in a pod. Peter and Paul, they're called.'

'Gosh, they're really alike,' Jo exclaimed. 'You needn't go to the trouble of having them both photographed, really. One would do!'

'Never. I have to have the two of them.' The little woman took the photo from Jo's hand. 'I can tell the difference, see. Nobody else ever could, but I can. So it wouldn't do for me to have just Peter, or just Paul. I'd always be looking for the other one.'

Jo stared at the two photographs and could see nothing different between them. 'Are they both in the same unit? It must be difficult for the others.'

'Well, they always make some difference, in the way they dress or something like that. Yes, they're always together, never been parted.' She sighed. 'It's to be hoped nothing happens to one of 'em. I don't know how the other would go on, I really don't.'

Jo looked at her with sympathy. She wanted to say that of course nothing would happen – but you couldn't say that these days. She sighed a little, too, and then turned to help lay the table. 'My mum and auntie are also identical twins so I know what it's like to have two people in the family who look the same.'

'Go on,' Mrs Dell said. 'And do you take after them, then?'

'No, I'm not a bit like my mum,' Jo said with a grin. 'Just the opposite. I'm lanky like my dad. My cousin Phyl's like them, though, small and dark, a bit like a wren.' She sighed. 'Phyl and me don't look a bit alike, but we're almost like twins ourselves. There's only a month between us and we've always done everything together. We were both Nippies.'

'Both *what*?'

'Nippies. Waitresses in one of the Lyons Corner Houses. They're really big restaurants in London. There were a thousand people working at Marble Arch, where me and Phyl were.'

'Well, I never did,' Mrs Dell said, as if Jo had told her she'd just flown in from the moon. 'Waitresses in a posh London restaurant! A thousand people! And now here you are in little Clun. Why, there's not more than three hundred in the whole village. Must seem proper strange.'

'Well, it's a bit different from chopping down trees, I can tell you!' Jo grinned. 'Although I wouldn't say Corner Houses were posh, exactly. They're really nice – had chandeliers and all before the war started and they had to take them down for

100

safety. But they're more for ordinary people – good food at reasonable prices. Mind you, we got a few famous faces in as well. They're good value, see, and everyone likes good value.'

'Well, I hope you won't be disappointed by the food you get here,' Mrs Dell said. 'Your tea's ready now. It's only plain old toad-in-the-hole, I'm afraid.'

'Toad-in-the-hole! That's one of my favourites,' Jo exclaimed, and she and Poppy drew up their chairs and fell to.

Mrs Dell had made the toad-in-the-hole with dried egg batter and sausages from the farm. They ate it with cabbage and boiled potatoes. For afters, there was stewed apple and custard, made with Bird's custard powder. They ate till they were full, and finished with cups of tea.

'That feels better,' Jo said, leaning back. 'As good as any Corner House meal. Maybe I'll be able to go up to the forest again tomorrow after all. All the same, I reckon I'll have an early night tonight. How about a stroll down to the bridge first, Poppy, see if any of the others are about? We'll help wash up first, of course,' she added in case their landlady should feel they were treating her as a servant.

It was still light as they sauntered out, feeling self-conscious in their breeches and pullovers. There were quite a few village people about, working in their gardens or chatting in doorways. The Sun Inn had its doors and windows open and they could hear voices and laughter, and the occasional snatch of song.

'That reminds me,' Jo said. 'I heard a rhyme about this place today.' She wrinkled her nose, trying to remember. 'It's something like this. "Clunton, Clungunford and Clun, They're the drunkenest places under the sun!"'

Poppy laughed. 'Better not let the locals hear you reciting that. Where are those other places, then?'

'Don't know. Must be near by, I suppose.' They came within sight of the bridge and saw Suzy leaning on the parapet, chatting with some of the other girls and a few of the men who worked with them. Jo and Poppy joined them and just as they did so another tall figure, also in breeches and pullover, approached and made to cross the bridge.

Jo looked up at him casually, and then stared. For a moment or two, she couldn't recall where she had seen him before. Then a picture flashed into her mind. A railway station on a cold Sunday morning. A cup of tea in the waiting-room. The steam of her train as it bore her away . . .

Josh – that was his name. Josh Taylor. He'd been at the lumber training camp at Culford, and now here he was at Clun.

She opened her mouth to speak, but before she could utter a word the men's faces changed. They scowled and spread out across the narrow bridge.

'What do *you* want?' one of them asked aggressively.

Jo turned her eyes upon him. She'd sat near him at lunchtime and they'd chatted easily. He'd seemed a nice sort of bloke, not at all unfriendly. Now, however, his face was set in a dark scowl and his arms were folded across his chest.

'I'd just like to get by, please,' Josh said quietly in his pleasant voice.

The other men snorted and one of them uttered a jeering laugh.

'Ay say, old chap, Ay'd just like to get by, please, if you don't mind too terribly, old chap,' one of them mocked in a high, false accent, and then went on in his normal voice, 'Well, what d'you reckon – shall we let him?'

'Don't see why we should,' the first man said. 'Perfectly good ford he can walk through. Don't need no bridge.'

Josh looked down at the water and Jo followed his glance. The river ran more shallowly over the ford, but he'd still get his boots and socks wet. There didn't seem to her to be any reason not to let him pass.

'Come on,' she said, 'let him through.' She looked up at Josh and he met her eyes. She saw his face change slightly and knew that he had recognised her. But he made no sign.

'You keep out of it! It's nothing to do with you.'

Jo flinched at the unexpected attack. Then her spirit rose

102

and she said heatedly, 'I don't know what it's about, but bullying's everyone's business. Let him through. He's not doing any harm.'

'And that's all you know!' The man turned on her. 'It's blokes like him what could lose this war for us. Cowards! Conchies! Can't fight, won't fight. Why, he wouldn't even fight *me*, not even if I punched him one on the nose. And why? Too bloody scared, that's why, and tries to make out it's because he's better than anyone else. Makes out he's got exemption. Well, he didn't ought to *have* bloody exemption, not while better blokes than he'll ever be are risking their lives.'

Jo stared at him, then turned to look at the tall man, a question in her eyes. He met her eyes again, but his expression told her nothing.

'Just let me through,' he said quietly. 'You're right, I won't fight. But I'll stay here till you let me by, and unless you want to stand here all night you might as well let me go now.'

The men stared at him, obviously debating silently whether to knock him down or just stand back and let him pass. In the end, the one who was barring his way shrugged and stood back.

'Better things to do than tangle with a conchie,' he said loudly. 'Wouldn't want to soil me hands by touching him anyway. But you can remember this.' He stepped into the tall man's path again and thrust his chin forward. 'We won't always let you go. You'd better watch yourself, up in them woods. Something might happen to you one day – some nasty accident, like. See?'

Josh stared at him for a moment, then turned away and walked on across the bridge. The others watched him, sneering and sticking out their feet so that he stumbled and tripped. As he walked on up the lane, they jeered after him.

He turned the corner out of sight, and they fell silent. Nobody looked at anyone for a moment or two. Then Jo said, 'What did you mean, calling him a conchie? Is that what he is? A conscientious objector?'

103

'Course he is.' The leader spat into the river. 'Why else would a bloke like him be here instead of in the army? Went in front of a tribunal, didn't he, and got round them to let him off and do some nice safe civvy job in a place where he wouldn't get bombed. Huh! Thought he'd get it easy. Got another think coming, hasn't he?'

There was a general murmur of agreement. Jo looked around at the hostile faces. She touched Poppy's arm.

'I'm going back to Mrs Dell's. I don't want to stay here.'

Poppy glanced at her in surprise. 'Okay. I'll come with you.' They walked away and back along the street to the other end of the village. After a few moments' silence Poppy said, 'What's the matter, Jo?'

'That man,' Jo said. 'The one they called a conchie. A CO. I know him.'

'You know him? How?'

'Well, I've met him and talked to him. He was at training camp, in the group ahead of us. He told me he was coming to Shropshire but I'd forgotten. His name's Josh – Josh Taylor.' She swallowed, wondering why she should feel so upset. 'He never said a word about being a CO.'

There was no reason, really, why Josh Taylor should have told Jo why he was in the Timber Corps. They'd only met for half an hour or so on a railway station and had a cup of tea and a chat together. Just to pass the time really. But he'd seemed so nice. He'd listened to her talking about Nick, and he'd been shocked and sympathetic about Nick's injuries. She'd felt comfortable with him. She'd felt he was someone she could trust, who could be a friend, and she'd been sorry to think they'd never meet again.

Now it seemed as if all that had been false. He hadn't told her he was a CO – and there was no reason why he should, she told herself for the hundredth time – but it was important all the same. It made a difference.

While Tommy Wheeler was being killed at Dunkirk, while Nick was being shot down in his Spitfire and burnt, while Mike was leaving his wedding, and Jo and Phyl's own

104

brothers were joining up and going to fight heaven knew where – while all that was happening, Josh Taylor and others like him were getting out of it. Going in front of tribunals, spinning a yarn about religious beliefs or whatever excuse they could think up, and being told that they needn't fight for their country. They could go and work out in the country instead. They could keep themselves and their miserable, cowardly skins safe.

'A lot of them went to prison first,' Poppy pointed out when Jo said all this as they walked back through the village. They leant on a wall, staring out across the valley towards the dark hill where they would be working each day. 'And I think they had a pretty miserable time while they were there.'

'Not as miserable as my Nick,' Jo said fiercely. 'Not as miserable as Tommy, or all those other men who got killed at Dunkirk. Or drowned at sea. Or bombed. What's a few months in prison beside all that? Why, they were even safe while they were in there! You don't hear about prisons getting bombed, do you!'

Poppy lifted her shoulders. 'S'pose not. But why are you so upset about this, Jo? It's only one man and we don't have to talk to him.'

Jo turned away from the wall. 'Oh, I don't know. I was just surprised. He didn't seem like a coward when I talked to him before. He seemed a really nice bloke. And when I first saw him just now, I felt really pleased. And when the rest of them started on at him, I thought it was awful. But when they said about him being a conchie – well, I dunno, I just felt sort of sick inside. I still do.'

Poppy stared at her. 'But why? I mean, I don't like the idea any more than you do, but it's not upsetting me, not like that.'

'Well, maybe that's because you haven't got a boyfriend who's been nearly burnt to death!' Jo flared. 'You haven't had to see what I've seen. You haven't had to see the chap you love all wrapped up in bandages so you can hardly recognise him. You haven't had to try to talk to him when he can't answer and you're not even sure he can hear you. You don't have to think about him having all those horrible operations when you're hundreds of miles away, and even then he'll still have scars. Maybe it's easier not to be upset when you haven't got all that on your mind all the time.'

She turned and walked away, her back stiff. Poppy stared after her, appalled, and then ran to catch her up.

'Jo! Jo, wait. I'm sorry – I didn't think. I shouldn't have said that. You're right – it must be awful to think about your Nick and then see someone like Josh Taylor getting away with it. It's just that—' She stopped abruptly.

'Just what?' Jo said, not slowing down, still looking straight ahead.

'Oh, nothing. I'm sorry, Jo. Really sorry. About Nick and everything.' She touched Jo's arm. 'Don't let's fall out. Not over some chap we hardly know and don't even have to talk to.'

'I wish I knew that for sure,' Jo said. 'I mean, suppose we have to work with him? I won't be able to keep quiet, Poppy, I just won't.'

'We won't. He's in a different gang to us, Jo, he'll probably be in a different place. We never saw him today, did we?'

'No.' They had arrived at Mrs Dell's gate. Jo paused with her hand on the latch. She looked at Poppy and gave an awkward little grin. 'Sorry I blew up.'

'I'm sorry, too, about what I said. I just didn't think.'

They went indoors together. Mrs Dell was knitting and listening to *Henry Hall's Guest Night* on the wireless. Poppy made a cup of cocoa and they sat drinking it and listening to the various acts. Then Poppy yawned.

'I'm almost too tired to move. I'm going to bed, or I'll never get up in the morning.'

'I might as well go, too,' Jo agreed, but she knew already that she wouldn't sleep. Tired as she was, the meeting with Josh Taylor had upset her somehow, and she knew that even if she did fall asleep she would be awake in a couple of hours. Or, worse still, in that strange, uncomfortable state of being half awake and half asleep, her brain churning out ridiculous thoughts and pictures that she couldn't get rid of.

I could have done without this, she thought as Poppy blew out the candle and settled herself down. Within moments, Jo could hear her quiet, regular breathing and knew that she was asleep. But for Jo, there was to be no peaceful slumber.

Instead, she seemed to spend the night in a succession of jumbled, half-conscious dreams of station waiting-rooms, hospital wards, of bandages and mutilated faces, of a tall, quiet man who refused to fight for his country, and of endless forests, stretching away into eternity, with each and every tree waiting for her alone to chop it down.

Chapter Nine

Meeting Josh Taylor seemed to settle a question in Jo's own mind – a question she wasn't even aware she was asking.

The first few weeks in the forest, however, didn't give her much time to think about her own life. There was too much to do, too much to get used to. If you tried for a hundred years to find something that was completely different from a Lyons Corner House, she thought, you'd have put forestry on the shortlist. And if you'd looked for somewhere completely different from London, Clun would have been at the top.

The forests were vast and silent, except for the calling of the birds and the chattering of squirrels. The lumber gangs soon changed that, though, with their noisy vehicles – tractors with snorting engines and rattling carts dragged by big horses – and their shouts and sawing and chopping. Then it was noisy enough. But the noise seemed to float away into the wide, clear sky. There was room for it.

Once they'd begun to get used to it, Jo, Suzy and Poppy started to meet early in the mornings and cycle up to the forest before the others arrived. They rode along the aisles between the towering brown trunks, feeling as if they were entering a great cathedral, listening to birdsong rather than organ music and watching out for red squirrels and pine martens as they scurried into the branches. The screech of a jay startled them at first, sounding as it did like the cry of someone in sudden pain, but a glimpse of the brightly coloured bird made them laugh at themselves and after that they looked more closely to see what else lived amongst the conifers.

'We're chopping down all the places where they live,' Jo said. 'What'll they do then?'

'Find somewhere else,' Poppy said unconcernedly. 'There's millions of trees here, Jo. We'll never chop them all down. There's still plenty of places for birds and squirrels and things.'

'That's right,' Suzy agreed, leaning her bike against a pile of logs ready to be carted away. 'We've got a war to win, remember?'

It seemed hard to remember the war, here in this peaceful forest. Jo looked at the great trees, wondering how long it had taken them to grow here, whether they'd been already tall when the last war – the Great War, as they called it – had been fought. The war to end all wars, that was supposed to have been, and now look what was happening. Even the trees were having to go into service.

They built a fire with scraps of shredded wood, piled up where the trees had been chopped down and then sawn into lengths. Many were to be used for pit-props, from the shortest ones, four feet six inches long, to the longest at nine feet. Making these was a large part of the loggers' work, and Jo thought of the pits they were to go into and the men who worked there. She held up a four-foot-six prop and imagined working in a tunnel no higher than that. You'd have to be bent double the whole time, she thought. And in the dark, too, with water dripping down from the roof and all the filth of coal and dirt and muck . . . No wonder Shirley's Owen didn't want to go back to Wales.

Once the fire was lit, the girls set billycans of water over the flames and then turned to and did some sawing to warm themselves up. By the time the rest of the gang arrived, on bikes, lorries and tractors, the water was boiling ready for the first mug of tea of the day.

'It's not a bad life,' Poppy observed as they cycled home

again, their muscles aching. 'I know we get tired but it's a healthy sort of tired. I tell you what, I've never appreciated a chair in my life like I do now!'

Jo had been to the railway station at Craven Arms that day. Riding on the top of a lorryload of pit-props, she'd made several trips back and forth, loading and unloading until she thought her back would break. She watched the poles in their coal-trucks, steaming away to the pits of Wales. Without them, the coal couldn't be mined, without the coal the country would come to a standstill – factories unable to work, planes and tanks and munitions not made, bread not baked . . . the list was endless. Without us in the forest, she thought, the war just couldn't go on.

She turned to find Josh Taylor at her side. He'd been working on one of the other lorries. The men had decided they had to work with him, but they didn't have to talk to him. He was a lonely, solitary figure and sometimes, when Jo saw him, she felt almost sorry for him. Then she thought of Nick, and hardened her heart.

Abruptly, she turned away again, but Josh reached out and laid one hand on her arm. Jo wheeled back, furious, but the look in his eyes stopped her angry words.

'Don't kick me when I'm down,' Josh said quietly. 'You're not that sort of girl.'

Jo bit her lip. There were tears in her eyes.

'How do you know what sort of girl I am? We've only spoken to each other once.'

'But we said quite a lot,' he reminded her. 'And I think we know each other quite well.'

Jo remembered her feeling as they'd stood on that other railway platform, so many miles away, that she had known Josh for years. She looked away from his eyes. They were too warm and they saw too much.

'We didn't know each other that well,' she said. 'Not well enough for you to tell me what you were.'

Josh sighed. 'Perhaps there wasn't time. Would it have made so much difference?'

'Well, of course it would!' she flashed. 'I was going to see my fiancé. You knew that, and you knew he'd been burnt. I told you about it, I told you about his plastic surgery. You knew everything about me.' Everything important, she meant. Everything, including the fact that she'd been a Nippy, that Nick had been shot down the day before their wedding. Before their wedding *should* have been. About the only thing he didn't know was that she'd refused for a long time even to go out with Nick, just because his name – Laurence – was the same as that of her hero in *Little Women*, while hers was Jo, and because that Laurie had married Jo's sister and not Jo herself, she'd thought any romance between herself and Nick would be doomed . . . How could I have been so stupid and childish? she thought, as angry with herself as she was with Josh. We could have been married.

We could be married now.

'It wasn't exactly the moment to tell you,' Josh pointed out, and she stared at him blankly for a moment. The thought that had slipped into her mind had whirled her away from the railway sidings at Craven Arms. 'I know what you mean,' he went on gently. 'You'd told me important things and I should have told you important things back. But there wasn't time. I couldn't say to you, just when you'd told me about Nick, that I'd refused to fight.'

'Why not? Why couldn't you?'

Josh was silent for a moment. Then he said, 'It would have upset you too much. It was more important that you should go to see him feeling cheerful. And there was another reason.' She looked up at him again, meeting his eyes once more. 'I didn't want you to look at me the way everyone else did,' he admitted. 'You see, everyone's right. I am a coward.'

Jo opened her mouth and closed it again. The bitterness in her wanted her to say yes, you are a coward, just like everyone says. But she had seen Josh at the bridge when the men refused to let him cross, she'd seen him in the forest working as hard as anyone else, she'd seen him refuse to fight even in his own defence. He'd never looked afraid, simply resigned. As if he understood. And he'd never apologised for his views.

'I don't think you're a coward,' she said slowly, 'but I'd like to know why you think the way you do.'

Josh looked at her and nodded slightly. 'I'll tell you some time. If you really want to know.'

Their eyes met. Then another train came in, and the shriek of its whistle and the surge of steam around them tore the moment apart. When the air cleared, Jo was alone and Josh was climbing aboard the lorry, ready to rattle back to the forest for another load of poles.

Jo went back to her own lorry. Her mind was in turmoil, yet there was one steady thought at the centre, like the stillness at the eye of a hurricane. It was the thought that had come to her as she stood talking to Josh, and now that it was there she could not understand why it had never come before.

She wrote to Nick that evening, as she did every night before she went to bed. She told him all the things she knew he wanted to hear, but this time she had something else to say. She had a suggestion to make – a *proposal*, she thought with a tiny, nervous giggle – and she felt a tingle of excitement and almost panic as she thought of Nick reading it. Say yes, she begged him silently, please, please say yes . . .

She folded the pages and slipped them into an envelope. And then she drew them out again and scribbled the tiny note with which she ended all her letters.

'PS: I love you . . .'

'Getting *married*?' Carrie Mason looked at the letter in her hand. 'Bill, our Jo says she's getting married!'

Bill dropped the *Daily Express* on Robertson, who was curled up on his lap, and stared at her. Robertson uncurled with a miaow of protest, and he and the newspaper fell in a tangle to the floor. Bill took no notice.

'Married? What, up there in that forest? What about Nick, then?'

'Don't be daft, Bill, it's Nick she's getting married to. She says she's written and told him there's no need to wait any longer. He can get a licence at the church down near the hospital and the next bit of time off she has, she'll go down and marry him.' Carrie lowered the letter and looked at him. 'What d'you make of that, then?'

'What should I make of it? They been engaged long enough.'

'Yes, but after he got so burnt – well, we never thought he'd live, did we, those first few days . . . ? And then he was poorly such a long time, and got all them operations to go through – well, somehow I started to wonder if it would ever happen. You do hear about girls going off men when they're, well, disfigured or maimed. And you can't really blame the girls either.'

'Nick's going to be all right. Jo said so, last time she was here. He's even talking about going back to flying, once he's got some of these ops out of the way.'

'I know, but all the same . . . Jo just never said no more about them getting married, that's all. I thought maybe they'd drift apart.'

'Well, obviously they haven't.' Bill reached down and started to pick up the pages of the *Express* and sort them into order. 'So I suppose we got all that expense to save up for now, have we?'

'Doesn't look like it. Here, you'd better read the letter yourself. She says it's going to be quiet, just them and any family that can get down there. No posh frocks or nothing. And you know they can't have a cake, not these days. I heard some people are hiring out wedding-cakes – just for show, you're not allowed to cut 'em!'

'Well, that's a relief,' Bill said, trying to sort out his newspaper. 'Mind, I'll want to stand everyone a drink to celebrate. We'd better get in touch with Nick's mum and dad, ask 'em what the local pub's like. What's that flipping cat done with page four – eaten it?'

Phyl and Etty too were surprised to hear of Jo's plans.

'I thought they were going to wait till after the war,' Phyl said, reading Jo's letter for the umpteenth time as they sat in the Chimney Corner. 'Or at least till Nick was finished with his operations. Jo's seemed quite funny about it, the last few times she's talked about him. And it was a shock to her when she saw his face that time.'

'Well, I suppose she's got over it,' Etty said. 'D'you think we'll be able to go to the wedding, Phyl?'

'Try and stop me! It ought to have been her and me getting married together. I'm not going to miss it now. Tell you what, I'm going to look through my clothes when we get back, see if I can't make something new. There's that red frock of mine, the armpits are all worn through but I could take the skirt off. If I had something pretty to sew on at the top, it'd be all right.'

'You could have my lace blouse,' Etty offered. 'It would look nice with that skirt.'

Phyl stared at her. 'But won't you want to wear it yourself?'

'I can find something else. You're the bride's cousin, she'll probably want you as bridesmaid. You've got to have something nice.'

'Matron of honour,' Phyl said. 'Don't forget I'm a married woman. I can't be a bridesmaid. Or any sort of maid,' she added with a giggle. 'Well, if you really don't mind, Etty . . .'

Jo wrote to all her friends to tell them the news. It hadn't been easy to persuade Nick, especially by letter, but once she'd got him to agree she threw herself into preparations. She spent her evenings making lists and writing letters, and Poppy complained that she wasn't thinking about anything else.

'You don't even know when this wedding's going to be,' she pointed out. 'You're just going to do it on the hop, and you'll have to come back here straight after. You can't make preparations for something like that.'

'I can. If everyone knows, they can be ready as soon as Nick says he's got some time off from the operations and I can get a few days' leave. Anyway, it's a *wedding*, Pop. The most important day of a girl's life. I've got to make preparations.'

Josh had been put on charcoal working. He disappeared from the logging gangs and joined a small group of men deep in the forest, who lived in a rough shelter and tended a huge bonfire day and night. The fire was buried beneath slabs of turf and mud which had to be kept damp to prevent the fire breaking through. Deep inside, the wood smouldered until there was nothing left but dense black charcoal.

Jo seldom saw him, but occasionally she was sent with a lorry to load the charcoal on to a lorry and carry it away. The mounds had been opened and cooled, but Josh and his companions were still black from the soft, crumbling soot. As the girls loaded the charcoal on to the lorries they too turned black. They made faces at each other, trying to laugh at their bizarre appearance.

'Gosh, this is the worst job we've ever had to do,' Jo panted, rubbing her nose and sneezing. 'Yeuch! It's getting everywhere.'

'And doesn't it itch when it gets there,' Poppy agreed. 'We're going to have to wash ourselves down in the river, Jo! Mrs Dell's never going to let us inside the house in this state.'

'Imagine what it's like working with it all the time,' Josh said, appearing at their side, totally unrecognisable until he spoke. 'I've given up all hope of ever being clean again.'

Poppy giggled. 'You'll have to get a job at the seaside as a minstrel!'

'Have you ever heard me sing?' he asked, and they all laughed. Jo caught herself up in surprise. What was she doing, laughing and chatting with this conchie, the man who wouldn't go and fight when people like Nick were being shot down in flames . . . ? Then she caught Josh's eye and once again the feeling that they'd always known each other swept over her. She remembered him saying that he'd tell her his reasons for not fighting, if she really wanted to know, and she realised that she did want to know.

Yet how could it matter to her? She was going to marry

Nick. What Josh Taylor did or didn't do, and why he did or didn't do it, wasn't of the least importance to her.

Her eyes fell and she turned away, but she knew that Josh had seen every thought, as if it had been written on her forehead, and she knew that somehow, whatever happened, he and she could never really be enemies.

It had surprised Jo when Nick hadn't fallen in at once with her plans to marry at the first opportunity. She'd written to him in a state of excitement, thinking that this would break down all the barriers that seemed to have grown between them since he had been shot down. Instead, he hadn't even replied for a week and then his letter had been disappointingly unenthusiastic. 'Do you really know what you're doing?' he'd written. 'Shackling yourself up to an ugly mug like me? I'm never going to be a film star now . . . Most girls would yell and run away.'

Jo knew, uncomfortably, that this had been her first reaction. But that was just shock, she told herself. His mum had been exactly the same. The real Nick was still there, behind the pathetic, puckered skin and the distorted mouth and nose. The boy she loved was still there. He wasn't any different.

'How can you really want to kiss me, looking like this?' he asked. 'It must make you feel sick to look at me . . . Just forget me, Jo. Find someone else. I'm not fit to be anyone's husband now.'

His letter only made Jo's determination stronger. Of *course* she wanted to kiss him. His mouth wasn't that bad. And the surgeons were going to put it right. He'd be like new. Maybe not quite the same as before – but still Nick. She held on to that thought. Still her beloved Nick.

At last he shrugged – she could almost see him doing it – and gave in. If it was what she really wanted . . . But she'd got to understand, he was going to go back to flying if the war was still on when they'd finished with him. He wasn't going to give in and sit at a desk. It could happen all over again, and even worse next time. He might end up with no legs, like that bloke Bader, and have to be pushed about in a wheelchair, like a baby in a pram.

'Douglas Bader doesn't get pushed about in a wheelchair,' Jo wrote back firmly. 'You get that licence. I'm coming down the minute I get leave, and we're going to get married.' She signed her name and then, with a smile, the PS she always added, 'PS: I love you . . .'

It was Christmas, however, before she got the leave, and by then everyone else was keen to go home to their own families. Jo made the long train journey from Craven Arms to Canterbury, and stumbled into the cottage Nick's parents were renting, almost dead with weariness, at nearly midnight. She fell into an armchair and gratefully accepted a mug of tea and then a bowl of lentil soup, made with a knuckle of bacon.

'Oh, that's lovely. I feel better now.' She looked at them. 'I'm sorry I was so late. The trains stopped everywhere. I think they even went out of their way, down little branch lines, and then came back again. I thought it would never end.'

'That's all right, Jo.' Mrs Laurence looked better than the last time Jo had seen her. Then she had been suffering from the shock of seeing Nick's face for the first time. Now she'd had time to get used to it, and to see him through the first few operations. She looked tired but more cheerful.

She took the empty bowl from Jo and refilled her teacup. Then she sat down and looked at her seriously.

'Jo, I want to talk to you—'

'Come on, Edna. Give the girl a chance to catch her breath.' Mr Laurence shook his head at his wife. 'Leave it till the morning.'

'Leave what till the morning?' Jo sat up straight, turning frightened eyes from one to the other. 'What's happened? What's happened to Nick?'

'Nothing's happened. It's all right.' Mr Laurence made a soothing motion with his hand, then looked at his wife again and shrugged. 'Well, it looks like you'll have to tell her now.

Not that there's anything to tell, to my mind. It's all in your imagination.'

'*What* is?' Jo asked again, and Mrs Laurence came and sat beside her.

'Ted's right. It's probably nothing. It's just that – well, are you absolutely sure about this, Jo? About getting married?'

'Of course I am. Why shouldn't I be?'

Nick's mother sighed. 'It's a few months since you saw him. Don't you think you ought to have a bit of time together first? Make sure you both feel the same?'

'What do you mean?' Jo's voice rose. 'D'you mean you don't think I'm sure? Look, I've written letter after letter to Nick—'

'I know. That's just it. *You're* sure – but is he?' Nick's mother shook her head. 'He's in a funny mood, Jo, it's no use saying otherwise. Up one day, down the next. I just don't think it's the time to get married, that's all.'

'Maybe that's just what he needs,' Jo said stubbornly. 'To know someone loves him. To know *I* still love him, just the same.'

'Well, so it might be. That's what Ted says. But you ought to be sure before you tie the knot. It's not as if you were going to be here with him, Jo. A few days, and you'll be off back to Shropshire. It's a long way.'

'I know that. But I don't have any choice. There's a war on.' Jo was silent for a moment. 'I suppose I could ask for a transfer . . . But I'm trained now, I'm part of a team. And I promised I wouldn't leave.' She turned to Mrs Laurence. 'It's going to be all right, I know it is. Don't forget, it was me who needed persuading in the first place! Nick was always sure.'

'Yes.' The older woman heaved another sigh. 'I expect you're right. Anyway, we'd better all get off to bed now. You've got plenty to do tomorrow if you're getting married on Wednesday.'

Christmas Day was on Friday. The wedding had been arranged for two o'clock Wednesday afternoon, so that as many people as could manage the journey could be there.

Phyl and Etty were coming from Bedford and the families from London. Shirley was hoping to get the day off from the Corner House and had arranged for neighbours to keep an eye on her father. Some of Nick's other relatives were coming, too, and the pilots he still knew in the squadron were going to do their best to make it 'if only for the beer'.

'Not that there's many left now,' Mrs Laurence said sadly. 'Too many have been shot down like Nick, and not all of them as lucky.'

Jo went to the hospital first thing next morning. She felt shaky and nervous. She knew that he'd had three operations since she'd seen him last, and there was still one to come, but Mrs Laurence had warned her not to expect too much. 'He's healed up well, but he doesn't look the same. He never will. They can't work miracles.'

'They are letting him out, though?'

'Oh, yes. They know he's getting married. And the surgeons don't want to work over Christmas, any more than anyone else. He's getting the week and then he's got to go in for the last one. You could wait till then, you know. Let him get over it all and then think about a wedding. It's not too late.'

'It is,' Jo said firmly. 'I don't know when I'll get leave again. We're getting married tomorrow, and that's all there is to it.'

She walked through the big doors of the hospital. Nick had been moved to a different part, now that he was no longer 'burns' but 'surgery'. She found her way to the ward and stood at the door, taking a deep breath.

A nurse, bending over a bed, turned and saw her. She came over and Jo saw to her surprise that it was the one who had nursed Nick before, the one who had been standing by when Jo saw his face for the first time. The two girls eyed one another.

'I've come to see my fiancé,' Jo said. 'I dare say he's told you we're getting married tomorrow.'

'Yes, he has.' The blonde girl's face gave nothing away. She pushed a curl under her cap and nodded towards the other corner. 'He's over there. He only has to wait to see the doctor, and then he can come out.'

Jo gave her a brief smile. The girl had, no doubt, done a lot for Nick, had looked after him and talked to him, but she was only a nurse after all. It was Jo he was going to marry.

She walked across the ward and stopped by his bed.

'Nick . . .'

The wedding took place the following afternoon.

Everyone was there. Phyl and Etty, Shirley, Jo's parents and Phyl's, the two mothers dressed in almost identical red coats they'd bought just before the war. Freddie and Norman. A couple of aunts and uncles, and some of Nick's family. They stood in the cold little church and sang 'Love Divine' with lusty voices, and they crowded round the happy couple as they came down the aisle and vied to be first to kiss the bride.

Jo clasped Nick's arm against her and let her happiness shine out. It *was* the right thing to do, she thought. I knew it would be. And Nick knows it, too. She glanced up at his face and saw the scars of the surgery overlaying the ruin of the burns. It was still a shock to see it, but she wouldn't let it repel her. When they were alone at last, she would prove that she didn't feel the disgust Nick was so afraid of. She would touch the poor, puckered skin and soothe the hurt. My poor Nick, she thought, and felt guilty that she hadn't been able to be with him during this terrible time, that even now they were married she would be leaving him again in a few days.

But that's the war, she thought. If it were the other way around, nobody would expect Nick to stay at home. Women have war work to do, too, and even though chopping down trees doesn't sound as glamorous as flying Spitfires, it's still got to be done.

They went to the pub, where a meal of Spam and salad and hot baked potatoes had been laid out. It wasn't up to pre-war standards, but you couldn't expect it. There were beer and lemonade to drink, and a sponge cake – Mrs Laurence had refused to hire a cake or to use a cardboard one, and half the village had contributed eggs and sugar. And there were plenty of speeches and a lot of laughter. Afterwards, the pub landlord brought in a wind-up gramophone and some records and they pushed back the tables and danced.

Jo joined in everything. She was determined to enjoy this, the most important day of a girl's life. She dragged Nick out on to the floor and made him dance with her, resting her head on his shoulder. He felt stiff and ungainly in her arms and she smiled up at him, trying to get him to relax.

'I can't. I feel as if everyone's staring at me. This is the first time I've been out of the hospital in a crowd like this. You don't know what it's like.'

Jo looked at him in dismay. The blackout curtains were up and someone had wrapped the light bulbs in red Cellophane to make the room seem like a nightclub. The dark shadows lay raddled across everyone's faces, and Nick looked no different from anyone else. All around them, their friends and relatives were dancing. It had been a happy day, a good day. It couldn't be spoilt now.

'Nobody's looking at you. And what if they were? Everyone here loves you, Nick. *I* love you.'

'You don't. You're just sorry for me.'

'*No!*' Her voice was louder than she'd intended and people glanced around. Jo tugged Nick to the door and pulled him outside. They shut the door quickly behind them and stood breathing in the cold night air. Jo shook his arm, unable to believe that it was all going wrong.

'Nick, why did you say that? It's not true.'

'Isn't it? Why did you suddenly decide we'd got to get married, then?' He turned his face away from her and walked away a few steps. 'I saw the way you looked at me when they first took the bandages off. You were disgusted. It made you feel sick. Well – didn't it?' He wheeled to face her in the pale starlight. '*Didn't* it?'

'No! All right, then, it was a shock. But it was the same for everyone. Your mother – I met her at the gates that day, she

121

was in a terrible state. But it wasn't digust, Nick. It was just – just . . .'

'Pity,' he said in a bitter tone. 'You're sorry for me.'

'Well, and why shouldn't I be?' she flared. 'What's wrong with being sorry for someone who's suffered? What's so awful about pity? Yes, I *am* sorry for you, I'm sorry you've been hurt, I'm sorry you've had to spend so long in hospital feeling useless, I don't see why I *shouldn't* be sorry for you. But that doesn't mean I don't love you. And I'm *not* disgusted.' She came close and reached up to touch his face, stroking her fingertip gently over the rutted skin. 'I love you,' she repeated softly. 'Can't you get that into your thick, stupid head?'

For a moment, there was utter silence. Nick stood without moving. Then, with a groan, he caught her in his arms and kissed her fiercely. Jo gasped and stiffened momentarily, then flung her arms around him and kissed him back. They broke apart, breathless, and she laughed a little shakily.

'We ought to go back inside.'

'No,' he said. 'No, I don't want to. I want to go home. I want to go home with you.'

Home, Jo knew, was the double bed they were to share in the cottage. Nick's parents had arranged to stay over Christmas at a small hotel in Canterbury. She smiled and kissed him again, quickly and lightly.

'I'll go in and tell them,' she whispered. 'You wait here.'

Phyl and Etty saw them go outside and exchanged anxious glances. A few moments later, Jo slipped back through the door and spoke to her mother, then to Mrs Laurence. She glanced around the room and came over to Phyl and Etty.

'Nick and me are going home now. He's – he's feeling tired.' She blushed as Phyl giggled. 'Well, we've only got a few days,' she said defensively. 'We don't want to spend all our time with you lot!'

'Course you don't,' Phyl said. 'You go off now, Jo. We'll make sure you're left in peace.'

Jo looked at her as if she wasn't quite sure what to make of this remark, then leant forward and gave her a quick kiss. 'Thanks, Phyl. And, Etty – thanks for coming. It's been a smashing day. Have a good journey back. And write as soon as you can.'

'We'll do that. And you let us know how you get on. Shame you can't take Nick with you, back to that forest, but we got a war to win first.'

They looked at each other for a moment. Then Jo gave a little shrug, as if she had run out of words, and turned away. They watched her bright chestnut head burn its way across the crowded little room and disappear through the door. Then they looked at each other and sighed.

'Well, that's it,' Etty said. 'I suppose we ought to go, too, Phyl. We mustn't miss the last train.'

They made their way over to Phyl's parents. Stan and May Jennings were sitting at a small table, having a drink with Jo's mother and father. Carrie Mason looked as if she'd been crying, but that was the privilege of the bride's mother. It didn't mean there was anything wrong.

'It seems such a sad way to start married life,' she was saying as Phyl and Etty approached. 'Poor Nick in such a state still, and Jo having to go off back to Shropshire. It's not as if she can get back for the odd day here and there.'

'I can't help thinking they should have waited,' May agreed. 'It's the same with our Phyl – she's hardly set eyes on Mike since their wedding. They won't hardly know each other by the time they get together again.' She saw the girls and broke off. 'You two just off, then?'

'Yes, we'll miss our train else.' Phyl kissed her mother and father. 'You don't need to worry about me and Mike, Mum,' she added. 'We'll be all right, no matter how long we have to wait. And I bet Jo and Nick will be the same.'

May smiled ruefully. 'Got ears like a hawk's, you have. Well, all right . . .' as the others burst out laughing '. . . you know what I mean. And we'd better be on our way, too, or we'll be stranded here. And there's nothing worse for your dad than to be stranded in a pub, you know that.'

'Not in wartime, anyway,' Stan agreed lugubriously. 'Not enough beer to go round in opening hours, let alone after. Come on, then, let's say cheerio to Mr and Mrs Laurence and then all walk down to the station together. Pity you girls can't come back to London with us tonight, instead of having to trek all the way out to Bedford for just one day.'

'That's not the way old Nobby Clark sees it,' Phyl remarked. 'Took us long enough to get him to let us off today – if we missed tomorrow as well, that'd be a hundred less b—' She broke off abruptly, flushing scarlet. In a moment of forgetfulness, she'd almost said 'bombs'. Hastily, she amended it to 'breakfasts' and turned away from her father's curious eyes.

Keeping their work a secret was increasingly difficult for Phyl and Etty. Phyl knew that her parents didn't really believe the story that they were merely doing the catering at an army camp. But nobody asked questions and nobody speculated. A lot of people had secrets in wartime, and walls had sharp ears – even if hawks didn't.

Jo and Nick stood together in the small bedroom at the cottage. Nick's head brushed the wooden beams and Jo's wasn't far short. She laid her hands on his arms and looked up at him.

'Well. Here we are – Mr Laurence.'

He looked back into her eyes. He was trembling slightly.

'Here we are – *Mrs* Laurence.'

Jo giggled. 'Is that who I really am? It sounds funny, as if I were your mother.'

Nick shook his head. 'You're not my mother. You're my wife.' He bent his head and rubbed his lips against her cheek. 'My wife . . . I didn't think it was ever going to happen, Jo.'

'Well, it wouldn't be happening now if it had been left to you,' she teased him. 'You are glad, aren't you, Nick? You're not having regrets? Those things you said just now – you don't really believe them, do you?'

Nick didn't answer. He let go of her and took the few steps to the window. He fiddled with the blackout curtains, as if making sure they were properly light-proof. Jo watched him anxiously.

'It's just that I can't help wondering a bit,' he said at last in a low voice. 'I've seen it with other chaps, Jo. Their girlfriends, even their wives, not able to take it when they see what's happened to them, what they look like. Some of them just go off and don't come back, ever. Some of them sort of try, but you can see they're not going to keep it up, they'll just stop coming or writing. Some of them – well, they stay out of pity, but it doesn't work. It can't.' He turned and looked at her, his eyes full of pleading. 'I was afraid it was going to be like that with us, Jo. When you wanted to get married, all of a sudden, it scared me.'

'Why? Why should it scare you?'

'It was as if you'd suddenly decided to dive into deep, cold water,' he said. 'You know – you look at it and you don't want to, but there's someone behind you saying you've got to. So you do, and—'

'And it's all right after all,' she broke in. She went to him and put her arms around him, gazing up into his face, willing him to believe her. 'You dive in and it's cold for a moment, and then it's lovely. You've done it, and you're glad. And that's what it's going to be like for us, Nick. We've done it and it's lovely, and we're glad. Aren't we? *Aren't* we?'

Nick stared at her. Then he pulled her roughly into his arms. He rubbed his puckered skin against her and kissed her on the lips, an urgent, bruising kiss. He leant on her, hard, and Jo took a step back and then fell on to the bed. Nick fell with her, his body thin and hard against hers, and she felt his hands fumbling at the buttons of her jacket. Half laughing, half startled, she pushed them away.

'I'll do it. It'll be quicker . . . Oh, Nick, I love you. I *love* you.' Their clothes seemed to be fighting back, but at last they were both almost naked in the flickering candlelight. They looked at each other and Jo gasped.

'Nick! I didn't realise—'

'Did you think it was only my face?' he asked harshly. 'You saw me in the hospital. You knew I was burnt all over. And now they've taken even the good bits away . . .'

The scars were partly from his burns, partly from the plastic surgery. Jo willed herself not to look away. She met his eyes instead, and then did what she had told herself she would do and touched his ruined skin with her fingers, tracing the ridges and furrows, breathing deeply as her heart skidded and kicked within her.

'I love you, Nick.'

He reached for her again and slid her bra strap from her shoulder. He slipped his hands under the waistband of her knickers and eased them down her buttocks and thighs. He knelt between her legs and laid his face against her smooth, unmarked stomach.

'Nothing's ever touched you, Jo,' he whispered. 'Nothing's ever hurt you.'

'Nick . . .'

Jo did the same as he had done and slipped his underpants off. She drew him up against her and they lay on the bed together, side by side, their bodies touching.

'Make love to me, Nick,' she whispered. 'Make love to me now. We've waited so long . . .'

Part Two

Chapter Ten

Phyl and Etty would never have believed, when they'd first arrived at Elstow, that by December 1943 it would be the size of a small town.

'It's like a little bit of London, dumped in the middle of nowhere,' Etty said as they trudged along the road to the canteen from the building where they spent their days filling bombs. A patrol of the depot police approached them, carrying Sten guns, and the girls moved aside to let them pass. 'Remember all that mud we had to tramp through when we first got here? And all the building works going on? We never thought it'd end up like this, did we?'

Phyl shook her head in agreement. 'Mind you, it's still pretty weird. Huge great cranes, our own railway, and those enormous mounds round the TNT magazines, and all that grass in between, what keeps catching fire. The whole place could go up in one almighty bang, and here we are walking about as if nothing's happening.'

'Well, nothing *is* happening,' Etty said. 'Nothing much, anyway.' They stopped as they rounded a corner to see a huge bomb being lowered carefully by one of the big cranes into a cooling pit. She grinned at Phyl. 'Just the odd blockbuster, that's all – nothing out of the ordinary!'

They laughed, then turned as Jenny and Kaye caught up with them. 'What's the joke?'

'Just thinking how quickly we've all got used to it here,' Phyl said, nodding towards the bomb. 'Eighteen months back, we'd have nearly fainted at the idea of walking past one of those. Now we don't take any notice.'

'Not surprising,' Jenny said, 'when you think we were probably stuffing that very bomb with TNT a couple of days ago.'

'Yes, and that's another thing. We're walking bombs ourselves, with all that much getting in our clothes and our hair and everything. A couple of years ago, we'd have fainted at the idea, now we just don't bother – so long as the laundry can wash our things hot enough to kill it off, without shrinking our best jumpers to the size of dolls' clothes.'

'You shouldn't be wearing your best jumpers to work, should you? Anyway, never mind about that. Who do you think's going to be on our *Workers' Playtime*?'

'How should I know?' Phyl asked. 'You know they never tell us till we get there, same as when it's broadcast on the wireless they never say where it's coming from.' She imitated the voice of a BBC announcer. '"And today we bring you from a factory somewhere in the Midlands—"' Then, catching sight of Jenny's face, pink with suppressed excitement, she broke off. 'Who is it, then? And how d'you know?'

'It's Arthur Askey!' Jenny gave a little crow of delight and skipped round them in a circle. 'I saw him coming through the gate in a big car! Mr Carter sent me down there with a message . . . I *saw* him! He's ever so little, just like they say, but he saw me, too, and he gave me a really cheeky grin and waved and blew me a kiss! Me, Jenny Harris – Arthur Askey blew *me* a kiss!'

The others stopped and gazed at her with envy. 'Arthur Askey? Honest and true? You're having us on!'

'I'm not. You'll see I'm not. Tell you what, I'm going to try and get his autograph. Here, d'you think he'll sing that song about the bee? I like that one, it's my favourite, I heard him do it on the wireless the other week when he was on *Henry Hall's Guest Night*. They say he's a real scream.'

'*I* hope he'll do the window-cleaner one,' Kaye said solemnly, and they all turned to stare at her. She returned their looks, straight-faced, and then Phyl let out a yelp of laughter and poked her in the ribs.

'That's George Formby, you idiot! Honestly, Kaye, you're a fool. Anyway, we'll never get Arthur Askey and George Formby on the same day. They only ever have one big star at a time.'

'We won't see either of them if you don't stop nattering and get a move on,' Etty said, pulling at Phyl's arm. There was a crowd of people now, all hurrying towards the biggest canteen, where the lunchtime shows were put on, and it was first come, first served for seats. The girls joined them in the scramble and, to Jenny's great delight, managed to push right through to the front and get seats near the stage.

Arthur Askey was a big star but, as Jenny had said, he was a very small man. What he lacked in size, however, he made up for in energy. He erupted on to the stage as if he'd been blown there by the explosives they worked with every day, shouting his slogan, 'Hello, playmates! How *do* you do?' And from that moment he took their breath away with a non-stop patter of quickfire jokes, ending, as Jenny had hoped, with his 'Bee Song'. By the time he had finished his act everyone was aching with laughter and the overseers were looking at their watches.

'I don't know which I liked best,' Kaye said. 'Him, or Tommy Trinder the other week. And that Max Wall, he was good, too.' She grinned wickedly. 'A bit blue, mind. Even the double meanings had double meanings!'

'There won't be time for the other acts,' Phyl whispered. 'I'm sure he wasn't meant to be on stage that long.'

'Isn't he funny?' Etty whispered back. 'I can see why Jenny was so pleased she'd seen him.' They settled back in their seats as another act came on, a trio of sisters who sang close-harmony songs, most of them about love and separation like the ones Vera Lynn had made famous – 'We'll Meet Again' and 'There'll be Bluebirds Over the White Cliffs of Dover' – which made all the girls cry and the men clear their throats. After that, there was a ventriloquist with a schoolboy doll and

131

then, to their great joy, Arthur Askey bounced back on to the stage again with three more jokes and another song. When they came out at last they had to run all the way back to the bomb hut, and Jenny had no time to wait for an autograph.

Nobby, whose work at Elstow had after all been deemed a 'reserved occupation', much to the disappointment of the girls who had hoped he'd be sent away, was standing at the door as they piled back in. He glowered at them and looked pointedly at his foreman's watch.

'Come on, now, we 'aven't got all day. There's a war on, *if* you ain't forgot all about it, and we got work to do. Get those overalls on and look sharp about it, and if I sees you loitering down round the gate hoping to get autygraphs another time, Jenny Harris, you'll be for the 'igh jump, and I do mean *'igh*.'

'Mr Carter sent me on an errand,' Jenny began indignantly, but Nobby had turned away. He was looking at Etty.

'I hope you've not got that engagement ring on again.'

'Of course I haven't,' Etty said. 'I've never worn it, not after that first day.'

'I dunno.' He was staring at her neckline. 'I remember you 'iding it under yer blouse. I wouldn't put it past you to try that on again. Wouldn't put it past any of you young madams.'

'I wouldn't—' Etty began, but he took a step closer and put his hand on the front of her collar and began to fumble with the button. Etty gave an exclamation, and Phyl and Kaye glanced at each other and moved swiftly to grab his wrist.

'Leave her alone!' Phyl ordered. 'If she says she's not wearing her ring, she's not wearing it. Let go of her!'

Nobby turned his small black eyes on them. His skin had thickened during the past eighteen months and looked coarse, pitted with blackheads and grease-filled pores. His hair was lank and greasy, too. He lifted his upper lip in a snarl.

'*You* let go! I got a right to make sure if I think she's being a danger to the workshop—'

'Our little Etty a danger?' Kaye gave a hoot of laughter and several other people glanced around to see what was happening. 'Why, Etty's about as much danger as Vera Lynn herself! Anyway, what makes you think she's wearing her ring, all of a sudden?'

'It's a spot check,' he said defensively. 'We're supposed to make 'em regular.'

'Spot check, my eye,' Kaye said. 'You just want to get your filthy hands on her, that's what it is. Anyway, all you got to do is ask her to lift her collar up and show you there's no chain or ribbon round her neck – see?' Kaye demonstrated, revealing that Etty's neck was bare. 'No need to try and undress her.' She let the collar fall back into place. 'You get your overalls on, girl,' she told Etty, 'and don't you take no notice of that filthy-minded pig. And you leave her alone in future,' she told Nobby, 'or you'll have me to reckon with.'

The overseer glared at her. 'And *you'll* have *me* to reckon with,' he blustered. '*I'm* boss here, in case you haven't noticed, and I can get you the sack, and if there's any more insolence from you, I will.' He watched, fuming, as the girls pulled on their protective clothes and rubber shoes. 'And if we weren't working full stretch to beat the Germans, I *would*,' he yelled after them as they disappeared towards their benches.

The girls ignored him. 'He's nothing but a bully,' Kaye told Etty, 'and bullies have to be stood up to. They're all cowards when it comes to the point.'

'All the same, he can be nasty,' Etty said nervously. 'Look how he followed that girl Jean about all last winter. She couldn't move without he was there, and when he saw she didn't want anything to do with him, he made out she'd been pinching money. He got *her* sacked. I don't want it to happen to me.'

'I don't know,' Jenny observed, 'I don't think I'd mind getting sacked. It's not exactly a little bit of heaven, working here.'

'No, but you don't know what else you might have to do instead. And they trust us here. It's valuable work. I don't want it to be made out that I'm a thief or something like that.'

'Nobby wouldn't do that to you. He fancies you, anyone

133

can see that. That's why he wanted to get his hands on you just now.'

Etty shivered. She remembered Maggie and the soldier who had fancied her. Maggie had ended up raped and half-dead in a grimy back alley. 'I'd rather he didn't fancy me, thanks,' she said. 'I'd rather he didn't take any notice of me at all.'

They went to their positions along the bench and began work. Someone had once said that making bombs was like stuffing sausage rolls and although to begin with they'd known it was nothing like that, they were so used to doing it now that they would almost have agreed. They worked quickly and efficiently, chatting as they did so. Every now and then an overseer would come round to watch them for a moment and tell them not to talk so much, but as soon as he had gone they would resume their conversations.

'How's your Jim?' Kaye asked Etty. 'Any chance of him getting home for a spot of leave?'

Etty looked up, her face flushing. 'Yes! I had a letter this morning – I was going to tell you. They've decided he can have some recuperation leave. Honestly, it seems awful to be pleased when your boy gets wounded, but at least it gets him out of the fighting, and if it means he can come home – well, I can't help being a bit glad!'

'Course you can't.' Phyl gave her a grin of delight. 'I just wish it was my Mike as well. Mind you, he did sort of hint in his last letter that he might be getting some leave as well – but you know what it's like, you never know for certain till they're at the door. Be a lark if they both got home for Christmas, wouldn't it?'

'That'd be all of us set up,' Kaye remarked. 'My Ken's going to be home too, and Jenny's bloke's never even gone away. Trust you to find someone in a reserved occupation, Jen.'

'That's right,' the other girl agreed equably. 'Too valuable, that's my John.' John was a policeman on the site, one of those who patrolled day and night armed with a Sten gun.

134

They had met a few months after the girls had arrived at Elstow and had clicked straight away.

The girls continued with their work and Etty tried to forget the scene with Nobby. But every now and then she glanced up to find his eyes on her, watching across the benches of the crowded factory floor. And she shivered, feeling again the touch of his thick fingers on her neck and the hot, sour smell of his breath upon her face.

The past eighteen months had seen no improvement in Alf Woods's condition. He now had three and sometimes four seizures a week, and was almost afraid to get out of bed in the mornings. When he did, he sat in an armchair, wrapped in blankets because he was afraid to light a fire, and waited miserably for Shirley to come home.

Shirley was at her wits' end. She had tried again to persuade him to go to Wales to be with Annie and Jack, but he shook his head and either flew into a temper or started to cry. When Shirley saw tears pouring down his cheeks, she bit back the words and put her arms around him instead.

'It's all right, Dad. I'm not going to make you do anything you don't want to do. If you want to stay here, we'll say no more about it. But we'll have to make some arrangements to see you're looked after, see? I can't go off to work easy in my mind if I'm worrying about you the whole time.'

'You'll not put me in the workhouse,' he whimpered. 'You'll not put me in the Union?'

'Don't be silly! I'd never do that, you know I wouldn't. I just meant I'll have to ask one or two of the neighbours to pop in on you while I'm out, that's all. Mrs Yates wouldn't mind, she's always asking me if there's anything she can do to help, and that nice Mrs Harrison, she'll help as well. It's *no good*, Dad,' she continued as he began to protest about having strangers poking about, 'I just can't go on as we are, and if you won't go to Wales, that's what we'll have to do. And they're not strangers, we've known them for years, and they won't be poking about, they'll just keep an eye on you and see you get your dinner and that.'

Her father opened his mouth as if to object again, but caught her eye and closed it again. He looked as sulky as a little boy and Shirley hid a smile, but there were tears in her eyes as well. He'd always been so strong, so much in charge, and now she was having to treat him like a child. And it's not as if he *needs* to be treated like that, she thought sadly. When he's not having a fit he's just the same as he's always been. It's only that he's so frightened of having one that he won't do the things he used to.

Epilepsy, the doctor had said, and confirmed Alf's diagnosis that it had come from the blow on the head he'd received in the accident. Nothing could be done to cure it but it could sometimes be controlled with phenobarbitone. He gave Alf a prescription for tiny white pills and Alf took them for a while, but was so sleepy and befuddled that he threw the rest away and refused to see the doctor again.

'Chucking money down the drain,' he told Shirley. 'We got to accept I'm like it and always will be. And I'm not having your mother brought back to look after me, so there's no use suggesting it.'

Shirley sighed. It was all very well, and she knew that her mother was better off in Wales with Jack, even now that the bombing seemed to have stopped, but it didn't make life any easier for her.

'Well, so long as you agree to let Mrs Yates and Mrs Harrison come in and give an eye to things . . .'

'Don't seem to have no choice, do I?' Alf growled, and Shirley, thinking that it was his choice that made it necessary, said no more. It was part of his illness, the doctor had said, that he should get a bit low. And there was always the chance that the bit of his brain that had been hurt might get better and Alf be his old self again.

Not until the war's over and Mum and Jack are back again, she thought, going into the kitchen to get their evening meal ready. And then we'll have a whole lot of different problems.

136

How's our Jack going to take to being in London again, when he's settled down on the farm as if he'd been born there?

A knock on the front door brought a smile to her lips. Owen was coming round for supper this evening and she'd managed to get some sausages to go with the bit of liver the butcher had saved for her. It would be a tasty supper, with some nice mashed potatoes and cabbage, and rice pudding for afters. At least Dad had managed to get that into the oven so that it could simmer slowly through the afternoon.

'Owen.' She lifted her face for his kiss. 'It's lovely to see you.'

Owen popped his head round the door of the back room to say hello to Alf, then followed her into the kitchen.

'Didn't think I was going to make it in time, *cariad*. I been down the recruitment office. You know what they're saying about the call-up?'

Shirley shook her head. She was peeling potatoes and dropping them into a pan of water. 'What's that?'

'Well, that Mr Bevin, he's decided we got to have more men down the mines, see. Shortage of coal. So he's going to direct some of the servicemen down the pit. And guess who'll be first!'

Shirley turned and stared at him. 'But you're not in the services yet.'

Owen's call-up had been deferred to allow him to support his family, his father having suffered with bad lungs ever since his own days of working in a coal mine. Now his father had died and his mother had gone to live with her sister in Chepstow, and Owen had confirmed his registration.

'No, but it's not them already in that's going to be sent. They're going to pick the new recruits, see. By ballot, so they say.' He snorted with derision. 'So they say! But they're not going to pass over a chap like me, are they, Welsh and from a mining family?'

'But you've never worked down a mine. That's why your dad came to London, so you wouldn't have to.'

137

'Won't make any difference,' he said gloomily. 'I'll get picked out of the hat, you see if I don't.'

Shirley finished the potatoes and put them on the gas ring. She started the sausages frying and began to wash the cabbage.

'Well, I can't believe that Mr Bevin's got time to go through the list looking for boys like you who don't even live in Wales any more. He'll be far more likely to pick the ones who're still there. But even if you get chosen, will it be any worse than having to go to Burma or Africa or somewhere like that, and fight? Or to sea and get drowned? Or in the RAF and be burnt to bits, like Nick?' She dropped the cabbage in the bowl of water and turned to him again, putting her arms round him and burying her face against his chest. 'I know it's selfish,' she said in a muffled voice, 'but I just want you to be safe.'

Owen held her against him. He thought of his father, coughing up coal dust and blood together from his damaged lungs. He thought of the mining disasters he had witnessed, the crowds of women waiting at the pithead to know if their men would be brought out alive or dead.

'Safe?' he said. 'There's nowhere safe these days, *cariad*.'

Chapter Eleven

Jim Pratt came home just before Christmas. He had caught pneumonia just as his wounds were healing, and when he arrived at the Devonshire cottage he looked pale and thin, his uniform hanging on him as if made for a much bigger man. Maggie and her mother met him on the platform of Tavistock railway station and rushed forwards to hug him.

'Jim! You're like a rake. Don't they give you nothing to eat out there?'

'Course they do. Feed us like fighting cocks. I've been *ill*, Mum.'

'Ill you might have bin, but I'd've thought they'd feed you up a bit to send you home,' Ivy Pratt said, looking him up and down. 'You were a fine figure of a man when I sent you off, Jim, and now look at you. A shadow, that's what you are now, nothing but a shadow.'

'Well, that's why they've sent me home – for you to feed me up again,' Jim said, grinning, and his mother snorted.

'On our rations? Well, I hope they've given you a few points, to help out. Now, you leave that kitbag alone, our Maggie can carry that for you. We got to go down those steps and catch a bus in the town. Then it's a bit of a walk to the house – think you can manage it?'

'Course I can,' Jim said, but he was looking white and exhausted by the time they had trudged through the lanes to the cottage. Ivy opened the front door and he almost stumbled into the small living-room, collapsing into the battered armchair beside his grandmother. He leant back his head and closed his eyes. Ada Pratt, also half-asleep until that moment, blinked at him.

'Here, that's our Jim, ain't it?' She'd been told a dozen times he was coming home, but each time it had come as fresh news. 'What's the matter with him? He looks all in. I thought he was supposed to be better?'

'He's been sent home to convalesce,' Maggie said, thinking that she had at least taken in the fact that he'd been wounded. 'That means he's better but ain't got his strength back. The walk was a bit much for him.'

'It's not just that.' Ivy went through to the scullery to fill the kettle. She came back and set it on the range. 'It's all that long journey he's had. Took the train seven hours to get from London, he told us. Seven hours! It's unhuman, that is. Like pigs in a truck.'

'Well, you're home now,' Maggie said. She sat down beside him, stroking his thin hand. 'And we got plenty of butter and milk and nice fresh eggs down here. Ma's even learnt to make clotted cream! You'll be as fat as a pig in clover, never mind pigs in trucks.'

Jim opened his eyes and gave her a wan smile. He really did look poorly, Maggie thought, and wished Etty could be here, too. But Etty had written that she couldn't get away from that army camp where she worked in Bedford. Daft, Maggie called it. She was only waiting on army officers at the dinner-table, when all was said and done – not exactly vital war work. They could've given her a few days off to be with poor Jim.

The kettle came to the boil and Ivy made the tea. Despite Lord Woolton's behest, she put in not one but two for the pot, and let it get really strong before pouring it into thick cups. As she handed Jim his, the door opened and the children burst in, wrapped in scarves and thick coats, their faces rosy with the cold.

'Jim! *Jim!*' Ginnie shrieked. She was twelve now but still the flaxen-haired, dainty fairy child she'd always been. She flung herself upon her brother, while her cousins, Billy and Freddy, and two-year-old Barry hung back a little, staring.

140

'Look at our Barry, wondering what all the fuss is about,' Maggie said, reaching out to pull her son closer. 'Come and say hello to your Uncle Jim, Bar. And, Billy, you don't need to look so daft – you know Jim.'

'Has he brought me a present?' Billy asked. At eight and short for his age, he had a deep, growling voice that sounded comical from such a small boy. Built square, like a box, his grandfather Sam Pratt always said, and he'd shoot up later on and be a big bloke, just like his grandad. There was a place for him down Covent Garden Market as soon as he was ready.

'Billy!' his grandmother scolded, and Jim gave a wry smile. 'There wasn't much to buy where I was. Sorry, kid. But I got one souvenir . . .' He turned and fumbled in the shabby canvas kitbag. Crumpled clothes and a tin of blanco piled up on the floor until he finally found what he was looking for and held it out to his nephew. 'It's a cap off a shell. Someone told me all the kids are collecting 'em.'

Billy grasped it eagerly, his face alight. 'Coo, it's beauty. Thanks, Uncle Jim. Nobody at school's got one as good as this.'

'All the way from the Front,' Jim said, and leant his head back again.

Maggie and her mother exchanged glances.

'He's wore out,' Ivy said in a low voice. 'He ought to go to bed.'

'Let him rest a bit here first. Then he can go up and have a proper sleep. I reckon he just wants to get used to being here.' Maggie looked around at the rough plaster walls, the beams in the ceiling, the small, many-paned window. 'It ain't much like home used to be, is it?'

Home, as Jim remembered it, had been a big, untidy house behind St Paul's Cathedral. There had been room for everyone in the sprawling family, and room for them to bring their friends as well. Sam Pratt had earned a good wage in Covent Garden and had been able to bring a lot of fruit and vegetables home, and Jim and Maggie had been bringing

141

home wages. Ivy went out cleaning at the local pub each morning, and often served behind the bar at night. The house was always full of people and kids, noise and laughter, with old Ada, Sam's mother, a permanent fixture in her corner with her stick and her black umbrella close to hand.

It was very different from this tiny, overcrowded cottage, with only women and children in it, with no Sam Pratt filling the house with his booming laugh, and no George and Gerry arguing over their Meccano.

And no Evie, Billy's mother, who had been killed when the house was bombed, and no Queenie, her baby daughter who had been buried with her in the ruins.

Jim lay in his chair, his eyes still closed, and let the memories overwhelm him. While he'd been away, fighting, it was the picture of the big ramshackle house that he'd held in his mind – it was that house he'd been fighting for. He knew it had been bombed, of course, he'd been back since then and seen Sam and the twins in their London lodging house. He'd even been down to the cottage once. But now, in his frail state, it was as if he had never been properly aware of it, as if the full meaning of it all had only just hit him. Home was gone, the family torn apart, and this cramped, dark little cottage in the middle of nowhere was all that was left.

A tear trickled from under one eyelid and slid down his cheek. Maggie saw it and swiftly wiped it away. She slipped her arm behind his head and lifted him against her.

'Come on, our Jim. Time you was in bed.'

Jim nodded weakly and let her help him to his feet. He swayed a little, looking round the room, and went through the door to the narrow staircase. Maggie followed him, ready to catch him if he should stumble, and ushered him into the tiny back bedroom where he was to sleep.

Ivy sent Ginnie and the children out into the scullery to fetch an apple each out of the box where they were stored. She glanced at her mother-in-law, sitting in her corner as if she'd been dumped there. For once Ada's eyes were open and watching her, small black buttons in a nest of wrinkles.

'I don't care what you or our Maggie says, our Ive,' she said in her rusty, rasping voice, 'that boy's not well. He wants looking after.'

Don't they all? Ivy thought with a sigh as she poured another cup of strong tea. Don't they all want looking after – all the boys out there, fighting for freedom or whatever it is this war's all about? And don't the rest of us, too, that have been struggling on, doing our best for four blooming years and still got no idea when it might end?

Don't we all just need a bit of looking after?

Alf Woods needed a lot of looking after.

'You'd best put me in a home,' he said to Shirley when she came home yet again to find him trying to clean up after a seizure. 'I'm not fit to be left on me own.'

'You don't have to *be* on your own, Dad.' Shirley tried to keep the exasperation out of her voice. She'd been alarmed lately by just how irritated, even angry, she was getting with her father. It wasn't his fault, she reminded herself. But that didn't seem to help when, tired after a day at the Corner House, she came in to find the furniture knocked over, cups or ornaments smashed and the smell of urine or faeces from soiled clothes. 'I've told you, Mrs Yates and Mrs Harrison would be only too glad to come in and sit with you as well as get you a bite to eat. But you've started locking the door against them. What's the point of that?'

'Don't want them walking in any time they please, that's what,' he muttered defiantly. 'Don't leave me no privacy.'

Shirley sighed. 'But you could really hurt yourself. It's a miracle you haven't already—'

Her father turned on her. 'Well, and what's a miracle, then? God's will, that's what it is. And if He sees fit to put a miracle or two my way, then who're you or those nosy women to tell Him not to? Eh? You leave Him and me alone, that's all I ask. And maybe when He's had a bit more practice with miracles, He might work a real one and stop me having all these blasted fits so I can go back to work and start living like a proper man again.' He stood at the sink and scrubbed in silence at his trousers, then burst out again. 'Don't you never think what it's like for me, Shirl? Don't you never think how I feel about all this? What d'you suppose I'd feel like, eh, coming to and finding old woman Yates staring at me, seeing me in a fit, knowing what happens, what I do? How could I ever lift up me head again, eh? Tell me that.'

Shirley's irritation vanished, leaving a dark, spreading sorrow. She put her hand on his arm and spoke more softly.

'You leave that now, Dad, and go and have a rest. I'll finish it and make us both a cup of tea before I start getting supper. Owen's coming round, too. He'll brighten us both up.'

Alf sighed and nodded. He dropped the trousers back into the grey, scummy water and dried his hands on the roller towel behind the door. Shirley watched him go back into the other room and thought sadly how old he was looking, his strong legs thin and wasted, his shoulders bent. Even if he did get better, she thought, even if a miracle did happen, he'll never be fit to work again the way he used to.

Supper was almost ready when Owen arrived. He came in and kissed Shirley, but she knew at once that her hopes that he would cheer them up were to be dashed. She looked at him anxiously.

'Something's happened.'

He nodded. He looked angry, frightened and bitterly disappointed all at once. He sat down on a chair beside the table and leant his elbow on the white cloth. Shirley and her father stared at him.

'It's come,' Owen said. 'My call-up. I got me papers.'

Shirley made a quick movement but the look on his face stopped her in her tracks. She waited again.

'It's the pit,' he said. 'I knew it would be. I knew it'd happen. Soon as I heard about that Mr Bevin, I knew. Ballot, my foot!' He raised his eyes towards her and she saw the hopelessness in them. 'I'm going back to Wales, Shirley. Back to the valleys. I'm going down the mines.'

There was a long silence. Then Shirley moved at last. She

ran to him and dropped to her knees beside him, cradling his head against her. She kissed his hair, his ears, his eyes, his face, finally his mouth. She held his head between her hands and looked into his eyes.

'Stop looking like that, Owen. It's not that bad. It's not bad at all. It's *good*.' She took a deep breath and looked up at her father. Alf was watching, bewildered. He had never properly understood Owen's fear of going down the pit, never been able to understand why anyone would rather fight and be horribly maimed or killed than mine coal.

'This is it, Dad,' she told him. 'This is when you've got to decide what *you're* going to do. Because I know what's going to happen to Owen and me.' Her eyes brilliant, she looked back into Owen's face, almost as bewildered as Alf's. 'We're going to get married. I'm coming to Wales with you, Owen. When you go down the mine, I'll be there to kiss you goodbye, and when you come up again I'm going to be there to look after you. We're going to be together. And as for you, Dad, you can come with us or you can go and live on the farm with Mum and our Jack, where you ought to have been all this time – but whichever it is, you're going to Wales as well, so just you make up your mind to it!'

Etty was waiting anxiously for news of Jim. She'd had a telegram to say he was coming home, and another one came from Maggie to say he'd arrived. A couple of days later a letter arrived through the post office box number everyone at Elstow had to use.

'He says he's glad to be back,' she told Phyl and the others as they sat on their beds at the hostel. 'He says Maggie's learnt to be a nurse at that convalescent home and he's being looked after like a king. He says it's so quiet down there, you wouldn't believe it.' She wrinkled her nose. 'I reckon we'd believe it, eh? Remember how quiet it was when we first came to Elstow?'

'Not any more, though,' Phyl said. 'Not with the factories going day and night.' She was darning stockings and she looked at them critically. 'I don't reckon I'll be able to get much more wear out of these. I'm darning darns now. I wish we could get some of those nylon stockings people keep talking about.'

'They don't last any longer,' Kaye said. 'They run like mad, and you can't darn 'em either.'

'No, but they look smashing on, and so long as you're careful they don't ladder. Oh, well, I suppose we're lucky to get lisle. I don't mind drawing seams down the back of my legs in summer, but it's a bit chilly at this time of year.'

'A *bit* chilly!' Jenny exclaimed. 'There's nowhere on earth as cold as this place. I'm wearing thick socks from now till next April, I don't care what I look like!'

'What else does Jim say?' Phyl enquired, rolling her stockings into a ball and throwing them at Jenny's head.

Etty had been reading her letter, oblivious of the other girls' chatter. She looked up, blushing, and said, 'Oh, not much. Just this and that, you know.'

The others laughed. 'All right, we can guess! Phyl, what about your Mike? Is he getting leave after all?'

Phyl also flushed with delight. 'Yes, he is! I heard today. He's getting a whole week over Christmas – isn't it smashing? We're going to spend two days with his family and two with mine, and then go off on our own for a bit.'

'Bit of what?' Kaye asked slyly, and Phyl's blush deepened. 'Don't look like that, Phyl, it's your patriotic duty. You're supposed to be getting on with the next generation, didn't you know that?'

Phyl stared at her. 'Kaye! Don't be so awful.'

'I'm not being awful. My Ken told me. That's why they're giving a lot of leave, and the men've all been told they've got to get their wives in the family way, or else there won't be enough people to keep things going after the war. Well, it makes sense, doesn't it, when you think how many won't come—'

'*Kaye!* Don't!' Phyl had gone white. 'It *is* awful. Talking like that – and you and Ken aren't even married. And

146

anyway, I don't know that I'd *want* to have a baby now, not the way things are. What sort of a world is it to bring a baby into? Not even knowing if it's going to have a father. Nobody knows what's going to happen. You might get bombed, and the baby with you – or Hitler might win the war and we'll all be slaves. I don't even want to *think* about it!' She sat on the bed, trembling, her head bent over the rolled stockings that Jenny had thrown back.

The other girls stared at her. Kaye looked awkward and unhappy. She reached out and touched Phyl's arm.

'Come on, Phyl. You know I never meant to upset you. It was just a joke.'

'Well, it wasn't a very funny one,' Phyl said shakily.

'Perhaps it wasn't, but I didn't know that till I said it. And it didn't come out like I meant anyway. Look, just forget I said it, will you? You and Mike have a good time and don't think about anything else for a few days. That's what me and Ken are going to do, I can tell you.'

'I don't know why you don't get married,' Phyl said, still a little tearfully. 'If he's going to be home for a week, you've got time.'

'Look, I said we were going to have a good time, didn't I? I never said nothing about getting married.' Kaye grinned and rolled her eyes, poking Phyl in the ribs. 'That was another joke, in case you didn't notice. And don't tell me you and Mike didn't do a bit of anticipating, because I won't believe you. Everyone does, these days.'

Phyl blushed again and looked up to protest, then caught Kaye's eye and grinned reluctantly. 'Well – maybe a bit.'

Kaye hooted with laughter and Etty stared at Phyl in astonishment. 'Phyl! You never!'

'Yes, we did.' Phyl looked at her defiantly. 'Why not? We knew he was going to go away. We didn't know if he'd ever come home. Look at Maggie's husband, getting killed when they'd only been married a few hours. I bet she's glad she and Tom got to know each other a bit better beforehand.'

'Yes, but that was Maggie. I mean – I thought you were

different.' Try as she might, Etty couldn't keep the shock from her voice, but she knew that it was tinged with envy. Working in a factory, she'd heard a lot of talk from the other girls about what it was like to 'go with' a boy and, despite the modesty instilled in her by the orphanage – born largely of ignorance – she hadn't been able to help feeling curious and oddly excited. And she knew that when she was last with Jim – so long ago, it seemed – she'd begun to want more than the kisses and caresses they'd shared.

'None of us is different, Etty,' Kaye told her. 'We're human beings, doing what comes naturally. That's all there is to it, and so long as you're careful there isn't any harm in it. None at all.'

'Careful? Oh – you mean . . .' Etty coloured and Kaye laughed again.

'That's it! That's the time when you *don't* want to find yourself in the family way.'

Like Maggie, Etty thought. But that hadn't been her fault – as far as anyone knew. And as far as anyone would ever know, because little Barry had still not shown the slightest resemblance to whoever might have been his father – not to Dave, whose girlfriend's brother had come to warn Maggie off, or to Andy, the young soldier whom Maggie had said was 'special', or to the soldier who had treated her so brutally. And Maggie didn't care now. Barry was hers, and no one else's.

Phyl was watching her, smiling a little. She seemed to have got over her annoyance and her smile widened as she began to laugh.

'I remember Mike trying to buy French letters! He went in the chemist's shop first and came out with a tube of toothpaste because there was a woman serving, and then he went into the barber's and had a haircut so he could get "something for the weekend". He'd only had his hair cut a few days before that, and his mum gave him such a funny look when he got home. I'm sure she knew what he was up to.'

'Mums always do,' Jenny said sagely, and Etty turned away. She had no memory of her mother, who had died when she was two years old, and she didn't think Jim was the sort to go and buy French letters for the weekend or any other time. He was the quiet one of the big, noisy Pratt family and he'd never even suggested that Etty should unbutton her blouse. She sighed a little.

Maybe she and Jim should think about getting married, too. They'd been engaged long enough. Maybe this leave was the chance they'd been waiting for.

Chapter Twelve

Christmas leave was given to as many of the workers at Elstow as possible. Neither Etty nor Phyl had gone home for Christmas the previous year, and since both had a husband or fiancé at home Mr Carter insisted that they must be amongst the first to go. Nobby Clark put up his usual objections but he was overruled and Etty and Phyl boarded the train for London in high excitement.

'Fancy going all the way to Devon,' Phyl said to Etty, a shade enviously. 'I wish Mike and me could go somewhere like that. I bet it's really pretty, even in winter.'

'Well, why don't you come down for the last couple of days?' Etty suggested. 'I bet they could squeeze you in somewhere and it'd be nice for Maggie to see you and Mike again. I think she gets a bit lonely down there, even with her nursing.'

'That's not a bad idea,' Phyl said. 'I'll ask Mike. I reckon he'd like it, too.'

They parted at Liverpool Street, Etty to go on to Paddington for the second part of her journey. It was a long way to go, especially with the trains as they were now – packed with servicemen going on leave and with other people lucky enough to be able to go home for Christmas – and they seemed to stop at every station and every tiny halt on the line. At each one, people got out and the passengers hoped for a bit more room, but invariably another lot got in, sometimes making it even more crowded than it had been before. Etty found herself starting off in the corridor, perched uncomfortably on her small suitcase, and it was a long time before she managed to get a seat. Even then she was squashed between a sweaty army sergeant whose coarse khaki uniform smelt of fish and rubbed against her face, and a naval matelot in square rig, whose lanyard kept getting caught in her coat buttons.

'Reckon we'll have to get married if this keeps happening,' he said with a grin, untangling the white cord. 'Got a sweetheart, have you?'

Etty nodded, smiling back shyly. She could tell he wasn't being pushy, just friendly. He nodded in a resigned sort of way.

'Story of my life. Still, I've got a nice girl now, up in Pompey. Just been for a weekend there.' He closed his lips, as if afraid he'd already said too much.

Etty wondered which ship he belonged to. Before the war, all sailors had had the name of their ship on a band around their cap, but these had been taken off now. No one was supposed to know which ship was in harbour or where, and you weren't allowed to say if you did know. That was the sort of thing that Muriel Chalk had got Irene Bond, the sixth of the group of Nippies, to listen out for at the Corner House, and that was why they'd both ended up in prison for spying. Just passing on the tiniest bit of information could end in men being killed.

The journey came to an end at last. For the final half-hour, the dark slopes of Dartmoor could be seen out of the window, and Etty stared at them, fascinated. They were capped with a dusting of snow, and after the flat expanses of Bedfordshire they looked like mountains. Etty had never seen real hills before, and thought she had never seen anything so beautiful, or so forbidding.

'It looks better in summer,' the sailor told her. He was obviously going to Plymouth. 'It's real nice up there then. But you can get lost, easy, and you don't want to go wandering about where there's bogs. You can get swallowed up for good in those old marshes.'

'I don't think I'll be wandering about anywhere like that,' Etty said. 'My sweetheart's been wounded and had pneumonia. He's supposed to be getting his strength back.'

'You'll have to treat him gentle, then,' the sailor said, and winked.

Jim was waiting at Tavistock station. Bidding the sailor a hasty goodbye, Etty almost fell out of the carriage into his arms, and Jim held her tightly. She buried her face in his coat as the train enveloped them in clouds of steam, and found to her surprise that she was in tears. She looked up at him, laughing and sobbing at the same time.

'Oh, *Jim*! Jim . . . I'm sorry – I don't know why I'm crying like this. I'm just so glad to see you. Oh, Jim, you look so *thin* – what have they done to you?'

'Thin? I'm like a pig compared to what I was a fortnight ago. You should see the dinners our mum keeps putting in front of me.' He hugged her tightly. 'Oh, Et, it's so good to see you. I've missed you so bad . . . Don't reckon I'm going to let you go again, ever. I'm just going to have to put you in my kitbag and take you with me . . .' He rubbed his face against her hair. 'You smell lovely.'

Etty laughed. 'I don't! I smell of coal dust and smoke and other people's sweat as well as mine. There was this sergeant, you'd have thought he was in a Turkish bath. And he had onion sandwiches. I must smell awful.'

'You don't. You smell of you.' He drew in a deep breath. 'Come on. Let's go down the town and get some tea before we go back to the cottage.'

They walked down the steep little steps to the town and found a teashop near the corner of the wide square. Jim commandeered a table in the window and Etty gazed out at the big church and the handsome buildings of the town hall. He ordered beans on toast and a large pot of tea, and grinned at her.

'Just like the old days at Marble Arch, eh?'

It wasn't a bit like the Marble Arch Corner House, but Etty didn't mind. She wouldn't have minded if it had been a hole in the ground. She gazed at Jim across the table, drinking in every detail of his appearance. He was thinner than before, and still pale, and he held one arm awkwardly as if it still pained him a bit, but he was still her Jim, his hair still tousled as if it would never lie down flat, his eyes crinkling when he smiled. And the same lovelight shone in his eyes when he looked back at her.

'Oh, Jim, it's been such a long time . . .'

'I know. It seemed like for ever.' He looked grave. 'You know I'll have to go back, as soon as I'm fit enough?'

Etty nodded. 'I don't want to think about it.'

'Nor do I. But there's something I want to say to you about that.' He hesitated and picked up her hand, looking at the engagement ring with its tiny diamond. Etty had put it on the minute she was outside the gates at Elstow. 'Etty, let's get married. I don't want to wait any longer. I don't want to go away again without knowing you're my wife. Let's do it, shall we?'

Etty gazed at him. Her heart was beating quickly. She tightened her hand around his.

'I want to, Jim. I've been thinking about it, too. But we can't this time, surely – not with Christmas the day after tomorrow? And I've got to go back the day after Boxing Day. And then you'll be sent away again . . .'

'Yes, but I reckon I'll be sent to a camp somewhere for a few weeks first, just to get properly fit again. We could do it then. I can get a licence and come to Bedford or you might be able to get a few days off. It's only catering, after all.' Even Jim did not know exactly what Etty was doing at Elstow. 'They can spare you to get married, surely.'

Etty hesitated. She wanted to tell him the truth, but this café with its customers sitting only a few feet away wasn't the place to do it. She looked down at the scratched surface of the table.

'I don't know. They're a bit funny about leave . . .'

153

'Look, if I can get it I'm sure you can. They *want* people to get married. It's supposed to be good for us!' He grinned at her. 'It'll be good for me and you, I know that.'

Etty laughed. 'I know it will, too. Oh, yes, I'm sure Mr Carter would let me have some time off.' He'd deal with Nobby Clark too, she thought. And once she was a married woman, Nobby would leave her alone . . . 'It will be lovely to be married,' she whispered, her eyes shining.

Jim twined his fingers with hers. 'I just wish it could be now,' he murmured. 'Today. I just wish we could be starting our honeymoon tonight . . .'

The whole family was there to welcome Etty when she and Jim trudged along the last few yards of the lane and came to the front door of the cottage. Even old Ada had been persuaded to put on her best shawl and pop her dentures in for the occasion. She grinned from her corner, the false teeth glowing with polish, and Maggie rolled her eyes at her brother and whispered that it couldn't be too soon before she took them out again.

'They make her look more like a skull than ever . . .' She pushed past Ginnie and Billy, and pulled Etty into a warm hug. 'Oh, it's good to see you again, you little scallywag. How've you been? How's our Phyl? Have you heard from Jo lately – or Shirley? I s'pose you didn't have time to go up Marble Arch to see her?'

Etty shook her head, laughing. 'I came straight here on the train. But I tell you what, I've had a letter from her and she's got some news – I'll tell you later. And Phyl's all of a tiz because she's seeing Mike again, and Jo's hoping to get home for a couple of days as well . . . Let me get in the door, Maggie, I'm letting in all the cold! And let me look at Barry.'

They shifted into the small living-room and Etty unwound her scarf and took off her coat. She looked around, her eyes bright, enraptured by the cosiness of the tiny cottage. Maggie picked her son up and set him down on the rag rug in front of the range and Etty knelt to hug him. He stood gazing at her, and stuck his thumb in his mouth.

154

'Oh, he's gorgeous,' Etty whispered. She touched his peachy face with one finger, remembering with awe the night he had been born. 'Maggie, he's *lovely*. Look at these gorgeous *curls*.'

'I know,' Maggie said proudly. 'Mind you, they're getting a bit long now. Dad says they make him look like a girl, oughter be cut off, but me and Mum want to keep them for a while longer. Kiddies grow up too quick as it is. Mind you, he's a real boy, a proper holy terror. Into everything . . . but I wouldn't be without him for the world. Nor would any of the rest of us – eh, Dad?'

Etty's head jerked up. Her mouth fell open and she stared at the figure who was filling the kitchen doorway, smiling broadly, his arms held out like a great, welcoming Santa Claus.

'*Dad!*'

Sam Pratt, who had told her to call him and Ivy Dad and Mum as soon as she and Jim had got engaged, gave a great bellowing laugh. He stepped forward and enveloped her in an enormous bear-hug, grinning over her head at the rest of the family who stood by as proudly as if they'd invented him.

'They never told me you'd be here,' Etty told him, emerging at last from the folds of the huge jumper Ada had knitted him. She turned to look accusingly at Jim. '*You* never told me.'

'We wanted to surprise you,' he said, laughing, and Sam nodded and immediately went into a string of rhyming slang.

'It was my bottle o' beer. I wanted to see those big brown mince pies of yours light up – you know you've always been good as a proper bricks and mortar to me, ever since our Maggie brought you back home for Ginnie's birthday party, looking as scared as a gingerbread house. I reckon our Jim sized you up that day, an' all. We could see you were special.'

Etty blushed. 'When did you come? Are you staying all over Christmas? Are the twins here, too?'

Sam nodded. 'We all come down together on the pouring rain yesterday. We got till the day after Boxing Day – same as

155

you – so we can go back together. They're out getting wood for the rubber tyre.'

Etty smiled. Sam was just the same and she was more convinced than ever that he made up half his rhyming slang as he went along. You had to listen hard and work it out for yourself.

Ivy looked anxious. 'They oughter be back by now. It's been dark this past half-hour. And supper's about ready to go on the table.' She looked at Maggie. 'Take Etty upstairs and show her where she's going to sleep. And if you want a bit of a wash, Etty, the sink's out in the scullery and I won't be straining no veg for about a few minutes. I didn't put 'em on to cook till I heard you at the door.'

Maggie lit a candle at the range and led the way up the narrow stairs to a small room with a big iron bed almost filling it. In one corner was a chest of drawers and there was a rail fixed across an alcove for hanging clothes. There was a small window with a deep window-sill, and Maggie set the candlestick on it.

'Cosy, ain't it?' she remarked. 'Me and Ginnie shares this bed, so we'll all have to squash up a bit. And my Barry sleeps in this little bed here . . .' She pulled a small truckle-bed out from underneath.

Etty nodded. She didn't mind in the least sharing with Maggie and Ginnie. It would be fun, she thought, especially all waking up together on Christmas morning.

'What about the others? How many rooms are there?'

'Three bedrooms, only one of 'em's more like a sardine tin. Gran has that one, and Mum and Dad the other, and the boys'll kip down downstairs.' She gave Etty a rueful wink. 'Not much room for you and our Jim to be on your own, but I've showed him one or two nice little spots outside. There's a cosy little hayloft just down the lane.'

'Maggie!' Etty protested, but she hoped Maggie was serious. It would be dreadful if she and Jim couldn't find an opportunity to be on their own. She remembered Jim's remark that he wished tonight could be the first night of their honeymoon, and then recalled Kaye's advice about 'doing what came naturally', and felt a twinge of excitement.

On their way along the lane from the bus stop just outside the village, they'd stopped in the shade of a cluster of trees, and Jim had taken her in his arms. His kisses had been both tender and urgent, and Etty felt the difference in them. Before he'd gone away, they had been the kisses of a boy, a boy who had time to wait. Now they were the kisses of a man whose time was limited, and her body had responded in a way that it had never done before. She felt the spreading heat tingling through her body, the weakness of limbs that longed to give way, and she clung to him as his body hardened against her, and felt her senses reel.

'Jim, I love you. I love you so much.'

'I love you, too, Etty. You're mine – you know that, don't you? You'll always be mine.'

She sensed a fear in him that he might lose her. She held him more tightly, digging her fingers into his shoulders through the thick army greatcoat. 'I'll always, always be yours, Jim. There'll never be anyone else for me.'

There ought to be more to say than that, different things that nobody had ever said before. But nobody had ever said them in just this way, nobody had ever meant them as much as she did. Nobody had ever loved as she and Jim loved each other.

'I want to love you properly,' he whispered. 'I want you to be properly mine.'

Etty thought of his words now and looked at the big iron bed, wishing after all that she didn't have to share it with Maggie and Ginnie. But if there was a nice little hayloft just along the lane . . .

Her heart beat faster against her ribs. They had three whole days. Surely there would be time for at least one walk together.

Jo, too, had been given leave to go home at Christmas.

The forest was dark and frozen. Shropshire was one of the

coldest counties in England and already there had been snow. The roads that the lumberjacks and -jills had built through the trees were slippery with ice and the ruts made by the tractors in the thick mud were like concrete. Logging was a cruel job in these conditions, and even through their thick gloves the girls could feel their fingers freeze. Thawing them out by a fire was even more painful, but it was something you got used to in the end. You just suffered it.

The fires that were lit in the forest were a comfort when it was time to break off for strong black tea made in billycans and cheese sandwiches toasted over the flames. Then the loggers sat round on fallen trees, smoking and eating, talking in their variety of accents – the soft, almost Welsh lilt of the locals which contrasted oddly with Jo's London accent and Suzy Beech's Birmingham twang. Only Josh Taylor spoke without any accent at all – 'practically BBC', someone once remarked with disdain.

Josh still wasn't fully accepted by the other loggers, but at least they seemed to have decided to leave him alone, Jo thought. Instead of deliberately blocking his way or making things difficult for him, as they'd done at first, they simply ignored him. They worked with him, spoke to him when necessary, made room for him near the fire, but he was still an outsider, never part of the general chat or banter. Only Jo had become his friend.

It was as though they had always been friends, she thought sometimes. There didn't seem to be a time when she hadn't known Josh, even though she knew exactly when they had first met, on that railway station when he'd bought her a cup of tea and she'd told him about Mrs Holt and cried. It was as if they were old friends even then, as if they'd known and understood each other all their lives.

And then she'd encountered him again, here in Clun on the bridge that first evening, when the men had refused to let him cross. And she'd found out that he was a conchie. A man who had refused to go to war.

Everything in Jo had recoiled from him at that moment.

Here was a man who had refused to fight, refused to take any risks, while her Nick and others like him were risking their lives every day. While her Nick was in hospital with those terrible burns, facing months of plastic surgery and still wouldn't ever look the same again. While her own brothers, Norman and Freddy, and Phyl's brother Ronnie, and all those other men and boys were fighting in Africa or Europe or Burma or heaven knew where else. While all that was happening, Josh Taylor and others like him were safe at home, spending their days doing ordinary peacetime jobs like chopping trees in calm forests, with birds and squirrels instead of bombs and bullets. Letting others get killed to save their own miserable skins . . .

'It's not like that really,' Josh said to her one day when, unable to bear her angry thoughts any longer, she had challenged him. They had encountered each other unexpectedly in the forest, early one June morning. Jo had cycled in with Suzy and Poppy as usual and then volunteered to go up to the charcoal burners' hut with a message. She had found Josh working alone, had stopped and given him the message and then turned away when he took her by the arm, turning her back to face him.

'Let go! Don't touch me!'

'It's all right,' he said quietly. 'I know you're a married woman now. I'm not going to make a nuisance of myself.'

'You *are* making a nuisance of yourself,' she told him clearly. 'You always will, until you stop being such a coward and go and help win this awful war.'

Josh sighed. 'I know it's difficult to understand—'

'It's not. It's easy to understand. You're scared.'

'You don't really believe that,' Josh said.

Jo opened her mouth and then closed it again. She met his eyes and saw the calm knowledge in them. Once again she had the feeling that they knew each other, had always known each other.

'It doesn't matter what I believe, does it?' she said, turning her head away. 'I'm not important.'

159

'Everyone's important,' Josh said. 'That's partly why I can't kill.'

Jo turned back to face him. 'But the Germans are evil.'

'Are they? All of them? The ordinary men and women like you and me, who didn't have any say in all this? The boys and girls growing up who don't even remember peace? The old men and women who just want to be allowed to live quietly in their homes—?'

'A lot of them fought in the last war,' Jo reminded him swiftly. 'They didn't worry about old people then.'

'Didn't they? Perhaps they were forced into it, just as we have been today.' He looked at her for a moment. He had let go of her arm and now he gestured towards a fallen tree. 'Let's sit down for a few minutes, Jo. I promised to tell you one day why I think the way I do. Let's make it today.'

'I've got to get back—'

'There's time yet,' he said, and Jo allowed him to lead her to the log. They sat down, side by side, and she waited for him to speak.

The forest was silent, or seemed so at first. But as they sat there, Jo gradually became aware of all the little sounds – the rustling of the leaves above them, the scamper of a small animal through the undergrowth, the movement of birds and squirrels in the branches. She could hear the thin piping of goldcrests, the harsh scream of a jay, the patter of a nuthatch's claws on the bark of a nearby tree. She could hear and identify all these things which a year or so ago had been unknown to her and, sitting here with Josh, she felt a slow, spreading warmth of contentment. This is what my life ought to be, she thought. This is where I'd like to spend it.

It seemed a very long way away from Nick.

'How's your husband now?' Josh asked, as if reading her thoughts.

'He's all right. He's back flying now. They've put him on bombers. They've – they've done as much as they can with the plastic surgery.'

'And? Has it helped him?'

160

Jo sighed. 'I don't know. I think he looks a lot better. But he'll always be scarred and he hates that. He doesn't talk about it much, but . . . sometimes I think he'd just like to be shot down again. He said once he wished they'd made a proper job of it.' Her voice trembled. She hadn't told anyone about the blackness of Nick's depressions, the nights when they should have been making love spent instead in torment. She had never given a hint of the dread she was beginning to feel when she got a few days off to go and visit him, or he came to Shropshire on a seventy-two-hour pass.

Perhaps if Phyl had been with her, she could have talked about it. But Phyl was miles away, too.

Josh watched her. He said in a quiet voice, 'I'm sorry. It's terrible that he should feel like that.'

'Oh, I don't think he does, most of the time,' Jo said in a brighter voice. 'He was just feeling a bit low that day.'

'You must wish you could see more of him.'

'I did think of asking for a transfer, so I could be closer. But he didn't want me to. He says he's better on his own, living with the squadron. He says it's distracting to fliers to have their families around.'

Josh said nothing. After a few moments, Jo said, 'So what about you? I really ought to be getting back soon.'

'I know.' He sighed a little. 'I wonder if you really want to know. Wouldn't you rather go on being angry with me?'

Jo stared at him. 'Whatever do you mean?'

'Sometimes it's a lot easier than understanding,' he said. 'Understanding means asking yourself questions.'

Jo shrugged. 'You're talking in riddles.'

'It's all riddles,' he said. 'Don't imagine I never question myself, Jo. Don't imagine I never wonder if I'm not just a coward, making excuses. I thought about it a lot before the war started, and I've never stopped thinking about it. I've made up my mind time and time again to go along to the nearest recruitment office and say I'll go wherever they send me. But—'

'Well, why don't you? Why don't you just do it? There's plenty of others who don't want to go, and *they* do it.'

'I can't,' he said, and to her surprise she heard a note of genuine despair in his voice. 'I just can't. I can't touch a weapon, you see. I simply can't do it.'

Jo stared at him. 'What do you mean? Why can't you?'

'They repel me,' he said. 'Everything they are, everything they mean. People being killed – hurt – injured, like your husband. I can't touch them. I would never, ever be able to use one. I would never be able to do injury to another human being.'

Jo's mind fumbled with his words. 'But suppose someone was going to kill you? Wouldn't you defend yourself?'

'I've asked myself that,' he said, 'a thousand times. Yes, probably I would – in the last resort. It's natural, isn't it? It's the survival instinct, you probably can't help it. But until I was in that situation – well, you saw me down at the bridge. I won't fight if I haven't absolutely got to.'

'And suppose it was your mother or your sister.' As Jo spoke the well-known formula, the question that all conscientious objectors were said to be asked when they went to tribunal, she realised that she didn't even know if Josh had a sister. She knew almost nothing about him. Except – she dredged up a memory from that first meeting – that he had a father in Brighton. He'd said 'father' specifically – not 'mother'. 'I'm sorry, perhaps I shouldn't ask that.'

'It's exactly the question you should ask,' he said. 'It's the question everybody asks.' He paused and then said in a very low voice, 'My mother's dead. She died when I was a boy, and it was partly the way she died that made me the way I am.'

Jo's heart thumped. She knew from his tone that she was going to hear something very private and very deep. She glanced around at the green summer light filtering down through the trees, wishing for a panicky moment that she needn't hear it, but she knew there was no escape. She could not get up and walk away from Josh now.

162

'What – what happened?'

'She was killed,' he said. 'We had a gun in the house. It was my father's gun. It wasn't a very big gun, just a small rifle that he used for target practice. At a distance, it wouldn't have been very dangerous, but close to and aimed at just the right place, it could kill.'

Jo gazed at him, fascinated, feeling slightly sick.

'He was teaching me to use it,' Josh said. 'I was twelve. He was always very careful. He taught me to clean it and to load it, and he told me never, never in *any* circumstances, to point it at anyone.'

The forest was very still. Even the leaves seemed to have stopped rustling.

'I was cleaning it one day,' Josh said. 'I was practising loading it. My mother came in unexpectedly and startled me. It went off.'

'Oh, *Josh*,' Jo breathed.

'I've never been able to touch a gun since,' he said. 'I can't do it. I've seen my own mother die. I killed her.'

'It was an accident,' she whispered.

'Oh, yes, an accident. But she died just the same.' Josh turned and looked at her. He took her hands. 'Nobody blamed me, not even my father. He blamed himself. He took the gun to a local gunsmith and gave it away. He wouldn't ever touch it again.'

'Oh, Josh.' Jo held his hands tightly. She could see the suffering in his face, the grief and despair in his eyes. 'Josh, that's awful.'

'I don't think I'm a coward,' he said, 'but I can't fight. I just can't.'

Since then, their relationship had deepened. They walked together, sometimes ate their sandwiches together, went for the occasional cycle-ride through the Shropshire lanes. Poppy and Suzy were curious but soon, like the rest of the timber workers, left them alone. Josh was accepted if not included, and Jo's championship seldom needed.

She told him that she was going home for Christmas and he came to the station to see her off.

'You'll be seeing Nick,' he said. 'That's good. You've been apart too long.'

'I know. It's not been good for us. I thought we could stand it – the separation – but it's been hard. In a way, it's worse that he's still based in England. If he were abroad, like Phyl's husband, it would seem more natural somehow. Something we couldn't do anything about.'

'I know.' Josh took her hands and looked at her. 'I'll miss you while you're away.'

'It's a shame you can't go home, too,' she said lightly. 'See your father in Brighton.'

Josh shrugged. 'It's a long way to go, and I can't ask for that much leave. You girls with husbands take priority. And Dad's all right. He's got his sister in Worthing, he'll go to her for Christmas Day. He'll have a good time.'

Jo nodded. She stood uncertainly on the platform, her hands still linked with his. She had a sudden feeling that she didn't want to go. A cold, dismal premonition, as if things were going wrong. She bit her lip and blinked back unexpected tears.

Josh saw them as he saw everything to do with Jo, but said nothing. He squeezed her hands a little more tightly and smiled at her.

'Your train's coming. Better get your bags together.'

Jo nodded and bent to pick up her suitcase and the haversack that contained her Christmas presents. During odd moments in the forest she had picked up scraps of wood and Josh had taught her to carve them. She had made models for each of her family – a cat for Alice, a mouse for Phyl and a dog for her father. They were simple shapes but she'd rubbed them down and polished them, and she was pleased to be able to give the people she loved things that she had made.

Josh let go of her hand. He fumbled in his pocket and brought out a small object, wrapped in brown paper.

'For you.'

Jo's eyes widened. She took it, looking at it questioningly.

The train was coming round the bend. Jo tore off the wrapping and revealed a small, carved elephant. It was round and smiling, its trunk held jauntily in the air, and she couldn't help laughing at it, even though there were tears in her eyes.

Josh smiled at her.

'It's just so that you know I won't forget. That we're friends, I mean.'

'Yes,' she said softly. 'Friends.' She reached up suddenly and kissed him on the cheek. 'And that's for you.' The train was pulling to a standstill, the steam rising around them. She felt another surge of longing and looked at him with sudden distress. 'Josh—'

'It's all right,' he said, his hands on her shoulders, urging her towards the carriage door. 'It's all right. Go and see your husband now. Go and see Nick. And ... have a happy Christmas.'

'Yes.' She climbed up into the carriage and turned to look down at him. 'You, too, Josh. Have a happy Christmas.'

The guard came along the platform and slammed the doors shut. He blew his whistle and waved his flag. The train pulled slowly out of the station.

Josh stood on the platform until it had disappeared. Then he turned and walked back through the cold, lonely lanes to the charcoal-burners' hut.

Chapter Thirteen

Nick was waiting at his parents' home, back in London. They'd given up the cottage once he'd left hospital, and put a double bed in Nick's old room. Jo would have preferred to go to her own home or – better still – somewhere totally separate, not belonging to either family, but she knew that with only a few days together nothing else was practicable. She found her way through the blacked-out streets and leant against the doorjamb, waiting for someone to answer her knock.

The door opened and Nick stood there, tall and still thin from his months in hospital. They stared at each other for a moment, then Jo put out her hands and he took them and drew her into his arms.

'Hello, Jo.'

'Nick – oh, Nick . . .' She laid her face against his chest and felt the hot tears rise behind her eyelids. He held her close and she felt his face against her hair. 'It's been so *long*.'

'Only because you're so far away,' he said, and she felt a shock at his words, and at his tone. 'If you'd gone into the ordinary Land Army—'

'I didn't have any choice! You know that, Nick. I had to go where I was sent. I could've been sent anywhere even in the ordinary . . . And I offered to ask for a transfer.'

He shrugged. '*I'm* not the one who's complaining. It was you who said it had been a long time.'

Jo stared at him. 'Nick, what's the matter? You – you haven't even kissed me yet. Aren't you pleased to see me?'

He looked at her for a moment and then his face softened. 'Of course I am, you daft ha'porth. And you haven't kissed me either! Come here.'

He pulled her against him and kissed her mouth. Jo felt the tears come again as she clung to him, letting her lips move with his, feeling the hard thrust of his tongue, the nip of his teeth on the soft flesh. His hand was splayed across her back, his fingers digging in through her thick greatcoat. Scarcely able to breathe and feeling that the kiss must end, she tried to pull back her head but he only grunted and tightened his grip.

'Goodness!' Jo said with a tiny laugh, when he finally let her go. 'Well, perhaps you are pleased to see me after all!'

'Of course I am,' he said, giving her an unfathomable look. 'Is there any reason why I shouldn't be?'

A worm of unease stirred somewhere deep in Jo's stomach. She smiled and shook her head. 'I hope not! Let's go inside, Nick, it's getting cold. I've come a long way.'

'Yes, so we've said.' There was a sudden edge to his voice. Jo bit her lip. He'd missed her, she thought, he was feeling neglected, like a small boy whose mother had left him with a neighbour for the afternoon. He'd be all right once they'd been together for a while and got used to each other again. He'd be all right once they'd been to bed.

Mr and Mrs Laurence were in the back room. They called it the 'dining-room' and the front room the 'sitting-room', as if 'front' and 'back' weren't posh enough. But their house was posher than Jo's parents' – it had a proper bathroom indoors, with a lavatory next to it on the landing, and the downstairs front room (sitting-room, she reminded herself) and the front bedroom upstairs both had bay windows. It was like Mrs Holt's house, she thought, where she and Phyl had lived when they'd first gone to London to be Nippies. They'd thought it was like a palace.

'There you are, Jo,' Mrs Laurence exclaimed, coming over to kiss her. 'You must be worn out. What a journey. I'll put the kettle on straight away, you must be dying for a cup of tea. Nick, take your wife upstairs. There's a jug of hot water on the washstand and some space in the wardrobe for your clothes, Jo.'

Jo smiled her thanks and followed Nick up the stairs. They stood in the back bedroom, decorated with cream wallpaper smothered in huge brown flowers and cramped with its double bed and wardrobe and washstand, and looked at each other. Jo saw the scars, still visible despite the best efforts of the surgeons, and the twist in his mouth that made him look different, more cynical, bitter. The skin around his eyes had changed, too. It looked stretched and smooth, so that even when he smiled there were no crinkles. She stepped closer and put her fingers up to touch him.

'Well?' he demanded harshly. 'Do I pass muster? I'm afraid I'm never going to look any prettier, Jo, if that's what you were hoping.'

Jo jumped back as if she had been stung. Tears filled her eyes as she stared at him.

'Nick, don't talk like that. I love you – it doesn't matter what you look like. You're the same to me whatever your face is like.'

'Am I?' He sounded as if he doubted it. He turned away and gestured around the room. 'Well, here it is, here's where we're going to enjoy a few more days' married life before you go back to your trees. You'd better do as you've been told and have a wash and hang your clothes up. Then you can come down and have a cup of tea. We'll probably have a nice game of cards afterwards and then all go to bed at ten o'clock like good little Englishmen and women – before we have our night of unbridled passion.' He stared at her. 'I suppose that's what you've been looking forward to? Lots of unbridled passion?'

Jo bit her lip. Her eyes smarted but she refused to let the tears fall. She had a feeling it was just what Nick wanted, in this bitter mood of his. She looked at him.

'I just wanted to be with you, Nick. That's all. It doesn't matter about anything else.'

He stared down at her and then turned towards the door.

'I'll see you downstairs,' he said, and went out.

Jo stood very still for a few moments, then she sank down slowly on the bed. She rested her elbows on her knees and buried her face in her hands. The tears she had refused to let fall came now, seeping through her fingers. Her throat ached intolerably and she wanted to give way to huge sobs, but knew that if she did so she would not be able to stop, and Mr and Mrs Laurence downstairs would hear her.

'What's happened to you, Nick?' she whispered. 'What's gone wrong? We loved each other – we were happy. We *would* have been happy, if only we could have got married before you were shot down. Why can't we be happy now?'

It was as if the burns had gone deeper than through skin and flesh, deep into the person Nick was inside, deep into his heart and soul, and left nothing but a hard, brittle shell.

Jo lifted her head and stared around the cold, brown room. Bleakly, she wondered if the real Nick was still there, deep inside. Or had he been destroyed for ever?

Mike was in full agreement with Kaye's remarks about the way Christmas leave should be used.

'She's right,' he said to Phyl as they lay together in the big bed at the Bennetts' house. 'Don't you remember me telling you that once? We've been given our orders. A bun in every oven by the time we go back, just in case we need to be replaced.'

'Mike! That's a horrible thing to say. I'm *not* an oven, I'm a person, and so would our baby be, if we had one. And you're not going to need to be replaced – and if you were, I wouldn't let our baby go – if we had one – as if we'd just had it for – for *cannon fodder*.' The last phrase was one she'd heard her father use about the young men who had gone to fight in the last war, the Great War. She rolled away from Mike, turning her back on him, the magic and delight of their lovemaking evaporated.

There was a moment of silence. Then Mike said in a shocked voice, 'Phyl. I'm sorry, Phyl. I never meant – it's just

169

the way men talk, I didn't even think – oh, God, Phyl, don't turn away from me. I'm sorry. It was meant to be a joke.'

'It was a horrible joke,' she said in a muffled voice.

'I know it was. It was a bloody *stupid* joke. Please, Phyl.' He stroked her bare back and then put his hand on her shoulder, trying to turn her towards him. 'Please. I've been away too long, I've forgotten how to behave when I'm in decent company. Phyl, I love you and I've missed you so much . . . I want us to have a baby, but not so that it can grow up and have to fight like me. I want it to have a good life, the sort of life we ought to be having now, the sort of life I'm fighting *for*. I want us to have our own family so that the world can go on like it should when all this is over. Phyl, forget what I said, please. *Please*. Turn over again. Look at me.'

Slowly, Phyl turned over. She looked searchingly into his face.

'I love you,' he repeated. 'I *love* you. I'm sorry, Phyl, I really am.'

'It's all right,' she said with a sigh, and wound her arms around his neck. He nuzzled his face into her breasts and she felt the tension ebb away from his body. She felt ashamed of her annoyance. 'It's just that . . . when we decide to have a baby, I want it to be for the right reasons.'

'So do I,' he said. He kissed her on the lips and Phyl relaxed against him. This was Mike, her Mike, and he was home for only a few days. Heaven knew when she'd see him again. It was crazy to waste their precious time together arguing.

'We won't talk about it any more,' Mike murmured. 'I won't mention babies again. It'll just be us – you and me. That's all I want.'

He began to kiss her breasts and her neck, and Phyl let her head fall back. She stretched her body against him and sighed with happiness. You and me, Mike had said. It was all he wanted – and all she wanted, too. The two of them, for these few precious days, and nobody else.

But Mike's words were like seeds planted in her mind, just

as in his lovemaking he might have planted the seed of a baby in her body. She woke later that night from a dream in which she held a baby in her arms, a tiny, dark-haired baby with Mike's eyes. She looked down into its small face and saw his smile, and she knew, in the dream, that it was all she had left of him. Mike had gone for ever, but his baby lived on.

Phyl woke with tears on her pillow. She felt for Mike, but she was alone in the bed and she sat up, suddenly stricken with terror. As she stared round the unfamiliar room the door opened and Mike came in, wearing his pyjamas and carrying two cups of tea.

'I thought you'd like a bit of spoiling.' He put the tea down on the floor beside the bed and slid between the sheets. He kissed her and poked his tongue into her ear. Phyl squealed and giggled.

'Don't! Your mum'll hear us.'

'Mum's gone to the shops,' he whispered. 'We can make as much noise as we like.'

'Haven't you had enough? You're greedy, Mike Bennett, that's what you are.'

'You bet I am,' he agreed. 'And why not? I've been going without for too long, and God knows when I'll get the chance again.' He slid his hands over her body. 'Phyl, I love you.'

'I love you, too,' she whispered. 'And I've been thinking.'

Mike groaned. 'My mum says that sometimes, and it always means trouble for Dad. What plan are you hatching now?'

'No plan. It's just – what you were saying last night, about babies. Maybe we should think about it, Mike. Maybe we ought to have one after all.'

Mike drew back a little and looked at her carefully.

'You're not just saying that because you think it's what I want?'

'No. I don't even know it's what I want,' she said honestly. 'I just said maybe we ought to *think* about it. It – it's a nice idea, and we *are* married after all.'

Mike studied her and then smiled. 'All right,' he said, 'we'll think about it. But we haven't got long, Phyl. A few days, that's all.'

'I know.' She gave him a slow, curving smile. 'So, what d'you reckon? Shall we?'

'Shall we what? Think about it?' He smiled back. 'Yes. Why not?' He reached over the side of the bed and picked up the cups of tea, handing her one. They drank, their eyes upon each other's face, and at last Mike took Phyl's cup and put them both back on the floor.

'Have you thought?' he asked softly, and she nodded, her eyes bright. Mike reached out a hand and stroked her bare shoulder and then her breast. He let his fingers trail gently down her belly and into the crease of her thighs.

'Let's do it, then,' he murmured. 'Let's have a baby.'

Christmas in Devon was like being in an old-fashioned Christmas card.

When Etty woke in the big, soft bed with Ginnie cuddled up beside her and Maggie still snoring on the far side, she found the room filled with a strange light and knew that snow had fallen. She slid out of bed and padded to the window, peeping out through the curtains. It had been dark when she and Jim had arrived last night, and she had no idea what she might see.

Patterns like trees were frosted on the ice-cold glass. She breathed a warm cloud on them and rubbed with the sleeve of her nightdress. The clear patch was like a miniature window in the real window, and she bent close to peer out.

'*Oh!*'

The world was white and rounded. There were humps that might be bushes or small trees, while the larger trees rose like giant feathers towards the lowering, yellowy sky. Immediately in front of the house was the garden, outlined by a low stone wall, and beyond were smooth white fields; and beyond those Etty could see the broad sweeping outlines of the moors.

She gazed at them. It had snowed in Bedford the previous winter, with a cruel, bitter cold, so that all the girls suffered from chilblains. The wind had scoured the bleak, flat fields and the ditches had been filled with ice as hard as iron. The hard white light had made their eyes ache, and the grey bruised sky had seemed to stretch on for ever.

'Blimey, look what's happened.' Maggie had woken and stood beside her, with Barry round-eyed with amazement in her arms. 'Must be six inches deep. And more on the way, too, I wouldn't wonder.'

'It's lovely,' Etty said in wonder. 'Oh, Maggie, it's going to be a real Christmas!'

Maggie regarded her with amusement. 'Well, what other sort is there? All right, I knows what you mean. All we want is a robin redbreast sitting on a tree stump. And Father Christmas driving his sledge across the sky with all those reindeer . . . Well, we won't get that but I reckon we'll have most of the other trimmings. We even got a turkey!'

Etty dressed quickly and ran downstairs. The family was already up and about, and Jim got up from his chair when he saw her, his face brightening. He gave her a quick kiss and George and Gerry, the twins who didn't look the least bit alike, grinned at her over their porridge. Sam wiped his mouth and planted a smacking kiss on her cheek, and Ivy brought her a cup of tea.

'There you are, ducks. And there's some porridge in that pan on the range. Pass Etty a bowl, George, you're nearest the cupboard. Good job you boys brought in plenty of wood last night.' She bustled back into the little scullery where she could be heard working the water-pump to fill the kettle.

The twins nodded. They'd recently had their call-up papers and were to go into the army in January. Ivy had wept when she'd heard and Maggie had felt a sick cold inside her, thinking of her Tommy, of Jim, of Nick and all the others who had been taken by this war and might not be given back. But nobody had said anything. Everyone felt the same, and there was no point in talking about it. You just had to carry on.

Maggie looked at her own son, Barry, sometimes, and

173

thought that she could not bear it if he ever had to go to war. She didn't see how her mother could bear it now, with three sons called up, a daughter already lost in the Blitz, and her husband left behind in London.

Still, they were all here together now, and all safe, or as safe as anyone could be these days. Devon hadn't been ignored by the Germans, but evacuation from Plymouth hadn't been considered necessary at first, until the Luftwaffe had proved it could send its planes down the South Coast and bomb the city flat. Then there had been the same nightly trek from the city out to the safety of countryside and moorland, until Exeter had its turn in the 'Baedeker' raids and the trekkers had come from a different direction.

However, the village where the Pratt family had been allotted their cottage seemed safe enough, and the nearby town of Tavistock had been barely touched. Ivy often said that they had a lot to be thankful for, and maybe that was how she managed to get through the war.

Etty sat down beside Jim and he pressed his arm against her side. She felt a warm glow of delight spread through her body. She knew that there was plenty to do to help Ivy, but later on they'd find time to be alone together somewhere. I wouldn't mind living in a place like this, she thought, looking around the tiny, crowded room. It's small, but that doesn't matter when there's a family to fill it up. She remembered the orphanage where she'd spent her childhood – a big, rambling building that had once been a school, with high ceilings and cold, bare rooms equipped with the minimum of scarred, beaten furniture.

'Where's Gran?' she asked, realising that the corner where Ada sat was empty. 'She's not ill, is she?'

'Old, that's all,' Ivy said, coming back to set the kettle on the range. 'She don't get about so early these days. You musta noticed a difference in her, Etty.'

'She looks smaller somehow,' Etty said. 'Sort of shrunk.'

'That's it. That's old age does that. She's past ninety, you know.' Ivy glanced at Sam. His mother had lived with them all their married life, and Sam had been apart from her only while he'd served during the First World War. Cantankerous though she was, she was a part of their lives and would be missed when she was no longer there. Ivy only hoped that she would survive long enough to go back to London, but the longer this war dragged on the longer it seemed likely to take.

They cleared away the breakfast things and the twins went out to do more wood-chopping. They'd dragged a fallen tree-trunk back from a nearby field and were steadily reducing it to logs. This morning they would have to clear the snow from it first, and when Jim and Etty went out to see how they were getting on they found them in the middle of a snowball fight with Billy and Freddy, who had come out to help, capering about squealing with excitement.

'Got you!' Gerry shouted as a handful of snow caught Jim full in the face. Jim spluttered and waved his fist, then bent for his own handful and soon they were in the thick of it, joined by Maggie and Ginnie and finally Sam, with little Barry staggering behind with a pair of his uncle's socks pulled on over his shoes. Ivy watched from the window and when Etty paused and glanced up she saw Ada's wrinkled old face peering down from the bedroom.

'Let's build a snowman,' George shouted, and they stopped snowballing and started to pile the snow up beside the log-pile. Soon it was five feet high and Gerry and Jim made a huge ball which they lifted carefully on top for his head. George ran into the shed and came out with a couple of lumps of coke for his eyes, and Sam produced a carrot for his nose.

'Can anyone spare a hat and scarf?' They all looked at each other doubtfully. It was too cold to give up warm clothes for a snowman. They all shrugged, then turned in surprise when Ivy came out of the cottage, carrying one of Ada's black shawls and a round black hat with a rather tired-looking feather in it.

'Gran sent these out. She says she ain't going nowhere so the old bloke had better have them.' She put the hat on top of the snowman's head and draped the shawl around his shoulders, and everyone stared at it and then began to laugh.

'It looks just *like* Gran!' Gerry spluttered. 'It's the spitting image!'

'Well, that should keep the German bombers away,' his twin agreed. 'No one'll dare come near us with Gran out here watching out. Pity the Government's never thought of it.'

Sam grinned. 'It ain't just the Germans she'll be keeping an eye on,' he told his sons. 'It's you lot too. You'd better get on with what you're meant to be doing, or she'll be after you with her brolly!'

Jim smiled. He went into the cottage and came out a moment later with Ada's old umbrella. He tucked it against the snowman, and the similarity was all but complete. All it needed, Etty thought, was a set of false teeth, but since Ada hardly ever put hers in these days it didn't really matter.

Jim came to stand beside her and took her hand in his. She looked up at him and he smiled into her eyes.

'Let's go for a walk,' he said softly, and they turned and slipped away from the others and walked down the lane together, towards the hayloft.

Maggie, trudging along the lane later on her way to the nursing home, saw them coming out of the hayloft. There was straw in Jim's hair and more sticking to Etty's back. She smiled and stood back in the hedge so that they wouldn't notice her. Not that they'd have noticed her if she'd walked up and shouted in their ears, she thought with a grin. They looked as if they were in a world of their own, a dream from which neither wanted to wake up.

Maggie's own world was very different now from the one she'd known in London. If she wasn't in the cottage or with her family, she was in the big house where the Canadian soldiers were brought to convalesce. She hurried about the wards, bringing meals and bedpans as required, seeing to their needs, and sometimes thought that maybe it wasn't so very different after all from being a Nippy – except that she'd never had to wipe a customer's bottom in the Corner House!

'Why aren't you a proper nurse?' one of the young men asked her one day. 'You'd be good at it. You've got the gentle touch.'

'Only while you're behaving yourself,' Maggie told him. 'You try anything on and you'll find I can pack quite a punch!'

He grinned. 'Haven't got the strength today, but I'm working on it. Don't tell me you haven't got a boyfriend already, though.'

Maggie shook her head. 'Too busy. Besides, who is there down here, at the back of nowhere?'

'Well, there's us. We're not a bad bunch of guys.'

'You!' Maggie scoffed. 'The halt and the lame! Anyway, I'm not interested in men. I've had my fill, ta very much.'

The young Canadian looked at her curiously. He was tall, she guessed, and had a square, merry face under a thatch of black curls. His eyes were so deep a brown that they looked almost black too. He was a nice-looking bloke, she thought, without being so good-looking he'd be conceited about it. His name was Carl Forrester.

'You can't mean that,' he said. 'A lovely girl like you, sounding so cynical. What's some guy done to you to make you feel that way?'

'Haven't got time to tell you,' she said briskly. 'Now, let's wash your face. Where's your flannel?'

'Gee,' he said, 'it's sure frustrating being all splinted up like this. If I only had the use of my arms—'

'If you had the use of your arms, I wouldn't come within a yard of your bed. I bet you're like an octopus, hands everywhere.'

'Octopuses don't have hands, but I wouldn't mind eight arms like they've got. What did human beings do wrong that they were only given two when things were being shared out?' Carl looked at her mournfully, but his eyes were dancing. 'You'll give me my dinner, won't you, Maggie?'

'I might. Or I might ask Nurse Pett to do it.'

He groaned. 'Oh, no, not Nurse Pett! She's a sadist, that one, d'you know that? She puts food into my mouth when it's boiling hot and she pinched me the other day, just because I wouldn't eat my greens. Pinched me! Is that any way for a nurse to behave? I ask you.'

Maggie grinned. 'That's nothing to what I'll do if you won't eat your dinner. Honestly, you blokes, you're just like a lot of babies. Why, even my Barry—' She stopped abruptly and turned away, rinsing out the flannel and squeezing it dry. The soldier looked at her.

'Yeah? Your Barry? Who's he, then?'

'Nobody.' She began to pack up the washing things, not looking at the young man. 'Nobody you need know about, anyway.'

'You can't go yet,' he said, watching her. 'You haven't brushed my hair and if Matron comes in and sees me looking like a scarecrow—'

'Oh, all right!' She leant over and began to brush the dark curls. She was trembling slightly. She wished she hadn't let Barry's name slip out. Carl Forrester was altogether too sharp and he knew perfectly well what effect he had on her. It was no good pretending she wasn't still interested in men. In her mind, she might deny it and even believe her denial, but her body still responded to a good-looking bloke.

'So who's this Barry?' he asked as her fingers touched his hair. 'Boyfriend? Husband?' He looked at her hands and saw Maggie's wedding ring. 'Oh-oh, sorry.'

'It's none of your business who Barry is. Now, do you think you're smart enough now to make eyes at Matron when she does her rounds? Or d'you want your nails cut and your eyelashes trimmed as well?'

He grinned. 'It's not Matron I want to make eyes at, Maggie, and if it's guys with short eyelashes you go for, you go ahead and trim 'em. Anything to make you smile at me.'

Maggie frowned at him instead. 'You're too cheeky for

your own good. I'm going to ask to be transferred to another patient. Another *ward*.'

'Maggie, you wouldn't do that. You wouldn't abandon a poor guy who's broken both his arms and a leg defending little old Britain. Why, if I only had the use of these poor old arms, I'd put 'em both around you right now and give you the biggest, smackingest kiss you've ever had in your whole life, married or not. Just to show you how much I think of you.'

'You'd have to catch me first,' Maggie said, and walked away, hiding a smile.

It was hard work, being an orderly, but it was fun as well, and satisfying. Maggie's warm, blowzy good humour was a hit with the men who were so far away from home and more than one had suggested a date. As they recovered, they were allowed to leave the hospital to walk around the village and go to the pub or into Tavistock, and naturally they wanted company.

'Why don't you come down the pub sometimes on your evenings off?' one of the other girls asked Maggie. 'Your mum would look after your kiddy, wouldn't she?' Most of them knew that she was a widow and had a little boy. 'You got to have a bit of fun sometimes. There's no harm in it – we just have a laugh, that's all.'

But Maggie shook her head. 'Ma's got enough to do, what with Gran and the other kids. It's not fair to leave her with them all the time.'

She watched them go wistfully. The idea of an evening in the village inn, with the other girls and the Canadians, was tempting. But Maggie was wary these days of temptation.

Carl Forrester was the biggest temptation she'd faced yet. The only way she could get his square, merry face and dark eyes out of her mind was to go home and give her full attention to little Barry. She would gaze at the blond curls that would soon have to be cut off, and the blue eyes so like her own, and feel a rush of love for him, a rush so powerful that there simply wasn't room for temptation.

Sometimes, even now, Maggie looked at him and wondered just who his father was – Andy or the soldier who had raped her so brutally and left her to die. But it didn't seem to matter so much any more. Andy was gone, probably dead, and the soldier, too. Barry was hers and hers alone.

Chapter Fourteen

Nick was called back from his leave abruptly, early on Christmas Eve. The bombing of Berlin had intensified and all personnel were needed. Jo went to the station to see him off and they stood on the platform, awkward with one another. She held his sleeves and buried her face in the lapels of his greatcoat, torn with pain.

'It's not fair. We haven't had a chance—'

'It's war.' His face was remote, his eyes looking through her. He bent and kissed her lips and then removed her hands from his coat. 'I've got to go.'

'I know.' Jo looked up at him, her eyes swimming with tears. 'Nick, I love you—'

'Take care of yourself, Jo,' he said, interrupting her. 'Don't chop your legs off in all those trees!'

'I won't.' Her eyes begged him to say more, but the guard's whistle shrilled in their ears and he turned away and climbed up into the carriage. He pulled the door shut and leant out, and she reached towards him. He took her hand and held it for a moment, squeezing her fingers.

'Goodbye, Jo. Goodbye . . .'

Jo stared at him. The train began to move. He was going away from her, out of her reach, receding. Their hands were torn apart and she could do nothing but wave, her other hand at her mouth and then wiping away the tears that blurred her sight. The carriages passed before her, each with a row of faces at the windows, until at last the train had disappeared round the bend and was gone.

181

Nick was gone.

Jo turned away, with all the others who had been saying their heart-wrenching goodbyes, and walked blindly out of the station. Inside her was an abyss, a dark, pain-filled abyss. She felt as if she might fall into it at any moment, dropping endlessly into an icy chasm. She wondered if she would ever see Nick again.

They had parted often enough before, and it had always been painful, but this time it was different. Before, Jo had known that it was as bad for Nick as it was for her, that he felt the pain just as acutely. Today, there had been that terrible, cold remoteness in him, and she had not been sure. She thought he might even have been glad to go.

It's the war, she told herself as she walked through the dreary streets, devoid of any Christmas lights or decorations. We're all fed up with it. We just want to get it over and done with. All Nick wants is to go and fly his aeroplane and do his bit to bring it to an end. And he's already been shot down once. He must be scared, deep down, however much he says he's not.

And she felt ashamed, as if she had not done as much as she could have to comfort and reassure him, as if she hadn't been the wife he needed and deserved.

For Phyl and Etty, the return to Elstow was like waking from a dream to harsh reality. They went back together on the train, looking out of the window at the frozen fields and the cold grey sky, feeling warm inside despite the weather.

'It was lovely, having you and Mike down in Devon with us,' Etty said dreamily. 'You didn't mind the squash, did you, Phyl?'

Phyl chuckled. 'Not a bit. I don't know as the twins were so thrilled, though, having to doss down in the passageway!'

'Well, we had to give you a room to yourselves, and that was the only one.' Etty gave Phyl a sidelong glance and then looked out of the window again. 'Me and Jim managed to get a bit of time to ourselves now and then.'

'Oh, yes?' Phyl caught the note in Etty's voice and gave her a challenging glance. 'And just what does that mean, Etty Brown?'

'Nothing.'

'Come on – you can't fool me.' Phyl studied Etty's face. 'You've gone all pink. You and Jim got together, didn't you! Properly, I mean. *You* know.'

'Do I?' Etty asked innocently, then blushed more deeply and turned back, a smile breaking out all over her face. 'Well, perhaps I do.'

'I'm blooming sure you do.' Phyl stared at her and then broke into laughter. 'Well, I'm blowed! You're a real dark horse, you are. I never dreamt you and Jim were up to anything!'

'We weren't. We just – well, we've been engaged a long time, and what with Jim getting wounded and having pneumonia and then going away again, we thought—'

'You thought what everyone thinks. It's now or never – or might be. It's all right, kid, I don't blame you. Done the same myself, didn't I? I reckon we're all entitled to take what happiness we can get these days. I hope you were careful, all the same!'

'Of course we were.' Etty hesitated, then said, 'We're going to get married though, the first chance we get. Jim thinks he'll be sent to camp for a few weeks and he might get a chance of a couple of days' leave before he goes away. I'm going to see about a licence and then he can come down to Bedford and we'll get married there. We won't do nothing special – no white frock, or cake or anything – we just want to be married.'

'Well, *you* might not do anything special, but the rest of us will!' Phyl told her. 'We're not going to let an excuse for a party go by. I bet Mr Carter'll be pleased, an' all.'

The train arrived at Elstow at last, and the girls got out, stiff from the long journey. They carried their bags through the village, past the Chimney Corner pub and down the road to the wire fence and big gates of the munitions factory.

Showing their passes, they made their way between the dark, looming buildings towards their hostel.

'Like walking back into a nightmare, isn't it?' Phyl muttered. 'Just think, there's thousands of tons of high explosive here. What an explosion it would make if someone chucked a match in the middle of it all!'

'Don't,' Etty begged her. 'I've only just got used to the idea of it myself. Oh Phyl, d'you think this war's ever going to end?'

'Well, it's got to some time, surely. Someone'll give in. And when it does—' Phyl stopped with a little scream. A dark figure had stepped out suddenly from behind a building and blocked their way. Barely able to see in the thick darkness, the two girls stopped and clutched each other.

'Who's that?' demanded a grating voice. 'Who's that wandering round at this time of night?'

'It's Nobby Clark,' Phyl exclaimed with relief. 'We thought you were a German! It's only us – me and Etty – back from our Christmas leave. We—'

'Oh, it's *you* two, is it?' Nobby Clark's voice was ugly with dislike. 'Carter's favourites, sent off to enjoy Christmas in the bosom of their families when the rest of us had to carry on slaving away here. And how were the boyfriends, eh? Live up to expectations, did they?'

Phyl said with dignity, 'I'm a married woman, Mr Clark, as well you know, and I spent my leave with my *husband*. And Etty's *fiancé* was wounded in action, and got pneumonia as well, so he's a hero. And, yes, we had a very nice Christmas, thank you for asking.'

Nobby Clark sneered. 'Oh, *had a very nice Christmas*, did you? Well, *ain't* that good to know? I been worrying about that at nights.' He shot out his hand and gripped Etty's arm so that she cried out. 'Well, and ain't you got a kiss for your friend Nobby what's been missing you so bad all this time, and what's *not* had a very nice Christmas, thank you for asking?' He rubbed his face against hers and Etty turned away in disgust and tried to pull her arm out of his grip. 'I see.

184

Not good enough for you. Got a *fiancé* to see to your needs. Well, you can forget all that now. You're going to have to *work* from now on, work like you've never worked in your lives. We got a war to win, or maybe you didn't know that. Maybe you thought all this was just a picnic—'

'Let Etty go,' Phyl said, her voice trembling with anger. 'You're drunk. Let us get past and go to our hostel. We've had a long journey and we want to get to bed.'

'Oh, you go on, then. You just go on. You're going to need your sleep, I can tell you that. I'll expect you on the benches at five o'clock sharp, see? And not a minute later.'

'*Five* o'clock?' Phyl echoed. 'But we're not meant to start our shift till seven.'

He grinned in the faint light. 'Spot of overtime. Only I thought we'd do it at the beginning of the shift rather than the end – just in case we needs to slip in an extra hour or two as well then, see? And what with you two being fresh back from your holidays—'

'All right, we get it,' Phyl interrupted wearily. 'Well, come on, Etty, if we're only going to be allowed five hours' sleep we'd better get to bed as quick as we can.' She pulled at Etty's arm and the two girls walked away quickly, leaving Nobby Clark sniggering behind them. They said no more until they were in the hostel, and then they looked at each other and sighed.

'Well, that's Christmas over,' Etty said. 'I reckon he's going to have it in for us more than ever now, don't you?' And she turned to climb the stairs, her joy dimmed, weighed down by the knowledge that Nobby Clark was going to go all out to make her life at Elstow more miserable than ever.

The first week of January was Shirley's last week at the Corner House.

Each day brought her closer to the final goodbye. She looked at it with eyes that seemed suddenly fresh, seeing the great restaurants, the kitchens, even the dressing-room and the dank little tunnel as if for the first time. The lights seemed brighter, the clatter of cutlery and dishes in the serving area sharper, the friendship of the other Nippies warmer than at any time since that very first day, when she had been so nervous and uncertain. Yet she knew it was all very different now. The chandeliers had been replaced by ordinary light bulbs, the decoration of the walls had grown shabby, the carpets worn. The china and glasses had been replaced by cheap utility ware, and the menus were restricted by rationing. Most of all, there were none of the Nippies who had started with her, and although Lyons still did their best to train the young ones to the same high standards, there seemed to be a lack somehow. And self-service was creeping into the restaurants, with the waitresses working now only in the smartest ones.

Every restaurant was smart once, she thought sadly. I even miss Mr Carter with his torch, peering at our hemlines to make sure our petticoats were the right length! And the lovely dishes we used to serve – Adam and Eve on a Raft, and Airship on a Cloud. Now it's plain old poached egg on toast, and only one egg at a time at that.

The Corner Houses were still as popular as ever, though. Everyone knew that standards had to change in wartime, and Lyons had done their best to keep their glamour and their reputation for good food and service at reasonable prices. Office workers, shoppers and servicemen on leave still poured in through the doors, and there were still queues stretching down the pavements outside to get a table.

'What are you going to do in Wales?' one of the other girls asked Shirley as they put on their uniforms before her last shift of all. 'Won't you have to sign up for war work of some sort?'

'I suppose so. I'll face that when it comes to it.' All Shirley wanted to do was get her father safely settled on the farm with his wife and son, and then settle down with Jim in their own home. She couldn't look any further ahead than that. The struggle to get her father to agree to the move had taken all her strength. He had used every argument he could think of until she'd wanted to scream, and in the end she'd just sat down and cried, asking him just why he wouldn't go.

'Don't you love Mum any more? Is that it? Don't you want to be with her? And what about Jack? He's hardly seen you for the past two years. He'll forget who you are. Is that what you want?' She lifted her head and looked at him. 'Maybe you just don't want either of them any more.'

'That's a terrible thing to say,' Alf said, his voice shaking as much as Shirley's. 'Of course I love your mother. And saying I don't want to be with her, or our Jack – that's cruel, Shirley. I never thought you could be so cruel.'

'Well, then, why won't you go and be *with* them?' she demanded. 'It's where you ought to be. They *want* you there.'

He stared into the fire. 'I want to be there, too. I just can't face it, Shirl, and that's the top and bottom of it. I don't seem to have the energy. And what about when I has a fit, eh? How's your mother going to feel, seeing me as helpless as a baby?' He looked at her, his eyes filled with fear. 'Is she going to love *me*? It's easy for me to love your mother, she's a wonderful woman, but how can I expect her to love a wreck like I've turned into?'

Shirley's anger evaporated. She went to him and put her arms around his shoulders, holding his head against her. 'Of course she'll love you, Dad. Of course she will. Just give her the chance. Don't you think you ought to do that? Don't you think she deserves it?'

Alf had given way at last. Perhaps he was just too tired to argue any more. And at the end of this week he and Shirley would leave the little house in which they'd lived ever since Shirley was born, and set off on the long train journey to South Wales. Their bags and boxes were packed, their furniture either sold or distributed amongst various relatives and friends to be looked after until they could come home again. There wasn't much anyway, Alf said, looking round the little rooms. Half of it had been old when they'd first got married and they'd never been able to afford good stuff. But there was a little table that had been his mother's and a dining-table and chairs that they'd saved up for before Shirley was born. He wouldn't want to get rid of those.

'You don't have to. Auntie Mabel says she'll have them. She's got that front room she's never had furniture in – anything you want to keep can go in there. It can just be stacked up.'

'And what if Mabel gets bombed out?'

'What if *we* get bombed out?' Shirley exclaimed in exasperation. 'It's a chance we all have to take, Dad. Now, what about this nice tea set of Granny's? You want that kept, don't you?'

'Blimey, I should think so. Your mother'd kill me if I let that go. It was her mum's wedding present.' He picked up a cup, gold-rimmed and decorated with roses. 'Your Auntie Ethel always thought it ought to go to her, you know, with her being the oldest girl, but she had the rings so it was only fair your mum should have this. She set a lot of store by this set.'

'I know.' Shirley had wrapped each piece in newspaper and packed them carefully in a cardboard box. She stood up and looked around. There was nothing left to do. A few old plates and cups had been left out, to see them through the last few days, and Uncle Reg had borrowed a handcart to collect the stuff they were keeping. The rest would go to the junk shop up the street.

As she began her last shift Shirley thought of Alf, sitting in the desolate room after his brother-in-law had taken away the best of their furniture. Without the things that held his memories, the house seemed unlike home and he'd looked out of place and miserable, sitting in his armchair staring at the fire. She'd hesitated as she'd looked in to say goodbye, wondering if she ought to leave him. He looked so lost, so shrunken, as if he were withering away. Don't have a fit this morning, Dad, she begged him silently, please don't have a fit.

A knock at the door signalled the arrival of their neighbour, who had promised to come in and keep an eye on Alf that morning. Shirley went to let her in, although Mrs Yates had a key. She came in, a small, wiry woman with a flowered pinafore tied over her frock and a scarf would turbanwise round her head.

'I hope he's going to be all right,' Shirley murmured in the narrow passageway. 'He doesn't look very well. I've half a mind not to go in . . .'

'Well, they can hardly give you the sack if you don't,' Mrs Yates said briskly. 'But you don't need to worry, Shirley. He'll be all right with me. I've got to pop out to the shops later on, but I'll only be half an hour, unless there's bad queues, and I got me knitting I can be getting on with. I'm doing army balaclavas.' She showed Shirley the khaki wool. 'You go on and enjoy your last day. You'll want to say goodbye to your friends.'

I've already done that, Shirley thought later as she served her customers with beans on toast or poached eggs. I've said goodbye to Jo and Phyl and Etty and Maggie. And even Irene. There's nobody left who means as much to me as they did.

She wondered if they would ever meet again in this big restaurant where they had sallied out so brightly to serve their customers, where they had rushed about with their silver trays held high above their heads, where they had laughed and flirted and sometimes made mistakes. She remembered the day one of them – had it been Etty? – had spilt soup down a man's neck, and the day Phyl had been accused, wrongly, of fiddling a customer's bill. And the day Irene Bond had scalded herself on the coffee-urn, and the time when Jo had tripped over a customer's handbag and sent a whole tray of dinners flying. It had seemed a disaster at the time, yet looking back now Shirley thought it was nothing. None of it had really made a difference to their lives. Not so long as they could stay at the Corner House, a little band of girls who had become friends in a place that had become like home.

Smiling at her last customer, picking up her last small tip, clearing her last table, Shirley felt almost as if she were betraying them. It was as if they'd left her there to look after the Corner House for them. To look after their place in life. And now she was leaving it, walking away. It would never, ever, be the same again.

I'll write to them, she thought. I'll write to them all and ask them to meet me here when the war ends. I'll ask them all to come to London so that we can have tea here together. So that we can start life again, in the Lyons Corner House at Marble Arch.

Chapter Fifteen

The villages around Merthyr Tydfil were grey and black. Grey with the stone and slate of the houses, and black with coal dust and soot. The skies seemed permanently clouded with smoke, and when it rained black streaks were left on windows and whitened doorsteps. It seemed to rain almost all the time.

Owen met Shirley at the railway station and they took Alf to the farm up the mountain at Nant-ddu. The snow had melted in the valleys but still capped the mountains and the huge piles of slag that surrounded the villages. There was snow piled up at the sides of the track leading to the farmhouse, and the worn tyres of the battered old van that Owen had borrowed skidded on the icy ruts. Alf sat with Owen in the front, staring morosely out of the window, while Shirley perched on the suitcases in the back. She watched her father anxiously, wondering if after all it had been wise to make him come.

Alf had barely spoken during the long train journey. He had sat with an unopened newspaper on his lap, staring out of the window as he was doing now, although Shirley was sure he saw nothing. It was as if his eyes were turned inwards, staring at memories, staring at a past that could never be recovered. It was as if he were afraid to see what was happening now.

'You'll see Mum soon,' she whispered, leaning on his shoulder. 'You'll see Mum and Jack. I bet they're getting excited now, don't you? I bet they can hardly wait to see us coming up the valley.'

He didn't answer. He wrapped his arms around his thin body as if holding himself together, as if he might fly apart if he let go. He's still frightened he'll have a fit, she thought pityingly. He's scared to death he'll shame himself in front of them all.

Owen drove the van slowly round the last bend and brought it to a stop in the farmyard. The rattling engine spluttered into silence.

Shirley gazed around her. The first time she had come to Nant-ddu, it had been summer and the slopes of the mountains had been rich with purple heather, the green fields speckled with creamy-white sheep and the farmyard bustling with hens and ducks. The tiny farmhouse garden, fenced off from the yard by low white palings, had been crammed with brilliant flowers – nasturtiums, geraniums, antirrhinums and big white daisies. The crystal stream had filled the air with its bubbling and small birds had flirted along its banks before being chased off by the big black and white cat.

Now, in midwinter, the scene looked bleak and empty. The mountainside was frozen, its covering of snow so thin that the dark, slaty earth and rocks showed through, making it look dirty, and the yard was muddy and smeared with dung. The garden that had been filled with flowers now sported nothing but a few tired cabbages, and the stream had frozen and even its icicles looked grey and miserable.

'My God Almighty,' Alf said, staring out of the window, 'what the hell have we come to? I reckon we oughter be taking Annie and our Jack straight back to London.'

Shirley felt a miasma of dismay creep over her body, like a thick grey cobweb. She wanted to tell him they'd been right to come, but she felt dreadfully uncertain. She looked at Owen, but at that moment the farmhouse door opened and her brother Jack rushed out.

'Dad! Dad! Shirley! You came!'

As if released from a transfixing spell, they scrambled out

of the van. Shirley held out her arms, but it was to his father that Jack ran first. He scrabbled at Alf's coat as if begging to be lifted up and swung round as if he were still a baby instead of a gangling young man of twenty-three, and then flung his arms around his father and buried his face in Alf's old tweed coat.

Annie Woods came after him. She looked thinner than Shirley remembered, and her face was more weatherbeaten, but she looked healthier – tougher – as if the life on this Welsh mountainside had given her strength. She watched Jack for a moment, a smile in her eyes, and then came to kiss Shirley.

'I'm glad you've come. I'm glad you've brought him. Now I can look after him properly.'

'I've done my best—' Shirley began, but her mother shook her arm and laughed.

'I didn't mean that, you silly ha'porth. I just meant it's my job and now I can do it. I was thinking of coming back to London, you know.'

Shirley shook her head. 'You don't want to do that. It's awful in London now. Bomb damage everywhere – and queues – and you never know when it's going to start again. There was the "Little Blitz" last year and there's talk of some new secret weapon they reckon's going to be worse than anything we've had yet . . . You're best off here, and Jack would be miserable.'

'You're right about that. I don't know how we're ever going to get him back to London, away from his precious sheep and pigs and chickens.' Annie turned to greet her husband. 'Well, Alf. And how are you?'

'I'm all right,' he said gruffly, not meeting her eyes. 'Nothing wrong with me. Lot of fuss about nothing, keeping me off work all this time.'

Annie nodded. If she hadn't trusted Shirley to take care of him, she would have come back to London long ago, bombs or no bombs. Instead, she had lived on the hope that he would eventually be persuaded to come to Wales. Now he was here and she intended to look after him, but she could see

193

that the time apart had created a distance between them, a distance it would take time to bridge.

'Come on indoors, Alf,' she said, slipping her hand through his arm. 'Come and sit by the fire. Mair Prosser's got a nice lamb stew on the hob, and Dafydd's dug some potatoes special. And I've just made a pot of tea, to warm you up after the journey.'

Jack let go of his father with some reluctance and turned to his sister. He nuzzled her like a friendly animal, and she kissed his round face and slanting eyes. He smiled his wide, slack-lipped smile.

'It's winter now,' he informed her. 'We had snow. The sheep made themselves a cave in it. I dug a path. There'll be snowdrops soon, Uncle Dafydd says, and then primroses and lambs. It'll be spring again, just like last year.'

'Yes, so it will,' Shirley said, hugging him and thinking just how much she had missed him. 'So it will. And do you know something, Jack? Me and Owen are going to come up the mountain and see all those things. Because we've come to live here, too. Not at Nant-ddu, but down in the valley. We'll be able to see you much, much more.'

Jack stared at her. He put out a stubby finger and traced her mouth, pulling the corners into a smile.

'You and Owen? You're going to live here, too?'

'In the valley.' She nodded. 'Owen and me are getting married.'

'Married,' he repeated, and then gave her a broad grin. He felt in his pocket and produced his mouth-organ – the same mouth-organ that Alf and Annie had given him one Christmas long ago, before the war began. He blew a swift trill on it, as sweet as a robin's song, and then nodded at her.

'I'll play for you,' he said. 'I'll play tunes at your marrying.'

If it hadn't been for Jack's mouth-organ, Shirley thought, the wedding could have been mistaken for a funeral. Held in the village chapel the next afternoon, it was attended by Owen's uncle and aunt and a few Prosser cousins, as well as Alf and Annie and Jack. Almost everyone wore black.

'It's their best clothes, *cariad*,' Owen said, seeing Shirley's face as she looked around the sombre gathering. 'It's a compliment.'

'Well, that's a comfort. I thought maybe it was a wake.'

'That's in Ireland,' he said, grinning. 'You're in Wales now, look you.'

Shirley made a face at him, but she knew that the sober clothes belied their wearers' warm hearts. The Prosser family was glad to see Owen marrying, although at the party held afterwards in one of the larger cottages they commiserated with him for having to come back to the valleys. 'We thought you'd got away when you da' went off to London.'

'So did I. Just my luck to be a Bevin boy. I still don't believe it was a fair ballot.'

'It's what's to be expected when the Government goes in for gambling,' the uncle said disapprovingly, and Shirley remembered that these chapel folk wouldn't countenance so much as a raffle. Having boys from all over the country picked out by ballot to work in their mines, while their own lads went off to war, must be like adding insult to injury.

'Nobody likes working down the mines, yet they don't want other people coming to do it,' she remarked to Owen as they stood alone for a moment before the next crowd of cousins descended on them.

He shook his head. 'It's all there is in the valleys, see. All the livelihood there is, unless you got a farm up the mountain like Uncle Dafydd. Nobody likes the pit but it feeds us and clothes us and puts a roof over our heads. This old war's soaking up the coal, see, and people are afraid there won't be so much left afterwards. And then it's strangers coming in, English. There've never been English in the valleys – except for very special ones,' he added with a smile into her eyes.

'Everything's changing,' Shirley agreed. 'Everything's changing everywhere. But at least we're going to be together,

Owen. And we'll all just have to wait and see what happens after the war.'

The sombreness of the wedding faded rapidly through the evening as the party spirit grew. There was no alcohol, but the Welsh didn't seem to need it to start their singing. Jack played his mouth-organ, as he had promised, and they listened to its music, in turn sweet and plaintive. Dafydd, sitting next to Alf and Annie, nodded as proudly as if Jack were his own son.

'He can make that thing almost talk. He can make it weep tears. He's a genius on the mouth-organ.'

Alf looked at him in surprise. 'A genius? Our Jack? Why, he's a damaged boy.'

'I know all about that. Mongol, they call him, don't they, on account of his looks. But I tell you, Alfred, he's as good a worker as any man I've ever had up on the mountain. Do anything with the animals, he can. And they love him. You can see by the way they go to him.'

Some of the men had started to sing to the music Jack was making. Their voices blended together, deep and high, throbbing through the room like a full church organ. The words were in Welsh, but it didn't matter that the Woods couldn't understand them, for the emotion was transmitted from the hearts of the miners through the singing air to the hearts of their listeners.

'We were told he'd never live past fifteen,' Alf said in a low voice. 'Twenty at the most. He's on borrowed time, Dafydd.'

'Then he can borrow as much as he likes.' Dafydd smiled broadly. 'I reckon it's the mountain air suits him, see. There's years left in him yet, Alf, years and years. Ah – listen to this now.'

The men fell silent. The group in the corner had begun to sing the Welsh song 'Myfanwy', and Jack was joining in, very softly. All around the room, the song was taken up by lilting Welsh voices until the emotion sobbed and sighed in the trembling air. The dirt and grime of the valley, with its mines and pits and slag-heaps; the nightmare of war that extended beyond the mountains that ringed the valleys and far beyond them to the world that struggled and bled; the fear and pain of those who had sent sons and brothers and husbands to war and did not know when they might come back or, perhaps, knew already that they would never come back – all these were set aside, if not forgotten, while the people of the valley listened to the song that meant so much to them.

When it finished, there was not a dry eye in the room, not even amongst the English.

Owen stood up and drew Shirley to stand beside him.

'I want to thank you all,' he said in English. 'I want to thank you for welcoming my wife to the valley and for giving us this happy night. I want to thank you for being my family and my friends, and I wish you all the happiness you've given us today.'

He spoke in Welsh then, for some of the people there knew no English, and when he finished there was a murmur of approval. Someone began to sing again, a noisy, jolly song this time, and they all joined in. Jack learnt the tune as quickly as he always did and began to caper with his mouth-organ at his lips, and others joined him in the tiny space to dance. In the midst of the clamour, Shirley turned to her mother and father and kissed them both.

'Owen and I are going now. He's borrowed the van to take us to our rooms. I'll see you as soon as I can.' She looked into her father's eyes. 'You'll be all right now, Dad.'

'I reckon I will,' he said, nodding. He had not had a seizure yet and felt as though he never would again. 'I never realised just how much I missed your mother. I wish I'd come a long time ago.'

Shirley gave him a look of fond exasperation. 'I wish I'd *made* you come,' she said, and then caught her brother's shoulder as he capered past. 'Goodnight, Jack.'

He looked at her, his slanting eyes seeming as they often did to see more than other people. 'You going to bed? You and Owen?'

Shirley blushed and laughed. 'Yes.'

Jack nodded in his matter-of-fact way. 'Married now,' he said, and lurched away, his mouth-organ once again at his lips.

Married now.

The words echoed between them as Owen drove the old van along the valley road to the next village, where they had rented two rooms in a tiny cottage, one in a long row set along the side of the mountain close to the mine. The moon had risen above the undulating skyline and rimed the pitheads and crags with silver, glinting on the white caps of the mountains. In the starkness of black and white, the scene looked dramatic and clean. In the morning, Shirley knew, it would look very different.

They came to the village and the row of small, mean houses. Owen stopped the van. It would have to be returned in the morning but for tonight it could be left here, in front of the middle cottage of the row. They climbed out, shivering, and Owen opened the front door.

Their two rooms were one upstairs and one down. They were to share the kitchen and the tiny, outside lavatory with the widow who rented the cottage from the mine-owner. They went straight up the stairs and into the bedroom.

Owen closed the door and took Shirley in his arms.

'Well, *cariad*,' he said, smiling in the darkness, 'here we are. Do you want me to light a candle?'

'Yes, please,' she said, and he struck a match and lit the candle that stood beside the bed. They looked at each other in the flickering light.

'Mrs Prosser,' he said wonderingly, tracing her lips with his finger. 'My wife. Shirley, I love you.'

'I love you, too, Owen,' she whispered, and offered her lips to his.

The small, crowded room, with its cheap furniture and its dull painted walls and its old iron bed, seemed a million miles away from the brightness of the Corner House. But in that moment, as Shirley and Owen held each other and pledged their love again, as they had already done in the chapel that afternoon, Shirley knew that she would not have gone back for the world. This gritty, noisy valley was her home now, and this man her husband, and his life was hers.

In the Clun forest, the winter was bitter.

'Shropshire must be the coldest county in England.' Poppy shivered as she and Jo got out of bed morning after morning to find the windows glazed with frost flowers. The only fire in the cottage was the range downstairs, and it was the girls' first task to light it and get the kettle boiling and the porridge on the simmer. Wrapped in thick jerseys over their shirts and breeches, they cut their sandwiches and took an apple each from the store in the shed. If all went well, they would have hot tea to drink and porridge to eat before they wheeled their bikes out to cycle to the forest. If the range was bad-tempered, as it often was, they would be lucky to see a flame before it was time to go.

They still went early, though. It pleased them to get to the woods first, when everything was still and quiet apart from the animals and birds, and they enjoyed starting a fire and getting the billy on to boil. Before the lorry arrived with the others, they would turn to with their saws or axes, and by the time the rest of the gang was there, frozen from their bumpy ride, Jo and Poppy were warm and glowing, ready to make the tea.

'You two aren't as bad as I thought you'd be,' Huw the Tree acknowledged. 'Getting handy with a saw, too. I wouldn't be surprised if you weren't quite useful, come the end of the war.'

Jo made a face at him, but she knew that from Huw this was high praise. He had taken a long time to come around to the idea of girls doing timber work, but he seemed to have accepted them now, as had the rest of the men. The only person who still wasn't properly a part of the gang was Josh.

Jo had avoided Josh since she'd come back from her Christmas leave. It was unkind, she knew, when they had been friends and he'd seen her off at the station and given her the little carved elephant. She'd seen the surprise and the disappointment in his eyes when they'd first encountered each other after her return, and she'd turned away with no more than a nod. But she had determined, during the long journey home, that their friendship must end.

'Did you have a nice Christmas?' Poppy asked her, the first morning they cycled to work together after the holiday. 'I bet Nick was glad to see you, wasn't he?'

'I think so,' Jo answered cautiously, and then, seeing Poppy's eyebrows go up, added, 'Yes, of course he was! It was lovely. But he had to go back on Christmas Eve. It spoilt things.'

'Oh, what a shame. Still, you had a bit of time together – better than nothing. And he's all right.'

'Yes.' Jo felt a weight around her heart. *Was* Nick all right? He'd been so different – remote, strange. It's all the worry and the strain, she reminded herself. It's all those operations he's had. You can't expect him to be the same.

'You know,' Poppy panted as they struggled up the hill, 'you've changed lately.'

Jo looked at her, startled. 'What d'you mean?'

'You're different. You used to be so – so bold and confident. So cheery, as if you knew everything would be all right in the end. You made us all feel better. But just lately – well, don't mind me saying this, will you? – you seem sort of subdued. As if you're not so sure any more.'

Jo was silent. She did mind Poppy saying it. She felt hurt and annoyed, as if she'd been accused of something wrong, something she hadn't done. She pushed her feet hard down on the pedals, making the bike go faster.

'I don't suppose there's many people who can keep cheerful *all* the time,' she said tersely. 'Specially these days. You're not always a ray of sunshine yourself, Poppy.'

'Oh, lor', now I've upset you,' Poppy said contritely. 'Look, Jo, I didn't mean anything. I'm just a bit worried about you. There's nothing wrong, is there? I mean, you and Nick – you're all right?'

Jo bit her lip. She felt like crying. Angrily, she said, 'Look, I told you, he had to go back the day before Christmas. How d'you think that made me feel? Why the hell should I be cheerful all the time, just to keep *you* happy, when everything in my life's going wrong? I mean – I mean, of *course* Nick and me are all right, of course we are, it's just – it's just that we never see each other and when we do – when we do . . .' To her horror, she found that she was crying, great noisy sobs that tore themselves up from her chest and wrenched at her throat. Her eyes blurred and her bike wobbled so that she almost fell. She scrambled off and started to push it up the hill, trying to control her tears and failing utterly.

Poppy got off, too. She walked beside Jo and tried to get her to stop by putting her hands on Jo's handlebars. Jo shook her off savagely. She stamped up the hill, shaking with the sobs that refused to stop coming, furious with Poppy, furious with herself, furious even with Nick. Why couldn't he have said he loved her as they waited for the train? Why couldn't he have given her a proper, loving kiss?

'Jo. Please don't cry. Please. I'm sorry – I shouldn't have asked. I never meant to upset you, you know that. Look, I won't say any more, I won't ask again. *Please*, Jo.'

Jo took a deep, shuddering breath. She stopped and leant on her bike, her head drooping. At last she regained some control and turned to her friend.

'It's all right,' she said drearily. 'I know you didn't mean anything. It's just – oh, you know. The war. The hell of it all. I wonder sometimes how we can all carry on.'

'I know,' Poppy said gently. She fished in her pocket and pulled out a khaki hanky. 'It's a bit grubby . . .'

Jo laughed shakily and took it. She blew her nose and wiped her eyes. 'It's even grubbier now. Let's get on, Pops. Let's get the fire lit and chop down trees and make pit-props for my friend Shirley's new husband, and do whatever we can to help win this bloody war. And just let's not *talk* about it – all right?'

They went on up the hill and along the track into the forest to the clearing where they were working. They said no more about Jo's tears, and Poppy said no more about Nick. But they were both shaken by the sudden outburst, and Jo knew that her distress was deeper than she would ever admit to Poppy, or to anyone else.

Much too deep to risk being friends with Josh again.

Chapter Sixteen

January ran into February, but the weather grew no warmer. The bombing over Berlin continued, and the RAF suffered heavy losses. Jo went to bed at night thinking of Nick, and woke each morning dreading the arrival of a telegram. Fear stalked the country, walking like a spectre beside the determination not to be beaten. Work – war work – seemed the only comfort, and friends the only support.

'What have I done?' Josh asked when he encountered Jo one Sunday afternoon near the castle. Jo had come out for a walk on her own. Poppy was ensconced by Mrs Dell's fire with that week's copy of *Woman's Own*, and refused to come out into the cold and, to tell the truth, Jo had been relieved to leave her behind. They were together so much that, good friends though they'd become, they needed a few hours apart.

It was bitterly cold, with a thin, scouring wind. She hadn't expected to meet anyone else, and nearly jumped out of her skin when Josh spoke to her. He was sitting on a low, broken wall as she came round the old keep, and stood up as she came near. He looked down at her, his eyes grave and questioning.

Jo glanced round as if to look for an escape, but he took her arm – so gently that she could have pulled away without any trouble. But his touch seemed to run through her like fire and she gasped in surprise. She stared up at him and opened her mouth, but no words came and to her bewilderment she felt tears prick her eyes.

'Have I hurt you in some way?' he asked quietly. 'Have I annoyed you? What is it, Jo? I thought we were friends.'

She shook her head blindly. 'I – yes. We were. I – I mean, no, we can't be. We can't be friends, Josh.' She looked at his hand on her arm. 'Please – let me go.'

'I'm not holding you.' His fingers were laid on her sleeve, open against the thick fabric. 'You can go as soon as you like, I won't prevent you. But I would just like to know why you won't speak to me now.'

Jo tried a little laugh. 'I've hardly seen you.'

'You haven't tried. But even when we have met, you've looked through me as if I weren't there. As you used to, when you first found out what I was.' A small frown appeared between his dark brows. 'Is it Nick?'

'What do you mean?' The words came out harshly. 'What do you mean, *is it Nick?*'

'Are you still angry with me because of what happened to him?'

Jo stared at him. She had almost forgotten her first reaction on hearing that Josh was a CO. 'No. No, it's not that. It's – it's nothing at all. Honestly. Please – let me go.' She shifted abruptly and his hand fell away, but he remained still, looking at her.

'Jo, friends are honest with each other. Isn't that right?'

'Yes,' she muttered miserably.

'So won't you be honest with me? Tell me what I've done to hurt or offend you? Whatever it is, I promise you it wasn't intended.'

'You haven't done anything,' Jo said with a sigh. 'It's nothing like that. It really isn't.'

'So, what is it, then?'

'I can't tell you,' she said, looking straight at him for the first time. She hardly knew herself, and could not have put it into words. 'I just can't tell you, Josh. I'm sorry. I just think it's better that – that we don't meet too much, that's all.'

Josh looked at her for a long moment. 'I see,' he said eventually. 'And will that make life easier for you?'

'Yes. Yes, it will.'

'Then that's what we'll do,' he said quietly, and turned away. 'But I'll be here, Jo. If ever you need anyone. If ever you need a friend who truly cares for you, you'll come to me, won't you? Promise me that, Jo.'

'Yes,' she said, not believing that she ever would. 'Yes, of course I will.'

There was a moment of silence. He looked back at her over his shoulder and their eyes met. Then Jo turned and walked away, into the bitter, scouring wind, her head down and her eyes watering.

It was only the wind, she told herself. It was only the wind that brought the hot, scalding tears to her eyes.

It was cold at Elstow, too. Phyl tried not to think about her chilblains and helped Etty plan her wedding. It was only going to be a simple one, Etty said, what else could they do? But Phyl and the other girls had made up their minds to give her a bit of a splash.

'You've got to have a new frock. You can't get married in something old.'

' "*Something old, something new*",' Etty quoted. 'Mind, I don't know what the "*new*" will be. A bit of ribbon in me hair, I should think, if I can only get hold of some.'

'A new frock,' Phyl repeated firmly. 'Let's have a look at what you've got, see if there's something we can change a bit.'

'It won't be new, then.'

Phyl gave her a look. 'It'll be as new as we can manage. Look, what about this green frock? You could take the bodice off and—'

'She can't get married in *green*,' Jenny interrupted. 'That's asking for bad luck.'

'We can't afford to be superstitious—'

'I'm not getting married in green,' Etty said definitely. 'I'm not getting married in a dark colour at all. I want something light.'

'Not white, then?' Phyl asked with a wink, and Etty blushed.

Jenny giggled. 'Tell you what, I've got a white frock at home. I haven't worn it for years. I'll ask Mum to post it down.'

'Well, that's the answer, then,' Phyl said triumphantly, but when the parcel came they saw that the dress, once a white cotton, had turned yellow all along the creases where it had been folded away for so long. They looked at it regretfully.

'What a shame,' Etty said. 'It's really pretty, too.'

'We could bleach it,' Phyl suggested. 'That'd freshen it up.'

The next time she was in the village she went to the shop and bought some Brobat. They poured it into a bowl and left the dress soaking in it overnight. In the morning, Phyl tipped it out carefully and rinsed it in the sink.

'Oh.'

'What's the matter? Hasn't it got rid of the stains?'

'Yes, it's got rid of them all right,' Phyl said sorrowfully. 'Trouble is, it's got rid of the buttons and half the dress as well.'

'Oh, no!'

She held the dress up for them to see. It dripped into the sink and they stared at it in dismay. The buttons had more or less fallen to pieces and the material was in holes. Etty put one hand to her mouth and Jenny looked about to burst into tears.

'That was one of my favourite frocks! I used to wear it all the time.'

'Well, you won't wear it no more,' Phyl told her. 'You've had it packed away for the past three years anyway, you can't have liked it that much. And it wouldn't have fallen to bits like that if it hadn't been going rotten.'

Jenny looked ready to argue but Kaye, coming in at that moment, came over to see what had happened and started to giggle. The others looked at her for a moment in injured silence, then Phyl grinned and began to laugh as well, and after another moment Jenny and Etty joined in. They took turns in holding up the ruined dress and bursting into fresh giggles, until at last they were all exhausted with mirth.

'Well, this won't help Etty get married in style,' Phyl said at last. 'What are we going to do? You said Jim was hoping to get leave soon, didn't you?'

'Next weekend, he thinks,' Etty said, and they squealed in dismay.

'Next *week*? You never said! When did you find that out?'

'Only this morning. A letter came. He's being posted the week after, so it's got to be then. Look, it doesn't matter about a frock. I can get married in anything.'

'You'll be getting married in your overalls at this rate,' Phyl said. They all jumped as the hooter sounded and she dropped the ruined frock back into the bowl. 'I'll see to that later. Come on, or we'll be late and that Nobby Clark'll be on our tails again. And we don't want to take any chances with our day off next week, not if it's going to be Etty's wedding day.'

Shirley thought she had never known such a grimy place to live as the little mining village where she and Owen had their rooms.

The very air was dirty. You breathed in grit and coal-dust all the time and if you blew your nose, your handkerchief was covered in black mucus. It rimmed your eyelids and got into your food, until Shirley felt she would scream. She thought of the bright cleanliness of the Corner House, and envied her parents and brother, high up in the clear, cold air of the mountain.

Then she would think of Owen, down the mine, and feel ashamed. Whatever it was like in the village, it was a hundred times worse below ground. She washed, ironed clothes and cleaned the rooms for him every day, and when he came off shift she had hot water waiting for his bath and clean clothes for him to put on. She felt lucky then to have a man at home, not risking his life hundreds of miles away, killing and perhaps being killed, and she washed his back tenderly as he sat in the tin bath, and kissed him, and never told him how much she missed London and her friends.

Owen worked as a haulier with the pit-ponies. He never mentioned the sweat and filth, the feeling that you were breathing and eating coal, the oppression of the thousands of tons of rock above your head. Instead, he told her about the ponies.

'Taffy's the one I drive most. Skewbald, he is – brown and white. Morgan Phillips looks after them, he's the ostler. Got sixty ponies to look after, he has.'

'Sixty! That's a lot.'

'Well, it's all he does, see. He feeds them and washes them down a bit, and cleans out their stables. He doesn't have nothing else to do.'

He explained how the pit-ponies sometimes wore leather head-shields to protect their faces from jutting rocks, or heavy blinkers to protect their eyes. They pulled the trucks of coal – 'drams', Owen called them – along rails from the coalface to the entrance of the mine. There was no deep shaft in this mine – you simply walked into it down the steep slope of the drift, and hauling the drams up the slope was hard work, even for the tough little ponies.

'Taffy can draw thirty drams a day,' Owen said with pride. 'He's a grand little chap.'

'It sounds ever such hard work.'

'It is. We have to run, see, all the time – we're not out for a Sunday afternoon jaunt. He gets his bait, of course, same as the rest of us – Morgan makes every pony a nosebag to put his face in while we has our sandwiches. He has a drink at the end of the shift, back in the stable. They get looked after all right, the ponies.'

Shirley finished washing his back and stroked his shoulders. The bathwater was black now and he stood up for her to pour a final bowl of water over his body to wash off the scum. He stood in the firelight, his muscles glimmering under the shower of water, and Shirley pressed her face against his wet chest.

'You look as if you've been doing body-building.'

'It's hard work,' he told her. He stepped out of the bath and stood naked before the fire, while Shirley dried him with a big towel. Then he put his arms around her and smiled down into her face.

'Not sorry you left London, are you?'

Shirley thought of the grit in her eyes and mouth, the soot and coal-dust that had to be cleaned from the windows every day, the sheer hard work of trying to get clothes clean, and shook her head. 'Not a bit sorry.'

'That's good.' He held her against him. 'Nor am I. You know, I think Mr Bevin did us a good turn after all.' He bent to nuzzle her neck. 'What about going upstairs? Is Mrs Davies in?'

Shirley shook her head. 'She's gone to see her sister.'

'So there's no one to see.' He swung Shirley into his arms and opened the door. Ignoring her protests, he carried her up the short flight of stairs to the tiny bedroom and laid her on the bed. She lay looking up at him and smiling.

'Take off those clothes, woman,' he ordered her. 'Your man wants you.'

Spring came earlier in Devon than in Shropshire, Bedford or Wales. By mid-February, snowdrops carpeted the woods and the birds had begun to sing. There were even a few days when the sun shone from a pale blue sky and you could feel a fragile warmth in it.

Maggie took Barry for walks beside the river. It came down from the moors, a rush of brown, clear water tumbling over the rocks, and Barry was entranced by its sparkle and its noise. He leant over the stone bridge, pushing his hair back out of his eyes, and watched for fish, shouting with delight when one jumped clear of the water. They were going to lay their eggs, Maggie told him, and make baby fishes, and he looked at her with some doubt.

'*Birds* lay eggs.'

'Yes. So do fishes.'

'Fishes can't climb *trees*,' he said, and Maggie laughed. Before she could say any more, uneven footsteps sounded behind them and they turned to see Carl Forrester coming along the lane towards them.

Carl's arms were out of plaster now but his leg was still giving trouble. He had a new plaster, which enabled him to walk with a crutch, but Maggie knew that he wasn't supposed to leave the hospital grounds.

'What are you doing out here? You're not allowed out yet.'

He grinned at her. 'Sure, but you won't tell anyone, will you? I just had to see if there was a real world out here still. And who's this little guy, hey?'

Maggie looked down at Barry. She had never explained to Carl about her little boy, partly because something had prevented her from allowing him to get too close to her and partly because she didn't want to see the disapproval in his eyes that she thought was inevitable once he knew the truth. But there was no getting away from it now.

'It's Barry. My little boy.'

'So *this* is Barry. Gee, I'm glad to meet you.' He held out his hand and after a moment's hesitation Barry held out his own small fist. The Canadian folded his fingers around the little hand and shook it gently.

'You're a fine fellow, aren't you? A grand little chap. So this is your mom, is it? Well, you lucky boy!' He glanced at Maggie, his eyes twinkling. 'And *you're* a dark horse!'

'It wasn't any of your business,' she said stiffly. 'I don't talk about Barry at work. It's separate.'

'Sure it is, but we're friends now, ain't we? We've known each other quite a while – six weeks, at least.' His face was full of merriment and warmth and Maggie was drawn to it despite herself. 'So, what have you seen in the river today, then, Barry?'

'Fishes,' the little boy said. 'We saw fishes. Mummy says they lay eggs. *I* don't think fishes lay eggs. *Birds* lay eggs.'

Maggie gave Carl a wry look. 'Nearly three years old and knows it all. And chatter! He'll talk the hind leg off a donkey.'

Carl laughed. 'They all do at this age!' He held out his hand to Barry. 'Well, fishes might not make nests, perhaps – though some even do that – but they sure do lay eggs. Now, what else is there to see? What's that little bird there, the one with the black suit and white bib sitting on that rock? Does he have a name?'

Barry studied the bird and shook his head. 'No. No name.'

'Oh, I'll bet he does. Tell you what, there's a book up at the hospital where I live, it tells you all about birds. Shall I look and see if it's got that bird in it, and next time I see you I'll tell you what it's called? Would you like that? Would you like to know what it's called?'

Barry nodded. His thumb was in his mouth and he removed it and looked commandingly at his mother.

'Man come to tea,' he said.

Carl and Maggie looked at each other. She felt a blush rise slowly up her neck and cheeks. 'I'm sure Mr Forrester doesn't want to come to our house. He'll have his tea at the hospital.'

'No,' Barry said. 'Come to tea with *us*. Please,' he added winningly, looking up through his lashes at her, and Carl laughed again.

'It's all right. I won't impose on you—'

'No,' she said, surprised by how much she wanted him to come. 'No, it's all right. Mum won't mind – she'll be glad to see someone new. You won't have to mind Gran, that's all. And our Billy will ask you for chocolate, but all the kids do that. It's because they hardly ever have any.'

'And I just happen to have a bar in my pocket, so that's OK.' He leant on the parapet of the bridge and Maggie realised that he looked tired. It was quite a walk down here from the house, she thought, especially on a crutch, and his arms couldn't be really strong yet.

'Come on,' she said, taking Barry's hand. 'The cottage is just along the lane. Come and have a cup of tea with us, and then I'll walk back with you. I'm on duty this evening anyway.'

'And that', Carl Forrester said, 'is the best news I've had today.'

He came to tea quite often after that, dropping in on his afternoon walks and bringing fruit cake or chocolate or chewing-gum for the children. Ivy liked him on sight and Ada took to putting it her teeth every afternoon just in case Carl dropped by. Ginnie and Billy hurried home from school and tried to claim all his attention as he sat in the armchair, his plaster stuck out in front of him, and chatted as if he'd lived with them all his life.

'Tell us about Canada,' Billy begged. 'D'you live on the prairie? Are you a cowboy in real life?'

'That's America, stupid,' Ginnie told him. 'Canadians have Mounties.'

'Oh, we have cowboys, too, and prairies,' Carl said, smiling. His teeth, Maggie noticed, were very white and even, as if he'd never had a moment's trouble with them. 'But I don't live in those parts. I hail from Ontario. We have a big river, and lots of lakes and forests near by. D'you know . . .' he leant forwards '. . . you could step outside our front door and cross the track into the forest and walk for three months without coming to another road.'

The children stared at him, open-mouthed.

'Where would you be when you came out the other side?' Billy demanded.

'Labrador. That's one heck of a long walk.' He nodded. 'Mind you, most people wouldn't be able to do that. Most people when they get lost in the forest just walk round in circles till they drop dead.'

His folk were farmers, he told Maggie as they walked back to the hospital, and his brothers had gone into the timber business. They worked in the forest all winter, cutting down trees and hauling the logs out or bringing them downriver lashed together as rafts. He'd taken on the farm but when the war started he'd joined up.

'Felt I ought to do something to help. Pa said he could

manage for a few months – but it's been longer than that now, and don't seem like coming to an end yet awhile.'

'When it started,' Maggie said, 'people said it'd be over by Christmas. What Christmas? That's what I'd like to know!'

They walked in silence for a few minutes. It was dark but there was a half-moon, and they could see the lane ahead of them, a pale strip between the dark Devon hedges. Then Carl said, 'What'll you do when it's over, Maggie? Go back to London and your Corner House?'

She shrugged. 'I suppose so. London, anyway – I dunno if they'll have me back at Lyons. Maybe they won't want Nippies then, and if they do I reckon they'll want younger ones. But I'll have to do summat to keep the wolf from the door, 'specially with Barry to look after.'

'Tell me to mind my own business,' Carl said, 'but nobody ever says anything about Barry's dad. Was he killed in action – something like that?'

Maggie sighed. She had known that this question would come sooner or later. To the villagers and the other girls at the hospital, all she ever said was that she was a widow. But she found now that she couldn't lie to Carl.

'I dunno where Barry's dad is,' she said. 'Tell you the truth, I don't even know *who* he is.' She sighed again. 'I'm not trying to paint meself white or nothing. I was married, but my Tom was killed at Dunkirk. And after that – well, I went a bit haywire. I thought of all those boys going off to war without knowing anything about women or love, and I, well, I just tried to help them a bit. So maybe it was one of them, I don't know.' She paused a moment. 'Or maybe it was the bloke that half killed me one night in a back alley. All right, I had it coming to me. And it don't matter now. I thought at first I wouldn't be able to keep the baby, 'specially not if it looked like *him*. But when I saw Barry—'

'He looks like you,' Carl said quietly.

'I think I'd have kept him anyway,' she said. 'He's my baby, see.'

They were almost at the gates. Carl stopped and turned to her. He took her hands in his.

'It doesn't make any difference, Maggie. It doesn't make any difference to me.'

Maggie stared at him in the faint light. She tried to pull her hands away but he wouldn't let her. She laughed a little shakily.

'All them exercises must be doing you good! Your hands are getting proper strong.'

'You know what I'm saying, Maggie,' he said. 'Don't you?'

Maggie met his eyes and then looked away. She bit her lips and shook her head.

'No. No, Carl, I don't know. I don't *want* to know. None of us knows where we're going. Nobody can make promises. I can't – you can't. It's no good.'

'But it will be one day. When all this is over—'

'When all this is over,' she said, 'I'll be going back to London and you'll be going back to Canada. We'll forget each other. We won't even want to remember.'

'We will. *I* will.'

'No,' Maggie said. She could feel the ache of tears in her throat. '*No*, Carl. Please.' She pulled her hands away at last and began to walk quickly up the drive. 'Look, I'm on duty in five minutes. I can't talk any more.'

'Tomorrow—'

'No,' she said, and turned to face him. 'Not tomorrow. Not ever, Carl. I told you, I'm finished with all that. It's just me and Barry now – see?'

Chapter Seventeen

Etty's wedding outfit had been sorted out at last. She was to wear a white blouse of Jenny's, embroidered in the evenings by Kaye with some coloured silks she'd begged from her mother's store. To go with it, Phyl was lending her a blue skirt and Kaye had found a woollen jacket that was almost the same colour.

'You look really smart,' she said, as Etty tried it on. 'Jim'll think he's marrying Princess Elizabeth.'

'I hope not,' Phyl remarked. 'She's only seventeen.'

'What about flowers?' Kaye asked. 'There's nothing about this time of year, only snowdrops.'

'I like snowdrops,' Etty said. 'I'll carry a bunch of them. We can pick them in the morning.'

'And afterwards we'll go down to the Chimney Corner for a drink,' Phyl declared. 'It doesn't seem much of a celebration—'

'It'll be enough for Jim and me,' Etty said quickly. She slipped out of the blouse and skirt and hung them on her rail. 'All I'm hoping is that he'll get the leave.'

Mr Carter was to give her away. He had always taken a special interest in her and when Etty, after much urging from the other girls, dared at last to ask him, he said he'd be delighted to accept. Etty was almost as overwhelmed at the idea of walking up the aisle on his arm as she was by the thought of getting married to Jim at last. She went into the big abbey church with Phyl and they gazed in awe along the nave towards the altar. Etty looked at Phyl.

215

'I never thought I'd get married in a church like this. As a matter of fact, I never really thought I'd get married at all, not till I met Jim.'

'Why ever not? All girls think about getting married.'

'Well, I never thought anyone would want me,' Etty said, as if it were obvious, and Phyl looked at her and remembered the thin, pale, timid little mouse that Etty had been when she first knew her. She'd jumped and looked panic-stricken if anyone so much as spoke to her, and even after she'd become a Nippy she was still tongue-tied with boys. Phyl thought of the time she and the other girls had more or less frog-marched Etty along on a date with that friend of Mike's and Tommy's – Charlie, that was his name – who was even shyer than Etty, and how the two of them had sat as stiff as ramrods and never uttered a word all evening. And yet after that they'd taken to going around together for a while, although nobody could ever make out whether they actually got around to speaking.

I wonder where Charlie is now, she thought.

She wondered too if it felt odd to Etty to be getting married in a church. Etty's mother had been Jewish, but Phyl knew that Etty had been brought up in a children's home, where she would have had to go to church like all the other children. And nobody knew what her father had been – or even if he'd had any religion at all.

They went out of the church and walked back to the site. As they went through the gates, an ambulance came out, and they turned to watch it speed down the road.

'It's going to Bedford,' Phyl said. 'Must be serious if they can't treat whoever it is in our own hospital. I hope nobody's been hurt.'

'We'd have heard if there'd been an explosion,' Etty said. Despite all the precautions, there were sometimes accidents and only a few weeks earlier someone had been killed in one of the sheds when a shell had burst. But there didn't seem to be any panic, nobody was running about with fire extinguishers or water-pumps, and it wasn't until they reached their hostel that they discovered what had happened.

'It's Mr Carter! He's been taken ill – a heart attack, they think. He's gone to hospital.'

'We saw the ambulance,' Phyl said, horrified. 'Oh, poor Mr Carter. Will he be all right?'

'He's not going to die, is he?' Etty whispered, sitting down on her bed. Her face was white and her eyes huge. 'Oh, Phyl, he was going to give me away!'

Phyl moved quickly to put her arm around the slender shoulders. 'He'll get better. I'm sure he will.' But she sounded unconvinced, and Etty turned sharply.

'How can you know that? We didn't even know he was ill till a minute ago. How can we find out?' She stared at the other girls. 'How did it *happen*?'

'He just collapsed. It was in the canteen. He'd collected his dinner and he was just taking it to a table when he just sort of staggered and fell over. The stew went everywhere,' Jenny said. 'You never saw such a mess.'

'Oh, who cares about the mess? It's Mr Carter I'm thinking about. He's always been so good to us. He's looked after us. Even when Nobby Clark's been down on us, we always knew Mr Carter would be on our side.' Etty shrugged away Phyl's arm and got up. She paced agitatedly around the room. 'How can I get married, with him lying at death's door?'

The others looked at each other in consternation. 'Etty, don't talk daft! Of course you can still get married. Someone else can give you away – one of the chaps'd do it. Jack Bryant, he'd do it, or Mr Arnold. You can't put off your wedding because of this.'

'I don't *want* Jack Bryant or Mr Arnold,' Etty snapped. 'I want Mr Carter. It won't be the same without him. And anyway, I'd be worried about him all the time. It'd seem so callous, just going ahead as if nothing had happened, as if he didn't *matter*.'

'But he'd never want you to put off the wedding,' Kaye urged her. 'He'd want you to go ahead. And what about Jim? What are you going to say to him?'

'He'd understand.'

'I don't think he would,' Kaye said. 'I think he'd be really upset, and hurt, to think that Mr Carter mattered more than him.'

'It's not that. Mr Carter's *ill*—'

'And Jim might be going away any time,' Phyl pointed out. 'You don't know when you might see him again.' She paused. 'Think of poor Maggie, and Tom.'

Etty sat down again. She hunched her shoulders, then let them drop. 'I don't know *what* to do.'

'Get married,' Phyl said firmly. 'What difference do you think it's going to make to Mr Carter? He's not going to get better any quicker just because you don't get married. In fact, it'll make him miserable when he finds out, and my mum always says that being miserable makes illnesses worse. You don't want to make him worse, do you?'

'No, of course not.'

'Well, then.'

There was a long silence. Etty stared at the floor and the other girls stared at Etty. At last she looked up.

'All right. I can see it don't make sense to call the wedding off, and I don't want to hurt my Jim. But I'm not having anyone else give me away. Not one of the other chaps, I mean.' She looked at Phyl. 'Will you do it?'

'*Me?*' Phyl nearly fell off the bed. 'How can *I* do it? I'm not a man!'

'Well, I know that. But it doesn't have to be a man, does it? The priest just asks who's giving this woman, and all that. It's usually the bride's father but I haven't got a father, and there isn't anyone else. Please, Phyl. You've known me longer than anyone else. I wouldn't even be here if it wasn't for you. If you hadn't persuaded me to be a Nippy, I'd still be grilling bacon in the kitchens and I'd never have met Jim. So really it *ought* to be you. Please.'

Phyl looked at Etty's imploring face and sighed. 'I don't think the vicar'll agree . . .'

'Well, we can ask, can't we? Let's go round there now.

218

Let's go and see him. We've just got time before supper.' Etty was on her feet. 'And we can ask him to ring up the hospital, too, and ask how Mr Carter is. Come on.'

Phyl stared at her and then looked comically at the others. 'Our Etty's getting a proper little bossy-boots,' she said. 'I've never seen her like this before. I hope young Jim knows what he's getting – or he might be in for a surprise.'

The others laughed, but they were equally amazed. None of them had ever seen Etty take charge before. But as they hurried back through the huts and sheds of the munitions site, Phyl remembered the night when Etty had gone down into the bombed cellar and helped in the rescue of the family that had been trapped. She had never faltered then.

Most of the time, Etty was the quiet little mouse she'd always been. But just now and then – when it was needed – she showed a determination as strong as anyone's. And once she did that, it was impossible to go against her.

I hope this wedding goes through all right, Phyl thought with a tremor of premonition. I hope nothing happens to Jim. Etty deserves some happiness in her life. And if I can help her find it – even through giving her away at her wedding – then I'm going to blooming well do it.

The vicar said it would be quite all right for Phyl to give Etty away and the two girls came out of the vicarage and looked at each other. After all the rush and excitement, it seemed too flat just to go back to the hostel.

'Let's go to the hospital,' Etty suggested. 'Let's go and see Mr Carter.'

'They'll never let us! It'll just be family, and anyway it won't be visiting-time.'

'What family?' Etty asked. 'Mr Carter's never mentioned any family. His wife died ages ago and they never had any children. And he stopped here over Christmas, didn't he? I bet there's nobody but us. Come on.'

She was off again before Phyl could think of another argument. It was a walk of two or three miles to the middle of

Bedford and the hospital, and Etty marched along with her head up while Phyl scuttered close behind, panting to keep up with her. She had given up all hope of making Etty listen to her, and could only go along with her and hope to get her back to the site in time for their next shift at eleven o'clock.

'They won't let us in, you know,' she puffed. 'They're ever so strict in hospitals.'

Etty didn't even bother to answer and Phyl rolled her brown eyes and followed her.

They came to the hospital at last and Etty stormed through the big doors. The hallway seemed to be full of people bustling about – nurses in starched uniforms, visitors with anxious eyes and brown paper bags containing presents for their sick relatives. A few had managed to scratch together bunches of snowdrops or evergreen leaves, and one was carrying an orange as though it were a precious jewel.

Etty stopped, at a loss for the first time, and Phyl tugged at her sleeve. 'We don't even know what ward he's in.'

'We can ask, can't we?' Etty snapped, and stalked up to an angry-looking nurse carrying a sheaf of papers. 'We're looking for Mr Carter. He was brought in this afternoon with a – a heart attack. We want to visit him. Please,' she added, her voice wobbling.

The nurse gave her an incredulous glance. 'You can't just march in here and start demanding to see people. Sit over there and wait.'

'But we want to know how he is,' Etty said. 'Isn't there anyone who can tell us?'

'Possibly, but you'll have to wait just the same. There are other people here as well as you, you know.'

'Come on,' Phyl murmured, and Etty allowed herself to be led over to a space on one of the crowded benches. The girls sat down and stared around them. Etty fidgeted impatiently.

'How long d'you think we'll have to wait?'

'I don't know. They seem pretty busy.'

'All I want to do is *see* him for a minute.'

'They won't let you,' Phyl repeated patiently. 'They only

let the family in for things like heart attacks. I'm sure that's what I've heard.'

Etty turned and looked at her. Her sallow skin was flushed and her brown eyes sparkled. She got up and walked over to the nurse, who was sitting at a table and writing things on her papers.

'I need to see Mr Carter,' she said clearly. 'He was brought in this afternoon with a heart attack. I'm his *daughter*,' she added emphatically. 'He'll *want* to see me.'

The nurse looked up at her. 'His daughter? Then why didn't you say so?'

Because she didn't think of it till now, Phyl thought, watching with dismay and admiration. She saw the nurse run her finger down a list and then glance up at Etty again.

'Your father's in Ward 10. You'd better go straight there. I can't promise they'll let you in, mind.'

She pointed the way and Etty set off again, with Phyl once more in hot pursuit. They walked rapidly through the maze of corridors, swerving to avoid trolleys with patients on them, almost colliding with doctors and nurses who frowned and made gestures to slow them down. But nothing would slow Etty down. She strode along, ignoring everyone else. She seemed to have grown taller, Phyl thought, taller and stronger.

'Why did you tell the nurse you were his daughter? They'll find out you're not, you know.'

'So what? They can't do anything to me. So long as I can see him first, it doesn't matter.' They came to a crossing of the corridors and she paused, looking for the sign to Ward 10. 'Phyl, you know what Mr Carter's been like all these years. 'Specially since we came to Elstow. He's treated us *all* like daughters – not just me. We can't leave him here all by himself.'

She was off again. Phyl followed, thinking about what she had said. She was right. Since coming to Elstow, Mr Carter had been like a father to them all. He'd chosen the ones who were to come to Elstow and he'd looked after them. He'd made sure they understood their work, that they were safe amidst the danger of high explosives. He'd listened to their troubles, he'd helped them when they had problems at home and needed leave, he'd stood up for them against the bullying of Nobby Clark. And he'd offered to give Etty away at her wedding.

Etty was right. They were *all* like daughters to him, and they couldn't leave him here alone when he was ill.

Ward 10 was tucked away from the main part of the hospital. Its double doors were closed and they had to peer through the round windows set in the panels. In the row of beds down each side of the long room, they couldn't make out one patient from another. Before Etty could push the door open, a nurse came out of the tiny office beside them.

'Only family visitors are allowed to see patients in this ward.'

'We know,' Etty said. 'We are family. We've come to see Mr Carter.'

'Mr Bernard Carter? He was admitted this afternoon. He's not very well. I'm not sure . . .' The nurse looked at them doubtfully. 'Are you close family?'

'We're his daughters,' Etty said, and then, seeing the nurse's sceptical glance move from her to Phyl and realising that nobody would believe they were sisters, added hastily, 'Well, *I'm* his daughter and this is my cousin, but she's like a daughter to him really, she—'

'Sorry. Immediate family only, I'm afraid.' The nurse held open the door, indicating that only Etty would be permitted to pass through. 'You can have five minutes.'

Etty gave Phyl a glance that was full of apology and followed the nurse into the ward. The door swung shut behind them.

Phyl watched them through the window. She saw them go to a bed that was curtained off from the rest of the ward. The nurse parted the curtains and they disappeared.

Phyl found a chair and sat down. Her legs were shaking.

She wanted to cry, and she wanted to hold back the tears. She locked her hands tightly in her lap and stared at the floor.

Mr Carter had been like a father to them all, and now he was in the hospital, locked away from all except Etty who had been brave enough to lie for him.

She knew that Etty would not leave after only five minutes, and she knew that she would not leave until Etty came out.

'I don't care if you're marrying the King of England,' Nobby Clark said. His face was red with fury, his small eyes mean and piggy. 'You was late for your shift last night and that means you got to make up the time. Both of you. And with that boss of yours off sick, that means there's a lot to catch up on and you can't have the time off.'

Etty and Phyl stared at him.

'But you've *got* to let her have the time off,' Phyl said, her voice shaking. 'She's getting *married*. It's all arranged.'

'So it can be blooming well *un*arranged,' he said. 'There's work of national importance to be done here. That comes first.'

'I'll work all next weekend,' Etty pleaded. 'I'll make up the time then, I promise. *Please*, Mr Clark.'

He gave her a look of disfavour. 'Oh, so it's *Mr* Clark now, is it? And *please*. Lick your boots, Mr Clark. Yes, sir, no, sir, three bags full, *Mr Clark*. Well, it's a pity you never thought to be so polite beforehand, when you didn't want nothing, that's all. And now you'd better stop all this jabbering and get on with some work, because that's what we're here for, *just* in case you've forgotten.'

He turned and stalked away along the production line. Phyl and Etty stared after him, and then looked at each other in dismay.

'He really means it,' Etty whispered. 'He's not going to let me have the time. Phyl, what am I going to do?'

'Well, to start with we'd better get on with our work,' Phyl muttered. 'He's looking this way. It won't help if we make him any angrier.'

Etty bent to her work, but her hands were shaking. She couldn't believe that even Nobby Clark could be so vindictive as to refuse her the time to get married. Not just because she'd gone to see Mr Carter in hospital.

She'd stayed an hour. The nurse had poked her head round the curtains and told her to go after the first ten minutes and then had not appeared again. Etty had sat beside Mr Carter, watching him and holding his hand. He didn't seem to be having any treatment. He was just lying there, looking faintly blue about the lips and on the eyelids, breathing heavily. His face was white, as white as the pillowslip on which his head rested. His grey hair was brushed back from his pale forehead and he was dressed in a white hospital gown. He seemed almost invisible.

Etty sat without moving, his fingers held lightly in hers. Her eyes were fixed on his face. At last, after a long time, she saw the minutest flicker of the shadowed eyelids. She leant forwards and spoke in a whisper.

'Mr Carter. Mr Carter, it's me, Etty. I'm here. I'm with you.' A tiny frown creased the white brow and she drew in a quick breath. 'You're in hospital,' she murmured steadily. 'You're going to be all right. I'm going to make sure you're all right. Mr Carter, it's Etty. Can you hear me? Do you know I'm here?'

There was a long pause. Mr Carter seemed to sigh and his head rolled slightly away from her. Fear gripped Etty's heart and she held her breath. Then she felt his fingers move, very slightly, in her hand and her heart seemed to kickstart into action again.

'Mr Carter. You're going to be all right. You've got to be all right. Please, Mr Carter. For me. For Etty.'

The curtains parted and the nurse looked in again, with a tall, white-coated man close behind. She stared at Etty and came quickly forward, pulling Etty's hand away from Mr Carter's. 'You're still here,' she said accusingly. 'I told you to go an hour ago—'

'He's going to be all right,' Etty said, ignoring her. She

looked past the woman at the man behind. 'Are you the doctor? He's squeezed my hand. He knows I'm here, he heard me.'

The nurse looked at her disbelievingly and took her watch from its breast-pin to check Mr Carter's pulse. There was a brief silence while she counted, and then she turned to the doctor. 'He does seem to have picked up.'

The doctor had tired eyes and a day-old stubble. He put his stethoscope to Mr Carter's chest. Etty, standing back to give him room, watched anxiously and saw him straighten up and look first at the nurse and then at her.

'He does. I'm surprised – I didn't think he would.' He glanced again at Etty. 'You're his daughter, I believe?'

Etty nodded. 'Well – sort of. Not exactly. More like adopted.' She felt herself blush at the lie.

He nodded and she realised that he wasn't really interested. He had a hundred patients to see, and none of them mattered either more or less than the others. Mr Carter had 'picked up' and he was pleased, in a professional way. Who Etty was didn't matter one jot. He simply didn't have either the time or the energy to care.

'Your father will be all right,' he said to her, preparing already to move on. 'He'll take a day or two to recover from this and then a couple of weeks to get his strength back. It wasn't a serious attack. He'll be back at home with you before you've had time to miss him.'

Etty nodded, her eyes full of tears. As he went out through the curtains, she moved closer to the bed again and took Mr Carter's hand in hers.

'Did you hear that?' she whispered. 'You're going to get better. You're going to be *all right.*'

When the nurse came back and told her to go, she made no objection. She gathered herself together and walked quietly down the ward and through the doors to Phyl.

It was no wonder that they'd been late for their shift, and

they'd been prepared for Nobby's wrath. But they'd never expected that he would go so far as to stop their weekend leave.

Chapter Eighteen

'It's not true!' Maggie stared at the letter she'd just ripped open and then looked up at her mother. 'I don't believe it. They *can't* do that!'

'Do what? Who?' Ivy looked at Maggie in alarm. Her daughter's face had flushed bright red and her eyes were snapping with anger. 'What on earth's the matter, our Mag?'

'It's Jim.' Maggie slapped the letter down on the table and flattened it with her hand. 'They've only stopped him and Etty from getting married, that's all!'

'Stopped him getting married? Why? What you talking about?' Ivy snatched the letter up and read it for herself while Ginnie and Billy stared, wide-eyed, and Barry started to thump with his fist on the breakfast table. 'But they can't do that . . .' she repeated, disbelievingly. 'Nobody could be that cruel.'

'Looks like Lyons can,' Maggie said bitterly. 'And I always thought they looked after their girls. Things've changed, Mum, since Etty went over to Bedford to work in that army camp. They just don't seem to care any more. She's worse off than if she was *in* the bleeding army.'

Ivy stared at the letter and turned it round in her hands, as if it would make more sense upside down. Then she shook her head.

'English wasn't never Jim's best subject at school. He just don't know how to explain things in writing. We'll have to wait to hear from Etty – maybe she can throw a bit of light on it.'

'Hasn't Etty got married, then?' Ginnie asked in a disappointed voice, and Maggie shook her head.

'Don't look like it. And there we was thinking about 'em all day Saturday, saying now Etty's getting dressed, now Phyl's doing her hair for her, now she's walking up the aisle, now they're coming out man and wife – and all the time, none of it was happening at all.'

'So what *was* happening?' Billy enquired, finishing the last crumb of his bread and Marmite. 'Couldn't Jim go as well? She couldn't get married without him, could she?'

'No, it's nothing like that. From what this letter says, it looks like Jim went just as they'd planned and then found out Etty wasn't allowed off the camp. I mean, I can't make no sense of it,' Maggie said, turning back to Ivy. 'It's not as if she's doing any special sort of work. She's only waiting at the bleeding table, for Gawd's sake. Why wouldn't they let her out?'

'Perhaps they think she's a spy, like that Irene,' Billy suggested, and squawked indignantly as Maggie aimed a clout at his ear. 'Well, I said *perhaps*.'

'Don't be so flaming daft,' his aunt told him. 'And get off to school or you'll be late and we'll get the teacher round here again, like last week when you never turned up at all. You, too, our Gin.'

'All right, all right.' Grumbling, the two found their coats and banged out of the kitchen. Maggie and her mother looked at each other again.

'It don't make sense,' Maggie repeated, and Ivy shook her head.

'It don't. You know, Maggie, sometimes I wonder about that place, I do really. There's a lot don't add up about it. Things Etty don't talk about, and the way she don't seem to have a proper address. I mean to say, a post office box number! It's as if there's something secret going on there.'

'You're not saying Billy's right and she's got into some sort of trouble? Bad trouble? I won't believe that, not ever.'

'No, I'm not saying that, course I'm not. I just think there's more to it than meets the eye, that's all. Well, that's war for you, I suppose.' Ivy looked at Jim's letter again. 'But I still don't see why she couldn't be let out for her own wedding.'

Jo, in Shropshire, had also received a letter, this time from Phyl.

You'll never believe what that miserable so-and-so Nobby Clark's done now. 'Only stopped poor Etty from getting married, that's all! And just because she stopped in hospital with Mr Carter and we got back late for our shift that night. It's not as if we're usually late, we're always on time and nobody works harder than Etty, but just because she wouldn't dance with him that time and just because she wouldn't let him kiss her and maul her about – well, he's just got it in for her, that's it and all about it, and if he hadn't had a proper excuse to keep her on overtime he'd have made one up. I don't reckon he ever meant to let her out to get married. And now poor Jim's gone back to camp without even setting eyes on her, and God knows when they'll get the chance again . . .

Jo read the letter in bewilderment. Phyl and Etty, kept in the camp because they'd stayed in hospital with Mr Carter? Why was Mr Carter in hospital in the first place? She searched the letter for clues, but there were none. And why was it so important that they were back on time for a shift at *night*? What meals did they have to serve then?

She wrote back at once, asking Phyl to explain, but the explanation, when it came, left her not much wiser. Mr Carter had had a heart attack but was recovering, so that was all right, but this other overseer, Nobby Clark, who didn't sound like any Lyons overseer Jo had ever come across, had insisted that they work all over the weekend without any time off at all. It didn't make any more sense to Jo than it had to Maggie, but after a moment or two she stopped wondering about it. The main thing was that Etty and Jim's wedding had had to be postponed, and it was a bloody shame.

'It's always happening,' Poppy said when Jo told her about it. 'People arranging weddings and the bloke having to go away the day before. Or straight from the church. Friend of mine said they went behind a haystack for half an hour, and that was their honeymoon! What's more, she got in the family way, too.'

'But it wasn't like that,' Jo said, frowning. 'It wasn't Jim who had to go away. And she's only a *waitress*, Pops. She's not doing anything vital.'

She still hadn't got over it next morning when she cycled up to the forest, early as usual. She was on her own, for Poppy had woken with a streaming cold and had almost fallen over when she'd tried to get dressed. Flu, Mrs Dell had said, and made her get back into bed. It had been going around all winter and it was a wonder the girls hadn't caught it before.

'You'll be next,' she told Jo, but Jo shook her head indignantly. She'd never had flu in her life, she said, and wasn't going to start now.

The days were lengthening and pale sunlight was already filtering down through the trees when she arrived at the clearing where they were working this week. She dropped her bike against a pile of logs and went to the store of firewood they kept built up near the circle of blackened earth and yesterday's ashes. Once she'd got the fire going and the can of water set to boil she would forage for more wood, to dry out until it was needed. She built a little pyramid of twigs, surrounded it with thicker sticks and then sheaves of bark, until it was strong enough to bear the weight of a few thin offcuts. Then she struck a match and poked it into the middle.

The kindling caught at once, and the bright flames crept up and spiralled from the tip of the pyramid. Jo sat back on her heels, watching with satisfaction. She had a pile of logs ready to hand for when the fire had really caught hold, and she waited, judging the exact moment for putting them on.

'Mind if I warm my hands a bit?'

Jo jumped. Josh Taylor stood a few yards away, watching her. He was wearing the usual uniform of brown breeches and green pullover, and his hands were in his pockets. She gazed up at him, too startled to think of anything to say for a few moments.

'You look very clean,' she managed at last. 'I mean, you're not covered in charcoal. Have they taken you off that?'

He grinned. 'Yes, thank God. And I'm glad I pass muster. I do try to bathe whenever I can.'

Jo blushed. 'I didn't mean – it was just that I was so surprised to see you there. I haven't seen you for ages.'

'No,' he said, coming a little closer, 'you haven't, have you? I rather gathered that was how you wanted it.' He held out his hands to the little blaze and cocked an eyebrow at her. 'D'you mind?'

Jo looked at his hands, then realised what he meant. 'Oh – no, of course not. It – it's cold this morning, isn't it?'

'But pleasant,' he said solemnly. 'And I think it'll be quite a fine day, don't you? Spring's on the way, the evenings are drawing out.'

'You're making fun of me,' Jo said.

'Not really. But we used not to have to be polite to each other, talk about the weather. We used to be able to talk properly.'

Jo stared at the fire and said nothing.

'What went wrong?' he asked gently. 'What stopped us being friends?'

'Nothing. I just . . .' She cast about for something to distract her and picked up a log to throw on the fire. 'Josh, I'm a married woman, I can't—'

'I'm not asking you to do anything you shouldn't,' he said. 'Just go on being friends, that's all. And you'll put the fire out if you put that great thing on.'

Jo put the log down. She stared helplessly at the flames.

231

'It's not what you're asking me to do. It's – oh, I can't explain, I don't want to talk about it. It's just not so easy as you think. And it's too late for us to be friends now.'

He looked at her. 'Why?'

'Because it is, that's all.' She threw the log on anyway and it obliterated the fire she had so carefully built up. 'Oh, damn!'

Josh pulled the log off and raked the embers together. Swiftly, he built another pyramid of twigs over the glowing sticks and they caught again. In a few minutes, the fire was burning as merrily as before, and he sat back and smiled at her.

'Just shows that the flame can be rekindled, even when you think it's gone out,' he remarked cheerfully.

'Very clever,' Jo said. 'But there has to be something left to burn.'

'And isn't there?'

Jo looked at him. His eyes were slate-grey, touched with green from the shadows of the trees around them. His mouth was firm, his brows straight. He looked calm and reliable and strong.

She thought of Nick's restless energy, his volatile temper. The unpredictable swings from laughter to tears. The scars that seemed to have gone deeper than his skin.

'You didn't have to make that fire burn again,' she said quietly. 'You could have just let it go out.'

'Would it have been better that way?'

'It might.' She stood up. 'In any case, it's your fire now. You can look after it and boil the water for tea. I've got some work to do.'

She walked away from him, along the track and between the trees to where she and Poppy had been working the day before. There was a pile of pit-props waiting to be loaded on to a cart. Jo began to heave them up in her arms.

What a muddle it all is, she thought. Poor old Etty and Jim, not able to get married after all. Phyl, always waiting for news of Mike. And me and Nick . . . well, that's the biggest muddle of all. And what wouldn't I give for a friend, someone I could talk to about it all. But Phyl's the only one, and she's hundreds of miles away.

You could talk to Josh, whispered a small voice inside her mind. But Jo shook her head and brushed at her hair as if swatting away a fly, and would not listen.

Etty couldn't believe it had happened. She'd worked the first part of the shift in a blur of tears and had her work passed back several times by Phyl to be done again. It was a wonder, she thought miserably, that she hadn't blown them all to kingdom come, and she pulled herself together with an effort and made up her mind to keep her mind on her work. But it wasn't easy, not when you knew you were going to miss your own wedding . . .

'He's not going to do it, is he?' she asked Phyl when they were finally released for a short tea-break. 'He doesn't really mean it.'

'Well, you can only ask him,' Phyl said, but they'd both seen the look in Nobby's eyes as he'd passed near them on his rounds. Here was his chance to get back at them for all the times they'd laughed at him behind his back, all the times they'd pushed away his roving hands or twisted away from his slobbering lips. It wasn't fair that a man could make girls' lives a misery like that, just because he was their boss, but there was nothing you could do about it. That was the way things were.

Etty plucked up all her courage and approached him as they came off shift. 'Please, Mr Clark, I'm ever so sorry I was late. You will let me have my weekend off, won't you? I did tell you it was my wedding.'

''S right, you did.' He stared at her sourly. 'What 'm I supposed to do, offer to give yer away?'

'Mr Carter was going to do that,' Etty said. 'He can't now, but Phyl can – we've been to the vicar and asked, and he said it would be all right. So—'

'Look,' Nobby Clark said, 'I don't give a bleeding tinker's cuss who gives yer away. Fact is, *nobody's* going to give yer

233

away, because there ain't going to be no wedding. See? Got it?'

Etty trembled at the look on his face and the nasty, sneering tone in his voice, but she stood her ground. 'You can't stop me, Mr Clark. Mr Carter gave me the weekend off. He told me—'

'And now he's not here. *I'm* in charge. And I say you can't. There's too much to do.' He made to turn away but Etty caught at his sleeve.

'*Please!*' Her voice was desperate. 'This might be the only chance we'll get. Jim'll be going away again soon. I might not see him for months – years, even. Please, Mr Clark, we've just *got* to be able to get married this weekend!'

He turned and stared at her, and a thin smile lifted on the corner of his lip. '*Got* to? Like that, is it? Bun in the oven, eh?' His glance shifted down to her slim waist. 'Well, who'd have thought it, eh? Little Miss Butter-wouldn't-melt-in-'er-mouth herself, expecting the patter of tiny feet. Not too sweet and innocent for a roll in the hay after all? No wonder yer in such a rush to get to the altar!'

Etty took in a deep, gasping breath. Then she swung her open hand at his face and cracked a slap across his cheek that sounded right through the workshop. There was a sudden silence as everyone near them stopped working and turned to stare. Nobby Clark put a hand up to his cheek and rubbed it, looking at his fingers as if he expected them to be stained with blood. Then he grabbed Etty's shoulder and jerked her close to him.

'That's it!' he hissed viciously. 'That's bloody *it*! Striking a superior – that's worth a couple of weeks in solitary. Don't forget this is an army camp and we works to army rules, even you stuck-up Lyons hussies. I'm going to see they throws the *book* at you, Etty Brown, the whole flaming bloody *book*. Your feet just ain't going to touch the ground!'

'Leave her alone!' Phyl had paused to talk to Kaye and came running as soon as she heard the slap. 'Leave her alone, you bully. She's getting married tomorrow. You can't report her just for a silly little slap.'

'And would it have bin a silly little slap if it'd bin me hit one of you?' he demanded. 'You lot are always on about bein' equal, ain't yer? Well, let's see how you like being equal now. I'm taking her to the boss and you might as well cancel the flowers and the choir tomorrow, because there *ain't going to be no wedding*. See? No wedding at all.'

He marched Etty away, while Phyl and the others watched helplessly. They knew that it was no use protesting. Everyone had seen and heard the slap, and Etty herself wouldn't deny it. Nobby was right.

There wouldn't be any wedding.

'He'll never forgive me,' Etty wept.

'Of course he will.' Phyl sat on the bed, stroking her hair. Etty hadn't been put into solitary for two weeks, but she'd been gated for that time, and wasn't allowed out of the camp. Nobody liked Nobby Clark much, but that didn't mean girls could get away with hitting him. If they did, the chief supervisor had said without a flicker of a smile, everyone would be doing it.

'How can he? We were supposed to be getting *married*. Instead of that, he's been dragged all this way for nothing, and he'll have to go back to camp and tell the others. They'll think I stood him up. They'll think I jilted him at the altar!'

'They won't. Anyway, what does it matter? Jim knows.'

'He'll never forgive me for being so stupid,' Etty wept.

The other girls looked at each other in despair. They'd all been in tears over Etty's cancelled wedding, and when they'd come into the room and seen the skirt and blouse that had been meant as her wedding dress hanging on the rail, they'd started crying all over again. Jenny rushed to hang the clothes in the cupboard, squeezing them in amongst the few garments already in there, and slammed the door on them just before Etty came in, red-eyed and sobbing. Now she'd

235

been lying on the bed, crying, for so long that they were afraid she'd make herself ill.

'You've got to stop crying, Et,' Phyl said gently. 'Look, why don't you write to Jim? Explain why it happened. He doesn't know anything, except that the wedding's cancelled because you're being disciplined. If you write now and we post it first thing tomorrow, he'll get it as soon as he gets back to camp. Then he'll understand.'

'But what can I say? It all sounds so stupid.'

'That's just because Nobby Clark's stupid. And spiteful. He's a nasty bit of work, Etty, and it was bad luck you had to cross him. But it wasn't your fault.'

'I told lies,' Etty sobbed. 'It's my punishment for telling lies.'

Phyl, Kaye and Jenny looked at each other. 'What lies?'

'I said I was Mr Carter's d-daughter. I said he'd adopted me. Now I'm being punished for it. They told us at the Home, you always get punished for telling lies.'

'Listen,' Phyl said, taking her by the shoulders and lifting her up, 'that was a white lie. And if you hadn't told it, they wouldn't have let you stop there with him and he *might not have got better*. D'you hear me, Etty? If you hadn't said that, Mr Carter might have *died*. It was a good lie, and I'm glad you told it.'

'But it's stopped me and Jim getting married.'

'Oh, for heaven's sake! Of course it hasn't! I don't know what else they told you in that Home, but I don't believe it works that way. I really don't.'

'You don't believe people get punished for doing wrong?' Etty said doubtfully. She sniffed and rubbed her red nose with a grubby hanky.

'Yes – no. Well, I suppose so, in a way. My mum used to say that if you did wrong you'd get your comeuppance, so I suppose that means the same thing. But what you said about Mr Carter – honestly, Etty, that wasn't doing wrong. It wasn't going to hurt anyone. It did good. You know it did. He was glad you were there. It helped him get better. He *is* getting better, you know. He'll be out of hospital next week.' A fresh thought struck her. 'And do you know what – when Jim gets leave again, you'll be able to get married then and Mr Carter'll be able to give you away after all. So everything will be all right. Won't it?'

Etty gazed at her. She blew her nose again and gave a wobbly little smile. The tears had, the others were thankful to see, stopped falling.

'I suppose so,' she said. 'If Jim manages to get leave again. If Nobby Clark doesn't do something else to stop it.'

'He won't,' Phyl said grimly. 'I tell you what, Etty, he won't – not even if I have to tie him to a blockbuster to keep him quiet!'

For Jim, the shock of being unable to marry Etty had almost driven him out of his mind.

He'd arrived at the gates of the munition site as arranged, and stood for a few minutes, wondering where Etty was and expecting her to come running along the road at any minute, breathless and apologetic. He'd even started to rehearse in his mind what he'd say to her: 'I know it's the bride's privilege to be late, but you don't have to practise already!' Or: 'Well, you were lucky to catch me – I was just going to run off with that pretty girl who came through a few minutes ago.' But when twenty minutes went by, and then half an hour, he'd started to get worried.

The sentry was eyeing him a bit strange, too. You weren't supposed to hang around military establishments, and even though Jim was in uniform, he knew he could still be challenged. He glanced at his watch, the one Etty had given him for his twenty-first birthday present, and made up his mind. Etty wouldn't have kept him waiting like this, not deliberately. He strode across the road.

The sentry snapped to guard position and Jim gave him a salute. 'Who goes there?'

'All right, mate,' Jim said. 'No need to get your rag out. I'm waiting for me girl. She was meant to be meeting me here at half three.'

'Oh? What's her name, then?' The soldier looked pugnacious. He'd dreamt of being able to arrest a loiterer and this soldier ought to know better than to hang about like this.

'Etty Brown. Look, it's all above board, we're getting spliced in the morning, see? Is there any way you can get a message to her? She's not usually late.'

'Etty Brown?' The guard narrowed his eyes. 'That her proper name?'

'Well, of course it is,' Jim said, bewildered. 'Well, her proper name's Esther, but nobody ever calls her that. Why, has something—?'

'Oh, *her*.' The sentry grinned. 'Coo, yes.' He looked suddenly more human. 'It's all over the camp about her. Poked the overseer in the eye, didn't she? Broke his nose, that's what I heard. Blood all over the shop.' He shook his head, still grinning. 'Reckon you might as well call your wedding off, mate, she's on jankers!'

'She's *what*?' Jim stared at him in disbelief. His head felt as if it had started to spin and there was a roaring in his ears like a Sten gun going off. A feeling of hot, savage fury threatened to overwhelm him. 'Look, if this is your idea of a joke—'

'"T ain't me that's joking, mate, and you needn't put your fists up to me neither.' The sentry's rifle came up to his shoulder as if it were on elastic. 'You'll be on jankers with her if you ain't careful.'

'But *why*?' Jim took a step back and lowered his fists, staring at them, bemused. He hadn't even realised he'd raised them. 'My Etty's as meek and mild as a little lamb. She wouldn't never hit no one.'

'Well, she hit this bloke,' the sentry said with some satisfaction. 'Mind, he had it coming to him by all acounts. Proper nasty little squirt, he is. First he kept pawing her and laying in wait for her, and then when she wasn't having none of it he—'

'He *what*?' All Jim's fury returned. 'He was messing about

with my Etty? Who is he? What's his name? I'll *murder* the slimy little bastard, I will, straight.' He stepped up to the sentry again and clenched his fist under the man's nose. 'Look, mate, I ain't threatening *you* so you needn't get free with your popgun, but if you don't get my Etty brought down here straight away, I warn you, *someone's* going to get hurt. And it'll be whoever gets in my way, see, because I'm going to see her. I'm going to find out what this is all about, and I'm going to kill that bloody overseer, whoever he is, with my bare hands, and you can tell 'em I said so!'

The guard brought his rifle up and held it horizontally under Jim's chin. He pushed hard and suddenly, and Jim toppled backwards and tripped over his feet to collapse in a heap in the road. He swore and started to scamble up, but the sentry held his gun at Jim's neck and put one boot on his chest. He yelled over his shoulder and three other guards tumbled out of the guardhouse. Jim sank back, staring at them in sudden fear. From his own training, he knew that if he caused real trouble he could get shot, yet, even as he knew this, his blind fury threatened to overwhelm him again and he began to shout.

'Look, I only want to see me girl, that's all! I'm not some bloody fifth columnist. We're getting married tomorrow – it's all bin fixed up. You can't expect me to turn round and go back without even *seeing* her, without even knowing what's gone on.'

'Sorry, mate,' one of the new arrivals said, 'we ain't allowed to give out no details about personnel on the site. It's all Official Secret, see.'

'But that's daft! She's just a waitress, that's all. She's a Lyons Nippy – she ain't doing nothing secret.' He looked from one to the other. 'Let me get up, mates. I ain't going to do nothing. I didn't come here to pick a fight, for God's sake.'

'Thought you said you'd come to get married,' one of them said with a guffaw. 'Can't see much difference meself!'

Jim gave a bellow of rage and launched himself at the man, catching him round the knees and bringing him crashing to the ground. The soldier yelled with surprise and kicked out, and the other two immediately joined in, wrenching at Jim's arms and shoulders to pull him away. Rifles clattered and for a moment he feared he really was going to be shot, and then he found himself on his feet between two of the men, his arms held firmly behind his back, while the first sentry stood before him, glaring.

'Right, mate. You asked for it. It's the high jump for you, and no mistake. You'll be bashing spuds for the rest of your sweet little life, and by the time we've finished with you your girl won't even know you. Even your own *mother* won't know you.'

Jim breathed hard and jerked his head to get the hair out of his eyes. His cap had fallen off and there was a trickle of something warm and wet running down his forehead. 'Come on, mate. How would you feel if it was your girl?'

'Yeah, come on, Alfie,' one of the others said unexpectedly. 'Lofty overstepped the mark there, you know.'

Alfie hesitated. He looked at Jim. 'I'm going to send for one of the officers,' he said. 'You bin causing an affray, that's what you bin doing, and it needs someone in authority to deal with it. You can explain to him.'

Jim sighed and stood miserably between the other two. The one called Lofty had a tight, scorching hold on his wrist but the younger one had loosened his grip. He knew there was no point in trying to escape. He'd never get away, and it would only make things worse. He slumped a little and then remembered he was a soldier and had done nothing wrong, and lifted his head, squaring his shoulders defiantly. Until now he'd had a good record, and he wasn't going to stand here looking like some sort of criminal.

The officer who came seemed to know all about Etty. He had Jim brought into the guardhouse and confirmed what the soldier had said. No, Etty hadn't broken Mr Clark's nose, or blacked his eye, but she'd slapped his face and given him lip, and Mr Clark had complained and demanded that she be punished. Jim had to understand that the work being done here was of a highly sensitive nature and behaviour like that simply couldn't be tolerated. Mr Clark was within his rights, and Etty was to be detained on the site to make up her lost time, and that was all there was to it. Worse, she wouldn't be allowed off the site for a whole fortnight.

'A *fortnight*?' Jim echoed in despair. 'But we was supposed to be getting married *tomorrow*—'

'I'm sorry,' the officer said. 'There's a war on.'

I know there's a bloody war on, Jim said to himself. That's why I'm in the flaming army and Etty's here. But he dared not say it out loud. He stared at the officer, his misery etched deep on his face.

'Ain't there *nothing* we can do, sir? If I could just *see* her – just for a few minutes – so she could tell me herself what happened—'

'I'm sorry, that won't be possible.' The officer could see from Jim's face that if he let him catch even a glimpse of his sweetheart he'd go overboard entirely. 'Look, I'll send one of her friends down to have a word with you. She can tell you all about it. But I can't do any more, and I'd advise you to cause no more trouble.' His voice, which had been almost sympathetic, changed to a warning. 'You could be put on a charge yourself, and you know it.'

'Yes, sir,' Jim said miserably, and slumped on the bench between the two soldiers. 'It's all right, you can let go of me. I ain't going nowhere.'

They brought Phyl down to talk to him. Her eyes red with crying, she sat beside him and told him all that had happened. 'He's been making a real pest of himself, but it wasn't anything worse than that till Mr Carter was took bad. I mean, I know in a way she didn't ought to have done what she did, but he was being such a pig. She had to stay with Mr Carter – she thought he was going to die. Even the doctors thought that. She never thought Nobby Clark would be so spiteful.'

'He can't do it,' Jim said, still bewildered. 'He *can't* stop us getting married.'

But he could, and he had. As Phyl tried to explain, Nobby

Clark had only to say that Etty must work to make up her time, and there was no Mr Carter now to gainsay him. And in the end, seething and bitter, Jim had to give up and go back to his own camp.

The other men were as bewildered and angry as he when they heard what had happened. If that bastard ever dared come anywhere near one of them, they said . . . but they knew their threats were empty. Nobby was never likely to be seen at their camp. And Jim was given no time to brood. Training now was intensive, and everyone knew that something big was brewing.

As the officer had said, there was a war on, and the war had to come first – before everything else.

Chapter Nineteen

Phyl's hopes that she might be pregnant had been dashed within the month, and she hardly knew whether to be glad or sorry. It wouldn't have been easy, having a baby now – she'd have had to leave Elstow and go back to her mother, and it might have been a toddler before it saw its father – but she would have had something of Mike to look after and cherish, they would have had something to work for and something to look forward to. They would have been a family.

As it was, she was more or less back to being single again. Living on an ordnance depot, sharing a bedroom with three other girls, working on a factory bench – not so very different from the kind of work she'd done and hated after she'd left school, before she and Jo had got the idea of becoming Nippies – and spending her evenings darning stockings or going to the Chimney Corner or one of the dances that were held on Saturday nights in the big community hall on the site.

She hadn't gone to the dances at first, but the sound of the music floating across to the hostel, where she and Etty sat listening to the wireless and doing their everlasting mending or knitting, had finally drawn them. They'd looked at each other and sighed and admitted they needed a bit of fun. And it didn't have to mean anything. Half the girls there were already engaged, some married, and nobody batted an eyelid. Everyone needed to let their hair down once in a while.

They went to the dances and learnt the new dance crazes – the jitterbug, the jive, the boogie-woogie. Phyl loved dancing and was soon shrieking with delight as a brawny soldier swung her up over his shoulder, and even Etty forgot to be shy as she twisted and turned nimbly under her partner's arm. When a waltz or a quickstep was announced, the floor was crowded with men and girls dancing close in each other's arms, and Phyl felt guilty sometimes that she let her eyes close and imagined it was Mike whose body was so close to hers. But the dream was over as soon as she opened them again, and she told herself it was nice to feel a man's arms around you and let your body move to the music – but that was all there was to it. At the end of the evening, she'd be going back to the hostel with Etty, walking with linked arms through the blackout and ignoring the whispers and scuffling sounds that came from the dark spaces between the huts.

'They wouldn't mind, would they?' Etty asked wistfully. 'Jim and Mike – they wouldn't mind us going dancing?'

'No, they wouldn't mind.'

'It's fun,' Etty said. 'I enjoy it. But it makes me miss Jim even more. You know?'

'Yes,' Phyl said, pulling on her pyjamas. 'I know.' And she got into bed and lay there, staring at the pale square of the window and thinking about Mike.

It was even worse, somehow, now that she knew she wasn't going to have a baby. It was as if that Christmas leave had taken them a step further, and then the step hadn't been there. Suppose he doesn't come home again, she thought, feeling as if cold, bony fingers had fastened themselves about her heart. Suppose we never get another chance. He'll be gone, and there'll be nothing of him left. Nothing, for the rest of my life . . .

Etty, in the other bed, was awake, too, thinking about Jim.

Suppose he doesn't come home again. Suppose we can't ever be married. Even though we had those few times in the hayloft, it'll never be like it should be. I'll never have been his wife. It won't be me they send a telegram to, it'll be his mum. It won't be me they send his belongings back to . . .

They turned over, almost simultaneously, so that the other would not hear the sound of their tears.

Nobby Clark was awake, too.

He'd been to the dance that night as well. He'd managed to persuade one of the women to go with him, a new one who'd recently joined his team. She was one of the Irish women they'd been bringing over and she had red hair and hard blue eyes and a raucous laugh. She'd sized Nobby up straight away as someone who could make life on the production line unpleasant if he chose, and decided to keep on the best side of him. That didn't include going as far as Nobby wanted after the dance, but she'd given him enough to make him hope there might be more next time.

Nobby was in a state of part satisfaction and part frustration, and as so often happened he found his thoughts turning to Etty Brown.

Whey-faced little niminy-piminy, he thought, and Jewish at that. But there was something about her – some look in her eyes, a tilt to her chin – and the way she'd hit out at him a few weeks ago, well, it made him want to chuck her over his shoulder and carry her off to some dark spot and give her a good seeing-to. That'd wipe the frightened little smile off her face, really give her something to cry about. Seeing her bite back the tears when he'd told her she wasn't getting the leave she wanted to get married had been good, but not quite good enough. He wanted to see her really howl.

Watching her on the dance floor tonight, he'd felt his frustration burn inside him like a black, consuming flame. Little tart, letting her skirt fly out and showing her knickers for all to see! Made out she was so pure, yet she'd still dance with any bloke who asked her. And what else would she do, eh? What would she get up to afterwards, on the way back to that hostel?

Nobby turned over in bed. He didn't have to feel like this, just because of some sluttish little Jew and a red-haired Irish doxy who liked the idea of teasing him along. He could do something about it, and he would. And he'd teach them both a lesson.

The Irish girl would enjoy it, he thought. But Etty wouldn't.

The idea inflamed him even more.

The Battle of Berlin continued throughout February and March. The RAF losses were enormous – over a thousand bombers and their crews lost since November. Young men of eighteen and nineteen years old, many of them on their first operation, were shot down. On the last day of March, over five hundred aircrew died in a single raid on Nuremberg.

Jo listened to the news on the wireless and scoured the newspapers. Nick wrote to her, but his letters were intermittent and scrappy. She imagined him, tired to death, lying on his bed and beginning a letter, then falling asleep after the first few lines. She ached with anxiety and the only comfort she could find was in the forest, with the trees.

They had become her friends. She walked by herself amongst them, touching their rough trunks, looking up into their swaying crowns. She picked up fir cones and rubbed them in her hands, finding an odd satisfaction in their roughness. She sat on fallen logs and waited for birds and squirrels to forget she was there and come back to the clearing.

As the days grew longer, she cycled back after work, just to be there by herself with the trees.

She saw Josh quite often. He had come back to the felling gang and worked with the other men, chopping and sawing. He went down into the sawpits to work as 'underdog' – the least favourite job. He was accepted now, so long as he was prepared to take on this and other unpopular tasks, and he worked quietly and without complaint. He sat just a little apart as they drank the tea boiled on the fire and ate their sandwiches, but he wasn't ignored as he had been. Men talked to him from time to time and they didn't block his way as they had done on the bridge.

One evening at the beginning of April, he went to the forest to retrieve his lunchbox, and came upon Jo, sitting on a log and staring out over the valley.

She turned, startled, and Josh stopped. They looked at each other for a moment and he took a step back.

'Sorry. I didn't know you were here. I just came for this . . .' He picked up his tin box from behind a pile of sawn pit-props and then glanced at Jo again. 'Are you all right?'

'Why shouldn't I be?'

'No reason, I just – no, that's stupid, you've got every reason to be worried. With all this news from Berlin and your husband in the thick of it.' He looked more closely at her. 'You haven't had bad news, I hope?'

'No.'

'You've been crying,' he said.

'So what? Can't a girl cry when she's on her own and she doesn't know when she'll see her husband again? What's so wrong with that?'

'Nothing,' Josh said quietly, 'nothing at all.' He hesitated, then said, 'D'you mind if I sit here for a bit?'

'It's a free country. I was just going, anyway.'

'No.' He caught her arm. 'No, don't go. Stay here with me for a few minutes. Please, Jo. We don't have to talk. Just . . . sit together.'

Jo shrugged. 'If you want.' She knew she was being rude and ungracious, but she couldn't help it. The words just seemed to flow from the tumult inside her. She picked up a stick and poked at the ground with it.

Josh said nothing. He sat down beside her. Jo stared at the pine needles and a tear dropped from her eye and made a tiny damp patch amongst them. The patch spread and grew.

'What is it, Jo?' Josh asked at last.

She shook her head, but the gentleness of his tone was too much for her. A huge, harsh sob thrust its way up from her throat and hiccuped out of her mouth. She choked and put her hands up to her face and began to cry in earnest.

Josh placed his arm across her shoulders, and she turned

towards him and laid her streaming face against his collar. Her shoulders trembled and heaved, and he tightened his arm about her. With his other hand, he began to stroke her hair.

'Oh, Josh,' she wept at last. 'Oh, Josh. I'm sorry – I'm sorry.'

'It's all right. You cry if you want to. Don't say anything. Just let it out.' He went on stroking her hair, soothing her with gentle fingers. 'Just cry, Jo. Cry as long as you like. I'm here. I'm here . . .'

'I can't – it's not that – I don't want – oh, Josh, I've been so horrible to you. I don't know – oh, *Josh*.' Her words came jerkily, disjointedly, and she shook her head with frustration. 'I can't *say* it!'

'Then don't try. Not yet.' He went on stroking. 'There's time. There's plenty of time.'

The sobs were beginning to diminish, replaced by long, shuddering sighs. She lay against him, shivering, and he wrapped her more closely in his arms. At last she sniffed and fumbled in the pocket of her breeches for a hanky. She blew her nose and lifted her head to give him a faint, wobbly smile.

'I have, haven't I? Been horrible to you. All these months – not talking to you, not looking at you, going out of my way to avoid you. And I didn't even know why.'

'I thought it was because of Nick,' he said. 'And because of what I am.'

Jo shook her head. 'It wasn't that. We were friends after I knew about that.'

She paused, then said, 'It was because of me. Because of what I thought and – and felt. Because I was scared to be friends with you any more.'

'*Scared?*' He sounded surprised, even hurt. 'What did you think I was going to do, for heaven's sake?'

Jo's eyes fell. Somehow, she had expected him to understand.

'I wasn't scared of you, Josh. I was scared to be *friends* because – well, I suppose I didn't think I deserved a friend like you, and because Nick and me—' She stopped abruptly. 'Because Nick wouldn't have liked it.'

Josh looked at her narrowly. There had been a different note in her voice then, one that didn't ring true even if the words made sense. He said slowly, 'But that's not why you were crying.'

'No. I said it wasn't.'

There was a moment's silence. The light between the trees was turning a dusky brown as the sun dipped below the rim of the hill. The sky was a burnt orange, marbled with wafting mackerel clouds, and the trees stood etched sharply black against its flaming colour. Somewhere close by a red squirrel chattered.

'Do you want to tell me?' he asked eventually.

'I don't think I can tell anyone,' Jo said sadly. 'It's just the same old story, I suppose – the war. Making everything go wrong.' She lifted her head and looked around them, at the burning sky and the dark green trees, the fallen logs piled near by with their fresh-cut auburn edges. 'And at the same time – if it hadn't been for the war, I'd never have come to a place like this. I'd never have known what the country is really like, and the forest. I'd never have lived this sort of life.'

'You'd have gone on being a city girl.'

'I suppose so. Living in lodgings, working as a Nippy in the middle of London, till Nick and me got married, and then we'd still have stayed there. We'd never have thought of leaving London.' She smiled suddenly. 'D'you know, I always wanted to live in the country. I used to fancy working with horses or being a farmer's wife. I wanted to climb trees and fish and swim in ponds or lakes or the sea. I used to read books about it. There was this book that was my favourite – still is. It's called *Little Women*, and it's about these four sisters. One of them's called Jo, like me, and she's a tomboy. She goes skating and gets into trouble in all sorts of ways, and she . . .' Jo's voice faltered suddenly. 'She makes friends with this boy, Laurie, they're really good friends and I always thought she'd marry him.' She bit her lip and the tears began

249

to fall again. 'Only she doesn't. In another book, he gets married to her *sister*, a nasty, stuck-up, spiteful little prig called Amy, and Jo gets this old German professor instead. The book says she loves him and they're happy, but she couldn't have been, it's *Laurie* she ought to have married. I don't know why the author did that. It spoilt the whole thing.'

Josh watched her. There was a small frown between his brows as he tried to untangle her story. At last he said, 'Why does it matter so much to you, Jo?'

'It doesn't! I'm just telling you, that's all. It used to matter to me when I was a kid, but it doesn't now.' She paused and then said, 'You know what my name is now. It's Laurence. *Nick's* name is Laurence.'

'So it's all turned out happily after all,' he said, half-teasingly. 'Jo's got her Laurie, and they'll live happily ever after.'

'Yes,' she agreed dully, 'they will, won't they? Once the war's over, anyway.'

'It can't be so very long now,' he said comfortingly. 'We're almost at the end of the tunnel. We must be.'

They sat in silence for a while, staring into the gathering twilight and thinking of the war. The heavy losses suffered by Bomber Command. The fighting in the Far East, in the African desert, in Russia, all over Europe. It couldn't go on for ever.

Josh tightened his clasp on Jo's shoulder again momentarily, and then lifted her to her feet. He rested his cheek briefly against her hair.

'Come on. We'd better be making tracks back, or it'll be too dark to see our way.'

Side by side, they wheeled their bikes back to the forest edge. Then they mounted and freewheeled down the hill to the river and started the climb up the other side to the village.

At Mrs Dell's gate, Jo stopped and looked at him. It was almost completely dark now but she could see the shine of his eyes and the gleam of his teeth. She put out a hand and touched his sleeve.

'I really am sorry, Josh.'

'I told you – it doesn't matter.' He paused. 'Friends again?'

'Friends,' she said, and turned to go in through the gate.

Spring had come to the Welsh valleys and hills just as Jack had predicted, and brought both primroses and lambs. Shirley and Owen saw them when they climbed the mountain to visit their families. They stood and laughed at the antics of the tiny creatures, and Owen promised that they would pick a big bunch of primroses on the way down to cheer up their rooms.

'It's lovely now,' Shirley said, watching a little group of lambs playing king-of-the-castle on a hillock. 'It's lovely to be able to come up here after being down in the valley all week.' Shirley was working in the office at the pithead, doing the men's wages. She felt close to Owen there, seeing the men go down the mine at the beginning of their shifts and come up again at the end. It was as if by being there she could keep an eye on him and know that he was safe, even though by now she'd heard enough stories of pit disasters to know that you could never be absolutely sure that the men were safe.

'Pity those poor old ponies can't come, too,' Owen remarked. 'I'd like to bring old Taffy up here, see him roll in the grass. That's the first thing they do when they're brought above ground, roll on the ground and kick their legs in the air. You can see them really enjoying it.'

'Someone told me they go blind through being down in the pit all their lives,' Shirley said, but Owen shook his head.

'They don't have very good sight, mind, so maybe it does strain their eyes a bit, but they don't go blind. Anyway, they don't come up to enjoy the view. Just to feel the sun on their backs and a bit of real green grass in their bellies.'

They came to the farm and Jack came rushing to meet them. His button face was screwed up with excitement. 'Lambs! Seen the lambs?'

'Yes, we've seen them,' Shirley said, laughing. 'Lots and lots of them.'

He nodded importantly. 'Jack helped born 'em.'

'*Did* you? All of them?'

He looked slightly less certain, but nodded anyway. Then, because he had had it impressed upon him that he must always tell the truth, and he knew what truth was, he added reluctantly, 'Uncle Dafydd born some.'

Owen and Shirley laughed and opened the gate into the small garden. Alf was there, digging. He straightened up as they came in and his face creased in a smile.

'I bet you never thought you'd see me doing this. Beans and peas I'm going to plant here, and some early carrots. Go lovely with a nice leg of Welsh lamb.' He winked. 'Not that we'd be likely to get such a thing, up here on this mountain, miles away from the butcher, mind!'

'Dad, you're beginning to sound more Welsh than the Welsh,' Shirley teased. She regarded him. 'You know, you're looking ever so much better. I knew it would be good for you, being up here.'

'It's being with your mother. And Jack. And Dafydd and Mair, of course, and having you down in the village.' Alf looked around at the sloping green valley and the stark grey crags of the mountain. 'Took me a while to get used to all this, but I reckon it's not so bad.'

The door opened and Shirley's mother came out. She kissed them both and said, 'The tea's on. Make sure you take those muddy boots off before you come in here, now, Alf.' Leading Shirley indoors while Owen stayed outside to find his uncle, she lowered her voice and said, 'What d'you think, Shirl? Does he look all right?'

'All right? He's a king to what he was. Is he having any fits now, Mum?'

'One or two. But they're not bad ones. The last one was – let's see now – a week ago Thursday. He fell over in the yard, but Jack saw him and pushed a bit of rope in his mouth to stop him biting his tongue. He's a wonder, that boy. Still can't tie his own shoelaces but give him a sick animal and he can work miracles. Not that your dad's a sick animal, of course!'

Shirley laughed, then said, 'A week ago Thursday. That's a lot longer than he used to go, Mum. He'd have them two or three times a week when he was in London.'

'So you've told me – now. But you ought to have told me *then* how bad he was. I'd have had him up here months before, or else come back.'

'He wouldn't let me.' They'd been through this before and Shirley had tried to explain, but she still felt that her mother hadn't quite forgiven her. She went to kiss Owen's aunt, who was pouring boiling water into the big brown teapot. 'We've had a lovely walk up the mountain.'

'And seen all Jack's lambs?' The round face creased into a million tiny wrinkles, all caused, it seemed, by smiling. 'That boy's a wizard. But it does upset him when one dies. Breaks his little heart, it does.' She poured cups of tea. 'There, now. That'll keep you going till tea's ready.'

Shirley sat drinking the tea with her mother and the kindly Welshwoman. She looked around the comfortable, shabby kitchen with its dresser crammed with unmatching crockery and the big table with plates piled with freshly cooked Welsh cakes and home-baked bread. It was always warm in here, the range kept burning with sticks foraged from the woods down the mountain and coal from the pits. You only had to scratch the ground here to get coal, Dafydd said, yet in places the soil was fertile enough to grow heather, and grass for the sheep.

Shirley knew that the hill-farmers were poor; they scratched a bare living from their thin mountain soil and tough, goat-like sheep. But the farmhouse, shabby as it was, was comfortable and it was home. It was a place where you could be content.

That's all I want for me and Owen, she thought, and for Mum and Dad and Jack and our Donald, wherever he is – just to be content.

A few hours later, she and Owen made their way back down the mountain. It was a long walk back to the village, but the soft April air washed over their faces like a balm and there was time to pick the primroses Owen had promised. They arrived at their rooms just as it grew dark, and filled an old enamel jug with water to stand them in.

With the tingle of the air still on their faces, they washed and went to bed, and lay together gazing out through the uncurtained window at the stars. I shall never be happier than this, Shirley thought, not even when we're old and grey and have a big family and perhaps even grandchildren. I shall never be happier than I am at this moment.

By the next evening, she was wondering if she would ever be happy again. For soon after Owen had gone down the pit for his day's work, running with the horse Taffy to bring dram after dram of coal to the adit, there was an explosion somewhere underground and by the time the Bevin boys and the miners should have been coming home for their baths and their suppers, the terrified women were gathering instead at the pithead. And Shirley was amongst them.

Chapter Twenty

'They say the roof collapsed, down near the bottom of the drift,' someone said, and a groan went up from the women. The nearer the entrance the accident had occurred, the more men were likely to have been trapped. Already a few had been brought up, shaken and bruised but not much hurt, and they were telling their story so that the rescuers would understand the situation.

'I dunno what started it.' One of the Bevin boys, a Cockney lad of about nineteen, was standing in the midst of a crowd near Shirley. She edged closer to hear what he said. 'We was just sittin' down with our bait, see, and there was this queer rumblin' noise from somewhere over our heads. It was like thunder. I thought that was what it was at first, and then old Rhodri, he said you'd never hear thunder that deep underground and it must be a cave-in somewhere. And then everyone started standin' up and shoutin' and tryin' to get to the drift. We'd just made it when the roof started to fall in.' He shook his head and Shirley could see the fear in his eyes, showing white against the coal-dust that ingrained his skin. 'I thought I was a goner, I tell yer straight. I never bin so glad to see the bloody sky in all me life.'

'How many men were behind it? How many are trapped?'

He shook his head, shocked and bewildered. 'I dunno. I dunno how far back it goes.' He swayed and someone caught him, and then he was passed along to the back of the crowd and someone said they'd take him back to the hostel where some of the Bevin boys were living.

Everyone turned to watch the entrance again. When the collapse had happened, they'd seen a huge cloud of dust and debris billow out of the gaping hole. Shirley, hearing the sound of the collapse from the tiny office where she worked, had looked out of the window and seen it, like a great black miasma of death. Too appalled to move for a moment, she'd simply sat and stared, and then as others began to shout and move, she'd cried '*Owen!*' and had run from the room to join the crowd racing towards the pit. Fear had gripped her, turning every limb to water and her heart to a heavy, leaden lump, and her head had been filled with visions of Owen, far underground, trapped beyond a vast pile of rocks and rubble; of Owen, caught in the fall, crushed where nobody could reach him. Every story she had ever heard about mine disasters came rushing in upon her mind.

The word went round the village like wildfire. Many people had heard the rumbling of the fall and knew what it meant. Women of all ages, children, miners off shift – all came running. Those who were accustomed to working under-ground ran into the drift and began to hack and scrabble at the mound of debris, while everyone watched in terror that there might be further falls and the rescuers themselves lost.

Shirley stood with her hands pressed to her mouth, listening to the soft Welsh voices around her. Many of them spoke in their own language and she couldn't understand them, but a few used English, and when she heard what they were saying, she wished she didn't understand.

'My old grandad, he was caught down a mine, took both his legs off . . .'

'I lost my da' in Black Pit in '29 . . .'

'I remember standing right here on this very spot that time when twenty men were trapped for a week, and when they finally got them out only two were still alive. Drank mucky water dripping down the sides of the tunnel, that's what saved them.'

I can't stay here and listen to this, Shirley thought. I can't bear to think of Owen trapped down there, his legs crushed under a pile of rocks and coal. Or slowly starving to death, licking the walls to stay alive. I can't.

But neither could she move away. Like all the other women present, she was caught between the unbearable horror and her desperate need to be there, to know whatever there was to know, to be present when – if, no, *when*, it had to be *when* – Owen was brought out. She had to be there to hold him, to feel his body, to look into his eyes. She would not think that it could end in any other way.

The day wore on. The first survivors had been taken away, back to their homes where their womenfolk would look after them. The Bevin boys, who had no mothers or sisters or wives, had been taken to their hostel. In a day or two they would be expected to report for work again.

Nobody else had yet been brought out.

Above the village, the sky was a tender, April blue. Away in the clear air of the combes primroses were growing and birds and animals going unconcernedly about their ordinary lives. Nests were being built, eggs laid, rabbits giving birth in burrows. But in the deeper burrows of the coal-mine men were waiting, behind a fall of rock that extended nobody knew how far. In the depths of the earth, beneath the weight of the mountain, Owen was waiting.

Shirley could not leave.

'You ought to have something to eat, *cariad*,' the chief clerk told her, coming upon her in the crowd. 'Been here all day, you have. It won't do your man no good to have you wasting away like a shadow, look, now, will it?'

'I can't eat anything. I'm not hungry.'

'A cup of tea, then. Look, they're making tea over there and giving it out. Go and have something, or you'll be ill. You can keep an eye on things from there, you'll know the minute anything happens.'

Shirley hesitated. She had never known Mr Evans to be kind or sympathetic before, but this was a time in which rank was forgotten. They all had men down the mine, men they loved and were frightened for. He had a son, she remembered, who had elected to work in the mine rather than serve in the forces. Reserved occupation . . .

'Go on,' Mr Evans urged her, and reluctantly she turned away and went over to the benches where tea was being poured from a big urn and penny buns handed out for nothing.

The blue of the sky faded and the setting sun burnished it with scorching pink. It didn't seem right, Shirley thought, to have such a lovely sunset on a day like this. It didn't seem right that the birds and animals should go on as if nothing had happened. The sky should have been black and the songs of thrushes silenced. Even the primroses should have folded their petals in sympathy.

The tea tasted rank and the penny bun was like ashes. She forced it down and went back to her position, her eyes fixed on the entrance to the drift.

Night fell.

On the first of April, the entire coast from the Wash to Land's End was closed off.

Only the people who lived there were allowed to move about in the ten-mile-deep band. They had to carry their identity cards with them at all times, and could be sent to prison if they were stopped and couldn't produce them. They weren't allowed out of the area without a permit, and nobody else was allowed in, unless they were considered vital to the war effort.

Visiting football teams and entertainers were classed as being vital to the war effort – the Government was well aware of the value of such pleasures to the morale of a nation which had been suffering now for almost five years. But the marriage of one young soldier to a girl who had once been a Nippy wasn't so important.

'They've stopped all leave,' Etty told the other girls, reading Jim's latest letter. 'He's been moved down near Portsmouth and he says they're not allowed off the camp. He doesn't know when he's even going to be able to see me again.'

'Oh, Et, I am sorry.' Phyl sat down on the bed beside her friend. She had heard from Mike and he was on the South Coast, too. 'It looks as if something really big's going to happen.'

'It's the invasion,' Etty said dully. 'Mr Carter says they're planning to invade. They'll all be going over to France and Germany, and we'll never see them again.'

'Don't say that. We're going to win the war. That's what it's all about.'

'We might win,' Etty said. 'But that doesn't mean a lot of men aren't going to be killed first.' She stared at her letter again and then held it close to her breast. 'I know we can't stop it. I know we've just got to let it happen. But if only Jim and me could have been married first! It's as if we're not meant to be, and we *are*, I know we are.'

Phyl and the others gazed at her helplessly. They were all in much the same boat. Except for Jenny, whose sweetheart was on the ordnance site himself, they all had a man away and only last week Kaye had heard that her Ken was a prisoner of war somewhere in Germany.

'I'm sorry,' Etty sniffed. 'I'm being selfish. At least I know Jim's safe at the moment. It's stupid to make such a fuss about getting married.'

'No, it's not,' Phyl said gently. 'It's not stupid at all. And it's worse for you, because you ought to have been married by now, and you would have been if it hadn't been for that horrible Nobby Clark.'

'I'd like to get back at him somehow,' Kaye said. 'I'd really like to wipe that nasty smirk off his face for him.'

'Don't do anything,' Etty begged her. 'You know what he's like. He'll find something worse to do to you. Anyway, it's too late now. Jim's trapped down there in Portsmouth and I can't even go to him because it's all closed off.'

It was clear that something big was happening. People didn't talk about it much in case it got through to the wrong

259

ears, but the movement of troops and the closing of such a huge stretch of coastline made it obvious. And if the girls at Elstow had thought they'd worked hard before, they worked even harder now. Their free time was cut down as they toiled at the benches, filling bombs and shells by the thousand. The competition between the various production lines was stepped up, with results published each week and awards made to the best teams. The sight of a huge blockbuster being lowered into its pit or hauled up again was commonplace.

'Those things are being dropped on ordinary people now,' Etty said. 'It's awful to think of them. Old women and babies and children and people sick in hospital . . .'

'You can't think like that,' Phyl said soberly. 'It's war. It's happened to us as well.'

Mr Carter was back at work now. He'd come back about three weeks after his attack, looking rather pale and thin but determined to carry on with his work. He told Etty he remembered her being in the hospital with him.

'You brought me out of it. I'm only sorry it was through me your wedding was ruined. I hope you'll ask me to give you away when you manage to fix it again.'

Etty smiled shyly at him. He knew she'd told the nurses she was his daughter, and he'd said he wished she was. 'We never had children, my wife and I. She was an invalid after she lost our first baby and there was never another chance.' He smiled at Etty. 'Perhaps I could adopt you!'

After that, he'd taken a special interest in her, and Nobby Clark's jealousy had increased.

The overseer had become obsesssed with the little half-Jewish girl. His eyes followed her all the time in the factory and outside she would catch glimpses of him watching her as she walked to and fro with the other girls. On Valentine's Day she'd found a badly made card at her place on the bench, with a picture of a flower cut from a magazine and stuck on the front, and scrawled on the inside the rhyme that roses were red, violets were blue, sugar was sweet and so was she.

She'd glanced up to find Nobby's eyes burning on her face, and knew he'd put it there. With a swift, angry movement she'd crumpled it in her hand and thrown it to the floor, and when she'd next looked at him his face had been black with anger.

'Pity you did that,' Phyl had murmured. 'He's a bad man to cross, Etty.'

'Well, I crossed him weeks ago, so that makes no difference,' she said. 'And I wasn't going to blush and come over all sloppy.'

Phyl looked at her. 'You know, you've changed. You'd never have stood up for yourself a year or two ago the way you do now.'

'It's the war,' Etty said shortly. 'Everyone changes. We've got to.'

But there was nothing she could do about the news of Jim. Unless she could find some way of getting through the permit zone and reaching him, down in Portsmouth.

On the second morning of the pit disaster, the clouds gathered overhead and a drizzle began to fall.

The women were still there. Some of them had gone home at some point during the night to snatch a few hours' sleep. The pit managers had spoken to them through a megaphone and told them that everything possible was being done, and they should try to rest. They went reluctantly and were back as soon as dawn broke.

Shirley had trailed miserably back to the two little rooms and Mrs Davies had made her sit down and drink a cup of tea and eat some toast before going to bed. They didn't taste any better than the tea and bun she'd had at the pithead, but she forced down as much as she could and then, hardly able to stand for weariness, stumbled up the stairs. The lumpy bed seemed huge without Owen and she tried to find a comfortable position without his body to snuggle up against, but her dreams were filled with nightmare scenes of empty black spaces, and she woke several times thinking she was on the brink of falling. By six, she was wide awake again, and pulling on her clothes.

'There won't have been any news, look,' Mrs Davies said, appearing with the brown teapot in her hand. 'We'd have heard. You'd much better have something hot inside you before you go.'

'They might have got through. They might not have let people know. Owen could be out now – in hospital or – or . . .' Shirley took the cup of scalding tea and drank it as if it were lukewarm. 'No, I can't wait for anything else – I'll just take a piece of bread in my hand . . .' She snatched up a crust and ran, her footsteps clattering up the street.

Other women were doing the same. Some had stayed all night, but as Shirley and her companions drew near they could see from the grey, tired faces that nothing had happened. The men were still trapped and the efforts to free them were still going on.

'Who've you got down there, then, *cariad*?' a woman asked her. She wore a black scarf over her head and her face was lined.

'My husband. His father moved to London because he was too sick to work in the mine any more, but Owen was picked as a Bevin boy so we had to come back. He's a haulier, he works with the ponies.'

The woman nodded. 'Both my boys are down there. I begged them not to go away to sea, told them they'd be safer here as well as doing "work of national importance", as they call it. Now look. Both of them, trapped down there just like their da' was, twenty years ago when they were little. I ought to have known better.'

Her lilting voice was like a threnody of regret. Shirley looked at her with pity. Both her sons. And her husband, too, gone when they were small boys.

The light was growing and through the misty rain they could see the entrance to the mine. The steep track, with its rails for bringing out the drams, dipped sharply under the looming rock. All around were the other drifts and the

262

opencast mines, great raw slashes of black in the grey hillsides. The clank of machinery clattered in their ears, for the other mines had to go on working just the same. Shirley looked up, beyond the gritty heaps of slag, to the true mountain beyond, and thought of her mother and father up there on the farm, in a different world. Had the news reached them yet? she wondered. Did Uncle Dafydd and Auntie Mair know about their nephew, buried under thousands of tons of rock and coal?

Mr Evans came to look for her.

'I'm sorry, Mrs Prosser, you'll have to come back to the office. The wages have to be done, see. People need their money.'

Shirley looked at him blankly. The men were down the mine, trapped. How could they need money? Then she thought of those who weren't down there, the men working in the other drifts, the opencasts. The men who hadn't been on that shift or didn't work down in the mine. The women who had to feed their families.

'But what if they come out?'

'You'll be told straight away.' His face was kindly. He had seen these tragedies before. His own son was there. 'And you can see from the window of the office.'

Shirley nodded and turned reluctantly away. She went back to the chair she had left the day before and stared at the columns of figures she'd been adding up. They didn't make any sense. She picked up her pencil and started again and slowly she began to work out the wages earned that week by the men who worked for the mine.

Davies. Llewellyn. Jones. The familiar, traditional Welsh names. And then the others – the names of the Bevin boys, picked at random from all over the country and brought to work the coal instead of fight. Smith. Cook. Carpenter. Berryman. Men – young men, boys – whose families would not be at the pithead to see them brought up, who probably didn't even know what had happened.

Prosser.

Her pencil stopped abruptly. Owen's name. Owen's shift, his wages, waiting to be worked out.

Owen, somewhere down there beneath her feet.

Shirley felt a wave of despair engulf her. She dropped the pencil and put her head in her hands. The hope that had sustained her and kept the worst of the fears at bay was swept away by the black force of surging terror. She imagined him crushed, bleeding to death, dying of thirst, alone and bewildered in the solid darkness. And the air running out, choking him. And more rocks, falling all around.

'Mrs Prosser. Shirley.'

Slowly, Shirley lifted her head. For a moment, she could not think where she was. The image of the black cavern had been so powerful that she had almost believed herself to be there. She looked, bemused, at the tiny, familiar office with its ledgers and its bundles of paper stuck on to spikes or hanging from hooks, and then turned to see Mr Evans behind her.

'They've got through. They've started bringing men out.'

Shirley was on her feet and following him out of the office, running along the gritty track to the crowd of people waiting at the pithead. She pushed her way through. Owen. *Owen*.

Men were coming out of the adit. They were walking, staggering between their rescuers. They were black with filth, their heads drooping, their backs bent. They stumbled along, exhausted, blinking in the grey light. The women pressed forward, searching their faces, seeking recognition.

Shirley pressed forward with the rest. She knew she didn't need to look into Owen's face to recognise him. She would know him by his shape, by his movements, by the way he walked. She would know him by her own sense of familiarity and love.

The men passed her, each one claimed by a woman – his mother, his wife, his sweetheart. Then there was a pause.

Shirley looked round her wildly. 'Is that all? Where are the others? There must be more, there must be! Owen – my Owen – he's not come up yet. Where is he?'

'It'll be the stretcher cases next, love,' said an old man

standing near. 'And they might not have got through to them all yet, see.'

'Might not have got through . . . ? You mean there might still be some trapped down there?' Angry with disbelief, she stared into his face and he shrugged and looked away. 'But *Owen . . .*'

He wasn't the only one. She knew that. She watched as a few more badly injured men were brought out on stretchers, just as the old man had said, but she knew somehow that Owen wouldn't be among them. After a while the trickle ceased and she turned and trailed back to the office. Mr Evans was right. People needed their money and it seemed that beyond the men who had just come out there had been another fall. The rest were trapped behind that, but the men said they'd heard the sounds of movement, of picks being smashed against the rubble and rocks being dragged away. So they were alive, those others, and eventually they would be brought out. They must be.

Provided there wasn't another fall. Provided they were all still alive. Provided no more had been buried.

By dinnertime, Shirley had finished the wages. She came out again and stood with the knot of people still waiting. The crowd was smaller now; there were no more than twenty men still down the mine. The rain had increased and now fell in a steady, monotonous downpour. The women's scarves were soaked and clung to their hair, and their faces were streaming as if with tears, but they would not move. They waited, patiently, because they had no choice.

At two o'clock in the afternoon, just twenty-four hours after the collapse, a rickety old van drove on to the yard, and Shirley turned and gave a cry of thankfulness.

'Mum! Dad! Oh, and Uncle Dafydd. Oh, thank goodness you're here.'

'He's not been brought out yet?' Her mother was out of the van and hurrying towards her. 'They've not found Owen?'

Shirley shook her head. 'There are about twenty still down there. They'll get through to them soon. They can hear them.

They're making a hole, so they can talk to them and find out what it's like and if – if anyone's hurt bad. Where's our Jack?'

'We left him behind. He wouldn't have understood. Mair's looking after him.' Annie held Shirley in her arms. 'Oh, you poor love.'

'I feel better now I know they're nearly there. Yesterday was worse.' Shirley clung to her mother. 'It's been awful. Not knowing . . . And yesterday they brought out three men who'd been killed. Hit by rocks. Mum, if Owen . . .' She began to cry.

'I know, love, I know.' Annie patted her shoulder. She gazed over Shirley's head towards the adit. 'Look! They're bringing someone out now.'

Shirley tore herself from her mother's arms and ran towards the drift. Her hands making fists at her mouth, she watched as more men began to stumble from the cavern's mouth. They were as black and exhausted as those who had come out earlier, and they stumbled as if they were on the edge of survival.

'*Owen . . .*' she breathed.

He wasn't there. They were bringing stretchers now, bearing still figures covered in blankets. With a little choking cry, Shirley pushed past the watching people and ran closer.

Eighteen men out of the twenty had been brought out. There were only two more to come.

Shirley's teeth bit into her knuckles. She tasted blood, but didn't notice it. She stared, unable to take her eyes from the gaping mouth of the mine.

Three men came out together – two rescuers with a miner half carried between them. A woman cried out and ran to take him in her arms. He hung there as if he were half-dead and the rest of the watchers could hear her sobs.

Shirley's eyes were fixed on the mine. There was only one man to come. It must be Owen. She prayed that he would be walking, that he'd stayed till last to help the others, that he was at least alive.

'It's a stretcher,' someone near her muttered, and Shirley closed her eyes.

'Come on, *cariad*,' Uncle Dafydd murmured in her ear. 'Bear up, now. Let's go and say hello to our Owen.'

Hello? she thought, the fear like an icicle penetrating her heart. Or goodbye?

With Dafydd and her parents beside her, she walked forwards. The men bearing the stretcher paused as they came close. They stopped, and Shirley looked down at the bundle of blankets and the face that lay so still and white, the eyes turned up to the heavy sky, and the tears streamed down her face and mingled with the rain that swept down from the lowering clouds.

Owen . . .

Chapter Twenty-One

News of the mining disaster wasn't reported immediately in the newspapers or on the wireless. News like that rarely was, until a week or so later. It was like the weather – there were no forecasts any more, and you weren't told that snow had fallen up to your eyebrows until ten days later, when you had probably noticed it anyway.

So it was that none of Shirley's friends, in London, Bedford or Devon, knew what she was going through. As if there were nothing at all out of the way, they just went on with their ordinary lives.

'You're wasting your time, you know,' Maggie told Carl. She had tried to avoid him as much as possible but he wouldn't let go. If she swapped duties at the house, she'd find him in the cottage when she came home, having a cup of tea with her mother and gran. As often as not, he'd have Barry on his knee, or be playing Ludo with Ginnie and Billy. He'd taken Billy fishing in the stream and once they'd caught quite a big fish, a trout, and had brought it home in high excitement, to be cooked for supper.

'I wish you wouldn't,' she said as they washed up together in the tiny scullery. 'I've told you, it's no use. I'm not going to Canada with you.'

'Well, maybe I'll stop on here for a while, then.' He scrubbed at the enamel dish Ivy had used for that night's toad-in-the-hole, which Ada had said was more hole than toad. 'Would that suit you?'

'*No.*' She stopped wiping the plates and looked at him with exasperation. 'Carl, you've got to take notice of me. I'm not interested in – in anything like that. I've got Barry to look after.'

He lifted the dish from the water and laid it on the wooden draining-board. His eyes were very serious.

'You know what I'm saying, don't you, Maggie? I'm asking you to marry me.'

Maggie stared at him and then let her eyes fall. She shook her head.

'I can't—'

'It's Barry, too,' he said. 'I'm happy to take Barry as well. He'd be our son.'

'*No!*' The denial shocked Maggie herself. 'No! He's *my* son.'

Carl gazed at her. 'But why, Maggie? Why won't you let me share him? I'd be a good father to him, I promise.'

'Barry doesn't have a father! He just has me. I've told you—'

'I know you have. It doesn't make any difference.' He took her by the shoulders and turned her, making her look at him. 'I love you, Maggie.'

Maggie felt the shock run through her. She closed her eyes and swayed a little. Carl held her firmly by the shoulders and she swallowed and opened her eyes again. He was looking directly into them.

'I love you and I want to marry you. And I want Barry to be our eldest son. Because there'll be others, Maggie. I believe in big families. Big, happy families.'

She shook her head. She felt as if she might drown. Her ears were filled with a rushing, pounding noise as if water were surging over a high fall.

'I don't know . . .'

'Well,' he said with a smile in his voice, 'that's an improvement on no. Maggie, I'm not going to rush you. You've got to take time to think. You need to turn it all over in your mind and we need to talk about it. You'll have a million questions. Ask them. Ask me anything.'

Maggie turned away and leaned against the edge of the sink. In the other room they could hear the wireless. It was Arthur Askey and Richard Murdoch. She remembered Etty writing to say they'd seen Arthur Askey in the works canteen, and how funny he was. She heard a burst of laughter from the wireless, joined by Ivy's rich chuckle and the children's giggling and even her grandmother's rusty cackle.

'I don't know what to say. I don't know what to ask. I just don't know, Carl. I feel I can't marry anyone. If Barry's father came back—'

'But you don't even know who he is!'

Maggie raised her eyes. 'I think I might. If I just saw him again. And then – then, maybe I'd know, Carl.'

Carl stared at her. He shook his head, baffled. Then he dried his hands on the roller towel behind the door and thrust them into his pockets.

'Well, maybe you're right and I shouldn't come here so much, Maggie. Maybe you'd better just take the time to think it over. But don't take too long, because I guess I won't be around here much longer. I'm practically fit now. I'll be going back to my unit in a couple of weeks.'

He turned towards the door and Maggie watched him, feeling a tearing pain in her breast. She wanted to reach out for him, beg him not to go. But she couldn't tell him what he wanted to hear. She couldn't tell him she would marry him.

'I'm sorry,' she whispered. 'I know it sounds daft. It sounds daft to me. But the last time I was with a man – I can't forget that, Carl. I just can't get it out of my mind. And not knowing about Barry – it's all too much.' She was crying now, crying as she hadn't done since those early days when she had first realised she was pregnant. 'I can't put it all behind me till I know. I just can't.'

Carl took his hands from his pockets and came over to her. He held her face between his hands.

'But you're never going to know that, Maggie. You can't spend the rest of your life wondering – and not living.'

'I just think one day I will,' she said. 'I just think I've got to wait.'

Carl studied her for a long moment. She met his eyes, knowing that he would see in them all the feeling for him that had grown during the past months, all the love and desire and passion that she had thought destroyed by the rape. He bent his head and kissed her, very slowly, and her tears wet their lips.

'Just be sure you don't wait too long, Maggie,' he said, and opened the back door.

Maggie watched him walk down the path. She waited for him to turn at the gate and lift his hand in his usual wave. But he walked away, without looking back.

They took Owen to the cottage hospital in the next village, for their own was full. He lay unconscious for three whole days, with Shirley at his bedside almost the entire time, and then he opened his eyes and gave her a weak, tremulous smile.

'Hello, Shirley. What are you doing in hospital, *cariad*? Hurt yourself, is it?'

Shirley laughed through her tears. 'It's you that's in hospital, Owen. Don't you remember the mine? The roof fell in.'

'The roof? In the mine?' He frowned a little, and flinched. 'My head hurts.'

'You had a bit of a bang.' She didn't tell him about the shock of seeing his hair matted with blood and coal-dust, the raw, gaping wound in his skull. A miracle he'd lived, the doctors had said. Another fraction of an inch and the bones would have been smashed in . . . 'Don't try to talk, Owen. Just go to sleep.'

He looked at her for a moment. She saw his lips move painfully, and bent to touch his cheek with her mouth. He gave a little sigh and his eyes closed.

Shirley sat beside him, weak with gratitude. The past three days had been touch and go, but the doctor had told her that if he came round and was lucid, if he knew her and seemed to understand what she said, he would pull through. She watched as he slipped back into sleep, and then gently removed her hand and went to find the nurse.

'What will you do when the war's over?' Jo asked as she and Josh climbed up Stepple Knoll.

They went for a walk most Sundays now. Poppy had found a boyfriend in the village and Suzy had met someone from Ludlow who cycled over to see her. Without ever talking about it, it had become accepted that Jo and Josh would meet by the bridge after Sunday dinner and set off through the forest or by the river or across the hills. As the weather grew better and the days longer, they took sandwiches and went for the whole day. Today, they were going to walk to Bury Ditches, the ancient hillfort at the top of the next steep little hummock, and then to Purslow and back through Sowdley Wood.

Josh considered her question. It was a game everyone played – a fantasy, like what you would do if you won the football pools and never had to work again. But there was a feeling in the air just lately that the time was coming when you'd have to think about it more seriously. The war really might be coming to an end. Not this summer, not by Christmas, but perhaps by the following Christmas, maybe even sooner.

It still seemed a long way off, though. The game could still be played.

'I don't know,' he said thoughtfully. 'I don't think I want to go back to London. Or to Brighton. I'm not sure I even want to go back to being an accountant. Working in an office is going to seem like being in a cage after all this.'

They were at the top of the knoll and paused for breath, looking out over the rolling hills. On the far side of the valley they could see the forest where they were working – a huge stretch of dense woodland with a great swathe cut into it. The kidney shape of Clunton Hill lay before them, and the little river Clun gleamed below as it wound its way through the valley.

'I don't want to go back to London either,' Jo said. 'But I suppose I'll have to, if it's what Nick wants. A wife has to go with her husband.'

Josh turned his head and looked at her. 'That's going to be hard for a lot of you girls. Being used to so much freedom – living your own lives, taking responsibility, going out into the world. And then having to go back to being housewives and doing what your lord and master tells you.'

Jo grinned. 'I've never noticed my mum doing what Dad tells her! Well, she does, I suppose, except that he never gives orders, but she gets her own way a lot of the time, too. She just lets him think it's what he wants as well.'

'All the same,' Josh said, 'you'll have to live the way you're expected to. You might not find it so easy.'

Jo was silent. She hadn't seen Nick for several months now, and their last meeting had been difficult and awkward. They just didn't seem to be able to connect any more. She knew that during the Battle of Berlin he'd been flying almost every night, and had had no chance of getting leave to come to Shropshire, but she'd hoped that after the long stint he would be able to get some time off. Instead, he told her that they were just as busy, and she knew from the news that Bomber Command was now concentrating on France. Something big was going to happen, and Nick's letters were brief and perfunctory, always apparently written just as he was waiting for the call to fly again.

'Well, I suppose it'll work itself out,' she said with a little shrug. 'It's not going to be easy for the men either, coming home after all the fighting and trying to settle down to ordinary life again. I mean, my Nick was a shopwalker in a Burtons menswear shop and now he flies bombers. He's in charge, he's a boss, and it's life or death. How's he going to take to going back into a shop and measuring people's outside legs?'

'I think it's *inside* legs that get measured,' Josh murmured with a smile, and then put out a conciliatory hand as Jo turned impatiently away. 'Yes, I know what you mean. It's going to be hard for a lot of people.'

'On the other hand,' Jo said, staring fixedly across the valley, 'it might just be so wonderful to know that we *can* live a normal life and we're not going to be bombed or have to fight any more that we won't care *what* we do.'

Josh glanced at her. There was an odd, brittle tone to her voice, as if she found her own words difficult to believe. He touched her arm gently.

'It'll be all right, Jo. You and Nick – once you're able to be together, you'll settle down. You'll have a home, you'll start a family and all this will seem like a dream.'

She turned and looked at him. 'Will it? Will it really? All this . . . ?' She waved her arm in a wide semicircle, encompassing the rolling hills and the forests. 'Just a dream?' Her lip quivered suddenly. 'But I don't want it to be a dream! It's real. It's what I want. I don't want to leave the forest, and Clun, and – and everything.' She bit her lip, as if the last word hadn't been what she'd intended to say, and then she looked Josh full in the face and said in a note of desperation, 'I don't want to leave *you*.'

There was a moment of silence. They stared at each other. Josh lifted one hand slightly and made a small movement towards her, then stopped. Jo's eyes burnt into his and her lips moved and trembled. An instant later, she was in his arms.

'Josh – oh, *Josh*.'

'Jo, we mustn't do this.'

'I know.' She clung to him, weeping. 'I know we mustn't. It's wrong, I'm a married woman, I love my husband – but – oh, Josh, just hold me now. Just for a few minutes. Just this *once*. Please.'

He held her close. She was lean and wiry in his arms, toughened by the work she did. But there was softness, too, in the shape of her, and her skin felt smooth against his cheek.

He closed his eyes, imagining it was for ever, and tried to hold the moment. Just this once . . .

Jo laid her face against his pullover. The strength of his arms around her, the warmth of his body close to hers, was like a haven. She felt as if she had been left out in the cold, starving, and had at last been let in to comfort and warmth. I don't want to move away, ever, she thought. I know I must, but . . . just this once . . .

Josh moved first. He released one of his arms and touched Jo's face with his fingertips. With a tender, stroking movement, he slid his hand down to cup her chin and turned her face up to his. She opened her eyes and they looked at each other.

'Oh, Josh,' she whispered.

'Jo,' he said quietly, and bent his head.

Their lips brushed and then touched in a kiss as light as a butterfly settling on a flower. Jo felt her body quiver and sensed the answering tremble in his. Then, gently, he put her away from him.

'Perhaps we ought to go back,' he said.

Jo shook her head violently. 'No! No, we can't go back. I want to walk. I want to be with you.'

'I'm not sure it's wise—'

'Oh,' Jo cried, 'who cares about *wise*? We've got all the rest of our lives to be wise. Josh, I thought we were friends!'

'We are.' He looked at her soberly. 'I don't want to do anything to spoil that friendship.'

'What do you mean? Why should it be spoilt?'

'You're married,' he said, and turned away.

Jo stared at him as he walked on along the track. Then she ran after him, tugging at his sleeve.

'I know I'm married! You don't have to tell me. Look, it was just a kiss. A little kiss. It was just friendly – because it's such a lovely day and we were thinking about the war and what we'll do when it's over – and I know we won't see each other again after that, and it just seemed so sad, that's all. It didn't mean anything else.'

'Didn't it?' he said.

Their eyes met and Jo glanced away, down at her feet. Then she lifted her head again and looked him directly in the eye.

'All right, it did mean something else. But it's never going to go any further, Josh. I do love Nick.'

'I know.' He sighed. 'But when you're so far away from him, and so unhappy, it would be all too easy to forget that, Jo.'

'Who says I'm unhappy?' she demanded in a tight voice.

Josh looked at her. Then he said, 'Jo, if we're to be friends – real friends – we have to be honest with each other. That's my condition. All right?'

'All right,' she said at last, in a small voice.

'And don't tell me you're not unhappy.'

Again, she looked him in the eye. 'All right, I won't. But don't ask me why.'

There was a short silence. Josh smiled. 'All right, Jo. It's your marriage and I've no right to ask questions about it. And we stay friends. Even though it may not be easy at times.'

'Why not? You'll make sure we don't do anything *unwise*.'

He gave her a wry look. 'Don't bank on it, Jo. I've got feelings, too, you know. And I'm not always sensible about them.'

They walked on in silence. Gradually, the awkwardness between them eased and they were able to talk more naturally and laugh again. They strode down the hill into Purslow and stopped at the village inn for a glass of beer, and then climbed to the ridge. They were in the forest now, not far from where the timber gangs were working, and they stopped for a last breather before the final descent to Clun. The pine-scented air was fresh and tingling in their nostrils. The sun was setting behind them, casting long shadows across the valley.

Jo sat down on a felled log and patted the rough bark beside her. After a moment's hesitation, Josh took his seat, leaving a small space between them. Jo glanced at it and said nothing. The slight constraint fell again between them, and then he turned to her and said almost savagely, 'This is no good, Jo. We can't go on like this.'

Jo stared at him. 'Like what?'

'*Pretending*. Pretending to be friends. Pretending there's nothing more between us, and if there is it's not important, it's small enough to be squashed down and hidden and ignored. It isn't *like* that, Jo, you know it isn't.'

'So what is it like, then?' she asked in a small voice.

'I'm in love with you,' he said flatly. 'I have been ever since that first day, when we met on that railway station. I didn't think we'd ever meet again – I thought you'd be sent somewhere down south so that you could see Nick more often. And then I saw you again on the bridge in Clun, and I couldn't believe my eyes. Or my luck.'

'But you knew – you knew about me and Nick.'

'I thought friendship would be enough. I thought just being able to see you would be enough. And then you found out what I was and I thought you hated me.'

'I did, for a while,' she whispered. 'At least, I tried to. I don't think I ever did, not really.'

'I thought you did,' he said. 'I thought about trying to get a transfer so that I needn't see you looking at me the way you did. But the thought of going away . . . I couldn't bear it. Even seeing you hate me was better than not seeing you at all.'

Jo was silent. She had never dreamt that anyone could feel so strongly about her. Nick had never talked to her like this. And she felt the answering beat of her pulse.

'I wanted to be friends,' she said. 'That time on the station – it was as if we'd known each other for ages. So easy . . .'

'It's as if we've always known each other,' Josh said.

They sat very quietly. Then Jo reached out a hand and laid it on Josh's. They turned towards each other and slowly he put his arm around her shoulders and drew her against him. Their kiss began again as lightly as the settling of a butterfly, then deepened. They clung together and he slid his hand up gently to cover her breast.

'Jo, I love you.'

'Josh . . .'

He held her away from him, looking down into her eyes. 'You can't say it, can you?'

'I don't know. I *want* to. But I love Nick. How can I love two people at once?'

'Perhaps you can. Perhaps it's possible – especially when one's so far away. But the real point is that you can't let yourself, isn't it? You're married to Nick, not to me, and he's the one you're going to make your life with. There's no future for us.'

'Only a present,' she whispered.

'Only a present.' He stood up, bringing her with him. 'Let's walk on, Jo. It's time to go home.'

Silently, she stood beside him. Then she slipped her hand into his and laid her head briefly against his shoulder. They looked down at the village, merging now with the shadows of dusk. The last bird twittered behind them and the forest was hushed.

Time to go home, she thought, and wondered where Nick was now.

Owen was paralysed. His back had been badly damaged and his spinal cord crushed just below his waist. It might heal in time, the doctors said, but no one could tell for certain. He might have to spend the rest of his life in a wheelchair.

Gradually, Shirley learnt the story of what had happened down the mine. The men had been working at the coalface as usual. Owen had just arrived with Taffy, ready to load the empty dram. The pony had been standing patiently waiting and Owen had fastened on his nosebag for a few bites while the coal was shovelled into the big iron tub. It was almost full when they heard the first distant rumble.

They paused and looked at each other in the unsteady light.

'Sounds like a fall somewhere,' one of the men said uneasily.

278

'It's a mile away,' another muttered with false confidence.

'It's not. It's right overhead. It's – gow, it's on top of us, it's—'

The rising voice, the panic, the yells of terror were all cut off by the sudden roar of rocks falling, displacing each other, scraping and smashing as the tunnel roof gave way. The study pit props splintered and flaked. Water flooded from somewhere, rose about their necks and then swirled away as suddenly as it had arrived. The lamps were extinguished and a thick, solid darkness blotted their sight. As the sound died away, Owen heard the frantic whinnying of a horse.

He did not know how long he had been unconscious. He came to several times, and drifted away again. He knew that he was lying on hard rock, its lumps thrusting painfully into his shoulders and back, but from the waist down he could feel nothing. The air was thick with coal-dust, and his mouth was gritty. It was hard to breathe; he didn't seem to have the power to lift the muscles of his chest to open his lungs.

When he felt about with his hands he realised that his legs were pinned beneath a pile of broken rock, but it hurt his arm to move and he didn't do it again for a while. He began to remember those last few moments, and it gradually came to him that he was in the mine, trapped, and that he might die there.

He tried harder to remember. He'd been standing at the coalface, waiting to load up Taffy's dram. He'd fastened the pony's nosebag on, just to give him a quick bite. And then they'd heard the rumbling.

Taffy.

In sudden panic, Owen tried to feel about again. The pony had been right beside him, snuffling and chomping in the sack strapped over his nose. He should be close by. He strained his ears but could hear nothing. No clink of harness, no rattle of hooves on the rocky ground, no snuffling or neighing.

He remembered hearing a whinny as the rocks began to fall, a high-pitched scream of terror and pain.

'Taffy,' he muttered. 'Taffy. Can you hear me, boy? Are you there?'

He knew that there were other men with him. He could hear them breathing and groaning. He heard one call out, asking if anyone else was still alive, and he answered feebly, but the man didn't reply. Perhaps he had imagined that his voice had sounded. After a while, the other man called out again, but this time Owen didn't have either the strength or the interest to respond. They were together down here, but alone. Neither of them could help the other.

Taffy must be dead.

A long time later, he saw a glimmer of light and heard another voice.

'Is there anyone here? Is anyone still alive?'

The voice sounded strong, as if its owner was properly conscious. Owen summoned up all his strength. 'I'm here. Owen Prosser. And there was someone else but maybe he's gone. I don't know . . .'

He heard a scuffling, scrabbling sound and felt a flicker of fear. The light came closer and he saw the lamp itself, fixed to a miner's helmet. Then a hand touched his shoulder and felt its way to his face. The voice sounded again, very close.

'Is that you, Owen?'

He recognised it now. Ivor, the man's name was. Ivor Evans. His father was chief clerk and people had wondered what the boy was doing down the mine when he could have had a nice, safe job up in the offices. But Ivor had said he'd chosen it. If he'd stayed above ground he would have had to go into the forces, and he knew mining, he could do better work here than learning to drive a battleship.

'Yes, it's me. I'm worried about my pony. Taffy, the skewbald. I don't know what happened to him.'

The light moved as the boy peered this way and that.

'He'll be all right. Who else is here?'

But Owen had used all his strength. He mumbled something and then floated away again. He came round to hear Ivor's voice once more.

'There's three of you here. One's unconscious and I think one's dead. Look, we've got a better place in the other tunnel. There's a few more chaps there, see, and we got a bit of light, too. I don't reckon there's anyone else here.' The light danced again as he turned his head.

Owen could see now that they were in a small space. The coalface here had been quite large, he remembered, with a good-sized tunnel running away from it and two or three more leading off. Ivor must have come through one of those. Now, the cavern was piled with fallen rock and coal. It gleamed black in the light from Ivor Evans's helmet. There was very little room, and no sign of a pony.

'Can you move?' Ivor asked.

Owen experimented gingerly. One arm was free but the other shot fiery pains right through his shoulder to the tip of his brain when he tried to shift it. He groaned.

'I think I've broken my arm. And I can't even feel my legs.'

Ivor peered down. He spoke again, subdued.

'They're under some rocks. It'll take a while to get you free.'

'What about the others? Silwyn and Trevor? And Ken Orchard, he was down here, too. And—'

'There's only Trevor and Ken.'

'But—'

'They might be on the other side of the rocks,' Ivor said, and Owen knew that he could have added, 'Or they might be underneath them.'

Talking was exhausting. Owen wanted to close his eyes and go to sleep. But before he did so he managed to ask one more question.

'Is there any way out?'

Ivor didn't answer for a few minutes and Owen had almost drifted away again when he heard the boy's voice, coming from a long way off.

'Only if we dig . . .'

Owen hadn't dug, and neither had Trevor Jones, an old miner who died as they lifted the last rock away from him, as if it had been keeping him alive until that moment. Neither had Ken Orchard, a Bevin boy from Nottingham who had a broken leg and a bang on the head but was otherwise unharmed. It wasn't until Ivor and his friends had spent almost twenty-four hours patiently scrabbling at the rocks, and they'd heard the sounds of men digging from the other side, that they knew there was a chance of getting out. And it was only after Owen had been in the hospital for almost a week that they knew he was unlikely to walk again.

'I don't remember much after they found us,' he told Shirley, lying in the high white bed. 'The doctor came down and looked at me. He said they had to be very careful how they moved me, see. And he gave me an injection. It must have put me out.'

'Yes, it did.' Shirley remembered her first sight of Owen, lying so white and still on that stretcher. For a moment, staring at the ashen face and the dark red blood clotted in his hair, she'd thought he must be dead. She'd flung herself on him and been swiftly dragged away. The doctor had looked almost angry.

'You don't want to kill him, do you?'

Shirley had stared at him. 'But he's already dead.'

'Nonsense. He's injured, but he's alive and going to stay that way. But he'll need you to be calm and sensible not having hysterics all over him.' The doctor had lowered his brows at her and Shirley had felt ashamed.

'I'm sorry. It's just the waiting – and the wondering. I didn't mean—'

'No matter. Now listen, your husband's got some serious injuries. We won't know the extent till we get him in the hospital, but with luck they won't kill him. Now let's get him into that ambulance. It'll do him no good lying about out here.'

Owen had no feeling in his legs. They lay in the bed with him, useless, no longer an active part of him. They might as

282

well, he said bitterly, be two feather bolsters.

'The feeling might come back,' Shirley said. 'The doctors don't know for certain.'

'I do,' he said. 'I know. And so do they, really. They're just trying to let us down gently, Shirl.' He turned his head restlessly. 'I'm going to be a burden on you. You'll be better off with someone else.'

'Owen!' Shock made her angry. 'Don't you dare say things like that. We're married, remember? For better, for worse.'

'You said it. It can't get much worse than this.'

'It could. At least you've still got your mind. You're not like poor Stanley that had half his head knocked in. They say he'll be a vegetable for the rest of his life, and it could be years.'

'I'm not going to be able to support you, though. I'm not going to be able to be a husband to you.'

'You're my husband,' Shirley told him firmly. 'And you're going to stay my husband. You don't get away that easily, Owen Prosser!'

'Easy?' he said. 'When I can't even run?' And he grinned – feebly, it was true, but still a grin. Shirley smiled back, though she felt like crying, and bent to kiss him.

'We'll be all right,' she whispered. 'We'll manage, together. We've still got each other.'

Owen reached up with his good arm and held her against him. Then he said, 'Have they told you if they've found Taffy?'

Shirley had been waiting for this question. While Owen had been unconscious, and sometimes delirious, he had asked repeatedly for Taffy. He had clutched her hand, begging her to feed the pony, to water him and brush him. 'He'll be waiting for me. He'll be wondering where I am.' Once or twice he'd been convinced that Taffy was in the room with them, waiting to have his dram filled. He'd reached out, feeling the air to try to pat the pony's nose. He'd fallen back at last into sleep, muttering the name 'Taffy' over and over again.

She was only surprised that he hadn't asked before.

'Yes,' she said, 'they found him. He was hit by a rock. He must have died straight away. He couldn't have known anything about it.'

It might have been true. He might not have died slowly, rearing his long neck back in agony, his belly crushed by coal. But she could hardly bear to think of that herself and she could not put the thought into Owen's mind. She said again, 'It was very quick. I don't suppose he even had time to be frightened.'

Owen moved his head, as if he were trying to nod. His eyes were closing again. His hand grew limp in hers and he slept.

Shirley watched him. She knew that Owen was not likely to get better. He would recover from his broken arm and from the knock on his head, but he would never walk again. He would never, as he had said, be the husband to her that he had been in the past few months.

Yet she had never loved him more than now, when he lay so helpless in the high hospital bed. He was alive. He had been returned to her.

Chapter Twenty-Two

April passed into May. Owen grew slowly stronger. In a few weeks, he would be allowed home, but before then Shirley had to decide where they should live. Two tiny rooms, one of them upstairs, would be no use for a man who needed a wheelchair. Not that they had a wheelchair anyway. How could they afford one?

'Come up to us, *cariad*,' Mair Prosser said to her. 'We've got the room, and your mam and dad are here for you, too. And Dafydd says he can make Owen a sort of little cart to get about the farm in. It's the best thing for you both.'

Shirley thought about it. They wanted to be independent, but it was impossible. And what were families for, if not to help when there was trouble?

'Yes,' she said. 'We'll come. But I want to work, mind.'

'Oh, there'll be plenty of work for you to do, never worry about that!' Mair said, laughing.

The preparations for the invasion were gathering pace. The South Coast was now one vast army camp, every spare bit of ground cluttered with tanks and lorries. Soldiers were everywhere. Bomber Command and the American Air Force were still flying to Berlin and other major German cities every night. The consumption of bombs and artillery seemed endless.

At Elstow, as at other ordnance factories, those bombs were being produced like cakes in a bakery. Long lines of them moved down the benches and conveyor belts and reached the end, to be transported to airfields and ammunition dumps. How many thousands would they kill? Etty wondered as she worked. But it was best not to think that way. You mustn't think that way.

There didn't seem to be any chance that she and Jim would be able to marry before he finally went away.

She knew he was somewhere near Portsmouth. His letters came regularly, short but loving notes that she treasured and tucked under her pillow at night. She wore her engagement ring then, too, taking it off with regret each morning. It felt like a betrayal of Jim, to put it in the drawer as if she didn't care. But the rules were strict and she knew that she dared not take it into the factory with her.

Towards the end of May the site had a visit from Field Marshal Montgomery. They had crowded into the canteen at lunchtime, expecting to see a famous entertainer like George Formby or Max Wall, and instead a rather stocky figure, wearing battledress and a beret, strutted on to the stage. They gaped at him and then someone realised who he was and shouted, 'It's Monty!'

'*Monty!*'

The cheer almost took the roof off. Monty had made his name in the desert of North Africa, commanding his troops. He was almost as famous and almost as revered as Mr Churchill. He stood on the stage, accepting the applause, and then stepped forward, his arms held high.

The noise slowly died away and everyone craned to hear what he had to tell them.

'I am visiting all the war factories I can this week,' he said in clipped tones. 'I want to tell you all the same thing. As the time approaches for our invasion of Europe, you are amongst the most valuable of all our workers. Your efforts in producing bombs and artillery are going to make all the difference on the day when we finally leave these shores and start to liberate France and Belgium and those other countries who are under the heel of the Nazi. That day . . .' He leant forward as if to tell them a secret. 'That day is to be called D –

D, for Day. And the hour of our invasion will be called H, for Hour. Listen to your wirelesses, and you will hear it announced. And you'll know that *your* bombs, *your* ammunition will be going with us and helping to win the war!'

The roof really did lift off that time, Etty thought as she cheered and stamped with the rest. What a man, to take the trouble to come and tell *them*, when there must be so much else to do. She felt that she couldn't wait to get back to her bench to start work again. Looking at the faces around her, she knew that everyone else felt the same.

'D-Day,' Phyl said as they hurried back after only the scrappiest of lunches, almost snatched from the hands of the canteen staff. 'It's not much of a name for something like that. You'd think they could come up with something more original. D-Day – it'll be forgotten in a few months.'

'Who cares about being original?' Kaye demanded, catching up. 'Just let's get over there and give Hitler a bloody nose. They've got better things to do than sit around thinking up fancy names. It's not as if anyone's going to bother to remember what they called it, after all.'

Nobby Clark was waiting for them at the door.

'I suppose you're all keen to do a bit of work for a change,' he sneered as they came in. 'Pity he couldn't have come round here a year or two ago. He could've had my job.'

'For once,' Kaye said, sweeping past him loftily, 'I entirely agree with you. It would have been a big improvement!'

Etty giggled and Nobby glared at her.

'Funny, was it? Well, let's see if you think this is funny, too. I've got a message for you.'

Etty stared at him. 'A message? Who from?'

'Wouldn't you like to know? You're wanted in the supervisor's office, at the double. And I'm coming with you, so quick march!'

With a frightened glance at the others, Etty turned and almost ran to the office in the corner. Jim, she thought, it's got to be about Jim. He's been killed. There's been an accident. Or it's Maggie, or Barry. Something awful . . .

Mr Carter was in the office, waiting for her. She gazed at him and he looked at her kindly, but she knew at once that she'd been right. Something was very wrong.

'Jim?' she whispered.

'I'm sorry,' he said. 'I've just been notified. He's deserted, Etty. He's run away from camp.'

'*Deserted?*' Etty whispered. 'My *Jim?*'

'That's what they call it.' Mr Carter sighed. 'I can't believe it myself. I know your Jim, and I'm sure he's not a coward. There's some reason for this.' He looked at her. 'Do you think he might be coming here?'

Etty stared at him. 'Here? You mean, coming to me?'

'It's the only thing I can think of. They've been in touch with his mother in Devon and his father in London and neither of them has heard anything – or, at least, they say they haven't. Who knows? But he's been talking a lot about you, apparently, and his friends say he was getting desperate at the thought of going away without being able to marry you. They think that's what he has in mind – to come here and get married. They think he'd go back then, but, of course, it won't be that easy – he'd be arrested as a deserter, no matter what the excuse.' He paused and sighed. 'I'm afraid he's in very bad trouble, Etty.'

Etty put both hands to her face. She felt sick and giddy. She swayed, and Mr Carter moved hastily to help her into a chair. Nobby stood watching, a sneer curling his lip.

'Don't just stand there, man!' Mr Carter ordered harshly. 'Fetch her some water. Can't you see she's almost fainting?'

Nobby went out. Mr Carter knelt and laid his arm across her shoulders.

'Put your head between your knees, Etty, dear. That's it. Oh, dear, what a dreadful thing. Poor Jim. Poor, foolish Jim.'

Etty gulped and sniffed. Nobby came back with a cup of water and Mr Carter held it to her lips. She sipped and coughed.

'Oh, Jim. My Jim. It's just because we love each other so much, Mr Carter. There'll never be anyone for me but Jim, and he knows that. He just wants us to be married. He'd go then, I know he would. They *ought* to have let us be married.'

'Etty,' he said tenderly. 'Etty.'

'It isn't fair,' she whispered. 'Jim never tried to get out of anything. He'd never desert. He's not a coward. He'd fight to the end – he just wanted to be married first . . .' Her words dissolved into sobs, and the tears dripped on to her hands. Mr Carter put his arm around her and held her. He felt her narrow shoulders quiver under his touch. She was such a little scrap, he thought, so thin and pale, yet there was an odd beauty in her face at times, an almost luminous look, and she had lovely eyes.

He glanced up and saw Nobby Clark watching them, and felt a shock. There was naked jealousy in the man's face, and bitter anger. Bernard Carter jerked his head at the door.

'You can go now, Clark. You ought to be back at the production lines, seeing that Etty's place is being taken by one of the key girls. She won't be working any more today.'

'Fat lot of difference that'll make,' Nobby retorted with a sneer, and went out, slamming the door behind him.

Etty looked up. 'What's going to happen? What will they do to him?'

Bernard Carter sighed. 'I'm afraid he's in serious trouble, Etty. The best thing he could do would be to report to a police station at once and give himself up. Otherwise he'll never be able to prove he isn't really deserting. If he turns up here, you'll have to try to persuade him to do that.'

'But if he wants to get married, couldn't we just do that first, quickly, and then go to the police?'

Mr Carter shook his head. 'Think about it, Etty. Unless you report him the minute you see him, you'll be an accomplice. And so would the priest who marries you and anyone else involved. He has to go to the police. And I'm afraid if he doesn't, and you give him any help at all, you'll be in trouble, too.'

Etty stared at him. 'That's awful. It's cruel.'

'We're at war, Etty,' he reminded her. 'And all the signs are that there's going to be an invasion soon. Think of what Field Marshal Montgomery said. It's a vital moment. We can't have our soldiers dashing off to get married, however cruel it seems.'

'But suppose he never comes back,' Etty said, her voice wobbling.

'It's the same for many others,' he said quietly. 'We're all having to make sacrifices, Etty, and some of us more than others.'

Etty sat silently for a moment. Mr Carter offered her the cup of water again and she took it and sipped absently. At last she said, 'I think I'd better go back to work now.'

'Back to work? Are you sure you feel up to it? You don't want to go and lie down for a while?'

'No, I don't. I'm not ill, Mr Carter. I've just had a shock, that's all. And there's nothing I can do about Jim, is there?' She raised her eyes and he was reminded of the time when she had gone down into the bombed cellar and given strength to the people still alive down there. 'Not till he turns up, anyway. And I've got work to do. I can't let everyone down.' Her mouth twisted in a wry smile. 'Not after what Monty said in the canteen just now.'

Bernard Carter studied her for a moment, then nodded. 'You're right, Etty. You go back to work. It's the best thing you can do. And if Jim turns up here . . .'

'You'll let me know straight away, won't you?' she asked, and he nodded.

'I'll tell them at the gate that if he does turn up, they're to notify me immediately and bring him to my office. I'll call you at once.'

Etty went back to the assembly line. They were working on some particularly difficult bombs today, a new sort that needed constructing and filling with extra care. The key girl gave up her place with relief and Etty took the position beside Phyl. Phyl gave her a quick, anxious glance but Etty shook her head.

'Tell you later.' She dared not talk about Jim now. She

could only manage to keep going if she didn't even think about him.

They worked in silence, aware that the job needed all their concentration. Etty tried again and again to turn her thoughts away from Jim, but her mind kept picturing him, running and hiding, trying to get through the prohibited areas that surrounded the coast, sneaking through lanes and alleyways, probably lost and bewildered in his attempt to reach Elstow. She knew that must be what he was doing. He'll never make it, she thought despairingly. He'll never get through. And if he does – what then?

He must realise they wouldn't be able to get married. He was coming to say goodbye. That's what it was. He knew he wasn't going to come back from this big invasion, and he just wanted to say goodbye.

Nobby Clark appeared at her elbow. His face was sour, twisted with contempt.

'Keep your mind on your work, Brown. I don't want the whole line put at risk just because your lily-livered coward of a boyfriend's done a bunk. Deserter! A fine soldier *he* is, I don't think. And just when we've had the privilege of a man like Monty to tell us what's what.'

A wave of shock ran along the line, through all the girls that heard his words. Etty was aware of Phyl's gasp and the sudden pause in the work. She bit her lip and tried to keep the tears back, but as Nobby jeered her temper flared and she whirled round.

'My Jim's not a coward! And he's not a deserter neither. He just wants to say goodbye to me before he goes away to fight – that's all. And if it wasn't for you, Nobby Clark, we'd be married by now and he wouldn't be feeling so desperate. It's *your* fault he's run away!'

'*My* fault? Well, that's a rich one, I must say. Went down there, did I, and forced him? Held a gun at his head? Put a knife to his throat? Told him Hitler was coming for him if he didn't do it? He's a coward, Etty Brown, and that's it and all about it, and you're aiding and abetting him. I bet you knew all about it. I bet you'll be next. Come tomorrow and you'll be off together, selling secrets to Germans!'

Etty drew in a deep breath. She felt the colour drain from her face, leaving her sick and dizzy, and then as quickly rush back. A surge of rage possessed her body and she stepped forward, both hands raised.

'Etty! No!' Phyl caught at her arm, but Etty shook her off. She could see nothing but Nobby Clark's sneering mouth, his small, contemptuous eyes. Vaguely, she heard Phyl's footsteps as she ran, but nothing else mattered to Etty than the hateful face before her, and she swung first one hand, then the other, slapping his head from side to side, intent only on wiping off the horrible smirk.

'You little *bitch*!'

Nobby staggered, caught off guard by her attack. Then he moved swiftly, grabbing both her wrists. His finger bit cruelly into her flesh. Etty cried out and struggled in his grasp. She kicked out and the toe of her shoe met his shin. Nobby yelped and pushed her backwards, and Etty fell across the bench and struck the shells that were waiting to be filled.

The explosion was not large, but it was enough to kill anyone close by. The other girls had stepped back, forming a horrified circle around the pair, and those that were nearest received ugly but minor injuries. Phyl, hurrying back with Mr Carter, was knocked over by the blast and broke her arm in the fall. Mr Carter himself lost his eyebrows and some of his hair.

Etty and Nobby Clark were killed instantly.

Chapter Twenty-Three

'I just can't believe it.' White-faced and shaking, Maggie read the telegram and handed it to her mother. 'Our Jim running off – and Etty killed. Our *Etty*. It don't seem possible.'

Ivy's face was blotched with tears. She held the telegram but didn't read it. She sat at the kitchen table, her lips working, moving her head slowly from side to side.

'Our *Jim*? Our *Etty*?'

Maggie repeated the words again and again, trying to make sense of them, trying to make them sound true. It was a joke, a horrible joke, it must be. It *couldn't* be true.

'If he'd bin killed in *action* . . .'

'Our Jim ain't dead,' Ivy said harshly. 'Our Jim's still alive.'

'I know. But what's going to happen to him? He's a deserter.'

'He *ain't* a deserter. He went to see Etty. To say goodbye.'

'I know that, too,' Maggie said dispiritedly. 'But they're not going to believe that, are they? They're going to say he deserted.'

The children had been huddled in an old armchair in the corner. Ginnie, clinging to Barry as if he were a doll, spoke up in a voice sharp-edged with anxiety.

'What do they do to deserters, Mum? Do they shoot them? Is that what they'll do to our Jim?'

'*No!*' Ivy turned on her youngest daughter. 'Don't you dare say such wicked things. Jim's not a deserter, and don't you ever forget it. He's brave and good and all he wanted to do . . .' Her voice trembled and broke into a shower of tears. 'He's not a deserter,' she sobbed. 'He's *not.*'

'Oh, Mum.' Maggie reached across to pat her mother's shoulder. 'Mum, try not to cry any more. You'll make yourself bad . . . Look, we'll know more when we gets a letter. Maybe they won't court-martial him after all. I mean, with this invasion coming up, they must have more to do than bother about one bloke that's run off to see his sweetheart. They'll probably just send him back.'

'That won't help our Etty,' Ivy wept. 'And it won't help Jim much either, to know she wouldn't be dead if it hadn't bin for him . . . What I don't understand is how she got killed anyway. She was only waiting at tables, for Gawd's sake. How could she have got mixed up with bombs and stuff?'

'I dunno.' Maggie looked at the letter again. 'I reckon there was more to it than that. I always thought there was something funny about that place, you know. She never seemed to want to talk about it much when she was here at Christmas. I asked her a couple of times if it was like being at the Corner House, or if anything funny had ever happened like used to happen to us sometimes, but she just changed the subject. I don't reckon she was waiting at tables at all.'

'Why?' Ivy stared at her. 'What d'you think she was doing?'

'Well, what do you think? Munitions, that's what it was. I'd bet my last brass farthing that's what it was. Her and Phyl, too.'

'Munitions?' Billy said. 'That's making bombs, ain't it?'

'Yes, it is,' Maggie said. 'And don't you say nothing to no one else about it, young Billy. It's meant to be secret, and if Etty could keep it secret so can you. Don't you say a word, see?'

She got up and went to the door where her jacket hung, ready to go out. 'I've got to go now, Mum. I'm on duty in twenty minutes. Will you be all right?'

Ivy nodded. She had stopped sobbing and her tears were drying on her cheeks. She wiped her nose and drew in a shuddering breath.

'I'll get your gran up in a minute. Gawd knows what this is going to do to her. You know what she's bin like lately, and a shock like this could be the end of her.' Her eyes filled again. 'I wonder if we didn't oughter let your dad know.'

'We'll talk about it when I get back.' Maggie came round the table to lay her hand on her mother's shoulder again. 'He knows about Jim, anyway. I s'pose they went to him when Jim first went off, same as they come to us. Gawd, it's terrible that Jim don't even know about Etty yet.'

'That's the first thing they'll do when they catch up with him,' Ivy said. 'They'll tell him what's happened. He's going to think it's all his fault, Maggie. He's never going to forgive himself.'

Maggie went out. Although it was now June, the weather was dull and chilly, with rain in the air. The trees dripped on her as she walked beside the river, and she looked up through the canopy at the leaden clouds and thought that even the skies were crying.

Poor Jim. And poor Etty. Maggie still could not believe that her friend was dead. Etty, who had joined the Nippies only at Phyl's persuasion, after the two of them had met working in the kitchen of the Marble Arch Corner House. Maggie remembered her then, small and thin with huge brown eyes, almost too timid to ask the customers for their orders. But she had such a lovely smile, and she was so polite and so helpful, she won the hearts of even the most irascible diners, and it had been a joy to see her blossom as her confidence grew.

Only Irene Bond hadn't welcomed Etty but, then, Irene Bond wouldn't have welcomed the King himself, and no one had bothered about her opinions. She'd done her best to cause Etty problems, both at the Corner House and in the hostel where they lived, but in the end it had been Irene herself who had finished up in trouble, and no one had been sorry to see the back of her.

Maggie thought of the day when she'd taken Etty home for the first time. It had been Ginnie's seventh birthday and they'd had a party. Etty had never been to a real home before, with a real family, and Maggie could still remember her wide eyes and awe as she came into the big, crowded room. Ada had taken to her straight away, and so had baby Queenie. Maggie's eyes filled with fresh tears as she thought of Queenie. It wasn't fair, she thought angrily, rubbing them away, it wasn't fair that so many people had to be killed. Girls like Etty, babies like Queenie, men like her Tommy. Haven't we lost enough people? she thought bitterly. Haven't we given enough to this bloody war?

'Hey. You're looking down in the dumps.'

Maggie jumped. She had paused to stare blindly at the brown, rushing water and she turned to see Carl leaning against a tree, watching her. Maggie stared at him for a moment, almost without recognition, and then turned abruptly back to the river.

'Hey, now,' he said more softly, coming closer. 'What is it? What's happened?'

Maggie turned and looked up into his face. She hadn't seen him to speak to since the day he'd walked out of the house and left her. She knew that he was to leave the hospital soon and she'd hoped – or feared – that he would go without coming to say goodbye. She didn't know now whether she was glad or sorry to see him, but there wasn't time to think about it. At the concern in his eyes, and at the first touch of his hands on her shoulders, she had begun to cry.

'It's not Barry?' he said sharply. 'Nothing's happened to Barry, has it? Your ma? The other kids? Gran?'

Maggie shook her head. She had kept the tears back for her mother's sake, but now they had been let loose it was like a dam bursting, and equally unstoppable. She leant towards him and he took her in his arms and held her close, murmuring and soothing her. At last her sobs ceased and she looked up at him, trying to smile. Her face was wet with tears and the rain was falling steadily upon them. She tried to smile.

'I dunno what's making you wettest, me or the rain.'

'It doesn't matter. Tell me what's happened.'

'It's our Jim. And Etty.' Her voice trembled again and she steadied it and then told him briefly what had happened. He listened in dismay.

'Say, that's just awful. And Jim doesn't even know?'

'He didn't this morning. Mr Carter sent us the telegram. He said Jim hadn't turned up there.'

'Look,' he said, 'you've got to go and find that brother of yours. Tell him. Look after him.'

'But nobody knows where he is! And when they do, they'll just – just take him away. Don't you realise? He's a deserter. They'll court-martial him.'

Carl whistled softly. 'What a mess. What a goddamned mess.'

'And Etty – Etty's been killed. She was my friend. We were like sisters. We *would* have been sisters.'

'Oh, Maggie.' He folded his arms about her again. 'My poor, poor Maggie.'

'I don't know what to do,' she whispered. 'I don't know what any of us can do except – except just carry on.'

'And that's what you're doing now?'

She nodded. 'I'm on my way to work. I might as well be doing some good.'

Carl nodded. 'I'll walk along with you.' They turned and began to walk along the path. It was getting slippery underfoot. Soon it would be too muddy to use and Maggie would have to go to work by way of the lane. She thought dully of the tasks she would do when she arrived. Taking round meals. Taking round bedpans. Talking to the men, trying to be jolly and cheerful. Once it had been easy to be jolly and cheerful, it had come naturally. Now it was more of an effort each day, and never more so than now.

'Is there anyone to speak for Jim?' Carl asked.

'His mates, I s'pose. They all know what he's like, and they know he wanted to marry Etty. His sergeant and captain, people like that. They all know he's not a coward. There'll be plenty to speak up for him.' She paused. 'But they're not going to have time, are they? Everyone knows something

297

big's going to happen. They'll have more to do than worry about one poor bloke who broke ranks to see his girl.'

They walked on in silence. At the gates to the big house, Maggie turned and put out her hand.

'Thanks, Carl. I'm sorry I cried all over you. Sorry I made you all wet.'

Carl grinned and glanced up at the sky. 'I think you had help!' He held on to her hand and drew her closer. 'I've been wanting to talk to you anyway, Maggie. That's why I was down at the river – I was hoping you'd come along that way. Look, it won't matter to you much now, but I just wanted to say I'm sorry. Sorry about the way I walked out on you. You've got a right to feel the way you do, and I don't have any right to ask any different.'

Maggie stared at him. A feeling of relief washed through her, and she realised just how unhappy she'd been at the thought that it was all over between them. Not that it made any difference, she thought sadly. I still think I've got to wait – just in case . . .

'I just want you to know I'm around,' he said softly. 'If you ever change your mind – or want to get in touch. I'd like to know what happens to you and the little guy. I meant what I said, Maggie – I love you. I want to know you're all right.'

He took two envelopes from his pocket and gave them to her.

'That's my unit. That'll find me, as long as this war's still going on. And that's my mom's address in Canada. If you ever need me, even after it's all over, she'll know what to do.'

Maggie looked at the two envelopes and nodded. She put them into her pocket and looked up at him again.

'I'm sorry, Carl. It's just that I have this feeling – if Barry's dad comes back, if it's the bloke I hope it is – well, he's got a right to his chance, hasn't he? If Barry's his kid . . .' She lifted her shoulders and let them drop. 'Look, I know it sounds stupid – why should he come back? Why should he look for me? And I don't even know what I'd do if he did. I wouldn't want to *marry* him. I don't s'pose he'd want to marry *me*. But I just feel I got to wait. I'm sorry.'

'Don't be,' he said. 'It's one of the things I love about you, Maggie, my darling.' And he bent his head and kissed her, and then walked quickly away into the rain.

Maggie walked slowly up the drive. Her mind was whirling. But even Carl could not occupy her thoughts for long.

Etty, she thought. Oh, *Etty*.

Jim Pratt arrived at the gates of the Royal Ordnance unit at Elstow just as they swung open to allow two large black cars to come out.

He stood back and bowed his head. It was obvious from the trail of sad faces following that this was a funeral. He wondered what had happened. Some accident, probably. Not everyone who died in wartime was killed in action.

He didn't bother to look at any of the faces. He was concerned only with seeing Etty before he was caught. He needed to see her face just once more. He needed to explain . . .

Jim was well aware of the fact that he'd been a fool. He'd done a crazy thing, breaking out and running off like that. It had been a moment of madness, and he'd known at once that he was an idiot. But there was no going back, even in those first few moments. As soon as he had jumped down from his lorry, he'd been branded a deserter.

Ever since their wedding had been cancelled, Jim had been in a state of despair. He kept Etty's photograph in his wallet and carried it with him all the time, taking it out to look at whenever he had a chance. He'd put it beside his pillow at night, staring at it until his eyes closed or someone put out the lights. Then he'd put out his hand for it and slept with it tucked under his cheek.

I ought to have married her before, he thought. I ought to have married her at Christmas, down in Devon. Why didn't I? Why didn't we find time? Why didn't we *make* that vicar marry us, even if it was Christmas Day itself?

He remembered the three times during that brief holiday when they had managed to slip along to the hayloft. Etty's slender body, quivering in his arms. The shape of her, the feel of soft skin and flesh over delicate bones. Her lips, so tender and so eager. The way she fitted against him, the shape their bodies made together, the rhythm and music of their love.

We *are* married, he thought, as near as makes no difference. Etty's mine and I'm hers, and a bit of paper don't make no difference. *God* knows we're married, He's seen us, He wouldn't say it was wrong for us to love each other the way we did. That's what He made us for, that's why we were given these feelings.

He had never known anything like the blind fury he'd felt when he'd arrived at Elstow to find that Etty wasn't allowed off the camp. He'd railed and shouted until the sentries had sent for someone in authority to come and quieten him down. Eventually, they'd brought Phyl, and she'd sat with him by the gates and told him what had happened.

After that, it was as if he went through the days in a dream. Parade, spud-bashing, cleaning his gun, polishing his belt . . . none of it seemed real. He followed the others like a robot. There was nothing in his mind but Etty. Etty, Etty, Etty . . .

He could not rid himself of the deep need to see her again, to say the words and make the promises that would tell the world they were man and wife. Then, when he came back again they could start their life together, without having to slip away to haylofts. They could be proud and open about their love, and nobody would have the right to keep them apart.

The need grew in him, like a monstrous plant that fed on his love and blotted out everything else. If I could just see her again once, he thought, just once . . .

The unit was near Portsmouth when the ban was announced. All movement in and out of the area, except for the military and permitted personnel, was to be prohibited. Jim's last chance to see Etty had gone.

The unit moved to be as near the beach as possible. The lines stretched for miles back from the coast, thousands of

300

men and trucks and tanks, the longest queue of a war that had become famous for its queues.

In a week, two weeks, they would all be shipped over to the Normandy coast. Huge concrete harbours had been built, which were to be towed over first so that when the landing-craft arrived the huge army could be disembarked quickly, ready to take the Germans by surprise. It seemed an impossible undertaking, but the planning had taken two years or more and now it was ready. All they had to do was await the word from the two great commanders, General Eisenhower and Winston Churchill.

Jim was in a truck parked in a lane a few miles north of Portsmouth. The invasion was being planned from a big house not far away. He'd seen the convoys bringing the leaders for their consultations. He knew it could not be long now. His chance would be gone, perhaps for ever.

I'm never going to see Etty again, he thought with a sudden flash of bright, searing clarity.

With a swift movement, he wrenched open the door of the truck and dropped to the ground. He heard his mate's startled cry but ignored it. He was running, passing the other trucks and tanks lined up in the lane. He jumped a gate, ran along a hedge, thrust his way between trees into a small wood. He zigzagged along a narrow path, turned to run along the edge, slipped in a ditch and lay prone, his face half-submerged in dirty water, listening for the sounds of pursuit above the pounding of his heart.

There were a few shouts. Miraculously, they faded into the distance. They were going the opposite way and, although he knew they would soon turn and come back, he had been given his chance.

Jim scrambled to his feet. Moving more cautiously now, employing all the training he had been given in silent, invisible progress across country, he began his journey to Elstow to see Etty.

Phyl was walking behind the hearse, with Mr Carter beside her. Behind them came Kaye and Jenny and some of the other girls. One had her arm in a sling, another a bandage round her head. They all looked pale and subdued, and most of them were crying.

Mr Carter looked defeated. He had always been fond of Etty, but had never realised quite how deep his feelings had gone. Since his wife Violet had died, he had focused more on the quiet little girl from the orphanage and had begun to think of her more and more as a daughter. When he'd offered to give her away at her wedding, it had been with as much pride as if he had indeed been her father.

Now she was gone, and the horror of it would stay with him for the rest of his life.

Phyl glanced up at him. She knew how he was feeling, for she felt the same. Etty had been like a sister, almost as close as her cousin Jo. Etty had shown her how to grate cheese without grating her fingers in the process, and how to whip up eggs so that they scrambled like cream, even in quantity. Etty had gone through training as a Nippy with her. They'd been to the pictures together, they'd gone to the Lyons Club at Sudbury to dance and swim and compete in all sorts of daft races in the Nippies' Sports Day. They'd firewatched together on the Corner House roof during the Blitz, and they'd huddled in the depths of the basement, listening to the crash of the bombs overhead. They'd come to Elstow together and worked on bombs instead of beans on toast, grenades instead of gateaux.

Now she was gone, and nothing would ever be quite the same again.

Phyl looked at the hearses. Two hearses, for two coffins. Nobby Clark was there, too, following Etty as he'd followed her about during these past few weeks. It was a bitter thought, that they would share their funeral service, and she was thankful that the vicar had listened to her pleas that the two should not be buried in the same grave. He'd found a tiny plot in one corner for Etty and another on the other side of the churchyard for Nobby.

She wondered how many there were mourning Nobby, and guessed that most of them were there for Etty's sake.

The hearses reached the gates. They were swung wide and the cortège passed slowly through. Phyl lifted her eyes, blurred with tears, and saw the little knot of people standing on the road.

There was a soldier there, oddly unkempt, with no hat and mud stains on his khaki uniform. Phyl's glance passed over him. And then, with a sudden feeling of disbelief, she looked again.

'Jim,' she whispered. '*Jim* . . .'

Mr Carter, walking beside her, caught her whisper. He looked at her, startled, and followed her gaze.

'Is it?' he murmured. 'Is it really him?'

'Yes! It's Jim. Oh, *Jim* . . .' Phyl broke away and ran to the side of the road. The soldier stared at her and she had a moment of doubt. Surely she'd been mistaken. Surely this rough-looking, unshaven man with his red-rimmed eyes and haggard cheeks could not be Jim, not the Jim who used to ride his motorbike with Etty clinging on behind, who used to come swinging up to the Corner House to take her out after work, who had caught her heart and loved her and given her his ring . . .

'Phyl?' he said wonderingly, and she knew that it was, and knew that he had no idea of what had happened. He did not know that it was Etty's funeral they were following; he did not know that the girl he loved lay in the coffin now being borne towards the big abbey church.

'Oh, Jim,' she whispered again, and took his hand in hers. Slowly, she drew him with her, back into the line, where Mr Carter put his arm around Jim's shoulder. Slowly, he let his steps match theirs as, horrifyingly, comprehension dawned.

When the funeral was over, they stood together at the graveside while Phyl wept against his shoulder. And then two military policemen stepped out of the crowd and led Jim away.

303

Chapter Twenty-Four

'They didn't even bother with a court-martial,' Jo told Josh as the timber gang paused to eat their sandwiches around the fire. The weather was still miserable for June, with a driving, misty rain, but the work went on just the same and Poppy had managed to keep a fire going long enough to boil water for tea. It made a cheerful glow in the dripping gloom of the forest. 'They just took him back and stuck him in his lorry again. More important things to worry about at the moment, the sergeant told him, but when the war's over he'd better look out!'

'Does your cousin say how he took it?' Josh asked, looking at the letter in Jo's hand. 'He must have been pretty cut up, arriving just as the funeral was being held. And then whipped away without even having a chance to find out what had happened. It's enough to send a chap right over the top, and he was pretty near it already, from what you say.'

'I think he was,' Jo agreed soberly. 'He must have been desperate to see Etty to take those sorts of risks. And then to find she was dead – I still can't believe it myself. Our little Etty! She was such a sweet little person, Josh, and she'd had a terrible life. It was only when she met Maggie and the rest of us that she started to be happy. And then Jim – it was such a lovely romance. They really thought the world of each other.' The tears came into her eyes again. 'I'm sorry, I just can't get over it.'

'It's not surprising,' Josh said. He wanted to put his arm around her and hold her close, to comfort her, but he contented himself with patting her knee. 'Look, put the letter away now or it'll get soaked. And Huw'll be wanting us to get back to work any minute.'

'I know.' She folded the letter and tucked it into an inside pocket. 'The worst of it is, she ought to have been *safe* where she was. I mean, all she was doing was waiting on officers. How *could* she have got killed? How could she?'

'A lot of queer things happen in war. Look, Jo, let's meet later on, down by the ford. We'll talk about it – if you'd like to.' He looked at her doubtfully. 'Maybe you'd rather not.'

'I don't know what I'll want to do,' Jo said hopelessly. 'But I'll come, Josh. I just – I just want to be with someone who'll understand.' She turned to look at him. 'I want to be with you.'

Huw the Tree was on his feet, shouting to the gangs to get started again. Their brief respite was over. They packed away their lunch tins and got to their feet, and Poppy stamped out the remains of the fire.

Jo worked mechanically for the rest of the day, her thoughts all with Jim and Etty. The anticipation of meeting Josh later shone like a point of bright light in the darkness of her mind. I just need someone strong to lean on for a bit, she thought. It ought to be Nick really, but he's not here.

I miss him so much, she thought, resting briefly from her work. I want him here with me. I wish he could come – just for a day or two – just so that we could be together for a little while and know that everything's all right.

Her eyes filled with tears again. Tears for herself, tears for Etty, tears for Jim and for Maggie and her family. Tears for the whole world, caught up in this mad conflict that seemed never to be at an end.

'Come on, Jo Laurence!' shouted Huw the Tree, appearing from the misty gloom of the forest. 'We're not here on our holidays, not here to admire the scenery. Don't you know there's a war on? Haven't you got no work to do?'

Jo sighed and lifted her axe again. Of course she had work to do. And of course she knew there was a war on.

★

It was a boy who brought the news. Running all the way from the village, he arrived in the middle of the afternoon at the end of the road the timber gang had built, and stood with heaving shoulders while he tried to gasp out the words. Work stopped as the men and women nearest the road noticed him, and gradually his urgency infected them and they gathered round, urging him to 'spit it out'.

'Must be something big to make you run all this way, Jem Davies,' Huw the Tree said. 'What is it, pub on fire or something? Out with it, boy.'

Jem shook his head and clutched his side. 'Stitch,' he whispered, and then managed, 'It's the invasion. It's started. It's D-Day.'

D-Day. The name that had sounded so dull now seemed to ring like a knell in the silent forest. They all looked at each other and Jo moved a little closer to Josh.

'Invasion?' Huw said. 'You mean we've invaded Germany?'

'Not Germany. France. It was on the news on the wireless. Me mam put it on the Home Service, she always does to get the one o'clock news. There's thousands of soldiers gone over to Normandy. They say they've been ready for weeks, waiting all round the coast, and now they've all got on to ships and gone, all at once. It's the end of the war! We're going to win the war!' He had got his breath back now and began to leap in the air, punching his fists at nothing. Huw caught him as he came down and spoke severely.

'Now, don't you go spreading rumours, young Jem. I knows you and your stories. Are you sure about this?'

'*Yes!* I told you, it was on the news. Thousands and thousands of soldiers, and sailors and marines. And the RAF, too – they're bombing like mad to stop the Germans getting there. We're going to win – we *are*!'

'Not as quick as that, we won't,' Huw said. 'There'll be a long way to go before we can say that. Them Germans won't give in easy. There'll be a lot more blood shed before we can say it's all over.'

'Oh, don't be so gloomy!' Poppy exclaimed, almost as excited as Jem. 'It's marvellous news. Jem's right – we're going to win. We must!'

'Pop's right,' one of the men agreed. 'It's what we need. The Germans are hard-pressed on the other fronts – this lot coming up behind 'em's bound to catch 'em on the hop. We'll have 'em on the run now, sure as God made little chickens.'

There was a roar of approval. The full importance of the news seemed to sink in then, and the men turned to each other and began to shake hands. The girls hugged each other, and then began to hug the men, too. Everyone began to kiss and hug everyone else, and even Huw the Tree found himself caught up in the celebrations.

Jo and Josh came face to face. They looked at each other, and then Jo flung herself into his arms.

'Oh, Josh! Josh! Will this really make all the difference?'

'It must,' he said soberly. 'It must.' He held her close and she knew that he was remembering Huw's words – that there would be much more blood shed before the end came – and she lowered her eyes, thinking of all the men yet to die in this cause. But for the moment they were still alive, and ready to fight; for the moment, there was hope for everyone.

'We'll talk about it later,' he said gently, releasing her as Huw called for a return to work. 'Down by the ford.'

'Yes,' Jo said, looking at him with shining eyes. 'Yes, we will.'

There was a great deal to talk about in the days that followed. The phrase 'D-Day' was on everyone's lips. Now they could understand why nobody had been allowed within ten miles of the South Coast all these weeks. Now they could understand the long lines of army trucks, the troops camped by roadsides and in fields. Now they could understand the strange, secret constructions that had been rising on the skyline of the beaches. Enormous artificial harbours, built of concrete, had been taken out to sea and sunk before being raised again and towed to Normandy! It was an idea that was almost impossible to grasp. The powers that be must have been planning it for years. How could they have known the war would last that long?

'I suppose if it hadn't, it wouldn't have mattered,' Sam Pratt said. He had come down to Devon from London to be with his family after the news about Jim and Etty. 'Nobody would have minded a bit of bees and honey wasted on concrete harbours if we'd managed to beat Germany before they was needed. Pity we didn't. It'd have saved our Jim, and poor little Etty.'

'And a few thousand others,' Ivy said sadly. She thought of Jim, gone with the troops to Normandy. And her other sons, Gerry and George, who had enlisted in the Parachute Regiment. 'They say they're setting up hospitals all along the coast now, for the ones what get wounded in the first few days. They know there'll be casualties straight away. Sam, I can't bear to think of our boys . . . Is this all we had them for? Is this why we went through all that trouble, bringing them up, just to see them killed? And Jim in such awful trouble . . . And Etty, *poor* little Etty . . .'

'I know. I know.' His huge hand patted her shoulder. 'I know, Ive. But it don't do no good to go upsetting yourself. They're alive now and, God willing, they'll stay alive. What we got to do is think about the ones that's left to us here. Our Maggie and her Barry, and young Bill and Fred, and our Ginnie. We can't do nothing about the boys, but we can do our best for the kids. Saucepan lids,' he added, realising that he'd almost forgotten to use his Cockney rhyming slang. 'Blimey, the other Pearlies'd have me guts for garters if they heard me talking English!'

Ivy smiled faintly. 'Pearlies,' she said. 'It seems a long time since we put on our pearly costumes for our Maggie's wedding, don't it?'

'It does, gal, it does. Yer, that was a good day.' He grinned reminiscently. 'Once we'd got over all that fuss about young

Jo's sister running off with the cat. Maggie was in a proper state, thinking they weren't going to make it.'

'It'll all come again, won't it?' Ivy asked. 'Once the war's over and we've got peace again, we'll bring the pearlies back, won't we?'

'Course we will, duck, course we will. Only there'll be a bit of sewing for you and our Mags to do first, mind. We lost all our costumes when that bleeding bomb hit us, and Gawd knows where we're going to get all them pearls from.'

A rattling sound on the ceiling made them both look up. Ivy sighed and began to get to her feet, but Sam stopped her.

'She's my mother – bit of bother. Coo, that's a true one and no mistake! I'll see to her. You stop here and get the kettle on for a cup of Rosy Lee. I'm parched with all this chinwagging.'

Ivy did as she was told. She stood at the sink, pumping the water and wondering how much longer poor old Ada would last. She'd been failing for months and now hardly ever left her bed. She came down on good days, but there wouldn't be many more of them. It took Ivy and Maggie all their strength to get her down the narrow stairs as it was, and once she lost the use of her legs completely it would be impossible. It seemed queer to have no Ada in the corner, with her lips tucked in over her gums and her false teeth grinning from the mantelpiece, but it was just another thing they'd have to get used to. And she was a good age after all. Nobody could last for ever.

'What's she want?' she asked when Sam came downstairs. 'The kettle's nearly boiling.'

He sat down heavily on the kitchen chair. 'Don't reckon she'll be wanting one. She's looking poorly, Ive. I'm not sure but what we shouldn't call the doctor.'

Ivy looked at him in alarm. 'She's been off colour the past few days. I thought it was just worry about Jim.'

'She's past worrying about Jim,' he said quietly. 'That noise we heard – I reckon that was her dropping her stick. She's in a sort of a faint – looking grey round the mouth, and

309

breathing heavy.' He got to his feet again. 'I reckon I'll go for him now, Ive. I don't think we ought to leave it no longer.'

Ivy watched him go, and then hurried up the stairs to the narrow little bedroom where Ada slept. She peeped in and saw that it was just as Sam had said. The old lady was lying on her back, her mouth sagging open, and there was a blue shadow around her lips. Her breathing was heavy and she was snoring.

'Ma! Ma!' Ivy touched the bony shoulder, realising suddenly how thin Ada had become. She used to be such a stout little party, too, she thought, sitting there in her corner in her black frock and shawl. And it wasn't as if she'd lost her appetite – she could still put away a good meal right up to the last few weeks, never mind she hardly ever used her teeth . . .

'Ma, are you all right? Wake up, there's a love. It's Ivy here, Ivy, what's been with you for years . . . Ma . . .'

There was no response. The old head rolled a little, but the crêpey eyelids didn't flicker, neither did the snoring stop. Ivy sat down beside the bed, holding the claw-like hands in hers, rubbing them gently as if it would bring the weary body back to life. Why didn't I ever see how thin she was getting? she thought. It's not as if I haven't had enough chance, washing her and dressing her every day, getting her up and down the stairs. It must have happened gradual, so I didn't notice, but I should have seen it, I *should* have done.

At last she heard footsteps outside and voices as Sam and the doctor came up the stairs. She stood up hastily, laying Ada's hand gently on the worn coverlet, and turned with relief.

'Oh, thank Gawd you're here. I didn't know what to do for her. Should I have given her some water? Only I was frightened she might choke—'

'It's all right, Mrs Pratt.' The doctor was tall and thin with white hair, brought back out of retirement when his son, also a doctor, had joined the army. He came to the bed and looked at the frail body, then picked up the thin hand and laid his fingers on the loose, tortoise-like skin of the wrist.

'She's a good age,' he said quietly. 'And peaceful. I should just let her slip away, quietly and naturally.'

Sam and Ivy stared at him. 'You – you mean she's going?'

'No doubt of it, I'm afraid, Mr Pratt. But she's in no discomfort. It's the end we would all wish for.'

Better than lying on a battlefield, drowning in your own blood, Ivy thought with a sudden dreadful vision of one of her sons, even now landing in Normandy. She gave a sudden sob and Sam moved to put his arm around her shoulders.

'We ought to get our Maggie home from the hospital. And there's the kiddies, too – they're at school, except for little Barry. He's gone down the farm to play with young Micky Brimacombe. But maybe it's best they're kept out of the way.'

'Well, I always feel it's better to let children say goodbye to a member of the family who's dying,' the doctor said. 'Especially one who's been as much loved as old Mrs Pratt obviously has. But it's up to you, of course.'

Loved? Ivy looked at the snoring body and wondered if Ada had indeed been much loved. Sitting there in her corner, grumbling toothlessly, catching the kiddies a crack with her stick or her umbrella if they got on the wrong side of her – had she really been loved?

'It's just that we're all so used to her,' she said. 'I mean, she's bin with Sam and me since the day we was wed. And she had a terrible hard life, losing her hubby back at the turn of the century in the Boer War, and being left with four little ones to bring up. Took in washing, she did – washed ninety shirts a week *and* starched all their collars separate. And her mum and dad knew young Henry Croft down the market, him what started the Pearlies – gave him his supper often, she used to tell me.'

The doctor nodded. Not much of this made any sense to him, but he knew that Ivy was shocked and needed to talk. But he had been up all night with a difficult birth at the other end of the village, and he'd had only an hour's sleep when Sam had arrived to ask him to come. He rubbed a hand across his face and said, 'It'll be a few hours yet. I don't think there's any need to bring the children home from school. I'll look in again later, but if there's any change, call me at once.'

Ivy nodded. She turned back to the bed and took Ada's hand in her own once more. The doctor turned away and Sam saw him downstairs.

'How long d'you reckon it will be, Doc?' he asked when they reached the kitchen door. 'Seems to me she's gone downhill since I come out to fetch you.'

'She's certainly deteriorating. It could be just a few hours – it could be a day or two. There's really no telling. But it'll give her comfort to have her family around her. We don't know just how much someone in that state is aware of what's happening around them, but they really do seem easier when there's someone else there to hold their hand and maybe just talk to them. Remember the good times, that sort of thing.' The doctor yawned suddenly. 'I'm sorry – not much sleep last night.'

He went off down the garden path and Sam turned back into the kitchen. He stood for a moment looking round. It looked suddenly much barer than it had before, and Ada's corner, empty of her presence for ever now, looked dull and untidy.

He saw her false teeth grinning at him from the mantel-piece. He took them down and looked at them, blinking a little. Her smile, he thought, even if she didn't have call to use it all that much. And now she'll never use it again.

Ada died that night, with Sam and Ivy and Maggie around her bed. The children had all tiptoed in to say goodbye – Ginnie tearful, the boys inclined to giggle from uncertainty and embarrassment, Barry unknowing and unconcerned, climbing on to the bed to give his great-grandmother a sloppy, soft-mouthed kiss.

'Night-night, Gran-Gran,' he said, and stumped off to the bedroom he shared with the others, where he could be heard murmuring the words over and over again. 'Night-night,

Gran-Gran. Night-night, Gran-Gran . . .' Eventually his voice faded and he fell asleep.

'Sam,' Ada said, suddenly and very loudly, startling them all, 'it's time you was in bed. Go on, now, before your dad comes home . . .' She moaned and rolled her head a little and Ivy looked at her husband.

'She's wandering. She must have heard Barry's voice and it took her back to when you was a baby.'

'The doctor said she might still be able to hear,' he muttered. 'That's why we had to be careful what we said. Talk about good memories, he said, and that's what we done.'

'It's nice she's remembering them. Times when you was a kiddy, and she still had your dad. Sam's gone to bed now, Ma,' she said more loudly to the still figure. 'All tucked up, he is.'

But Ada made no response. She lay snoring, until at last her breathing began to be more laboured. She moaned a little and twisted her head about, and Ivy took her hand and tried to soothe her.

'It's all right, Ma. It's all right. You're just going to sleep. You're just going to have a nice long sleep . . . Sam, d'you think we ought to get the doctor back? D'you think she's suffering?'

'I don't see as there's anything he could do, love. She's sinking, and that's all there is to it.' He bent closer and put his mouth close to his mother's ear. 'Take it easy, now, gal. It ain't going to be hard. Just you rest easy, and let it come natural. It ain't no good fighting it no more.'

'She always was a fighter,' Ivy said, tears creeping down her cheeks. 'She never let nothing go by her.'

'That's how she come to live so long. That, and you looking after her so well. You done a good job, Ive, and you never complained, not like some would've done.' He stroked his mother's withered cheek. 'That's it, gal. You just let go, now. Just breathe easy and let it all go . . .'

The papery eyelids fluttered and opened. Ada's rheumy

eyes stared straight into her son's face. A tiny frown made one more crease amongst hundreds on her brow, and then she smiled her old toothless, gummy smile.

'You bin a good boy, Sammy,' she said in a voice like the rustle of dried leaves. 'And you picked a good wife. You look after her, now, and those kiddies. I'm too tired . . .'

She caught her breath and her head came up suddenly from the pillow. Her eyes opened wide, as if she could see something beyond the room, something that dazzled her and made her blink. Her mouth worked as if she were trying to say something more and she reached out, waveringly, with shaky hands. And then her throat rattled, her body stiffened momentarily, and she relaxed and fell back, her eyes still staring at whatever it was she thought she had seen.

There was a moment's quiet. The absence of the snoring gave the room an almost eerie silence.

'She's gone,' Ivy whispered. 'Sam, she's gone. Oh, Maggie . . .'

'It's all right, Mum. It's all over.' Maggie gripped her mother's hand. 'She never suffered. It was a beautiful—' Her voice cracked and she choked back a sob. 'It was a beautiful way to go.'

'It was better than our Evie had,' Sam said quietly. 'Better'n poor little Queenie, too. She had a hard life, but she was lucky at the last.'

'Yes.' Ivy sat gazing at the old face, still holding the chilling hand. 'Sam, there's some pennies in my purse. Fetch a couple of them up here, will you, and I'll put them on her eyes to keep 'em shut. We'll tuck her up here nice and comfy tonight, and tomorrow we'd better get the nurse in to lay her out. She won't get a proper Pearly funeral, and that's a shame, considering what she done for young Henry Croft, what started Pearlies, but we can't help that. We'll give her the best send-off we can manage.'

Maggie crept downstairs and put the kettle on. She knew that her mother and father would want some time alone with the old woman, and after that they'd need a cup of tea. And in the meantime, she had her own memories.

Gran, bustling round the house, sweeping and scrubbing floors and helping look after them all when they'd been youngsters. Gran, marching down to the shops or the market to haggle over groceries, her black umbrella brandished like a lethal weapon. Gran, failing in health, her knees swollen, sitting more and more in her corner, smiling her toothless smile or putting her teeth in for special occasions. Gran, pretending to sleep the day Tommy had come home unexpectedly so that he and Maggie could slip upstairs together. Gran, never short of a grumble.

We'll miss her, she thought. We'll miss her really bad.

Chapter Twenty-Five

For a week, the news was full of D-Day and reports from the coast of Normandy. Thousands of British and American troops had gone over, and this time – unlike the earlier disaster at Dieppe, when so many Canadians had been killed – the invasion was a success. With a fleet of six thousand ships, fifty miles wide, all setting sail together from points along the South Coast and protected by over twelve thousand planes of the Allied air forces, it could hardly be anything else. The enemy was, at last, overwhelmed and on the run.

'We're winning,' Jo said exultantly. 'We're winning at last. It won't be long now.'

She had managed to get a few days' leave to go home. Phyl, still shaken by Etty's death, had been given a week as well, and the two families rejoiced to have at least two of their members back with them. All the boys were away now, except for Jo's brother Eric, who had returned from his evacuation home in Kent on leaving school and now worked as an errand boy. And Bill and Carrie had agreed to let Alice, who had been begging to come back now that the bombing had stopped, come home, too.

'She's not bringing that other cat with her, mind,' Bill warned his wife. 'One's enough in this house.'

'She knows that. He's getting old anyway, that Solomon, and the old couple wouldn't want to let him go. Anyway, she'll be too pleased to see her Robbie again to worry about other cats.' Carrie paused, then added, 'She does want to bring Ossie, though.'

'*Ossie?* The *boy?*'

'Well, yes. Just for a few days' holiday. They're good pals and she wants to show him a bit of London. You can understand it.'

'A *bit* of London's about all there is left to show him,' Bill said. 'We had the Blitz, now we seem to be getting all these gas explosions. There was another one yesterday, the mains have bin weakened, so they said. It's just one thing after another . . . Where's he going to sleep?'

'Well, in our Freddy's bed, I suppose. Eric won't mind sharing the room. There's no harm in that, is there?'

Bill sighed. 'I suppose not. And the Tawes have been good to our Alice, so it's only right we should give their boy a bit of a holiday. They'll probably be glad to have the house to themselves for a few days. It's hard on an old couple like that to have two youngsters landed on them, and one a stranger. I don't suppose they minded having Ossie, he's their own grandson, but our Alice—'

'There's nothing wrong with our Alice,' Carrie said quickly.

'I'm not saying there is. But she's not their own flesh and blood, is she, and you can't deny she's got a will of her own. Never ready to take no for an answer – that's her trouble and always has been.'

'Well, she's a sensible girl now, and doing well at school, according to that letter we had saying she could stop on till she's fifteen or even sixteen if she wants to.'

'I'm not so sure about that,' Bill said, frowning. 'To my mind, she ought to be leaving this summer, now she's turned fourteen. She could still stop on in Devon and get a job down there till the war's over.'

'We won't get the billeting paid if she does that. Anyway, why not let her stop at school another year or two? It'll help her get a better job.'

'Better job?' Bill repeated in astonishment. 'What sort of a better job? There's plenty of jobs for a girl like Alice, in a shop or a hairdresser's or something. She'll be getting married in a few years and have her own home to look after. She don't want any more education to do that. Our Jo never did, and she done all right.'

'We don't know what things are going to be like after this war's over,' Carrie argued. 'There might not be many jobs about for young girls, not when all the men come back and want to take over again.'

Alice and Ossie arrived only a few minutes after Jo had walked in the door, and the house was suddenly filled with exclamations and laughter.

'Look how she's grown!'

'A proper young lady now.'

'And look how brown our Jo is – you look as if you've been abroad on your holidays!'

'Holidays!' Jo retorted. 'It's not much of a holiday, being a lumberjill, I can tell you! And this isn't sunburn, it's rust. It's never stopped raining since Christmas.'

'Where's Robertson? Where's my Robbie?' Alice, her fair hair streaming down her back, went out to the kitchen and opened the back door. 'Robbie! *Robbie!* I'd have thought you'd have kept him in so he'd be here to say hallo to me,' she complained to her mother, returning to the living-room.

'You try keeping that cat in when he wants to go out,' Carrie answered. 'He nearly tore the door down when he got shut in by accident one day. Claws like carving knives he's got. He'll be back when it's teatime, never you fear.' She looked at Ossie, standing shyly in the doorway. 'Come on in, Ossie, love, don't stand there. Make yourself at home.'

Jo looked at her sister. 'You're nearly as tall as me now. You'll be able to be a Nippy, too, if you go on growing like that.'

'A Nippy!' Alice exclaimed, tossing her head so that her hair swung. '*I'm* not going to be a Nippy. I'm going in the Civil Service.'

'The Civil Service? First I've heard of that,' her father said. 'What's put that idea into your head?'

'My teacher says I've got the brains to do it, and if I stop at school till I'm fifteen and then do a shorthand–typing course, I could be a secretary.'

'A *secretary*! Well, you got big ideas, I'll say that, never mind a brain. And who says you're going to stop on another year? Your mother and me's been talking about that and we think you ought to leave school and come home and get a job here.'

Carrie turned to him, her eyes wide, and opened her mouth to speak, but Alice got in first. 'You were keen enough for me to go away when the war started. I'd have thought you'd be pleased I want to stop there now.'

'You were never supposed to be going there for good, as well you know. And now the bombing's stopped and all our troops are over there – well, it seems a good time for you to come home. You'd be leaving school in a few weeks anyway.'

Alice looked sulky and Jo hid a smile, thinking how often she'd seen that lower lip stuck out when Alice had been smaller and couldn't get her own way.

'But that's just it, Dad. I don't want to leave school. I want to stop on and get some qualifications.'

'*Qualifications?*' Bill echoed, as if Alice had asked for an elephant for Christmas. 'What's a girl like you want with qualifications? You'll be getting married and—'

'Don't let's start arguing when the girls have hardly got in the door,' Carrie interrupted. 'We can talk about all that later. It's lovely to see you both, and you, too, Ossie. Jo, you're nearest the kitchen door, put the kettle on, there's a love, and we'll have a bit of cake with it. I got some dried fruit a few weeks ago and made a nice Dundee to celebrate.'

'A Dundee cake!' Jo exclaimed. 'Well, that *is* a welcome home.' She went out to the tiny kitchen and filled the familiar old kettle and set it on the gas, then stood looking around. The kitchen was just as she remembered it, the walls

319

distempered in a pale green and the gas stove with its bowed legs standing in one corner, next to the cupboard Bill had made. The green American cloth on the table was looking the worse for wear, but Jo would have been disappointed if it had been replaced. She wanted everything to stay the same, the way she remembered it from before the war.

She took some cups down from the hooks beneath the cream-painted shelves and got the milk out of the meat-safe outside the back door. I wonder if I'll manage to see Nick while I'm here, she thought wistfully. She had written to tell him about her leave but had received no answer – not surprising, since he must be flying day and night, with the invasion on, but she still hoped he'd manage to write, or even scrape a few hours to be with her in London. I could go down to the airfield, she thought. They'd probably not let me in but we could meet outside. Just to see him for an hour or so, even for only half an hour, would be better than nothing.

With thoughts of Nick came other thoughts, of Josh. Since Etty's death they had become even closer, and she knew, guiltily, that she was very nearly in love with him. Only the thought of Nick and the presence of Nick's wedding ring on her finger kept her from admitting it. She twisted it now as she waited for the kettle to boil, and tried to push Josh from her mind. You couldn't love two men at once. And she was *married*. It was Nick she loved. *Nick*.

Once the war's over, she told herself, once it's all done with and we can be together, everything will be all right.

'Whatever are you doing out there, our Jo?' Carrie exclaimed, coming out into the kitchen. 'The place is full of steam! It must have been boiling this past five minutes!'

Jo jumped. 'Oh, goodness! Sorry, Mum – I was day-dreaming.' Hastily, she spooned tea into the pot and poured the boiling water on top. 'There. One for each person and none for the pot! That'd please Lord Woolton.'

'It pleases me, too,' her mother said. 'This rationing don't get any easier. You brought your book, I hope?'

'Yes, of course I did.' Jo glanced at her mother. 'This

business about Alice . . .'

'Nothing's been decided. I don't know why your dad said that, I'm all for her stopping on. And when you think he was the one that was so keen for her to go in the first place . . .'

'I suppose he'd like her back, now the bombing's stopped.' Jo began to pour the tea, then paused, the pot held up. 'What's that funny droning noise?'

'I don't know. Sounds like an aeroplane, doesn't it?' Carrie looked at her doubtfully.

'Not like one I've heard before,' Jo began, and stepped back quickly as her father and sister came through the door. 'Dad, what d'you think it is?'

'It's that secret weapon Hitler's been on about,' he said, half-jokingly. He opened the back door and peered out, and his voice changed sharply. 'Blimey – look at that! You can see it up there. A sort of plane – a miniature one, with little stubby wings . . .' He shaded his eyes with one hand as the others crowded out behind him, staring up at the sky. 'What the bloody hell *is* it?'

'It can't be a—' Jo began, and then, as they watched, she drew in a breath and put her hand to her mouth. 'Oh, my God, it's coming *down* . . .'

The droning engine of the tiny plane stopped abruptly. There was the briefest pause and its nose dropped and it began to plunge earthwards. It fell past the skyline of the buildings and then there was an enormous explosion. The ground shook and a huge cloud of dust, smoke, rubble and flame rose into the air.

'*Down!*' Bill yelled. 'Get *down*! Carrie – Jo – Alice! Ossie, get down on the ground, *quick!*'

They lay half in and half out of the kitchen door, clutching each other and shaking. The sound of the blast died away, leaving silence. After a long time, Jo raised her head gingerly and saw her father doing the same.

'What on earth was that?' she whispered.

'I dunno, gal. I reckon it's what I said – Hitler's secret weapon. He's been threatening it and I suppose he reckons

321

now we've started to invade he'd better use it.' Bill stood up cautiously and dusted himself down. 'And I'll tell you something else – all them "gas explosions" we've been hearing about, I reckon they're the same thing.'

'Bombs?' Jo asked, getting to her feet. 'Sort of . . . flying bombs?'

'That's just about the size of it,' her father said grimly. 'You hit the nail right on the head there, our Jo. I reckon that's just what they are – flying bombs.'

The flying bombs were called V1s but they very quickly acquired other names – buzz-bombs, or doodlebugs. By the time the Government admitted that the country was under attack once more, and Herbert Morrison made his announcement on the wireless, there had been over seventy explosions, killing hundreds of people. Most of them fell on London, and people learnt to listen for the menacing drone and the swift cut-out of the engine which presaged the explosion. If the sound went on past you, you could breathe again; if you were directly below it when the drone stopped, you hadn't got much chance.

'They're aimed at London,' Bill said as the two families ate supper together on Jo's third night at home. Phyl had arrived on the evening of the first explosion, which had damaged the railway line and held her up for several hours. 'It's only a few that don't make it and drop on places like Portsmouth and Dover instead, so we're practically copping the lot.'

They were back to spending nights in the air-raid shelter. The buzz-bombs came over during the day, too, but as Phyl said, you couldn't let the Germans drive you underground all the time. And she wanted Jo to come with her to the Corner House.

'What's the point of going there?' Stan Jennings asked. 'All your mates have left, haven't they?'

'Well, the ones we knew best, yes. But there are still a few there. Anyway, we want to go and see the old place.'

'I don't know—' Bill began, but Carrie caught his eye and

he fell silent. They'd had all this out already. The girls were over twenty-one now, and living away from home. 'We can't tell them what to do any more,' Carrie had said.

Stan and May thought the same. You might not agree with what they did, but you just had to bite your tongue and say nothing. You could ask them to be home at a reasonable time, though. 'Otherwise your mother'll worry, you know what she is. 'Specially with all these doodlebugs. They're coming over all the time now, and there's no warnings given, there just isn't time.'

'We won't be late, Dad,' Phyl said. 'And it's light till gone eleven, with the daylight saving, so we won't even be coming home in the blackout. You don't need to worry about us.'

'I do, all the same,' May told her sister when the girls had gone out for a walk after tea. 'She's not the girl she used to be. Life and soul of the party, our Phyl always was, and now she's so pale she looks like a ghost, and hardly got a word to say for herself.'

'She's still upset over poor Etty,' Carrie said. 'You'll have to give her time. Maybe it'll do her good to go up to town tomorrow.'

'Can me and Ossie go, too?' Alice begged. 'Please. I want to show him Buckingham Palace and all that.'

Carrie sighed. 'I suppose so. But you mind and do what your sister tells you, all right? No more running off.'

Alice made a face. 'Mum, that was years ago. I don't do that sort of thing any more.'

Her mother gave her a look that said she would if she felt like it, and Alice grinned. She'd already made up her mind to go to London anyway, and her mother knew it. She also knew, although Alice did not, that she and Bill had decided that their younger daughter was to go back to Devon the day after tomorrow, and Bill had even agreed that she could stay on at school, if only for the discipline. 'She still needs telling,' he'd said, 'and if her parents aren't there to do it, her teachers are the next best thing.'

They set off next morning, heading straight for Marble

Arch. From the top of the bus, they were able to point out to Ossie all the landmarks – or at least, those that were left, Jo remarked wryly. But it was surprising how many there were: lots of the old churches, including St Paul's Cathedral which had so miraculously withstood the bombs and flames of the Blitz; the tall, thin Monument, commemorating the Great Fire of London nearly three hundred years before; the rather battered Houses of Parliament with the tower of Big Ben standing untouched, and the two great bridges, London Bridge and Tower Bridge.

'See, there's still quite a lot left,' Phyl said when the tour came to an end. She was looking brighter. 'Let's go to Marble Arch now and then walk through Hyde Park to Buckingham Palace and catch the train at Victoria. I reckon Ossie will have seen all he wants to of London by then!'

They wandered along Oxford Street and arrived at the Corner House. Outside, Phyl and Jo stopped and gazed up at the façade. They exchanged glances and smiled waveringly.

'Feels a bit funny, doesn't it?' Phyl whispered. 'Remember that first day, Jo? When we went to the Strand Corner House after we'd seen the Coronation procession? That was when we first got the idea of being Nippies.'

Jo nodded. 'And then we wrote in and got asked to come for our interviews . . . I thought I'd never get me hands clean enough, what with working in the greengrocer's shop and everything.' She held out her palms and looked ruefully at them. 'And now they're even worse. All rough and hard, and black as the ace of spades. I'd never get taken on as a Nippy now.'

'Nor me.' Phyl's hands were stained with yellow from the explosives she worked with. She caught Jo looking curiously at her and said hastily, 'It's that curry they make at Elstow. It's impossible to get off your skin.'

'How d'you get curry—?' Jo began, but Alice was pushing open the big doors and beckoning impatiently. 'All right, we're coming! Wonder if old Turgoose is still here,' she whispered to Phyl as they followed Alice and Ossie into the big, familiar room. 'Oh, my – *doesn't* it feel queer to be back?'

It was just ordinary sausages and beans and chips or shepherd's pie now. The plates of cakes were not so fancy, and there weren't so many different kinds. The teacups were utility and the glass chandeliers had gone entirely, replaced by plain cloth lampshades.

Yet the atmosphere didn't seem very different. A seater still came forward to greet them and show them to a table, and a Nippy, smart in her black frock and white apron, came swiftly to hand them a menu and take their order. Jo and Phyl glanced at her uniform, noting the buttons still sewn on with red cotton and the white cap perched jauntily on the girl's smooth head.

'Nippies have been wearing this outfit ever since they started,' the girl informed them as she caught their gaze. 'It's quite smart, isn't it, but you wouldn't believe how particular they are. Mustn't sew the buttons on with white cotton. Oh, no, red it's always been and red it's got to stay!'

Phyl and Jo exchanged glances and began to giggle. The girl looked hurt and Phyl hastened to apologise.

'We're not laughing at you. It's just that we were Nippies ourselves till a couple of years ago. Well, I still am, I suppose,' she said quickly, remembering once again that everyone was supposed to think she was waiting on army officers. 'Only I'm not in a Corner House now, I'm at Els—in Outside Catering. But we used to work here.'

'Here? In this Corner House? Coo-er.' The girl gazed at them. 'I bet you can see a few changes.'

'Not that many,' Jo said with a grin. 'For instance, old Goosy Gander over there used to look at us like a dead fish, just the way she's looking at you now!'

The girl turned and caught the supervisor's eye. With a wink and a little grimace, she whipped out her notebook and began to write busily. 'I'd better get on! What d'you want?'

'Big pot of tea, beans on toast all round and a plate of assorted fancies,' Jo said, before anyone could speak. 'It's what you'd have chosen anyway,' she said to them as the

Nippy hurried away. 'And you don't get a choice at home, do you?'

'That's why we'd like one when we come out,' Alice said. She turned her head, surveying the busy restaurant, and then turned back quickly and stared at the table. 'She's coming over. The one you said looked like a dead fish.'

Jo and Phyl smiled as the floor supervisor approached. They'd always got on well with Miss Turgoose, who had been strict enough but never unfair, and they were pleased to see that she was smiling, too. She came to a stop beside their table.

'Phyllis! And Josephine. How very nice to see you. Are you on holiday?'

'Just a few days' leave, Miss Turgoose,' Jo said. 'I'm working in a timber camp in Shropshire now – we're part of the Land Army really – and Phyl's at Elstow. But I suppose you know about that since it's a Lyons.'

'Elstow. Oh, yes. Rather a mysterious sort of place, but we don't talk about it here. Least said, soonest mended.' She frowned a little, and Jo guessed she was thinking of Irene Bond, who had said too much to the wrong person. 'Well, it's good to see you again. And do you think you'll be coming back to us once the war's over?'

Phyl shrugged. 'I don't know, Miss Turgoose. I don't suppose so. My hubby'll be back then, and Jo's will be coming out of the air force. I suppose we'll have to wait and see what they do.'

'Of course, you're both married women now, aren't you? I don't suppose you'll be working at all, then.' Miss Turgoose gave them another smile. 'Well, it's good to see you again and I hope you'll come back to see us again when the war's over. Everything will be different then.'

They watched her go and Phyl said, 'Tell you what, Jo. We ought to make a date to see the others here – Maggie and Shirley, I mean – when the war's over. Have a bite to eat together and catch up on all that's happened. I know a lot of it's been pretty bad,' she added soberly, 'but there've been good times, too, haven't there? It'd be good to see each other again.'

'Yes,' Jo said, 'yes, that's a good idea. We'll do that. I'll write to them both. It'd be smashing to see them again.' She turned as the Nippy appeared again at their elbow. 'Here, that looks as good as in the old days. Just look at the size of the pot of tea!'

'It's on the house,' the Nippy said, smiling. 'Miss Turgoose said so. And you're going to have the best selection of cakes we've got.'

'There,' Alice said as she picked up her fork, 'now aren't you sorry you called her a dead fish?'

After their meal they walked through Hyde Park, as Alice had suggested. They came to Hyde Park Corner and sauntered down Constitution Hill, to show Ossie Buckingham Palace. After peering through the gates for a while, they made their way towards Victoria Station.

'It's been a handsome day,' Ossie said. 'Mind, I wouldn't like to live in London. Too noisy for me. I like the countryside and the animals and trees and such. But 'tis good to come an' see the sights.'

'Well, you're going to see another sight now,' Alice told him. 'An Underground station and an escalator. A moving staircase, silly,' she added, giggling at his mystified expression.

They came round the corner and saw the façade of Victoria Station. It was the end of the afternoon and already people were hurrying to go home from work. Laughing at Ossie's bewilderment, the three girls jostled each other to buy tickets, and then, just as they were about to step on to the escalator, they heard the sound that everyone had come to dread.

'A doodlebug!' Jo exclaimed. 'Phyl – Alice – Ossie – get under cover. *Quick!*'

The station had become a mêlée of people struggling to find shelter. Those nearest the entrance stared fearfully into the sky, trying to spot the deadly weapon. Everyone knew

327

that there was really no point in trying to hide – if the engine cut out just above, you'd had it. If it didn't, you were safe – for the time being. But even the blast could do damage over a quarter of a mile. People had been killed by debris hurled into the air from a bomb that had fallen three streets away.

Let it go past, please let it go past, Jo prayed. She reached out to pull Alice and Phyl close to her, and saw Alice grab Ossie's sleeve. *Please*, don't let any of us be hurt. If anything happens to our Alice – just when Mum and Dad thought it was safe for her to come back – I don't know what they'll do. And Phyl. And Ossie – he's only come for a couple of days, it wouldn't be fair . . . Please, *please*, don't let anything happen to them . . .

The doodlebug's swift flight seemed to be bringing it straight for them. Jo held her breath. It was almost overhead. It was past now, surely it was past . . . *Please, God, please, let it go past* . . .

The engine cut out.

There was a tiny, dreadful silence. It was as if the earth had momentarily held its breath. And then a noise that filled the head, an explosion that seemed to come from deep beneath the ground yet swirled all around, beating and pounding at the mind, ripping bodies apart, tearing at the skin and the muscle and the blood. Jo felt as if she had been lifted into the air, as if she were being tossed about on a wave of solid sound, hurled against a wall that was harder than anything she could have imagined, yet somehow did not, could not, exist, and then thrown down again as if in a temper by some giant child having a ferocious tantrum. She heard a terrible clatter and a mighty crash, as if the entire station had been torn apart and dropped from a great height, each brick singly; and then a smashing of glass, a screeching of tortured metal. The afternoon was suddenly dark, and the soft summer air filled with choking, filthy dust and debris that got into your nose and your eyes and your mouth. It was like swimming in the depths of a suffocating morass of dirt and slime.

The noise died slowly away. Very gradually, Jo became aware that she was lying on a lump of twisted, jagged concrete. She moved cautiously and felt a sharp pain in her wrist. If that's all I've done, she thought, I'm lucky. And then . . . *Where are the others?*

'Phyl! Alice! Ossie!'

All around her, people were crying out and calling. Some were screaming in evident pain, others groaning. A baby was howling in fear. A man was shouting to everyone to keep calm, help would come soon, and a woman was weeping bitterly that her Jackie had been killed, he was here beside her, dead, she knew he was. And an old lady asked hopelessly, over and over again, for 'our Janet'.

Jo found she could move. Carefully, she drew up her legs and pulled herself into a sitting position. Then on to her knees. Something lurched and she gasped and clung to the concrete lump. Over in a corner there was a further crash, as another lump of debris fell.

'Phyl!' Jo called again, in panic. 'Phyl, are you there? Alice, are you all right? Ossie? Ossie?' She stopped as dust filled her mouth, and coughed violently. 'Oh, what's happened to you all?'

The dust was clearing a little. She could see daylight through the wrecked entrance to the station. People were coming from the street, running to help. Somewhere in the distance she could hear the bells of a fire engine and ambulance.

'Jo?' A wavering voice from near by brought her heart leaping in her chest. She peered around her in the murk.

'Phyl? Is that you? Are you all right?'

'I think so. I think I got knocked out. What was it?'

'A doodlebug. Don't you remember? We're at Victoria. We had Alice and Ossie with us, only I don't know what's happened to them. Oh, Phyl, if anything's happened to our Ali—'

'She's here,' Phyl said, and now Jo could make out her figure, half lying beneath a huge piece of timber. 'They're

329

both here. At least, I think . . . it looks like Alice's shoe. She had those sandals on, didn't she?'

'Yes. What do you mean? Is that all you can see? She – she's not buried, is she?'

'I'm not sure,' Phyl whispered. 'I can't see properly. But I'm sure it's her foot. Only – oh, Jo, she doesn't seem to be moving . . .'

Chapter Twenty-Six

By the end of June – less than three weeks after the first bomb had fallen – nearly two thousand people had been killed by V1s, and over five thousand seriously injured. The Government's dismissal of the first few as 'gas explosions', announced to prevent panic, soon became futile. Everyone knew that a new and dreadful weapon was being employed against them, and the excitement and optimism of D-Day were overshadowed by this fresh terror.

The bombs fell indiscriminately. There was no attempt to target them at military establishments, although of the hundred and twenty worshippers killed at the Guards Chapel in Wellington Barracks, not far from Buckingham Palace, half were servicemen. And there might well have been soldiers or sailors or airmen in the pub where twenty-four were killed, or the shops or offices or streets and houses where the bombs dropped from the sky to shatter lives as well as buildings. But all of the two hundred office workers enjoying their lunch-break at Bush House, home of the BBC, were civilians. And the terror was even worse than during the first great Blitz.

The ugly, stubby-winged flying bombs came over in a steady stream, arriving too swiftly for the sirens to be sounded. The harsh rattle of anti-aircraft guns sounded from every corner, and some were brought down by barrage balloons. But even these were liable to explode. The only thing you could do was listen, and then wait. And hope.

Fourteen people were killed in the doodlebug attack on Victoria Station that day. But Alice Mason wasn't one of them, and she and Ossie were finally dug out of the rubble under which they lay half-buried. Miraculously, they were unhurt. A steel plate had fallen across them, held up by an iron girder, and they lay beneath it, trapped, filthy, terrified, but untouched.

'It's like a miracle,' Carrie said when they finally got home. 'Oh, if you *knew* what I've been through, worrying about you all. I was sure you'd all have been killed. We heard it on the wireless, you see, that there'd been a bomb at Victoria, but when your dad got home he said not to worry, you probably weren't anywhere near. But I knew you were, I just *knew* you were.'

'Well, we're all right,' Jo said. 'I must say, I feel a bit shaky, though. It was horrible, Mum. All those hurt people and bodies. It took me back to the day poor Auntie Holt was killed. I thought we'd finished with all that.' She sat down suddenly and put her head in her hands. 'Oh, God, this war, it's awful. It just goes on and on. Isn't it *ever* going to stop?'

Carrie laid her hand on her daughter's shoulder. 'It's all right, Jo. You have a cry. It's reaction, that's what it is. You're bound to feel a bit shook up.' She addressed her twin sister over Jo's head. 'It's their husbands these two want at times like this,' she said in a low voice. 'I mean, they've had hardly any married life. It's unsettling for a young woman and when she gets this kind of a shock as well—'

Jo's head jerked up. 'All right, Mum, I can hear you. And I tell you what – you're right. It's Nick I want, and he ought to be here. It's not fair that I'm left all alone like this. I'm sure he could have got leave at some time to come and see me. I mean, it's not as if he's overseas – we're in the same country. It's daft!'

Carrie sighed. 'I know. But you've heard the news, same as the rest of us. Those pilots are flying all the hours God sends. I'm sure he'd come and see you if he could.' She turned to the younger children. 'You might as well know now, Alice and Ossie, you're going straight back to Devon tomorrow, on the first train. They're saying everyone's got to go that doesn't have to stay and, much as I like to have you at home, I can't put up with the worry of it. I want you safe. And you, too, Jo – you ought to get back to Shropshire.'

Jo shook her head. 'Not without seeing Nick. And if he won't come to see me, I'll go to him. I'm going to go and see him – tomorrow. I don't care *what* they say!'

'Go and see Nick? But how can you? He's not allowed off the airfield—'

'So he says,' Jo said bitterly. 'But I don't know anyone else who's married to a pilot and not seen him as much as me and Nick. *Everyone* gets a few days' leave some time or other.'

'But suppose he's on duty.'

'Then I'll wait till he's not. He can't fly for ever, Mum. He's got to have a few hours off. Anyway, he ought to be pleased to see me. He ought to be thrilled to think I've taken the trouble.'

She got up early next morning and caught the train to Chichester. Most of the restrictions on travel were being lifted now that the troops had left and there was no argument when she asked for her ticket. She sat on the train, looking out at the fields and the rolling Downs, thinking of Nick.

I'm looking forward to seeing him, she told herself. I'm so excited, I can hardly bear it. And it's no wonder I feel a little bit nervous, too – anyone would. I wonder if he's got my telegram. I wonder if he'll be at the station to meet me . . .

She clenched her hands in her lap and tried not to think about Shropshire, about the village of Clun which had somehow become her home, about the people there who had made her welcome. Her friends, Poppy and Suzy. Her landlady, Mrs Dell. Huw the Tree and the other men. And Josh.

His face was very clear in her mind. Lean and brown, with straight dark hair and brown eyes. Very straight eyebrows, a smooth, calm forehead. Long hands, with tapering fingers. Strong fingers. Gentle fingers . . .

A firm, strong mouth that could break into a smile as sweet as a baby's.

The train was almost at the little station near the airfield. Jo wrenched her mind away and thought again of Nick. I hope he's waiting for me, she thought. Oh, Nick, please, be at the station. I want to see you. I need to see you.

PS: I love you . . . I love you . . . I *do* . . .

Carl had gone. His convalescence over, he had returned to service, and all that Maggie knew was that he'd probably joined the troops in the invasion. She walked with Barry and the other children beside the river, watching the June sunshine glitter on the tumbling waters, and wondered why she hadn't known she would miss him this much.

He's the best man I've ever known, she thought sadly. If things had been different . . . we could have made a life together. But with him living in Canada and me in London . . . and with me having Barry, and not knowing who his dad was . . . how could it have worked?

All the same, she all too often caught herself imagining what it might be like to live in Canada. Her ideas of the country were hazy but Carl had told her about lakes and forests, and beautiful cities of modern buildings, and from films she had seen – mostly of either Hollywood or the Wild West – Maggie had cobbled together an image of wild open spaces and glamorous party living that seemed a world away from the streets of Cockney London and the terror of the war. It seemed a long way, too, from Devon, with its narrow lanes and treeless moors. It seemed both alluring and alarming.

Anyway, she thought, I couldn't leave Mum. Not while she and Dad are having to live apart. And then there's Billy and Ginnie and little Fred. And I don't even know why I'm thinking about it! He might have thought something of me while he was here, but it won't last. Why should it, with all those other girls in Canada, just waiting for their men to come home?

She sat on a rock and watched the children playing beside the river. If only Tommy had never been killed. But Tommy seemed a long way away, a long time ago, and she didn't even have their baby to remind her of him. Instead, she had Barry, and he didn't remind her of anyone.

I'd just like to *know*, though, she thought moodily, staring into a clear brown pool at the fish that darted beneath the rocks. I'd just really like to know . . .

Nick wasn't at the station. Jo swallowed her disappointment and set out to walk to the airfield. In less than half an hour she was at the gate. The corporal on guard listened to her request and shook his head.

'Sorry, love, we can't send out messages for personnel. He's probably on duty, see. They're on call all the time, those boys.'

'But he's my husband,' Jo pleaded. 'We haven't seen each other for so long. And I've got to go back to Shropshire tomorrow. I'm in the Timber Corps – the Land Army. It might be months before we get another chance.'

The man looked at her and sighed. 'Look, I'm sorry. I can see you're upset, but what would we do if everyone came to the gate asking to see their chap? It's just not on.'

'But everyone *isn't* here,' Jo said. 'It's only me. Please. I must see him. I – I'll stay here all day. All night. There's got to be *some* time when he could come, even if it's only for half an hour.'

The corporal sighed again. He glanced around and caught sight of a young airman strolling past and called him over. The boy came, looking curiously at Jo. He couldn't be more than eighteen, she thought, and saw the wings on his shoulder. I wonder how long he'll survive, or whether he'll end up marked and disfigured like Nick . . .

'Go and see if you can find this bloke,' the corporal said, writing down Nick's details on a scrap of paper. 'Tell him his missus is at the gate with his sandwiches.'

The boy looked surprised, but went off, and Jo gave the corporal a grateful glance. 'Thanks. I won't be a nuisance to you. I'll go over the road and wait there. Sorry to have given you any trouble.'

'It's all right,' the corporal said. He grinned suddenly. 'I tell you, if you were my missus I wouldn't keep you hanging about. Some blokes don't know how lucky they are!'

Jo blushed and smiled back, then went to stand by the hedge on the opposite side of the road. The airfield stretched away behind its wire, and she knew that normally anyone who loitered here would be sent on their way by the guards. I'd better not stop here too long, she thought, or that chap'll get into trouble, and that would be a shame when he's been so helpful . . .

Lost in thought, she had been watching the tall figure walking down the airfield road towards the gate for several moments before it dawned on her that it was Nick.

'*Nick!*' she screamed, hurling herself across the road. 'Oh, Nick, *Nick*! I didn't see it was you – I didn't realise – I didn't think you'd be able to come.' She flung her arms around his neck. 'Oh, it's so good to see you.'

'All right, all right.' He disentangled her arms and gave her a quick kiss. 'Let's get away from here. We'll walk down to the village, we can get a cup of coffee there. I don't have too long, mind,' he warned her. 'I'm on duty at midday.'

'I don't mind. Well, I do, but it's so good to see you – I'd have been happy with just five minutes.' She clasped his hand in hers as they walked along the lane. 'Oh, Nick . . . Are you pleased to see me?'

'Of course I am.' He gave her hand a quick squeeze. 'But didn't you get my telegram?'

'Telegram? No. Maybe it came after I left. I got the earliest train I could.'

'You should have waited,' he said. 'You didn't know I could get out. You could have had a wasted journey.'

Jo looked at him. 'I'd rather that than not try at all. Didn't you want me to come and see you, Nick?'

He sighed. 'It's difficult. We're on duty so much. I can't ever be sure—'

'Well, never mind. I'm here now and you *have* managed to get out, and we can have an hour or two together at least. It's better than nothing.' She looked up at his face. The scars were less livid now, but he would never be entirely rid of them. His whole cheek was stretched and shiny, with puckered edges. The pull on his lip gave his mouth a sneering, sardonic look, and the twinkling amusement that had danced on his face when she first knew him, and which had attracted her so much, had disappeared.

They came to the village. It was very small, but amongst the cluster of cottages there were an inn and a tiny teashop. The pub wasn't open, but Nick pushed open the door of the teashop and they went inside.

'Good morning. You're early customers. What can I get you?' The middle-aged woman who bustled out, in a green flowered apron, gave Jo a curious glance and then turned her attention to Nick. 'Oh, hello, Squadron Leader – I didn't realise it was you. Everything all right?'

'Yes, thanks, Polly.' His reply was brief and the woman gave him a surprised look. 'Pot of coffee, please, and maybe a couple of your fresh scones. This lady's come on a very quick visit so we just want to have a quiet chat.'

'Of course.' Polly disappeared through the kitchen door, and Jo and Nick sat down.

Jo was beginning to feel uncomfortable. Why hadn't Nick introduced her as his wife? The woman obviously knew him. 'D'you come here a lot?' she asked.

'Now and then. Look, Jo, I think we'd better have a talk. I didn't want to do it while the war was still on, but since you're here . . . Oh, thanks, Polly. Yes, that's fine. It's okay, we'll see to ourselves now.' He watched as Polly, clearly knowing her place, closed the kitchen door behind her. 'Will you pour, Jo?'

'Yes, all right.' She lifted the coffee-pot. The joy of seeing Nick was evaporating, leaving her chilled and almost frightened. 'Nick, is anything the matter?'

'Why?'

'You seem – you seem different.' She swallowed. 'You don't seem . . . very pleased to see me.'

'Of course I'm pleased to see you,' he said, but his tone was so flat that she put the pot down with a little bang and looked at him in sudden anger.

'Nick! I'm not a fool. I can tell when you're lying.'

'What do you mean, lying?' His voice was sharp. 'If you've only come here to start an argument—'

'No!' Terrified now, she stared at him. 'Nick, don't talk like that. We've only been together a few minutes – and it's been so long – we can't start quarrelling. Please.'

'Well, don't start calling me a liar, then,' he grumbled. 'I didn't have to come out, you know. I could have just said I was on duty.'

Jo couldn't believe her ears. She gazed at him, trying to find the Nick she knew – the old, teasing, merry Nick – behind the cold, shiny mask of his face. I know his scars make him look different, she thought, but there ought to be something . . . I ought to be able to see in his eyes if he's the same. If he still loves me . . .

Quietly, she said, 'There *is* something the matter. You're going to tell me, aren't you, Nick? You said we had to talk about something.'

'Yes.' He let his eyes drop and began tracing patterns on the table with one finger. 'The thing is, Jo, we've made a mistake.'

'A mistake? What do you mean? What sort of mistake?'

'Getting married,' he mumbled. 'We shouldn't have done it. I didn't really want to, but you went on about it so much, and in the end I—'

'*I* went on about it? But you wanted to get married! We were going to have a double wedding with Mike and Phyl. If you hadn't been shot down—'

'Oh, yes, I know all that.' His tone was impatient, dismissive. 'But after that, things changed, didn't they? You changed.'

Jo gazed at him. '*I* changed?'

338

'Yes,' he said. He looked up and met her eyes. 'When you came to see me in hospital. And that first time, when I had the bandages off and you saw what I looked like. Don't bother to argue about it, Jo, I saw it in your eyes. You were disgusted—'

'*No!*'

'You were. I could see it. You could hardly bring yourself to touch me, and as for kissing me—'

'I couldn't kiss you! You were all burnt.'

'And that was just as well,' he said coldly, 'because I think if you'd had to, you'd have been sick.'

There was a tiny silence. Then Jo said in a shaking voice, 'That's a terrible thing to say.'

'I think it's true.'

'It was a shock. Your mother was shocked, too. She met me at the door, she tried to stop me going in. She didn't want me to see you that morning.'

'Because she knew what effect it would have,' he said. 'She knew you'd be disgusted.'

'Nick, I *wasn't* disgusted.'

'What were you, then? Horrified, dismayed, revolted? Be honest, Jo – you told me just now I was lying. Well, I can tell when you are, too. So why not come out and say so?'

Jo shook her head. Tears were blurring her sight but she kept her eyes fixed firmly on Nick's face. Blindly, she felt for his hand.

'Nick, please. Is this why you haven't been writing so much? Is this what's been eating you all these months? All right, I was shocked, I was horrified and dismayed, but I wasn't disgusted or revolted. I really wasn't. I was *sorry* for you.'

'Oh, and that's supposed to be better, is it?' he broke in. 'So that's why you married me, is it, why you insisted? Because you were *sorry* for me. Not because you loved me, but because you were *sorry* for me. Am I supposed to go through life tied to someone who's just *sorry* for me? Is that your idea?'

'No! Nick, you're twisting everything. Of course I loved you – *love* you. I *wanted* to be married to you. And I don't see what's wrong with being sorry that – that such an awful thing had happened to you. Anyone would be.'

'There's a difference', he said, 'between being sorry that it happened and sorry for me. Don't you see, Jo? I wanted to be *loved*, without any of these other things coming into it. I just wanted to be like we were before.'

'But we could have been,' she said. 'It's only you who keeps dragging your injuries into it.'

'Well, they do happen to matter rather a lot to me,' he retorted.

Jo sighed. Her earlier flare of anger had died down in her distress, but now it was growing again, out of exasperation and frustration. 'Nick, what is it you want, exactly? For me not to take any notice of your burns and not to care at all, or for me to agree that they matter? It seems to me you don't even know yourself.'

'And you certainly don't,' he said, 'or you wouldn't be asking me such a question.'

Jo let go of his hand and ran her fingers through her hair. She felt a desperate sense of things slipping out of control. This isn't why I came, she thought. I just wanted to see him again. I just wanted us to be together for a while.

'Nick, why are we quarrelling like this? Why won't you believe me?' She looked at him again. 'Is there something else wrong? Is there something you haven't told me?'

The silence this time was longer, and as it stretched between them and filled the tiny room, she began to realise that she knew what he was going to say. A cold dread gripped her heart, and she felt her world sink away. She closed her eyes briefly and had a sense of spinning through space.

'Tell me, Nick,' she said at last, opening her eyes again. 'Tell me what it is.' And then, when he still didn't answer, 'Tell me *who* it is.'

Maggie walked on beside the river. Billy and Ginnie had grown bored and decided to go up to the moor, where a flock of lambs were playing king-of-the-castle on the rocks. Barry, fascinated by the water, scurried along in front, stooping now and then to pick up a stone and throw it into the swirling water. He stopped by a pool, fed by a glittering waterfall, and crowed with delight at the shower of sparkling drops that fell endlessly into the brown depths. Maggie watched him and smiled.

'You won't want to go back to London when all this is over, will you?' she said. 'You and the others – you've turned into proper little country folk. I can't see you taking to the streets again.'

Barry took no notice. His fair curls fell across his face as he bent over the water, and he pushed them back impatiently. She really would have to get his hair cut . . . Maggie reached out, anxious that he might fall in, but he shook himself away from her hand and scrambled down on to a half-moon of shingle that made a little beach in a bend of the river. The trees hung their green leaves over his head like a shady umbrella. He squatted on his haunches and gazed intently into the water.

'Looking for fish?'

Maggie jumped, her heart kicking as she turned to see the tall soldier standing in the shadow of the trees, watching her. For a long moment they stared at each other, and then he came closer and held out both hands.

'Hallo, Maggie . . .'

'It can't be,' she whispered. She stared at the dark curls, the brown eyes. He looked older, harder, the soft lines of boyhood gone from his face to leave it lean and tough. She thought of the warmth of his lips, the eagerness of his hands and body. The trembling innocence and the tenderness of their lovemaking.

'*Andy . . .*'

They stared at each other as slowly she took his out-stretched hands. She wondered whether they should kiss, and saw the same indecision in his face as well. Quickly, she

341

glanced away, to where Barry was still intent on watching for fish.

'How did you know I was here? How did you find me? Or maybe you weren't looking. Perhaps it's just coincidence . . . Andy, how *are* you?'

He laughed. 'I'm fine. Look at me! I've been through the mill and come out the other side – ready to go back and give a hand with the last push now. We're nearly there, you know. The war's ours now, though it'll still take a while to convince the Germans.'

'But what are you doing down here, in Devon?'

He looked at her seriously. 'I came to find you, of course. I went to your old home and found what had happened. A neighbour told me where to find your dad and he gave me your address here. And your ma sent me this way, said you were out with the kiddies.' He glanced incuriously at Barry. 'I gather you lost your sister as well?'

'Yes. She was killed. And—' And Queenie, her little girl, she was about to say, but he broke in, squeezing her hands in sympathy.

'And so you've taken on the youngsters between you. Well, that's just like you. Warmest heart I've ever known.' He gave her a twinkling grin. 'We had some good times, Maggie, didn't we?'

'I hope so.' He didn't know about the other soldier, the one who had raped and beaten her in the alley. 'I hope you were happier for them, Andy.'

'Oh, you bet I was! I went off that last morning feeling like a king. You certainly knew how to make a bloke feel on top of the world, Maggie.' He squeezed her hands again. 'I suppose that's why I've always wanted to come back and find you. I wanted to see you again – just once.'

Maggie gazed at him. 'You just wanted to see me again – *once*?'

'That's right. You see, you did something for me that night – letting me love you the way you did. You turned me from a boy into a man. I know what they said about you, Maggie –

that you were a bit easy, that you'd go for anything in trousers – but it wasn't true, was it? You were doing it for us – for boys like me who didn't know what it was like to be with a woman.'

Maggie felt the colour flood her face. She glanced again at Barry, pushing back his hair as he reached to try to catch a darting fish. The other children had vanished.

'Yes, you're right,' she said honestly. 'I went with a lot of boys like you, Andy, because I'd lost my own man, my husband Tommy, and I knew how much difference it made to him, to know what a bit of loving could be like, before he went. I don't do it any more, though.'

'Well, no.' He, too, looked at Barry, and Maggie caught her breath. There was something in the turn of his head . . . But the moment was gone, almost before she had recognised it, and the grin back on Andy's face. No, that wasn't Barry's smile. Barry's smile was hers, as all his other features were hers, too. She gave a little sigh.

'I don't suppose you do,' Andy went on. 'You'll have found someone else by now – someone who wouldn't want to share you. Isn't that right?'

Maggie looked at him again. He had changed so much – grown up so much. This man was barely recognisable as the boy she'd taught to make love. Once again she wondered why he had come. Just to see her once – or for something more?

'I don't know,' she said. 'There's someone I'm friendly with, but that's all it is. At least, I think so.'

Andy smiled. 'That's all right, then. It's going to be more, I can tell. And that means it's OK for me, too.'

'What do you mean?'

'I mean there's someone else for me as well,' he said, grinning. 'But I couldn't quite take that last step and ask her to marry me – not until I'd seen you. You see, I'd always felt there was something special between you and me, and if it was still there, well, I might have had some tricky decisions to make. But if there's someone for you, too – well!'

'You'll ask her to marry you,' Maggie said.

343

'That's it,' he agreed cheerfully, and took her hands again. 'Maggie, it's been smashing to see you again. And I'll never forget you. You were my first – and you set the standard for all the rest.' He glanced at his watch. 'Look, I've got to go. I just got a train down for the day and if I dash I can catch the next one back.' He bent forward and gave her a swift kiss on the cheek, then dropped her hands and turned away. 'Be happy, Maggie. And look after your sister's kiddy – it'll be good practice for when you have your own!'

He gave Barry a quick, friendly wave, and then leapt up the bank. At the top, he turned and grinned down at her.

'Cheerio . . .'

There was a minute pause, a tiny slice of time in which nobody moved. Then Maggie, speechless, saw him lift one hand and push his fingers through his dark curls. And then he was gone.

Her mind reeling, she turned back and looked down at her son. Fair curls, dark curls – what did the colour matter? What mattered was that Barry had exactly the same way of pushing back his hair. He did it more and more, an unconscious gesture that he hadn't learnt from anyone else. A gesture that was in his blood.

At last, Maggie knew for certain who his father was. And with the knowledge she was, at last, set free.

'Tell me, Nick,' Jo said quietly.

The scarlet colour flooded his face and he looked away. 'I don't know what you mean,' he began, blusteringly. 'Are you accusing me of – of—?'

'Oh, Nick, stop playing games. You started this after all. You said we had to talk. Well, what about? There's someone else, isn't there? You've found someone else and that's why you haven't been writing, why you can never get leave to see me. And now you're just looking for excuses to say it's my fault. Well, you can at least be honest with me. You can at least come right out and say it's true, and tell me who she is.'

344

'That wouldn't make any difference,' he muttered. 'You don't know her.'

Jo took in a deep breath. The fears that had tormented her had now come out of the shadows and she could face them. Yet until now it had never occurred to her that Nick might have found someone else. Until now, her fears had all been that their drifting apart was her fault. Until now, she had been tormented by guilt – guilt because she had failed him in some way, guilt over her feelings for Josh.

She stared at him. 'So there *is* someone?'

'Yes, there is,' he said loudly. 'And why not? You're never around, and *you* don't write all that much either. You talk about me, but you're not much better, Jo. All that way away in Shropshire. Why couldn't you have got a transfer to be nearer me? I don't think you even tried.'

'You never wanted me to,' she whispered. 'I suggested it once and you said, no, it would be a distraction, you just wanted to concentrate on your flying. You didn't want it even when we got married . . .' She bit her lip. 'You really didn't want to get married, did you? What you said just now – that was the *truth*.'

'Oh, so at least I'm not a liar now.' He caught her eye and then looked away. Jo felt hot, spiky tears come to her eyes. She had hoped so much that this meeting would put things right between them. Now she knew that she'd never allowed herself to realise just how wrong they were.

'Come on, Nick,' she said. 'Tell me about her. Tell me what you want to do.'

'All right,' he said suddenly. 'All right, I will.' He met her eyes again, defiantly this time. 'She's a nurse. You've met her, only you wouldn't remember. She was looking after me when I was in the burns unit. She was the only one – *the only person*', he said savagely, 'who didn't look at me as if I was a – a reptile or something. She used to change my dressings and she was so gentle, so – so matter-of-fact about it all. She didn't gasp or look away or feel sick, and she didn't treat me

345

as an object of pity – she just treated me like a *man*. As if I was no different from anyone else.'

'But *I* never thought you were any different from anyone else,' Jo whispered. 'You were still my Nick. Look, she was used to seeing things like that – we weren't. You can't blame us for being upset at first. But we got used to it, we—'

'Got used to it,' he said with bitterness. 'Yes, that's just about the size of it, Jo. You got used to me being ugly. But it wasn't easy, was it? Oh, yes, I saw you looking away, I saw you *steeling* yourself to look me in the face. You can't say you didn't. How do you think that made me feel? What do you think it was like for me, thinking that any day you were going to tell me you couldn't take it, that it was all off between us? Every time you came to visit – every letter you wrote – no *wonder* I didn't want you around, no *wonder* I didn't want letters!'

Jo shook her head blindly. 'You're doing it again. You're twisting *everything*. I never did say that, did I? I never did write to say it was all off. I had to *persuade* you to get married. I *wanted* to be your wife. All this is in your mind Nick, and you've got everything wrong.'

'So why', he asked in a hard, low tone, 'haven't we ever been able to make love properly?'

Jo drew in her breath. She felt the colour drain from her face. She looked down at her hands and thought of all the times they'd tried, the agonising nights when she'd stroked and caressed and kissed him, trying to arouse him, bewildered by his impotent frustration. The times when he had turned away, silent and bitter, the times when he had rounded on her and taken her savagely in his arms, his kisses rough and painful as he'd tried, uselessly, to force himself into her. The times when he had lain beside her and beaten the pillow with his fists as she'd quivered with tears, not knowing what to do next and praying that either sleep or dawn would release them both from this prison.

'I thought it was because of your burns,' she whispered.

'Or because you were so tired from flying – or something like that. I knew it would come right someday . . .'

'Well, that's more than I did. I didn't think it would ever come right. But I'll tell you this, Jo.' Again the bright, hard spark of defiance was in his eyes. 'It's come right for me now. So it couldn't *ever* have been my fault, could it?'

Jo gazed at him. She felt sick, as if the world had suddenly fallen away from her and she was swinging alone through some dark, rushing void. She put both hands to her face and kept them there for a few moments, trying in the warm darkness of her palms to find something to cling to. But there was nothing.

'So it was all my fault,' she said at last. 'Even that.'

'Well, it must have been, mustn't it?' he said triumphantly. 'Because when I'm with Amy—'

'*Amy?*'

Jo was on her feet. Her chair tipped and fell behind her with a crash, and Polly looked through the kitchen door, startled, and began to remonstrate. Jo ignored her. She laid both hands flat on the table and stared furiously down into Nick's startled face. 'Did you say *Amy?*'

'Yes,' he said. 'That's her name. Amy Pearson. What's that got to do with it?'

'You *know* what it's got to do with it. You know bloody *well* what it's got to do with it. Don't tell me you don't remember why I wouldn't go out with you in the first place – why I didn't want to get involved with you, even though I really fancied you. Don't tell me you've forgotten *Little Women*!'

'Little *women*?' he repeated blankly. 'Jo, what the hell are you raving about? Have you gone completely off your rocker?' He glanced round at Polly. 'Look, I'm really sorry about this. I'd never have brought her here if I'd realised – I think she must be having a breakdown of some sort – I'll get her out.'

'Don't you touch me!' Jo screamed at him. 'Don't you dare touch me! And I'm *not* having a breakdown!' She turned to Polly as well. 'This is my husband – you didn't know that, did you? You probably thought that *other* woman was his wife, that nurse he brings in here, that – that *Amy*!' She whipped back to face Nick, who was scarlet. 'You know perfectly well what I'm talking about. The book, *Little Women*. Jo and Laurie in the book, who ought to have got married and instead he dumped her and went off with her nasty, spiteful, selfish little sister. Her sister *Amy*.' She drew a deep shuddering breath. 'I *knew* it would never work out right,' she whispered. 'I knew you'd go to her in the end.'

Suddenly overwhelmingly weary, she sank down on another chair that Polly had swiftly placed near her. She put her elbows on the table and sank her head into her hands and began to weep. 'Oh, Nick, how could you? How could you do it? When I loved you so much . . . so very, very much . . .'

Polly and Nick exchanged glances. Red-faced and embarrassed, he mumbled something about taking Jo out, putting her on the next train back to London. But the older woman shook her head.

'I don't know the rights and wrongs of it all, and I don't want to know. But this poor young lady's had a bad shock, whatever way you look at it. She needs a nice cup of tea and a sit-down out of the way before she goes anywhere. I'll take her into my back room.'

Nick stood up and looked helplessly at the bent head of his wife. Awkwardly, he fumbled in his pocket and took out his wallet.

'Look. I've got to go back now. On duty, you know. But take this . . .' he held out a pound note '. . . and get her a taxi when she feels better, will you? And, er, it doesn't matter about the change. I'm sorry – I really must get back now.'

Polly looked at the money and then pushed his hand away.

'I don't think she needs your money, Squadron Leader. I'll see she gets the train all right. And it doesn't matter about the coffee and scones either. You can pay me for them next time – when you bring the other lady here.'

Nick flushed again. His scars stood out, livid, against the crimson skin. He opened his mouth to speak, an angry light in his eye, then thought better of it. He turned on his heel and walked out of the tearoom, slamming the door behind him.

Polly bent and touched Jo's shoulder.

'It's all right, love. He's gone now. And if you ask me, you're better off without him. You come along with me now, and sit quiet for a bit. And then we'll get you back to London or wherever you come from, all right? There'll be someone there to look after you, will there?'

'Yes,' Jo whispered, lifting her wet face and fumbling for a hanky. 'Yes, there is. Thanks, Polly. Thanks ever so much.'

When she got back to London there would be her mother and father, her aunt and uncle and her cousin Phyl to look after and console her. But suddenly she knew where she wanted to be most of all. She wanted to be back in Shropshire, back amongst the trees and the hills and the valleys.

Back with Josh.

Chapter Twenty-Seven

As autumn began to colour the trees, so the end of the war seemed to be coming closer, and colour about to return to the lives of those who had endured the long darkness.

The restrictions which had been so hard to bear were beginning to lift. The coastline ban was removed and holidaymakers were once again allowed to go to the beach. From Penzance right the way along to Dover, where a few months ago thousands of ships had set sail to take tens of thousands of men across the Channel, the beaches were now thronged with deckchairs brought by those who still had them, or with people lying on towels or old blankets. You'd have thought, Bill Mason said when he and Stan took their wives to Brighton for the day, that the war was over already.

'Except for the beer,' Stan remarked sourly. 'They don't seem to have given a thought to all the blokes who'd want a drink to wet their whistle after that train ride. Half the pubs are closed and those that are open won't sell you more than a pint! It's back to rationing all over again.'

'Never mind,' Carrie said, turning her face up to the sun. 'It's just lovely to be here and think that it might really be all over soon, and our boys back home again.'

'And our girls,' May reminded her. 'I'll be glad when our Phyl's left that place near Bedford. She's never looked well all the time she's been there, and that young Etty getting killed really shook her up. And your Jo looked like a ghost when she went back to Clun last time she was down.'

'Yes, well, we all got our own ideas about what happened

there,' Carrie said, tightening her lips. 'That marriage was never right, you know, not from the start. It's my belief what happened to young Nick turned his brain a bit. He was never the same again, you know.'

'It's a shame, though. It don't do a young woman no good to have marriage troubles. Is she still sticking to what she said – that she won't go back to him, even after the war?'

Carrie shook her head. 'I don't know what to make of it, to tell you the truth. She's more than hinted there's someone else – for him, I mean, not her, of course – and she's going to see about a divorce. But I said to her, you just think it over careful before you do anything rash, my girl. Marriage is for life, that's what I've always brought them up to believe – and you the same, I know, May – and no matter what's happened she and him ought to give it a proper chance. You can't say they've had that, not the way things have been. They've never even lived together, not properly. But you can't tell these girls. They've had so much freedom, they think they know it all.'

May nodded. 'They're going to find it hard to settle down when things get back to normal. There's Phyl, too, hardly seen her hubby apart from those few days they had together at Christmas. I did wonder . . .' She lowered her voice. 'I did wonder if she might not have had a bit of *news* for us after that, but apparently not. I must say, I never thought we'd have to wait this long to be grannies, Carrie. Phyl and Jo are twenty-five now. We were three years younger than that when they were born.'

'And it'll be a good while longer at this rate,' Carrie said. 'Well, that's the way of the world, May. There'll be plenty of babies born as soon as the war ends and the boys come home. And the girls,' she added with a wry smile. 'One ain't no good without the other. Here – there's my Bill waving at us. Looks like he's managed to find a pub with some beer after all!'

High on the Welsh hillside above Merthyr Tydfil, Shirley and Owen were sitting looking down over the valley below the farm. Owen was in his wheelchair and Shirley perched with her knees drawn up on a rock beside him. They had come as far along the old track as Shirley could manage to push, and now sat gazing down into the quiet combe, while behind them lay the black slashes of the opencast mines and the wheels and machinery of the deeper pits.

'It's a lovely place,' Shirley said quietly.

'As long as you don't turn round and look the other way.' Owen's voice still held the trace of bitterness he'd never been entirely able to get rid of, and Shirley reached out and took his hand.

'You're alive, Owen. Let's be thankful for that.'

'And a useless burden to everyone.' He shook his head. 'I'd have been better off to go with poor old Taffy. You know, Shirl, if he'd been the one to survive without the use of his legs, he'd have been shot to put him out of his misery. Pity they couldn't do that to me.'

'*Owen!*' Shirley almost threw his hand back at him. 'You're *not* to talk like that! I've told you over and over again, if you go on being so stupidly sorry for yourself, I'll walk out of the house and down the mountain and never come back. If you can't be thankful to be alive, if you can't appreciate a lovely day or living in such a lovely place – if you can't even be glad you've got *me* – well, there's no point in me *being* here, that's all.'

She folded her arms over her knees and stared angrily down into the narrow little valley. A tear or two dripped on to her arm and she brushed them impatiently away. There was a little silence.

'I'm sorry,' Owen said humbly. 'I'm sorry, *cariad*. I know I promised I wouldn't keep on like that. It just seemed to sort of come out, see, without me even knowing I was going to say it. It's like I can't help it somehow.'

Shirley felt her heart soften. She got up and stood behind Owen to put her arms around his neck and bend her face to his hair.

'I'm sorry, too. I shouldn't snap at you like that. I know it's awful for you, being stuck in this wheelchair. I'm horrible.'

'You're not!'

'I am. I'm really, really horrible.'

'All right, then,' Owen said after a pause. 'You are. Really, really horrible.' They both laughed and Shirley nuzzled his neck. 'In fact,' he went on, 'if I wasn't in this old chair *I'd* have been the one to walk out, months ago, so maybe you ought to be glad I'm tied down like this, a prisoner.'

'That's what you are,' Shirley said cheerfully. 'A prisoner. My prisoner. And I tell you what – you're never going to be let go, see?' Her face sobered suddenly. 'Oh, I'm sorry, I shouldn't have said that – it'd be the best day of my life if you could stand up and walk.'

'It'd be the second best of mine,' Owen said. 'The best was the day I married you, Shirley, *cariad.*'

Shirley kissed him and they stayed close for a few moments. Then she sat down again on her rock, this time keeping his hand in hers.

'What shall we do after the war, Owen?'

'I don't know, *cariad.* I don't know what a chap like me can do.' He stared moodily across to the far slopes, his momentary brightness fading. 'It's what bothers me, see. I *am* useless.'

'You're not. You can do lots of things. You're good with your hands, you can mend things and make them like new. And you can still do the work you used to do at Lyons – look how good you are with the farm books. Uncle Dafydd says he doesn't know how he managed without you.'

'It isn't enough to keep me, though, is it? It isn't enough to keep me and you after the war. We won't want to trade on their hospitality any more once this is over. We'll have to make our own lives then, Shirl.'

'I know.' She frowned and then said slowly, 'I've been thinking about it, Owen. We could do something together – using the things we're both good at. Like you doing accounts and me being a Nippy. I learnt a lot then, you know. I could use what I learnt.'

He grinned at her. 'Set up our own Lyons Corner House, you mean? Here in Merthyr Tydfil?'

She smiled back. 'Not a Corner House, no – not a proper one. But a teashop, perhaps. Our own teashop. Where people could come for a snack, lunchtimes, or tea when they're out shopping. Nothing expensive, just ordinary, simple things.'

Owen stared at her. 'And where would we get the money to do that? It takes a bit to set up a business, and there'd be cups and things to buy, and all the cooking—'

'I could do that. And Mum might help – I've got a feeling they'd like to stay on in Wales, she and Dad. You know how much better he's been, and how much our Jack likes it here, too. He'd never settle back in London.' She was sitting up straight, her eyes bright. 'I had a look round last time I was in Merthyr. There's nothing there for people, and they wouldn't want much, just a cup of tea and a bun or some beans on toast – that sort of thing. And some home-made cakes when we can get the ingredients. And there's plenty of places to rent – shops, with living accommodation over the top. Cheap, too.' She paused and then added, a little wheedlingly, 'There's even a corner shop that would be just right . . .'

'So you *do* – want to open your own Corner House!' Owen exclaimed, and Shirley laughed.

'*Our* own Corner House, Owen. Ours. What do you think?'

He twisted his head to look at her. She was half sitting, half kneeling. Her eyes were very bright and her hands gripped his tightly. He could feel the passion and excitement transmitting themselves through their clasped fingers.

'I think you're a scheming woman,' he said slowly, smiling. 'And I think it's a great idea! As soon as this old war's over, eh? The very minute they declare peace.'

'The very minute,' Shirley agreed, and sat back on her heels. She rubbed her face against his sleeve. 'Oh, Owen, I do love you. And I don't care what you say, I'm *very* glad you're alive!'

'So am I,' he said softly, gazing down at the valley. 'So am I.'

Towards the end of August came the news that Paris had been liberated. The newspapers were full of pictures of the American troops marching down the Champs Élysées, with the Arc de Triomphe like a proud symbol in the background. Within a few days, they had advanced as far as the Mediterranean, while at home the danger from the dreaded V1 doodlebug was declared to be over.

The war would be over by Christmas, Field Marshal Montgomery prophesied, but the older and more cynical of his listeners, who had heard this before too many times, shuddered. And almost before the words were out of his mouth came news of Hitler's next deadly weapon – the V2.

'They're trying to say it was gas explosions again,' Jo said as she and Josh sat on the bridge, looking at the *Daily Express*. 'Fancy digging up that old story! Nobody's going to believe it. I had a letter from Mum yesterday, too. She says they're awful, even worse than the doodlebugs. You don't hear anything at all until they're right overhead, and then there's a sort of thunderclap and a noise like an express train, and then the explosion. There's no time to do anything.'

'Is she sure it's bombs?' Josh asked. 'I mean, if you really don't hear anything coming . . . I don't see how anything could go that fast. It would have to be faster than the speed of sound for you not to hear it coming.'

'Well, I don't know anything about that. She says everyone reckons it's bombs, anyway.' Jo folded the newspaper. 'I hate reading these things now. The only good thing in here is Rupert Bear . . . I think you're right, Josh. If everyone refused to touch weapons, there wouldn't be a war at all.'

'It'll never happen, though,' he said, looking down into the clear water of the little river Clun. 'People like fighting. They think it's the only way to settle an argument. And sometimes, when I think about Hitler and what he's done, I wonder if they're not right. Maybe when you get someone like him, fighting is the only answer.'

'But all these innocent people being killed? People who don't want to fight but are forced to? Or just stay at home and get killed anyway? It wouldn't be so bad if it was just the politicians, all put in a ring to fight it out amongst themselves, but everyone else gets swept in, too. It's so unfair.' Jo shook her head. 'Perhaps they ought to settle it with the Olympic Games, like the Greeks used to. See who was best at the sports and let them rule. It couldn't be any worse.'

'And perhaps Hitler would have won that way, too,' Josh said with a rueful smile. 'Look how he made sure all the young men did exercises and got fit during the thirties. And look at the way he took over the Games when they were in Berlin.'

Jo got off the parapet of the bridge and dusted off the seat of her breeches with an impatient gesture.

'Oh, I don't know – it's all too difficult. Let's go for a walk, Josh.'

They strolled across the bridge and past the church to climb Clun Hill. It was one of their favourite walks, and when they reached the top they stopped and gazed out at the familiar view. Josh slipped his arm around Jo's shoulders and she leant against him and sighed.

'Penny for them?'

She smiled. 'Worth far more than a penny. I was just thinking how lovely it is here. I'm not sure I'm going to want to go back to London when all this is over, Josh.'

'What would you like to do?' he asked.

'Oh, I don't know. Country work of some kind. I always did fancy it, you know. Used to pet the baker's horse and wish I could live on a farm – that sort of thing. Phyl used to tell me I'd hate it if I ever tried it – all hard work and cold winters and mud – but I've really enjoyed being a lumberjill. And there's not much harder work than that, or colder or muddier.'

'You enjoyed being a Nippy, too, though, didn't you?'

'Yes, I did. I liked being with the people, and it was good to be doing something active – but I'd hate to be stuck indoors again, even in a Corner House. I want to feel free!' She stretched her arms wide and lifted her face to the sky. 'I've learnt so much out here, Josh – about trees and animals and birds, and all sorts of things I never even knew existed when I was in London. Maybe I've changed, but I don't feel I could ever go back.'

'And what about Nick?' he asked quietly.

Jo let her arms drop to her sides. Her face fell, too, and Josh looked as if he were sorry he'd mentioned the subject.

'Oh, *Nick* . . . well, I'm definitely going to see about a divorce. I don't know what you have to do to get one, but I'm going to do it. Someone told me I'd got to prove adultery – and he admitted that, though he might not in front of anyone else, and I don't know if that's proof anyway. But someone else told me I could get the marriage annulled.'

'Annulled?' Josh said. 'But why? Surely you can only get that if – if—'

'If it was never consummated,' Jo said quietly. 'That's the word. I looked it up.'

Josh stared at her. 'But – wasn't it? D'you mean to say that you never – he never—'

'We never had "full sexual intercourse",' she said, as if repeating a lesson. 'I looked that up, too, when I went to the library in Ludlow last week. And we never did.' She gave Josh a quick, blushing glance. 'He – he couldn't seem to manage it, you see. It wasn't for want of trying,' she added ruefully.

'Oh, *Jo*. My poor Jo.' Josh put his arm around her shoulders again and held her tightly. 'What you must have been through . . .'

'It wasn't very nice for him either,' she said fairly.

'No, but . . . Are you sure you've got it right, Jo? You could have the marriage annulled on those grounds? Even if he's . . . impotent?'

'But he's not. According to him, anyway. He seems to be

357

able to do it all right with this *Amy* person.' There was a note of bitterness in Jo's voice, and Josh gave her another comforting squeeze.

'It won't be pleasant, Jo. I don't know much about these things, except that an aunt and uncle of mine divorced years ago. It was a big case. They had to go to court and give evidence, and they had to get other people's evidence as well. And then it was all reported in the newspapers for everyone to see. And in your case, well, you might have to have medical evidence as well. You've got to be very sure before you start it.'

'I know,' she said. 'I am sure.'

For a few minutes they were silent. They stood together, gazing out over the rolling hills. The conifer woods where they had worked together for so long were scarred with great bare expanses, a testament to the labour of the Timber Corps. In places there were stretches of deciduous forest as well, a patchwork of golden yellow turning to bronze. In the valley below, the little river ran like a length of blue ribbon, tossed down by a careless child.

'Jo,' he said at last, 'if you do go through with this, you'll need support. You'll need someone to talk to to help you through. You know you can always turn to me, don't you? I'll always be here.'

She smiled, still looking across the valley. 'But you'll want to get on with your own life, Josh. You don't know where I'll be – and you don't know where you'll be either.'

'I shall be where you are,' he said quietly.

Jo turned and looked at him, as if searching his face. She opened her mouth, but he laid his fingers over her lips and spoke quickly, his voice husky.

'Jo – I meant to wait to say this. I wanted to make sure things were settled between you and Nick. I didn't want to come rushing in where I'm not wanted. You might have decided to try again. But if you're really determined, well, I may as well say it now.' He paused and she watched him, her eyes wide above his splayed fingers. 'Jo, I want to ask you to

358

marry me. As soon as you're free. I want us to be together for the rest of our lives. We'll live in the country, find a smallholding or something somewhere, rent a few fields, grow vegetables or keep sheep – whatever we can do. We'll live the rest of our lives in peace, the way people like us ought to live.' He gazed at her, and she saw the burning light deep in his eyes and knew that this was what she had looked for in Nick, and never found. 'You don't have to answer me now, but—'

With a muffled squawk, she pulled his fingers away from her mouth. Her eyes alive and dancing, she laughed at him and exclaimed, 'I *can't* answer you as long as you keep gagging me like that! Is this what our married life's going to be like, Josh? Am I never going to be allowed to speak?'

'You mean, you *will*?'

'Of course I will, you big buffoon!' she retorted, flinging her arms around his neck. 'I love you! You must know that. You probably knew it before I did myself.' She kissed him, and felt in him all the response Nick had never made. 'I told myself it was wrong, you know,' she said when she could speak again. 'I wouldn't let myself even think about you. I felt so guilty! But when Nick told me about – about *her*, well, I just wanted to get back to you. It was all I wanted. And you're *everything* I want.'

They laughed again and, caught up in the delight of their love and their promises, caught each other's hands and began to whirl in circles on the top of the hill as if in some wild, crazy country dance. At last, panting and breathless, they collapsed on the grass and lay gazing into each other's eyes, still laughing, reaching out now and then to kiss and then breaking away in a fresh burst of joy.

'Tell me,' Josh said at last, 'in this book you're always going on about – *Little Women* – was Jo actually happy with the man she married?'

Jo looked at him and thought for a moment. Then her lips twitched and she began to grin.

'Well, yes,' she admitted. 'She was, really. I just didn't want her to be, I suppose. I wanted her to be happy with Laurie. But now I can see that that would *never* have done!'

Everything was looking hopeful. People were beginning at last to make plans for the end of the war. 'Over by Christmas' sounded less of a dream, more of a possibility. You could dare, at last, to look forward to a normal life. To peace.

And then came Arnhem.

It looked all right to begin with. People on the South Coast were once again at the forefront of the action, watching in awe as the huge Horsa gliders floated overhead, carrying tanks and guns as well as paratroopers. It seemed impossible to believe that such flimsy craft, however big, could carry such massive loads. But in this war it seemed that nothing was impossible. Hadn't huge, towering concrete 'harbours' been built on the beaches and towed across to Normandy, an idea that must have seemed impossible yet had worked with such effect? There didn't seem any reason why the equally crazy idea of filling gliders with tanks and troops shouldn't be equally effective.

It should have been easy. Dropping from a silent sky, the paratroops should have been able to converge on and seize the essential railway bridges of the Lower Rhine before it was even known they were there. The big Horsas should have been able to land soundlessly, releasing their heavy artillery into the unprepared countryside. The operation should have been over before the enemy even realised it had begun.

But it didn't work that way. One of the gliders crashed, and in it were the plans for the invasion. As soon as the enemy realised what was happening, they swung into action. The bridges that were supposed to have been seized were blown up, and when the parachute brigade arrived, it was to a welcome of German sharpshooters who picked them off as they floated helplessly down. In ten days of savage fighting, over a thousand men were killed and nearly seven thousand taken prisoner. Only two and a half thousand escaped across the Rhine, by swimming or by stealing boats, and the last of the British and Polish troops trapped at Arnhem itself surrendered, after holding the bridgehead for nine days. For the last three of those days, they had no water and the lowest possible rations. They were attacked by flamethrowers.

George and Gerry Pratt were among those who parachuted down to that terrible welcome. Gerry escaped the shots and was taken prisoner. George was killed before he even reached the ground.

Chapter Twenty-Eight

Autumn ran into winter, and winter into spring, and still the war wasn't over. The fighting in Europe and the Far East seemed to have grown even fiercer, and while the armies advanced over the land and the navies fought at sea, so the air forces spread across the sky. German cities were bombed without mercy, as London and other British cities had been previously, and the American Air Force concentrated an attack on Tokyo. It was as if the entire world were being rocked by explosions.

'It's just not getting any better,' Maggie said in despair. 'I mean, they're making it *seem* better, taking away the blackout and liberating Greece and all that, but it ain't really. Not when so many people are still being killed.' She thought of her brothers – George, killed by a German sniper, and his twin Gerry, taken prisoner on the same night – and sighed. 'I dunno what we done to deserve all this, Ma.'

'Nor do I.' Ivy's overflowing figure had shrunk and her mass of hair, once – like Maggie's – a vibrant yellow, had turned grey and hung, thin and lank, to her shoulders. Her skin was wrinkled, her eyes faded and she looked almost as old as Ada had done. She moved heavily through the days and it seemed that nothing could lift her depression. Maggie wondered sometimes if her mother would ever be the same again.

But who would? We've all been changed by this war, she thought as she began her duty at the hospital. The Canadians had moved on long ago and it was now used as a convalescent home for British officers. They weren't as easygoing as the Canadians, and didn't seem inclined to exchange banter with the nurses and orderlies, but Maggie didn't mind. The signs now were that the war really was coming to an end, and she was beginning to think about what she would do afterwards. Go back to London, she supposed, and set up home again with her mother and father and the kids. Not that they were kids now – Ginnie was fifteen and working in a shop in Tavistock, and Billy talking about joining the navy as a boy seaman – but Barry was still little, and he was her first priority.

Maggie had given up all hope of hearing from Carl again. Since he had left to rejoin his unit and had gone in the D-Day invasion of Normandy, she hadn't heard a word. He must be dead, she thought sadly, and bitterly regretted that she had let him go without at least telling him how she felt. I loved him all the time, she thought. I just needed to know about Barry's father, and once I knew, it was like a window opening in my mind. I'm really glad it was Andy. He was special once, and I'm thankful it wasn't that other horrible man, but once I saw him, I knew there wasn't anything special any more. He was just someone I'd loved a little bit, for a little while.

And it wasn't as if he were even interested in Barry. It wouldn't have been fair to tell him – not when he was just going to start his life with someone else.

No, there was nothing to regret there. All her regrets were for Carl, who had gone without knowing what she felt, who had left thinking there was no future for them, who might even have died without knowing what it was like to hold her in his arms and love her properly. Who hadn't been given the loving she had given so freely to Andy and the others, and who had been the very one who – apart from Tommy – she had most wanted to love.

You're a fool, Maggie Wheeler, she told herself. A blind, stupid fool.

And then, suddenly, the end was in sight.

'A matter of weeks, Mr Churchill says!' Phyl exclaimed to

363

Kaye and Jenny as they made their way to the workshop. 'It was on the news just now, while you two were in the bathroom – they're saying that Hitler and that Eva Braun have killed themselves! And so's Goebbels, and they think Goering's been shot dead. That's nearly all of them gone, and good riddance. It must come to an end now. There's no one left to run it – not on their side, anyway.'

'How will they get it all to stop on the same day?' Kaye wondered. 'I mean, they've got to let all them people know out in the jungle and in Burma, and God knows where else, as well as all over Europe. I don't see as how they can. It'll take months to make everyone stop.'

'Mr Carter says the Japanese won't give in so easy,' Jenny said. 'It's a different war, see, they weren't fighting for Hitler, just for themselves. So they won't stop just because he's copped it. And Mr Carter says they won't give in anyway, because they just never do. They'd rather die.'

'Well, that's all right,' Kaye said. 'I don't mind. Perhaps we could make a really huge bomb to send over and drop on them. Then we'll all be happy.'

Phyl gave her arm a squeeze. Kaye's brother had been taken prisoner by the Japanese and was working on the Burma railway. There had been terrible stories about the conditions there, and everyone who had a relative in the Far East was worried sick about them. It was even worse, they said, than being in a German POW camp.

Worst of all, though, were the stories coming from the German concentration camps, where the Jews had been herded like animals at the beginning of the war. Everyone had now heard the tales of the horrors seen when the Allies had entered these camps for the first time – piles of naked bodies, not much more than skeletons, heaped up in trucks to be taken away and burnt, and some of them, even more horrifyingly, still pitifully just alive. The newspapers had published photographs and you couldn't look at them without feeling sick. It was said that the American generals –

Eisenhower, Patton and Bradley – had cried and actually been sick when they saw them, and the troops had just stood there, unable to believe their eyes.

'It proves the war was right,' Jo said soberly when she read the reports. 'It proves we were right to fight Hitler. You just can't let an evil man like that take over the world.'

'You're right about that,' Josh agreed. 'But I still can't accept the idea of all those innocent people being killed – ours and theirs. I still couldn't pick up a gun and go out to kill other men in cold blood, Jo, not when I know they're probably as good as me.'

She turned into his arms. 'It's a dreadful problem. But it's almost over now, and perhaps people really will remember what's happened and make sure it never happens again. Perhaps it will have done good in that way, too.'

'I hope so,' Josh said. 'I really hope so.'

It really was coming to an end. And for the Corner House girls, there was only one place they wanted to be.

'You know we said we'd meet up again when all this was over,' Shirley wrote to the three who were left of the six who had begun together as Nippies, all those years ago. 'Well, let's do it. Owen and me have got to go to London in a couple of weeks to help clear out the old shop his uncle ran, and sell up – and if anyone else could be there, too, we could have a cup of tea and a natter one afternoon at Marble Arch. Is there any chance? I'd love to see you all again.'

The others looked at the letter and felt a leap of excitement. Of course it could be possible! Leave still wasn't easy to get, but everyone knew the war would be over soon, and why shouldn't they want to go home and be with their own people to celebrate it? Jo asked Huw the Tree for a few days off, and Josh said he'd come a few days later. Phyl, still saddened by Etty's death, wasn't sure she could face the Corner House without her, but when she told Mr Carter about the idea he said of course she must go. Maggie, who had missed the streets and life of London, jumped at the idea and Ivy said she wouldn't mind looking after Barry – 'It's time you had a bit of fun with your old mates.'

They agreed to meet at lunchtime on 8 May. Shirley and Owen would be travelling by train a day or two earlier – a difficult job with Owen in a wheelchair, but they were determined to manage it – and Jo could come down from Clun and stay with her mother and father. Phyl, too, was coming and the two families would have their own celebration. The boys had all, miraculously, survived the war and would be home at any time. People were saying that POWs were being repatriated already, and some of the troops being sent back. You just didn't know when they might turn up.

Alice came home, too. She had grown tall, like Jo, and her fair hair had deepened to just the same shade of burnished chestnut. She was fifteen now and in her last year at school in Devon. After that, she was talking about training as a teacher.

'I don't know what she wants to do that for,' Bill grumbled. 'Job in a shop or a hairdresser's ought to be good enough for that young lady. All these ideas about careers – I'd have thought girls would be looking forward to being able to settle down a bit once this war's out of the way, and being content with their home and family.'

'It's seeing their older sisters going off and doing other things, like Jo and Phyl,' Carrie said. 'It's unsettled everyone. Look at our Jo, now, talking about divorce and bringing home another chap even while she's still married. I still don't know as we're doing right, letting her ask him to Sunday dinner with us.'

'I'm flipping sure we're not,' her husband said. 'And he's a CO, by all accounts. You know what that means, Carrie. It means our boys have been risking their lives to save his skin, while he's been hiding away in them trees. I don't like it. I'm not sure I'll be able to bring meself to be civil to the man.'

Carrie sighed. 'I know. I feel the same, but what can you do? I mean, I know Jo thinks a lot of him, and I know things haven't been right between her and Nick – but I still think they ought to be giving theirselves a chance to sort things out, not going off at half-cock like this. Still, you can't live your lives for them. We got to take a back seat now, Bill.'

Bill scowled. He wasn't used to taking a back seat in his own house. But Carrie was right. The war had changed things. It had taken their lives and turned them upside down and shaken them like an old shopping bag, and you never knew what might fall out when you did that.

'Don't let's let it spoil things, Bill,' Carrie said, seeing his face. 'It's going to be a celebration. The end of the war – I can hardly believe it. And all our girls home, and the boys on their way. It's not a time for arguments.'

He looked at her and his brows untangled themselves as he let his mouth widen in a slow smile. 'You're right, Carrie, love. It's a celebration. We won't let anything get in the way.'

By 7 May, everyone knew that the end was almost upon them. The girls were home, and the city buzzing with anticipation. Every house was turned upside down as people searched for flags and bunting, put away after their last outing at the Coronation in 1937. Haberdashery shops had run out of red, white and blue ribbons, which had been bought by the yard to tie on prams, bikes, cars and even pet dogs and cats as well as in girls' hair. The sound of hammering went on late into the night as neighbours climbed ladders to nail the decorations to the their houses, and by morning the city was ablaze with patriotic colour.

'Today! It's going to be today!' Alice picked up Robertson and swung him in her arms. 'Goodness me, you're heavier than ever! Oh Robbie, I've missed you *so* much!'

'Why don't they announce it straight away?' Phyl grumbled, as she helped her mother decorate the front window next door. 'Why have we got to wait for three o'clock? I mean, they're not going to tell us it's not happened, not after all this. Why can't we just go ahead and *celebrate*?'

'We'll be doing that soon enough.' May smiled. 'And aren't you going up to town this morning, to meet your friends? You'll hear about it sooner than us, I dare say.'

'Don't be daft, it'll be on the wireless.' Phyl flew to the door as Jo knocked and came in. 'Oh, you look smashing! I like the way you've twisted all that ribbon into a scarf . . .' She darted back into the room and kissed her mother. 'We're off now. See you when we see you!'

'Not too late, now,' her mother called, going to the front door to wave them off. She smiled at her sister, standing on next door's step to do the same thing. 'Not that we can tell 'em what time to come in any more – and both of them married women!'

'Shame they can't have their husbands with them,' Carrie agreed. 'Not that our Jo'd be all that pleased to see hers, the way things are going . . . But your Phyl'd like to have her Mike, I know. No news there, I suppose?'

May shook her head. 'All we know is they could come home at any time. There was a couple of soldiers walking down the street yesterday – my heart turned over, thinking it might be him – but it was that young chap from round the corner and a mate of his he'd brought home for the night. But I dare say Mike'll surprise us soon. I just hope it's before Phyl goes back to Bedford.'

'They'll be bringing her back from there soon, too, I dare say,' Carrie said. 'Won't want Lyons girls waiting on them once they've got their own men back. It'll be nice for you to have her back in London.' She sighed. 'My Jo, too, though I don't know what she means to do. She doesn't say much at all.'

'They'll make their own lives,' May said. 'Same as we made ours. It's just that they've had a later start, but maybe it'll stand them in good stead, when all's said and done. And it'll be good for them to be back at the Corner House today. Just like coming home, in a way.'

'Just like coming home.'

Phyl and Jo turned the corner into Marble Arch and spoke at the same moment. They looked at each other and laughed, then gazed up again at the familiar façade of the Lyons

Corner House. Jo put out one hand and touched the white stone wall.

'I feel like stroking it. I feel like *hugging* it!' There were tears in her eyes. 'Oh, Phyl, to think we're back here again after all this time – after all that's happened – and it looks just the same.' She wiped her face with the back of one hand and grinned shakily. 'I don't know why I'm being so soppy over a *building*!'

'It's not just a building, though, is it?' Phyl said. 'It *was* our home, in lots of ways. It was our life, working here. Lyons made you feel like that. They made you feel like a family. It *is* like coming home.'

'Yes, it is.' Jo gave the wall another stroke and a little pat. 'I'd better stop doing this! They'll be coming to take me to the loony-bin. Come on, Phyl, let's go inside and see if the others are there yet.'

'They're not,' a familiar voice said, behind them. 'They've just arrived. Hello, Jo – hello, Phyl. Oh, it's just *smashing* to see you again!'

'*Maggie!*' Phyl shrieked. 'And Shirley! Oh, how are you? Look at you, Maggie, you've lost weight, you look like Anna Neagle! And Shirley, you haven't changed a bit. Oh, isn't this lovely? And the war's going to be over – any minute now it's going to be *over*! I can't believe it!'

'Three o'clock, it's going to be announced,' Shirley said, her face full of laughter. 'That's what they said. Three o'clock. And I tell you what, we ought to go down to Buckingham Palace because the King and Queen and Mr Churchill and everyone will be out on the balcony and everyone will be able to see them. What d'you say?'

'*Yes!*' Phyl let go of Maggie and flung her arms around Shirley. 'Yes, we'll do that! Only let's go in and have something to eat now, because I'm *starving*!'

'That sounds like the Phyl we all know and love.' Maggie grinned. 'Come on, then. Let's see what Nippies are made of these days.'

Nippies, it seemed, were few and far between, and they

were either very young or middle-aged. Only one restaurant was serving now, the others having gone over to self-service. Office and shop workers were queueing up with their trays, but the girls turned up their noses at this idea and went to sit down. They wanted to remember the Corner House as it had been.

Their Nippy, a young girl with red hair and a merry face, came to them and asked what they would like. The menu was restricted, as they'd known it would be, and it didn't take long to choose. The girl hurried away and they began to look around them.

'They've done their best,' Jo said. 'But it's looking a bit shabby, isn't it? I suppose they couldn't get paint and paper. And there's thin patches in the carpet.'

'I dare say they'll soon smarten it all up,' Phyl said. She looked at Shirley. 'What will you do? Will you come back? Are you and Owen going to take over the shop?'

Shirley shook her dark head. 'We're staying in Wales. We're renting a shop there and we're going to run it as a – you'll never guess – as a teashop! There's a place next door we can live in, on the ground floor, and I'm going to do the cooking and waiting, and Owen'll do all the paperwork. Mum's going to help me – she and Dad are staying in Wales, too. It suits Dad. He got better as soon as he was away from London with Mum, and as long as he lives a quiet life, he's all right. And we'd never get Jack away from the farm!'

'Well!' Maggie said, as Shirley stopped to draw breath. 'If that ain't a turn-up for the book! Our little Shirl, striking out on her own. We'll all come and have tea there, Shirl, and that's a promise. How about you two?' she asked, turning to Phyl and Jo.

The cousins glanced at each other. 'I don't know what me and Mike will do,' Phyl said. 'Look for a place to live, I suppose, and look for a job. I don't really care much, so long as we're together. But I don't want to live in Bedford, that's for sure!' She looked down at her hands, stained with explosives that she still couldn't tell the others about. 'It'll always remind me of our Etty.'

The others were silent for a moment, thinking of the girl who had lost her life. After a few minutes, Jo said, 'I don't suppose anyone ever saw any more of Irene Bond, did they? Me and Phyl spotted her that time on a bus – clippie, she was – but we never heard no more. Nasty, spiteful little cat.'

The others shrugged. Nobody was particularly interested in Irene. They looked at Jo instead, and she blushed and told them about Nick, and about Josh.

'That's a shame,' Maggie said. 'You and Nick were a nice pair. I'd have put money on you stopping together once you'd got that daft book business out of your head. Still, there it is. I hope you do better with your new bloke.'

'I will,' Jo said quietly. She hadn't mentioned the name of Nick's new love. 'He's a good man, and we've known each other a long time now. But how about you, Mags? How's Barry? I bet he's a real little boy now, isn't he?'

'He is! A proper little monkey. Always climbing trees or getting into mischief. I don't know how he's going to take to coming back to London. Mum's coming back, see, she wants to be back with Dad as soon as they can find a place, so I suppose I'll come back, too. Dunno what else I'd do.' She sighed a little, and Jo caught the pensive expression on her face.

'Hasn't there been anyone else, Maggie? I thought – well, I knew you wouldn't feel very much like it for a while, not after what happened, but I'd have thought you'd have some feller after you.'

'Me? No!' Maggie laughed, then made a rueful face and said, 'Well, there was one.' There was a pause as the Nippy brought their meal and set it out on the table. 'Canadian, he was,' Maggie went on. 'We got on real well. But . . . you know how it is. I couldn't see no future. And then he went away, and I never heard no more. He was in the D-Day invasion, I suppose . . .' She let the sentence trail away and the others nodded. They knew what she meant. The

Canadian had either died or just decided he wasn't interested in the yellow-haired Cockney girl.

'There'll be someone else for you, Maggie,' Shirley said comfortingly. 'I'm sure there will.'

They fell silent for a few moments. The food was as good as Corner House food had ever been and they smiled at each other and began to reminisce. 'Do you remember when they told Phyl she was too short to be a Nippy and she said she'd stand in a bucket of muck every night till she grew?' . . . 'D'you remember that customer who used to buy a box of chocolates on the confectionery counter, 'specially to give whoever served him?' . . . 'What about that man who said Phyl had cheated him? That was that cat Irene, meddling with the bill and trying to get her the sack, wasn't it, Phyl?' . . . 'D'you remember the man who drank two whole bottles of wine and fell under the table? It took Mr Carter and three of the porters to get him out!' . . . 'Do you remember . . . ?' And so on, and so on.

At last they had finished. Maggie drained her teacup and looked round at them.

'It's nearly three! Look – they've brought in a wireless and set it up in the corner, so we can all hear. They did that before, remember? Let's stop and listen, and then we'll go to the Palace.'

The restaurant fell silent. Staff and customers alike were still as the radio was tuned to the BBC Home Service. As the chimes of Big Ben sounded across the room, Jo felt tears come to her eyes and looked around to see that others were just as affected.

'This is London.' The sombre announcement, used only for the most momentous occasions, had been heard more than once during the past six years. But now there was a hidden joy in the announcer's voice, an undercurrent of excitement, and it rippled through the listeners as they tensed and strained to hear the words they had longed to hear.

The broadcast was coming directly from 10 Downing Street, from the lips of the Prime Minister himself, Mr

Winston Churchill, who had led the nation through the turbulent years. It was his voice, rolling and mellifluous, which had heartened them in their darkest hours, not with false optimism but with plain, stark reality and a bulldog determination not to be beaten. He had promised them nothing but toil, blood, sweat and tears – but he had also shown them a vision of broad, sunlit uplands, a vision which had kept them going through terrors and hardships that perhaps even he had not dreamt possible. And it was he who was telling them now what they had achieved.

'The German war is at an end,' he proclaimed at last. 'Advance Britannia! Long live the cause of freedom! *God save the King!*'

As he spoke those last words, everyone leapt to their feet and broke into a storm of cheering. The girls hugged each other. They hugged their Nippy, who had been coming to give them their change from the bill. They hugged the people at the next table, and – telling the Nippy to keep the change – they ran out into the street and hugged people who were passing by. They took hands and danced in a circle on the pavement, and then they hugged each other again.

'It's over! It's over! The war's *over*!' It was almost too much to believe. After all the long years . . . 'It's over, it's over, it's *over*!'

'Let's go to the Palace!' Maggie cried, and they turned as one and joined the crowds who had the same idea and were already thronging across the road to Hyde Park and through to Hyde Park Corner.

'It's even more exciting than the Coronation!' Phyl exclaimed, catching at Jo's arm. 'Remember how we went to see them on the balcony then? The King and Queen in all their robes, with their crowns on, and the two little princesses with their tiaras? I thought nothing in the world could ever be better than that day – but this is! This is like life starting all over again!'

'It *is* life starting all over again,' Jo said. She knew that it wouldn't be easy for her and Josh to begin with – a divorce in the family and a man who'd been a conscientious objector were shocks that were hard for Carrie and Bill to bear. But away from London, in the hills of Shropshire or Hereford-shire that they had grown to love, she knew that she and Josh would be happy. They knew themselves and each other thoroughly; they knew the life they wanted to lead. The years stretched ahead into contentment, and that was all they asked.

The girls swept on, past Hyde Park Corner and across to Constitution Hill. People were massing already around the gates, or climbing on the Queen Victoria Memorial to get a better view, and you could see that there were even more coming, a huge crowd advancing up Birdcage Walk and the Mall and still more from Buckingham Palace Road itself and Buckingham Gate.

The Palace was at the centre of the excitement. And as the four girls came into view of the balcony, they saw the doors open and an enormous cheer rose into the air as the King and Queen themselves stepped out, with Mr Churchill beside them.

'Hooray!' Maggie yelled, beside herself with excitement. 'Hooray, hooray, horray! Hooray for the King! Hooray for the Queen! *Hooray for Mr Churchill!*'

Someone began to sing 'Land of Hope and Glory', and the song was taken up until the entire crowd had joined in, and they could see that Mr Churchill himself was singing the words as well. Tears poured down every face, and people hugged each other, as joy mingled with sorrow for those who would never come back. But there could not be too much grief on this day, and soon arms were waving in the air again and voices were calling out and cheering. It seemed that there would be no end to it.

'If only Mike could be here,' Phyl said, and Jo squeezed her arm.

'He will be, soon. And I'll have Josh, and you can see Shirley's happy with Owen. It's Maggie I feel sorry for. I reckon she thought a lot of that Canadian, you know.'

Phyl nodded, and then lifted her head to cheer again. The

King and Queen waved down, and Churchill gave his famous V for Victory sign, his cigar clamped as usual between two fingers. 'They look as happy as we are,' she said. 'Oh, he must feel so pleased. He must feel he's done such a good job.'

Maggie gazed up at the faces above and for a moment she was sober, thinking of Tommy. *We really did love each other,* she thought sadly, *and we'd have had a good life together. And I couldn't even have his kiddy to remember him by . . . But I've got Barry instead, and maybe in a funny way that's much the same, because it was Tom I did it for . . . And now he's gone, and so have Andy and all the others, and it's just me and Barry from now on. Just Barry and me . . .*

'Maggie,' said a voice, quietly in her ear. '*Maggie.*'

Maggie stood quite still. *I'm dreaming,* she thought. *It can't be true. Not here. Not today. Not in all this crowd . . .* She turned, slowly, and looked into the face of the man she had thought never to see again.

'*Carl.*'

'Oh, *Maggie,*' he said, and pulled her into his arms, 'Maggie, I thought I'd never find you!'

He bent his head and kissed her. Maggie, half laughing, half crying, clung to him, trying to speak, almost choking on her words. *Carl,* she thought. *Carl! It can't be! It can't be!*

'How did you find me? How did you know? In all these people . . . I'm dreaming, I must be. Oh, *Carl.*'

'If you're dreaming, so am I,' he said shakily, 'and let's hope neither of us ever wakes up . . . Maggie, I've wanted you so much! Tell me you've wanted me, too. Tell me you've missed me.'

'Oh, Carl, of course I have. But I don't know how you found me. I don't know how you *could.*'

'I went down to Devon, of course. Asked your mom. She told me you were coming up to meet the other girls.' Maggie glanced around to see them staring in astonishment. 'And I went to the Corner House and got there just as you all came rushing out. I followed you – thought I'd lost you a few times, people kept getting in the way, then a great crowd cut across from another street. Anyway, I finally managed to catch up with you and – and, Maggie, tell me, put me out of my misery – you *are* going to marry me, aren't you? You *are* going to come to Canada with me?'

'Oh, *yes!*' she exclaimed. 'Oh, yes, Carl. Of course I am!'

The rest of the day, and most of that night, went by in a blur. The girls and Carl stayed for hours outside the Palace, cheering and calling for their King and Queen. Now and then the doors opened and various members of the Royal Family and the Government came out and waved, and once Phyl was certain she caught sight of the princesses themselves, down in the crowd. At last, with the darkened skies lit as they had not been lit for years by streetlights, searchlights, torches and bonfires, the doors closed for the last time and the crowds began to disperse.

But for London, the party went on. The pubs stayed open, the fountains played in Trafalgar Square, and every street was filled with dancers. Exhausted but happy, the girls said goodnight at last and Maggie and Carl wandered off, arms entwined about each other's waist, into the night, while Shirley went back to Owen, and Phyl and Jo set off to go back to Woolwich.

'Oh, Phyl, wasn't that lovely?' Jo sighed happily. 'I'll never forget a minute of it. And fancy Carl coming to find Maggie, just at that moment. I did like him, didn't you, Phyl? I think Maggie'll be ever so happy with him.'

'Mmm. And going to Canada, too. It'll be a whole new life for her. And d'you really think it'll be all right for you and Josh?'

'Oh, yes. Nick wants the divorce as much as I do. I'm sad in a way. I thought everything was going to be so good for us – but I reckon the war's changed a lot of people's lives, Phyl, and maybe we've been luckier than most. And he did change. And Josh, well, Josh is different. He's right for me. I know he is.' She smiled, thinking of his arrival the next day. 'He'll be there in time for the street party! It's just a shame Mike can't be, too.'

It was late when they finally arrived home, and they giggled as they thought of their fathers, waiting for them with their watches in their hands. But late as it was, the street was still alive with people. Light poured out of every open front door and window, and someone had brought out a gramophone. As Phyl and Jo came down the street, they heard the strains of Vera Lynn's voice, singing 'We'll Meet Again', and when they turned the last corner they saw the line of a conga come snaking out of the Jennings house.

'Look at our Dad!' Jo exclaimed. 'And yours, Phyl! I never knew they could kick so high. And there's our Auntie Ethel, and your dad's brother, and – and . . .' Her voice faded and then she drew in a deep breath, gripped Phyl's arm and whispered, 'Phyl, who's that? It – surely it's – but it *can't* be . . .'

'It's Mike,' Phyl breathed. And then she gave a great whoop of joy. 'It's *Mike!*'

She shook off Jo's hand and threw herself forward. The conga line faltered and then broke as the young soldier, still in his stained and battered uniform, tore himself free. He opened his arms wide and Phyl disappeared into them as he caught her up and swung her into the air. The conga line gathered itself together again and continued, and Jo, sobbing with emotion, found herself dragged into it, to snake away up the road and in and out of all the other houses.

The war was over. And the girls had come home.